"My head is full of daydreams and nonsense…"

Amos narrowed his eyes. "You aren't nearly as out of touch with things as you would like your family to believe. I believe you're quite smart and intuitive."

Deborah's expression changed to a mix of shock and…pleasure? "You think I'm smart?"

"I told you that you need to tell me where you're going."

She gave him a tight smile. "You weren't here." She turned toward the buggy. "You want me to help you with finishing up?"

He should press the issue, but he didn't want to argue with her, didn't want to scare her away. "I would like that. Next time, tell someone where you're going. I know you don't understand or believe it, but I do feel responsible for everyone."

"But you're not. I can take care of myself."

But he wanted to look after her. "Sometimes your family may not notice you, but I do."

And she rewarded him with a sweet smile that made his brain a little fuzzy.

W9-BRX-451

Mary Davis is an award-winning author of more than a dozen novels. She is a member of American Christian Fiction Writers and is active in two critique groups. Mary lives in the Colorado Rocky Mountains with her husband of thirty years and three cats. She has three adult children and one grandchild. Her hobbies are quilting, porcelain-doll making, sewing, crafts, crocheting and knitting. Please visit her website, marydavisbooks.com.

Leigh Bale is a *Publishers Weekly* bestselling author. She is the winner of the prestigious Golden Heart® Award and is a finalist for the Gayle Wilson Award of Excellence and the Booksellers' Best Award. The daughter of a retired US forest ranger, she holds a BA in history. Married in 1981 to the love of her life, Leigh and her professor husband have two children and two grandkids. You can reach her at leighbale.com.

MARY DAVIS

Courting Her Secret Heart

&

LEIGH BALE

His Amish Choice

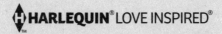

LOVE INSPIRED BOOKS

ISBN-13: 978-1-335-47014-0

Courting Her Secret Heart and His Amish Choice

Copyright © 2019 by Harlequin Books S.A.

The publisher acknowledges the copyright holders of the individual works as follows:

Courting Her Secret Heart
Copyright © 2018 by Mary Davis

His Amish Choice
Copyright © 2018 by Lora Lee Bale

www.Harlequin.com

Printed in U.S.A.

CONTENTS

COURTING HER
SECRET HEART

Mary Davis

Dedicated to my awesome sister Deborah Spencer.

A special thanks to Melissa Endlich
and the editorial team at Love Inspired and to
Sarah Joy Freese and WordServe Literary Agency.
I'm so thankful to work with you!

No man can serve two masters: for either
he will hate the one, and love the other; or else
he will hold to the one, and despise the other.
Ye cannot serve God and mammon.
—*Matthew 6:24*

German Proverb: *Wer zwei Hasen auf einmal
jagt bekommt keinen.*
"He who chases two rabbits at once
will catch none."

Chapter One

Elkhart County, Indiana

Deborah Miller ran to the clump of bare sycamore trees at the far edge of the pond on her family's property. Fortunately, the latest round of snow had melted and the ground had dried, so she wouldn't be leaving tracks.

Several ducks squawked their disapproval of her presence. With indignation, they waddled and flapped onto the frozen water.

Deborah cringed. "Sorry to disturb you. I'll bring you some bread crusts tomorrow."

The largest tree in the grove had a tangle of many trunks from its base, creating an empty space in the center. She scurried over and dropped her green, tan and white camouflage backpack into the hollow. A sprinkle of dried leaves on top, and no one would ever find it. Truth be told, she could leave her pack out in the open and no one would likely notice it. It would blend in with the tree's patchwork bark.

She took off for the house, running between the stubbly winter cornfield rows. She was going to be late. She'd lost track of time, which was her usual excuse, but this time it was true. She could be gone all day and no one in her family ever noticed her absence. Or if they did, they never mentioned it. Apparently, keeping track of so many girls was too much trouble to bother with. Seven. And she was right smack-dab in the middle. Not the oldest. Not the youngest. Not anything.

Of late, everyone was fussing over Hannah and Lydia, who were both planning to marry this fall. Although no one was supposed to know, since neither wedding would be officially announced until late summer or early fall, but a lot of celery would be planted in the garden this spring. After all, they couldn't have Amish weddings without celery.

It had been a *gut* photo shoot today. The sun was shining, and though cold out, it had been a perfect day. Even if by some strange chance her absence had been noticed and she got scolded for being gone, it wouldn't dampen her mood. Nothing could spoil today.

Deborah pulled her coat tighter around herself as she slowed down and entered the yard, finding it oddly quiet. She needed to look as though she hadn't been in a hurry and just lost track of time, as usual.

Chickens pecked at the ground, but no people could be seen. Where was everyone? Were *all* her sisters in the house with *Mutter*? That was peculiar. One or two were often outside at this time of day. Unusual to have caught them all in the kitchen.

An Amish man came out of the barn, carrying two empty buckets.

Who was he? She'd never seen him before. Though dressed Amish, she had to wonder if he belonged to their community. His light brown hair peeked out from under his black felt hat. The brim shaded his face. Just the type of rugged Amish man that Hudson, her photographer, had repeatedly asked her to find for photo shoots. What was this stranger doing on their farm?

She approached him. "Who are you?" Her words puffed out on little white clouds.

"I'm Amos Burkholder. Who are you?" He smiled.

A warm, inviting, disarming smile. The kind that could make her forget her purpose. A smile she wouldn't mind retreating into. She mentally shook herself free of his spell. "I'm Deborah Miller. I live here. What are you doing on our farm? And where's my family?"

"Deborah? I was told the whole family went to the hospital. What are *you* doing here?"

"Hospital? Why?" Her family went to the hospital and hadn't noticed her absence? It figured.

"Bartholomew Miller had an accident. An ambulance came. Bishop Bontrager asked me to take care of things here until you all returned and your *vater* was able to work again."

"My *vater*? Accident? What happened? Is he all right?"

"I don't know the details. But if the bishop thinks your *vater* will be well enough to work his farm again, then I think he will be all right eventually. Would you like me to drive you into Goshen to the hospital?"

Deborah shook her head. "If I hitch up the smaller buggy, I can drive myself."

"I'll hitch it."

"Danki." Deborah ran into the house to grab her bag of sewing. In case she had a while to wait at the hospital, she wanted to have something to keep herself distracted from too much worry. When she came back out, Amos wasn't much further along in getting the buggy ready.

Impatient, Deborah stalked over to the horse standing in the yard and took hold of the harness on the other side from Amos.

He stopped his progress. "I'm capable of doing this myself."

Deborah hooked the belly strap. "I know." What Amish person didn't know how to hitch up a horse to a buggy by themselves by age ten or twelve? "If I help, it'll go faster."

After a deep breath, he got back to the work at hand. Once the buggy was hitched and ready to go, he climbed in the side opposite her and took charge of the reins.

She put her hands on her hips. "What are you doing?"

"Taking you into town."

"I told you that I can drive a buggy myself."

"I know and have no doubt you're capable, but you're flustered over the news of your *vater*, and it would be best if you don't drive in your present state."

"Present state? What's that supposed to mean?"

He tilted his head. "Are you getting in? Or would you rather walk to town?"

With a huff, she climbed aboard and plopped down on the seat. "You are insufferable."

He handed her a quilt for her lap, then gently snapped the reins and clucked the horse into motion. "If by *insufferable* you mean *helpful*, then *danki*."

Why was she being so ill-tempered? This wasn't like her. Maybe it was the news of her *vater* being injured. Or maybe it was her guilt of being away from the house when it happened. Or maybe it was because she knew she had been doing something her *vater*, her family and the community would frown upon. Or maybe it was all three. Whatever the reason, Amos didn't deserve her poor attitude when he was being so helpful and kind. "I'm sorry for being difficult. I'm worried about my *vater*."

"That's understandable."

She blew into her hands to warm them, then slipped on her knitted mittens. "I haven't seen you before. Do you belong to a neighboring community district?"

"*Ne.* We live on the other side of the district. We moved here a year ago from Pennsylvania. We're at church every other Sunday. You've even been to church at our farm. We obviously haven't made a memorable impression on you. Or at least I haven't."

How could she not remember him? "Tell me a little about your family to remind me."

"I am the youngest of five boys. The two oldest stayed in Pennsylvania and split the farm we had there."

"I think I know who you are, or at least your family. I'm the middle of seven girls."

"I know. I've seen you in church along with all your sisters."

He'd noticed her?

"Tell me something, is Miriam spoken for or being courted by anyone?"

Evidently, he had his eye on her sister, who was a little over a year older than herself. That meant, it hadn't been Deborah he'd noticed at church, but her sister. Disappointing. Someone else who overlooked her. "Timothy Zook seems interested in her."

"Is she interested in him?"

"Some days *ja*, and others *ne*. Miriam likes a lot of boys. She can't seem to decide which one she likes most. She's so afraid of choosing the wrong man to marry, we fear she'll never marry at all." Deborah pulled a face. "I probably shouldn't have told you all that. Please don't hold it against her. She's a very wonderful sister."

His chuckle held no humor.

Was it truly Miriam she didn't want him to think of poorly, or herself because of her derogatory words? Why should she care what this man thought of her? But she did. "Can you hurry? I need to know how my *vater* is."

"I'm going as fast as the *Ordnung* allows."

"But this is kind of an emergency. You would be allowed to go faster."

He thinned his lips. "This isn't an emergency. Your *vater's* being well looked after. Whether it takes us five minutes or five hours to get there will have no bearing on your *vater's* condition."

He was right, of course, but she had already missed so much. She very much wished they were going by car. "When was my *vater* hurt?"

"First thing this morning."

So long ago? He must have gotten hurt soon after she had slipped away. Now she really did feel guilty.

Like Amos said, if she got to the hospital with everyone else or in the next hour, she wouldn't have been able to make a difference. But at least she could have been with her family. And know what was going on.

She settled her nerves for the plodding, boring journey. "Do you miss Pennsylvania?"

"Ne."

That was a sharp reply.

"But you grew up there. Your friends are there. The rest of your family is there. Don't you miss any of them?"

"Ne."

Again, his single word sounded harsh.

"There's nothing for me back there. This move was supposed to be *gut*."

But she sensed it wasn't. She wanted to press him, to understand why he seemed to harbor bitterness toward the place where he'd grown up, but doubted he would tell her anything. After all, they were basically strangers.

Eventually, Amos pulled in next to several other buggies outside the hospital.

She jumped out. "You don't have to stay. I'll get a ride back with my family. *Danki*." She trotted inside. She inquired at the information desk and soon found her family, with all her sisters, as well as several other community members. Her *vater* sat in a wheelchair, waiting to be discharged.

His left arm rested in a sling, and his left leg was in a cast and propped on a pillow on one of the wheelchair's leg supports. He'd chosen neon green. Would the church leaders approve of the color? Probably not, but they wouldn't be able to do anything about it until he had the cast changed in a few weeks.

Thirteen-year-old Naomi made a face at her.

Deborah ignored her younger sister, who liked to stir up trouble, and hurried over to him. "*Vater*, are you all right?"

Vater gave her a lopsided smile. "I'm feeling great. They gave me something for the pain. But I don't have any pain."

"There you are, Deborah." Her *mutter* frowned. "I was wondering where you'd gotten off to. Did you go to the vending machines without telling me?"

Vending machines? Hadn't her *mutter* noticed that Deborah had only just now arrived? That she'd been absent all day? Was she truly invisible to her family? Did any of them even care? No wonder she could be gone for hours and hours without repercussions. No one ever realized her absence.

Amos joined them then. "How are you doing, Mr. Miller?"

Vater waved his hands aimlessly through the air. "It's Bartholomew. I don't have any pain."

Deborah turned to Amos. "I thought you left."

"If you would have waited, I would have walked in with you." He turned to *Mutter*. "I brought Deborah."

Mutter gave Deborah a double take. "You weren't here? Then where were you?"

Oh, dear. "I went for a walk, and before I knew it, I had gone farther than I realized, and it took me a while to get back home."

"Oh." *Mutter* turned back to the nurse behind *Vater's* wheelchair. "Are we leaving now? I want to leave now. I have supper to start."

"We need to wait for the doctor to sign the release papers."

How had any of them survived infancy and childhood with *Mutter* always forgetting things? Well, mostly forgetting Deborah. She didn't have trouble with the rest of her daughters. Just her middlemost one.

The familiar pang of being left out twisted around her heart. One of these days, she might decide not to return. Would her *mutter* even notice? Probably not.

Well, it *had been* a perfect day until she'd come home and found out her world had been turned upside down.

Amos's inviting brown gaze settled on her. She wished now the buggy ride had taken longer. His look of sympathy warmed her heart. Well, at least *he* acknowledged her presence.

Amos studied Miriam, who smiled at everyone in the hospital waiting room. Did she truly like a lot of young men? Or was she just really nice? He'd been fooled by girls before. More than once. His gaze shifted back to

Deborah. She stood on the edge of the crowd, with them but not really a part of them. How could no one have noticed she hadn't been with the family when they left for the hospital? Or at least once they arrived. He admired how she seemed to take that in stride. The hospital lights didn't spark the red hints in her hair the way the sun had.

Deborah turned to him, and he smiled at her without thinking. Her green eyes seemed as though she could see his broken heart. There was something more to her than met the eye. Something he couldn't quite figure out. Like she had some sort of secret. Probably just his own guilty conscience. He didn't want to look away, but he did.

From down the hall, a man stared at him. It was his cousin Jacob. His shunned cousin Jacob, who'd left the Amish church and community. He glanced back at the crowd of his fellow Amish waiting for Bartholomew to be released.

He moved around the crowd to Bishop Bontrager. "I have something I need to take care of. Will you let the Millers know that I'll meet them back at their farm?"

The bishop nodded. "*Ja. Danki* for agreeing to lend them a hand. Bartholomew is going to be laid up for some time. Will your *vater* be able to spare you to stay on at the Millers'?"

"*Ja.* I'm sure he can." His *vater* had already declared the farm not big enough for Amos. He glanced in the direction where Jacob had been. "I won't be far behind everyone." As he hurried down the hall, he threw a glance back over his shoulder at Deborah and almost went back to her, but didn't. When he turned the corner, he came upon his cousin, who was leaning against the wall. Jacob looked strange but *gut* in his *English* clothes, jeans and a hooded sweatshirt. They suited his cousin. "What are you doing here?"

"I saw you drive up with one of the Miller girls. Quite a collection of Amish you're with. None of them *your* family, though. *And* the bishop."

"Bartholomew Miller broke his leg." Amos glanced back to make sure no one had followed him. "The bishop asked me to help out at their farm while they took him to the hospital."

Jacob nodded. "You seemed pretty content with all of them. Are you still interested in leaving?"

Amos's insides knotted. This would be a life-changing decision, but he didn't see the use of the Amish life anymore. His *vater* didn't have land enough for all his sons, and the Amish girls here seemed no different from the flighty ones back in Pennsylvania. Except Deborah. She seemed different. But that was what he'd thought about Esther. And Bethany. "*Ja*, of course I am."

"It might take a few weeks to get everything set up. I'll be in touch with more information."

"I'll wait to hear from you." Once away from the community and no longer having to keep this a secret, he'd feel better about his decision. "I should go before they get suspicious." Amos could be shunned just for talking to an ex-Amish member. But once he left, he would be shunned and turned over to the devil and excommunicated from the church, as well.

"See you soon." Jacob walked off in the opposite direction of the waiting room.

Amos peeked around the corner. None of his Amish brethren remained, only a handful of *Englishers*. He straightened before heading down the hall and out to the buggy parking area.

The only buggy that remained was the one he'd driven into town. Deborah sat on the buggy seat, rubbing her mitten-clad hands briskly together. She turned in his direction, and his heart sped up.

He stopped beside the vehicle. Though she wore a *kapp*, the sun once again ignited the hints of red in her hair around her face. "What are you still doing here? Why didn't you go with the others?"

The quilt lay across her lap. "All the other buggies were full."

That was a little sad. She'd been left behind. Now he felt bad for making her wait.

She picked up the reins and tilted her head. "Are you getting in? Or would you rather walk?"

Throwing his words back at him? Little scamp. But she'd lightened his mood. He climbed in and extended his hands for the reins.

She moved them from his reach and snapped the horse into motion.

He couldn't believe she'd just done that. It was audacious. "I should drive."

"Why?"

"Because I'm the man and you're a woman."

She set her jaw and kept control of the reins. "I'm quite capable, *danki.*"

She certainly seemed so, as well as a little bit feisty. He wanted to drive, but unless he wrestled the reins away from her, it didn't seem likely. "Did I do something to upset you?"

"Ne." Her answer was short and clipped.

"It certainly seems like I did. No one else around for you to be angry at."

She tossed the reins into his lap. "Take them if you want to drive so badly."

Now he had vexed her. He didn't want the reins this way and was tempted to leave them where they were, but that wouldn't do for the horse to have no guidance. With the reins in hand, he pulled to the side of the street in front of an antique store and stopped. "If I haven't upset you, then what has?"

She took a slow breath, and for a moment, he doubted she would answer him, but then she let out a huff of white air. "It doesn't matter."

"*Ja*, it does. Tell me." Why did it bother him so much that she was upset? He should just let it go and get back to her family's farm.

"My family went off to the hospital and didn't notice I wasn't with them."

That could be quite upsetting, but he'd thought that hadn't bothered her. He'd been wrong. "They were probably all worried about your *vater*. Focused on getting him the care he needed."

She sat quietly for a moment, and he could almost feel her mood shift. "You're right. I was being selfish. Only thinking of myself. I have a habit of doing that. *Danki*."

He smiled. *"Bitte."* He liked that he could help her and appreciated her honesty. Something he'd found lacking in others.

She waved her mittened hand in the air. "Shall we go?"

He lifted the reins but then paused and handed them over to her. "You can drive."

The smile she gifted him with and the spark in her green eyes as she took the reins warmed him all over.

Chapter Two

Amos sat forward on the buggy seat as the Miller farm came into view. What would people think of him not driving? He was the man, after all. He *should* be driving. Instinct told him to take the reins, but something held him back. He gritted his teeth, hoping no one would be out in the yard.

Deborah pulled on one rein and slackened the other to turn into the driveway.

Though several buggies, the chickens and two cats were scattered about the yard, fortunately no people were in sight.

She stopped the buggy in front of the house. "Do you mind putting this away by yourself? I want to see how my *vater's* doing."

He gladly took the offered reins. "I'd be happy to." He breathed easier having the strips of leather in his hands. How foolish of him, but he couldn't help feeling that way. "Tell your *vater* not to worry about the animals. I'll take care of everything."

"*Danki.* But I think he probably still has enough pain medication in him to not worry about much of anything right now." She jogged up the porch steps and into the house.

He stared at the door for a moment, feeling a sense of loss. But that couldn't be. He hadn't lost anything. At least not anything new. With a shake of his head, he drove the buggy to the barn. After unhitching the horse, he put the animal in a stall, then parked the buggy in its space inside the barn. Being an open buggy, it needed to be protected from the elements. With the harness put away, he brushed down the horse and fed him.

His encounter with his cousin Jacob played in his head. He needed to get off his *vater's* farm and experience the outside world more than he had on *Rumspringa*, with a different purpose this time. If he wasn't going to have land to farm and would have to work in the *Englisher* world anyway, he might as well live there, too, and be a part of it.

Amos would have left the first time when Jacob suggested it if there had been some place for him to go, but today was a different matter. The image of Deborah standing on the edge of her family at the hospital tugged at his heart. She needed him. This family needed him. Bartholomew needed him. And he needed them so he wouldn't have to be on his family's farm until he left for *gut*. This would make the wait more bearable.

He heard the humming of a female enter the barn. Deborah? He peeked out of the stall he was in as someone disappeared into the stall with the milking cow, but he couldn't tell who. He brushed down the front of his coat and trousers to remove hay particles, then stepped into the stall doorway.

Miriam glanced up at him with a smile from where

she sat on a three-legged stool. *"Hallo*, Amos Burk-holder."

His smile sagged a bit. *"Hallo."* This was *gut* that it wasn't Deborah. He shouldn't be thinking of her. "Your job to milk the cow?"

She leaned her head against the animal's side and began the task with a *swish-swish-swish*. *"Ja."*

"Do you and your sisters trade off with this duty?"

"Ne, I like milking. There is something soothing about it. It's just me and Sybil."

"I'm sorry. Would you like me to go away?"

"Ne."

He wasn't sure if he was disappointed or not at having to stay. "Tell me about your sisters."

"What do you want to know?"

"I don't know. I figure if I'm going to be working on your farm, I should know a little about everyone."

She nodded. "Hannah and Lydia are twins—identical. Hannah is the ultraresponsible one. Lydia is the peace-maker. They are both being courted and will likely get married this fall. Then comes me. A lot of people say I'm the positive one. I do try to see the *gut* in situations."

That was not how Deborah had described her. What was it she had said? That Miriam liked a lot of boys. Likely, there wasn't one young man in particular who had caught her attention yet.

"Then Deborah. After her comes Joanna. She's the *gut* one. Not that the rest of us aren't *gut*, but she was an easy baby and has always been easy to please. She's also quite shy. Naomi's thirteen and can be moody. She likes to be the center of attention. And lastly is carefree baby Sarah at eight. She is easily everyone's favorite, and the sweetest of us all."

Everyone got a description except Deborah. "What about Deborah?"

"What about her?"

"You gave everyone a little description except her."

"Did I? Hmm. Deborah is...irres—rarely here."

Was she about to say *irresponsible*? True, Deborah hadn't been around when her *vater* had been hurt, but that didn't necessarily make her irresponsible.

When Miriam finished milking, Amos hoisted the full bucket and carried it to the house.

Miriam opened the door to the kitchen and allowed him to enter first. The kitchen bustled with female activity. He was used to just his *mutter* in the kitchen, alone, doing all the work by herself.

Deborah looked up from her task of churning butter with the youngest girl and smiled at him.

He responded in kind.

Her gaze flickered away from him to where Miriam appeared, and Deborah's smile faltered, then she pushed her mouth up in a less genuine smile, but one of encouragement.

He wished he could bring back that first smile. What had caused the change? More important, how could he bring back the first smile?

"Right this way, Amos." Miriam motioned with her hand for him to follow her. "That goes in the back fridge until morning."

Amos aimed his apologetic shrug toward Deborah as he obediently complied. When he returned, Deborah's *mutter* stood in his path.

Teresa Miller put her hands on her hips and gave him an impish smile. "We do so love company, but you can't walk through my kitchen without introducing yourself."

"I'm Amos Burkholder."

"Which one of my daughters are you courting?"

"Um, none. I'm here to help out on the farm while Bartholomew is healing."

Shock and concern wiped away the older woman's smile in an instant. "What? What's wro—"

One of the older girls hooked her arm around her *mutter's* shoulders and escorted her out of the kitchen. "Let's go see how *Vater* is doing."

Another of the older sisters stood in front of him. "Supper will be ready in a little bit. We'll call you when it's ready."

This must be Lydia, the peacemaker. The one who left with their *mutter* must have been Hannah, the ultra-responsible one. Or it could be vice versa. He wasn't sure. He nodded and went back outside to finish up some chores.

Soon, another one of the sisters came out to retrieve him. "Supper's ready." She kept her head down.

"*Danki.* I'll head in with you." He walked to her side. "I didn't mean to upset your *mutter* earlier."

Her head remained down and her voice soft. "You didn't. She was just worried about *Vater.*"

It had seemed like more than worry. But then, what did he know?

This shy girl must be Joanna. It would probably be best if he didn't stress her by trying to hold a meaningless conversation just to quiet the silence.

Inside, he washed up and waited to be told where he should sit at the table.

Bartholomew sat alone at the far end of the table, his broken leg propped up on a chair. The women still scurried to and fro.

The youngest, who looked to be more like five than eight, crashed into him and wrapped her chubby arms around his waist. "Broffer Amos."

He wasn't sure what to make of this little one. "*Hallo*, Sarah."

She giggled.

One of the twins, he guessed Lydia, hurried over and disentangled the young one from him. "I'm sorry about that. She likes to greet people with a hug."

"That's all right." He gazed down into the upturned face of Sarah. Her slanted eyes and flat nose told him all he needed to know. Down syndrome. "I'm very pleased to meet you."

Lydia smiled at him but spoke to Sarah. "Go sit down. It's time to eat."

Sarah grabbed his hand. "Sit by me."

He looked to Lydia, who gave him a nod. He sat, and quickly the others did so, as well. Bartholomew blessed the food, and everyone served themselves except Sarah. Hannah, who sat on her other side, dished up for her.

Bartholomew grimaced in pain. His medication had probably worn off. "Amos, I certainly do appreciate you coming to help out in my hour of need."

"I'm glad to be here."

Teresa tilted her head. "Hour? It'll be a mite more than that." Her anxiety from earlier had been erased.

The girl directly across from Amos crinkled her nose. "I bet you don't even know who all of us are."

Center of attention. "You're Naomi."

He went around the table and named each of the family members.

Naomi narrowed her eyes. She obviously didn't think he could do it.

He wasn't so sure himself but had guessed right. Miriam's descriptions had helped. When he'd named Deborah and she smiled at him, something inside did a little flip. That was the smile he'd been looking for. He wanted to stop and stare at her but knew he shouldn't.

He cleared his throat to regain his train of thought and shifted his attention to Bartholomew. "I could, of course, travel home each night and return in the morning, but I would be able to get more work accomplished if I stayed on here."

Bartholomew swallowed his mouthful of food. "What did you have in mind?"

"I thought I could sleep in the barn."

Teresa spoke up. "I won't hear of that. The barn is no place for a person in winter."

Bartholomew gazed gently at his *frau*. "What would you suggest, *Mutter*?"

"Joanna and Naomi can move in with Miriam and…" She waved her hand in Deborah's direction. "And her sister."

A sadness flickered across Deborah's face, and Amos's heart ached for her. He knew what it was like to be hurt by family.

Naomi leaned forward. "I don't want to move rooms and be crowded in."

"Hush," Bartholomew scolded his daughter, and she huffed and folded her arms. Then he turned back to his *frau*. "You would have a young man who isn't a family member under the same roof as our daughters?"

Teresa's gaze flittered around the table, and the inappropriateness of the situation registered on her face. "Oh. I…"

Amos didn't want to cause a fuss. "I don't want to

displace anyone. The barn will be fine. There's an old woodstove still connected in the tack room. I can move a few things around and set up a cot." It was preferable to home.

With supper concluded and the arrangements settled, Amos headed out to fix up his new but temporary living quarters.

He located some firewood and lit the stove. Then he made a clearing in the center of the room and set up the cot that was used when an animal was sick and someone needed to stay in the barn to keep a watchful eye out.

A gray tabby rubbed against his leg. He crouched and petted him. "What's your name, hmm?"

The cat sauntered over to the stove, sniffed it and lay down in front of it.

"Don't get too comfortable. You can't stay in here at night with the door closed. You can warm yourself until I find some blankets."

When he exited the tack room, Deborah stood outside his door with an armful of quilts. She smiled. "We thought you might need these." She handed him the pile. "There's a pillow, as well."

"*Danki.* These'll be better than the horse blankets I was planning to rustle up."

"*Bitte.*" Her gaze lingered on him a long moment before she turned to leave.

He wanted to say something to make her stay. But what use would there be in that? Instead, he watched her walk out.

The following morning, Deborah stole glances at Amos throughout breakfast. Several times, she caught him looking back at her.

Vater hadn't come to the table for breakfast. Fortunately, his and *Mutter's* bedroom was on the main floor, so he wouldn't have to go up and down the stairs with a broken leg and injured arm. Though *Mutter* had scurried around the kitchen earlier, she had gone in to sit with *Vater*. Since *Vater's* accident, less than a day ago, *Mutter* had acted stranger than usual. One moment she sat calmly, and the next she scampered about like a nervous squirrel looking for lost acorns.

Amos drained the last of his coffee. "*Danki* for breakfast. I should get to work."

"Would you like another cup?" For some reason, she didn't want him to leave yet. It was nice having another man around the farm. Or was it that it was just different for all the girls? Or was it having a kind, handsome, eligible man around?

His mouth curved up into a smile that tickled her insides. "*Danki*. Maybe later." He gazed at her for a moment before trudging outside.

After he left, she stared at the door for a bit longer than she should before she turned to her sisters. "What do you need me to do?"

Lydia had taken charge of the kitchen cleanup. "I think we have everything covered."

Her sisters bustled around, busy at work. Even Naomi helped, and Sarah had her little job of sorting the silverware. The only other one not there, besides their parents, was Hannah.

Deborah headed for her parents' room and peeked in around the door frame. "Is there anything I can do? Anything you need?"

Mutter held a plate while *Vater* ate with his *gut* arm. Hannah gingerly tucked a pillow under *Vater's* broken leg. "We're *gut*. See if the others need help in the kitchen."

Deborah gave a weak smile. She'd already done that. "*Vater*, I'm praying you heal quickly."

"*Danki*."

She left. With nothing to do inside, she headed outside and found Amos in the barn.

He stood below the hayloft, staring up at the underside of the floor above.

"What are you doing?"

He turned to her, and his mouth pulled up at the corners. "Trying to decide the best way to fix this."

She liked his smile. A lot. She stood next to him and looked to where he pointed. A hole roughly the size of a laundry basket had opened up through several of the boards, and hay hung down in the opening. "What happened?"

Shifting, he stared at her. "You really don't know?"

"Know what?"

"Your *vater* fell through there and landed here on the floor. Fortunately, there weren't any tools, boxes or barrels for him to get further injured on."

She pictured her *vater* falling and gasped. She hadn't thought to ask just how he'd gotten hurt. All she knew was that he had fallen.

"The boards look pretty rotted. They should have been replaced long before now."

"Why hadn't he done that?"

"He was probably too busy with running the rest of the farm on his own to notice. I'll check all the boards and build a new loft floor if need be. I figure I can do some of the regular maintenance he couldn't get to and repair what needs repairing until I… Until it's time to plow and plant."

"Do you think he's going to be in a cast that long?"

"Hard to say. Some people's bones heal faster than others'. But even if he's out of the cast, his leg will be weak. He'll need time to regain his strength."

"What can I do to help?"

He chuffed out a chuckle. "What? I'm sure there's plenty to be done in the house."

"Hannah and Lydia are taking care of *Vater* while overseeing the breakfast cleanup as well as the early prep for lunch. Everyone's busy with their regular duties, leaving nothing for me except free time." She didn't even have a modeling job today. That would have been nice to get her mind off *Vater* being hurt.

"This isn't woman's work."

"If you haven't noticed, my *vater* has seven girls. We've all done a bit of carpentry, livestock tending and even some plowing. So let me help."

"*Danki* for the offer, but I can manage."

If she was a man, he'd accept her help. "Well, I have nothing else to do, so I'm not leaving." She backed up to a covered feed barrel, pushed herself up and sat. "If you won't let me help with the labor, I'll supervise from here." The truth was, she just wanted to be out here with him.

He stared at her hard for a long moment. "*You* are going to tell *me* how to fix this?"

"It's either that or put me to work." The work would go faster if he allowed her to help. Would he be too stubborn and insist on doing it alone? If so, he deserved to have a more difficult time than need be, *and* he deserved to have her comment on every little thing he did.

"Fine. But you have to do as I say. I don't want you getting hurt, as well."

She hopped off the barrel and saluted him.

He shook his head at her playful gesture. "First we need to determine how sturdy the rest of this floor is." He handed her a shovel, and he grabbed a pitchfork for himself. "Tap the underside of the boards with the end of the handle." He demonstrated with his implement.

Deborah poked at a board to show him that not only did she understand his elementary instructions, but that she could also follow his directions as ordered. Then she smiled.

He worked his mouth back and forth, presumably to keep from smiling himself. His effort created a cute expression.

She studied her shovel from tip to end. She didn't like the idea of lifting the heavy metal blade up and down. The repetitive movement would give her sore muscles, for sure. After looking around, she leaned the shovel against the wall and grabbed a push broom. Putting her foot on the head, she twisted the handle several times, freeing it. This was lighter. Much better for repetitive motions. She twirled it around once and went to work tapping and poking. "Tell me about your family."

Amos shrugged. "Like what?"

"Parents. Siblings."

"I have two parents and four brothers."

Not very forthcoming with information. She was going to have to work harder at learning anything about him. She would start with something easy and hope he got the hint and freely offered up more details. "What are your parents' names?"

"Joseph and Karen."

At least half the boards she poked at were usable for the time being, although they would need to be replaced soon. The other half of them were splintery and soft. "What about your brothers?"

"James, Boaz, Daniel and Titus."

She felt like growling and poking *him* with a stick. Couldn't he give her more information? Did he not want to talk to her? Well, she wasn't about to work in silence. Her sisters chatted all the time while doing chores. "Where do you fit into all of them?"

"Youngest."

Really? Nothing more than that? She did growl now, softly to herself, and jabbed her stick at the next board. It poked through, splintering the wood in half. Hay showered down on her from between the dangling halves.

Amos rushed over and pulled her out of the way as one of the jagged pieces broke free and shot straight down to where she'd been standing. She could have been seriously injured.

Caught off guard by his action, she lost her balance and grasped at his sleeve. Her body twisted, and gravity did the rest of the work, landing her in a pile of straw.

Between her yanking on his sleeve and his trying to catch her, he lost his footing as well and landed in the straw beside her with one arm stretched across to the other side of her. His eyes went wide. "Are you all right? Did you get hurt?"

He looked so adorable in his worried state that a giggle escaped her lips before she could stop it.

His mouth pulled up at the corners. "I guess that means you're not hurt."

She nodded and wrestled her chortling under control.

He plucked hay off her cheek and forehead. "You're covered."

She imagined she was but didn't help him, liking his ministrations.

His hand stilled, and he stared down at her for a long moment.

What was he thinking?

Clearing his throat, he pushed himself up to his feet, then offered her assistance. His hand was large and strong. And warm.

As soon as she was on her feet, he released her quickly as though embarrassed, and stared up at the ceiling. "Too many of the boards are rotted beyond repair, and the ones that are serviceable won't be for long. It would be best to replace the whole floor. I'll take the wagon into town and order the necessary lumber."

Now he was chatty? Or had their little moment made him uncomfortable? She missed the moment of closeness they'd just shared. Would they have another one in the future? She hoped so.

Chapter Three

The next morning, Amos was sent into town by the oldest twin, Hannah, to pick up some medicine for Bartholomew Miller. Though identical in most respects, he noted that Hannah had a worry crease between her eyebrows, which helped him to differentiate the two sisters.

He now drove back along the paved road. Floyd plodded along. The rhythm of his clip-clopping hoofbeats lulled Amos's thoughts—thoughts that drifted to his cousin. Jacob was *gut* to help Amos. Amos wouldn't know what to do on the outside. Having his cousin's guidance made him feel less anxious about the whole endeavor. Jacob knew all about Amos's hurts back in Pennsylvania. How Esther had let him court her and led him to believe she cared for him, only to turn down his offer of marriage. Then when he'd arrived in Indiana, the situation was nearly repeated with Bethany.

Then his thoughts turned to the Millers' farm. The work there was *gut*. Gave him purpose. And being around all those women would give him insight into the female mind. Maybe then he could figure out what he'd done wrong in the past.

Up ahead, an Amish woman meandered in the middle of the two-lane country road.

What was she doing?

A car came down the road, honked and swerved around her.

She sidestepped but didn't move to the side of the road.

He snapped the reins to hurry the horse. When he pulled up beside her, he said, "Ma'am?"

She faced him but didn't really look at him.

"Teresa? Teresa Miller?" He hauled back on the reins.

"Ja." She raised her hand to shade her eyes from the morning winter sun.

"What are you doing out here?"

"I was going somewhere." She chuckled. "But I seem to have forgotten where."

That didn't explain why she was in the middle of the road. He jumped down. "Come. I'll drive you home."

"That would be nice. *Danki.*" She climbed into the buggy and waited.

How odd. But other than her being in the middle of the road, he couldn't put his finger on what exactly was off about this encounter. He got in and took her home.

When he drove into the yard and up to the house, the twins rushed outside without coats on. Hannah opened the buggy door and took Teresa's hand. *"Mutter*, where have you been? We've been looking for you." A forced cheeriness laced her words.

"I went for a nice little walk." She patted Amos's arm. "But I was safe."

Hannah helped her *mutter* out and exchanged glances with Lydia. Hannah's gaze flickered to him. *"Danki."*

"Bitte." Amos held out the paper sack with the prescription. "Here's your *vater's* medication."

Lydia took it. *"Danki."* The women rushed into the house, leaving Amos to wonder.

Women. They behaved strangely. How was a man to figure them out? Maybe it was impossible, and he should give up on them altogether.

A while after Miriam had completed the late-afternoon milking, Amos headed to the house for supper. Though he'd been mulling over this morning's incident with Teresa all day and wanted to ask about it, he decided not to embarrass her by mentioning anything.

He stepped through the kitchen door into barely ordered chaos. One girl went this way while another went that way and two others looked to be on a collision course, but both swerved in the appropriate directions and barely missed running into each other. The women seemed to almost read each others' minds with each one going in a different direction. How did they ever get anything accomplished? But somehow they managed to pull supper together.

Maybe there was some order to their mayhem he couldn't detect. That men in general couldn't. He would like to figure it out but sensed he could spend a lifetime and never understand women. He should give up even trying anymore.

Teresa Miller smiled and came over to him. "My brother stopped by and brought some of your things. They are in a suitcase by the front door."

"Your brother?"

"Ja. David. He wore that blue shirt I made him for his birthday."

Hannah gave a nervous-sounding giggle, and the

crease between her eyebrows deepened. "She meant *your* brother."

He didn't have a brother named David. Maybe she meant Daniel.

"*Ne*. I didn't—"

Lydia put her arm around Teresa, effectively distracting her. "*Mutter*, did you get the cake frosted?" The two walked to the far side of the kitchen.

Why did the twins seem nervous? Calling someone by the wrong name was common enough. Most everyone had done it. How many times had he been called by one of his brothers' names? If he had a cookie for every time, he'd be fat.

Hannah spoke to Amos. "Why don't you take your suitcase out to the barn? It's going to take a few minutes to get everything on the table."

Was she trying to distract *him*?

"All right." He snagged the case and headed out to the barn. That had been strange. But then this had been a bit of a strange day. And he was surrounded by women who didn't behave or think like men. They were mysterious creatures whose sole purpose was to confuse and distract men.

He set the case on his bed and saw, out of the corner of his eye, the tabby dart in. When he turned to look, the cat dashed back out. What had scared it? He leaned to look on the other side of the potbellied stove, where the cat had run from.

A tiny kitten with its eyes still closed was lying on the ground. It raised its wobbly head and let out a small mew.

Amos picked it up. "Where has your *mutter* gone?" It seemed females of all species acted strange. He stepped out of the room and scanned the dim interior of the barn.

From the hayloft, the tabby trotted down the slanted ladder with another kitten hanging from her mouth. She ignored Amos and darted into his room. She quickly came back out and meowed at him. Then she put her paws on his leg and meowed again.

"I have your little one." He crouched down and she took the kitten from him.

He followed her into the tack room. "How many little ones do you have?"

She obviously liked the warmth of the stove for her babies. She looked from him to beside the stove and back again.

He waved his hand. "Go on. Get the others. I'm not going to make you sleep in the cold."

She darted out.

Amos snagged an unused crate, put in a layer of straw and then an old towel. By the time the *mutter* cat returned with number three, Amos had the crate with the two kittens in it next to the heat.

The tabby peered over the edge of the box, jumped in with the third kitten and lay down.

"I'll figure out how to keep the door open and stay warm later."

When he headed back to the house, all the girls sat silently at the table, hands folded in their laps. No one fluttered about. He could have waited until later to take out his suitcase. It didn't matter now. He sat next to Sarah as before.

As well as Bartholomew, Teresa and one of the twins weren't at the table. Which twin was here? She had the crease between her eyebrows, so she must be Hannah.

After the blessings, Hannah jumped right into conversation. "Now, tell me about the barn. Are you comfortable out there? If you would rather return home, I'm sure we can manage. You must miss your family."

He actually didn't miss his family as much as he'd imagined he might, and he preferred the barn to home. Maybe leaving the community wouldn't be as hard as he anticipated. "I'm quite comfortable. *Danki*."

Hannah continued, "We wouldn't want to keep you or put your parents in a bad position by insisting you stay."

He glanced around the table. Except for Deborah and Miriam, the younger girls paid no attention to Hannah's words. "My parents and brothers can manage quite well without me." His brothers would be running the farm soon enough without him; they'd might as well start now.

Deborah glanced from Hannah to Miriam, seemingly trying to figure out things, as well. She shook her head and went back to eating.

Miriam stared hard at him and then stabbed a cooked carrot. "If you change your mind, we'll understand."

A distraction attempt? Now more than one sister appeared to be trying to get rid of him. Eligible women were always trying to get rid of him. Women were strange indeed. "I won't. I promised Bishop Bontrager that I would work here while your *vater* is recovering." If he wasn't planning to leave altogether, he might be tempted to ask Bartholomew if he wanted to hire him on afterward to help ease his burden.

Neither Hannah nor Miriam seemed pleased with his answer. Didn't they want their *vater* to have help?

Typical strange behavior for women.

The following Monday, Deborah studied Amos as he watched Miriam. Her sister stood at the clothesline hanging the laundry. She didn't know he was observing her. And *he* didn't know that Deborah was studying him.

How fortunate for Miriam to have someone look at her the way Amos did. Maybe someday someone would regard her in such a manner. But probably not. At least not in her Amish community. The only time she'd ever been noticed was in the *Englisher* world.

Tugging her coat closed, she slipped out past the garden that had been harvested and canned last summer and fall. Spring planting was still a couple of months off.

She hurried out to the cluster of bare sycamore trees near the pond at the edge of their property. After retrieving her backpack from the tangled base of the largest tree, she headed for the meeting spot. No one would miss her. They never did. *Vater's* trip to the hospital had been proof of that.

Deborah tramped through the still-fallow field. This year would be the year this field was planted again. She came out the other side and dashed down the road. At the intersection, an idling car waited. She opened the passenger door and climbed in. Then she switched to English. "Sorry for making you wait."

The older woman pointed toward Deborah's seat belt. "I don't go anywhere until your seat belt is on."

Deborah grabbed the belt, pulled it and snapped it into place. One of the many differences between automobile travel and riding in a buggy.

The woman put her car into gear and pulled out onto the road. "I thought you might not be coming, and I was about to leave."

Deborah was glad the woman hadn't. "Thank you for waiting."

"This is certainly a strange place to be picked up. I've

driven a lot of you Amish and always go to a house, not the side of the road."

"I didn't want to bother anyone." Deborah hoped the woman didn't suspect she was sneaking out. Deborah usually had another woman drive her, one who didn't ask so many questions or insinuate things.

She was relieved when the woman dropped her off at her destination. "Thank you for the ride." She paid the woman for her gas and time.

"Do you need me to come back and return you to where I picked you up?"

"No, thank you. I have a ride." Fortunately, her regular person could take her back.

She hustled away from the car before she could be further delayed and nearly ran into an *Englisher* woman with multicolored hair. "*Entschuldigen Sie*—I mean, excuse me."

The young woman stared a moment as though trying to figure out who Deborah was before she scurried away.

Deborah shrugged and ducked into the restroom of the combination gas station/convenience store to change from her plain Amish dress into a pair of jeans and a sweatshirt, and let down her hair. Where it had been twisted into place in the front, it kinked, and where it had been coiled in the back, it waved. When she wore these clothes with her hair freed, she felt like a different person. What would Amos think of her appearance? Disapprove, for sure.

She hurried to the photography studio and entered silently.

Hudson stood behind his camera, giving instructions to the model sitting on a fake rock wall in front of a backdrop featuring an old building. He had dozens of such roll-down backdrops. From urban to countryside, woodlands to deserts to mountains, all four seasons and various weather, and fantasy backdrops with mythical creatures, medieval castles, Gothic arches, waterfalls and stone stairways in the forest.

Hudson, in his late twenties, had ambitions to move to New York City and become a famous photographer. His wavy, shoulder-length blond hair and dashing good looks meant he could likely succeed on the other side of the camera, as well. When she'd first started modeling for him a year ago, she'd developed a crush on him because of all his praise and attention—two things she rarely received at home.

His assistant, Summer, was the first to see her approaching. She leaned in and spoke to Hudson in a hushed voice.

He pulled back from his camera and swung in Deborah's direction. "Debo! There you are."

When she hadn't wanted to use her real name, Hudson had dubbed her Debo. She didn't much care for it, but it was better than using Deborah and risk being discovered. Because of all the makeup and fussy hair, no Amish would guess that was her even if they ever found out. The likelihood that any of them would see her in one of these *Englisher* catalogs was slim to none. If they did, they wouldn't recognize her.

He walked over to her and gripped her shoulders. "You're my best model. Go see Lindsey and Tina for wardrobe, hair and makeup." He stared at her a little longer and was probably assessing the condition of her features today.

"What is it? Is something wrong?"

"It just amazes me how different you look from when

you go into the dressing room and when you come out again. Lindsey and Tina are miracle workers. If I didn't know both women were you, I would never guess you were the same person."

Deborah counted on that. If her Amish community knew about this, she would be shunned. If the media found out she was an Amish girl modeling, they would exploit that. But Hudson and his team kept her secret, and as long as they did, she could continue to model. She wasn't hurting anyone and wasn't doing anything illegal. The money she earned would help her and her future husband buy a house and farm. She would quit as soon as someone special took interest and asked to court her.

Today's shoot was for a high-end clothing catalog. She would be transformed with makeup, and her hair would be curled and fluffed. It was fun to be pampered like this. It still gave her a chuckle at the variety of clothes *Englishers* owned and wore—different clothes for every season, every occasion and various times of day.

For her, spring and summer meant she could put away her sweater and coat and didn't have to wear shoes or stockings most of the time, going barefoot. Same dress, just fewer layers. Her biggest decision was whether to wear her green, blue or yellow dress. She wore far more outfits on a single photo shoot than she owned. Where did *Englishers* put them all? She would hate to have to wash the lot.

Once she had been rendered unrecognizable and dressed in a long, flowing summer dress she could never imagine owning, she returned to the main area of the studio.

Hudson smiled at her. "There's my favorite model."

He positioned her in the shot and took a lot of pictures. Same instructions he usually gave her.

Strange to be wearing a summer dress in the middle of winter. Strange to be wearing an *Englisher* summer dress, period. She moved automatically and let her mind wander. Back to her family's farm. Was Amos still gazing at Miriam? Had her sister taken notice of his attention? Part of her hoped not.

Deborah focused on the hand snapping in front of her face.

Hudson stood less than a foot away. "You're distracted, Debo. I don't know where you were, but I need you here."

Was she distracted? *Ja.* She supposed she was. "I'm sorry." Her mind kept flittering back to Amos. Why? He wasn't her beau. Until a little over a week ago, she'd barely known he existed. Now she couldn't shake him from her thoughts. He was like a mouse in the wall, always scratching. Always capturing her attention. Always crawling into her daydreams.

She tried to push Amos from her thoughts and focused on Hudson's instructions.

After four hours of changing clothes and hairstyles and having hundreds of photos taken of her, relief washed over Deborah when the shoot was over. After changing into her own *Englisher* clothes and scrubbing off the makeup, she left the dressing room.

Hudson gathered the five models around him. "A mostly great shoot today." He gave Deborah a pointed look.

Her performance was in the part not included in the "mostly great."

"I need all of you back here tomorrow and for the rest

of the week. The client wants the photos this weekend to present to his marketing department Monday."

The other models grabbed their coats and purses and headed out.

Deborah hung back. "I don't know if I can come every day."

He gave her a hard look. "Debo, I need you. You have to come."

"I'll try."

Surprisingly, she did manage to escape the farm each day, although some days were more of a challenge than others.

On Friday, Hudson praised them all for their hard work.

Deborah headed for the exit with aching feet and a tired body. Her body from constantly moving, and her feet from being shoved into impractical shoes. Her brain hurt as well from repeatedly forcing Amos out of her thoughts.

"Debo, hold up." Hudson trotted over to her. "You want to grab a cup of coffee?"

How many times in the past had she hoped for just such an invitation? She shook her head. "I'm sorry, Hudson. I need to get home."

"But we ended early. Certainly you don't have to rush off so soon."

"I have been gone too much from home this week." Not that her family noticed her absence. "And you have photos to edit for your client."

"Next Wednesday, then? I have a shoot. I'll see you then."

She shook her head again. "I need to stick around home for a while."

"If you had a phone, I could call you with opportunities."

She couldn't risk him calling their phone. That would be disastrous for her. She finally escaped, all the while her mind wandering back to Amos.

Amos looked out over the Millers' fields, which were to be plowed in the spring. He couldn't help but think of them as partly his. Since he'd already planned out the plowing and planting, they sort of felt a little like his fields. Of course, they weren't *his* fields, and he might not even be here to do the work. But if he was, he would take pride in that work.

Bartholomew appreciated everything he did around the farm, so Amos worked harder and enjoyed it so much more here than he ever had at home.

Here, even the little things he did mattered. *He* mattered. Bartholomew had never had a son to help him with all the work around the farm. How had he run this place without sons?

But on the flip side, Amos's *mutter* had been alone doing the house chores, cooking, cleaning and laundry for six men and boys through the years. How did *she* do it without help?

On the far side of one of the fields, a woman emerged from a bare stand of sycamore trees nestled next to a pond. She walked across the field he would plow in the not-too-distant future. If he was still here. Bartholomew should have his cast off by then, but he wouldn't likely be up for all the physical work yet. Maybe Amos should stay long enough to help with that.

The woman came closer and closer.

Deborah.

Where did she go all the time? She had disappeared every day this week and would be gone for hours. He was about to find out.

With her head down, she didn't see him approaching. He stepped directly into her path a few yards in front of her. She seemed to be talking to herself, but he couldn't make out all the words. Something about nothing wrong and not hurting anyone.

She kept walking with her head down. The words became clearer. "Everything will be fine. No harm done."

When it looked as though she might literally run into him, he cleared his throat.

She halted a foot away and jerked up her head. She was so startled to see him there, she took a step back and appeared to lose her balance on the uneven ground. Her arms swung out to keep herself upright.

He reached out and took hold of her upper arms to stop her from tumbling to the ground. "Whoa there."

She gasped. "I'm sorry. I didn't see you."

"Where have you been all day?"

"What? Nowhere." She tried to pull free of his grip, but he held fast.

He shook his head. "You've been somewhere. You've left every day this week and been gone for most of the day."

"I—I went for a walk."

"Where? Ohio?"

She twisted her face for a moment before his joke made sense. "We have a pond just over there by those trees. I like to sit there and watch the ducks. It's a nice place to think and be alone. You should go sometime."

"I did. Today. You weren't there."

Her self-satisfied expression fell. "I was for a while, then I walked farther."

He sensed there was more to her absence than a walk. "Where?"

"Why do you care?"

"With your *vater* laid up, I'm kind of responsible for everyone on this farm."

She rolled her eyes. "I'm fine. I can take care of my-self."

How could she not understand the role of a man?

"May I go now?"

He realized he still held on to her upper arms. He didn't want to let her go but did. "I don't want you to leave the farm without telling me where you're going."

"Are you serious?"

He gave her his serious look.

She huffed and strode away.

Would she heed his request?

Where *did* she go every day? He had wanted to fol-low her, was tempted to. He almost did once, but he real-ized it was none of his business and turned around. But curiosity pushed hard on him. He still might follow her if she didn't obey. Just to see. Just to watch her from a distance. Just to know her secret.

Something inside him feared for her. Feared she would walk out across this field and never return. Feared her secret would consume them both. She was a mystery.

A mystery he was drawn to solve.

Deborah heaved a sigh of relief. She marched the rest of the way through the field, resisting the urge to run. After two weeks, Amos Burkholder already paid more attention to her comings and goings than her own family had her whole life—they never expected much from her and thought her an airhead. Fanciful. Her head full of dreams and nonsense.

Well, she did have dreams. And to prove to everyone that she was someone to be noticed, not an airhead, she'd become a church member younger than any of her older sisters at age sixteen, the same year as Miriam, who was a year and a half older than her. She'd basically skipped her *Rumspringa*. But Naomi had run away in a fit of selfishness and sent the family into a tizzy. Miriam hadn't seemed to mind having her special day of joining church ruined, but Deborah had.

No one had congratulated her or told her how wonderful it was that she'd joined so young, that she must be the most dedicated Amish woman ever. Anything to be noticed, just once.

Instead, the whole community had gone on a search for Naomi and found her, hours later, sulking under their porch. She'd walked home by herself, having somehow slipped out of the service, probably under the guise of needing to use the bathroom. She'd stayed hidden even when she'd known people were searching for her. She'd hated that so much attention was being paid to others.

It had been the last straw for Deborah. She'd tried to get her parents' attention and had given up several times, but she'd thought joining church so young would get their attention for sure. If only for a moment. She had just about succeeded until Naomi had pulled her disappearing act. Even after their parents had scolded her younger sister, Deborah gave her a round of her own. After that, Naomi made sure to steal any attention that might be portioned out to Deborah.

Deborah decided that with Naomi always wanting the most attention, Deborah would never get her fair share, so she'd decided to take advantage of being the invisible one. She let Naomi suck up all the attention she could get from the family. Sarah, being the baby and having Down syndrome, naturally got a goodly amount of attention, as well. Joanna and Miriam both took everything in stride and seemed to almost be invisible as well, but they seemed to love it, as though it was their crowning glory to be overlooked. Always quietly in the background.

Well, that wasn't *gut* enough for Deborah. Wasn't she as important as any of the others? Wasn't she just as much in need of being noticed? Wasn't she as worthy as any of the others?

So, she took advantage of her invisibility and realized that her family never really noticed when she wasn't there. If it had been her missing that day instead of Naomi, when would her family have noticed? Certainly not as soon as they had for Naomi. It might not have been until the family was ready to leave for home in the late afternoon, instead of before the service even ended. Maybe not even until nightfall when she wasn't in her bed. Maybe never. But Hudson had noticed her.

She had experimented with being gone from the family for longer and longer periods of time, until she could be gone all day without hardly a notice. She would claim to go for a walk and be gone for hours. When she returned home, she would be told to get her head out of the clouds and keep track of time. Didn't she know they worried about her?

Worried? But they never came looking for her. When she told them that, they said she'd always been a wanderer and she always came home and she could take care of herself.

She had to admit that she had been self-sufficient from an early age. Everyone attributed it to when her *mutter* was so sick while carrying Joanna, that even at two, she somehow knew something had been wrong with *Mutter*, and it was best if she didn't cause a fuss. She'd learned to be quiet from all the shushing from adults and her three older sisters at ages four and three. They all knew to be quiet and not cause any more trouble for the family.

So, Deborah wandered farther and farther from home. Until she ended up at the edge of a photo shoot over a year ago.

Though she tried to stay hidden, the photographer, Hudson, had seen her and said she'd be perfect for the shot. A contrast between two worlds: the outside—*Englisher*—one and the Amish one. She hadn't wanted to do it. She knew she shouldn't. Hudson told her that there would be no harm in it. That none of her Amish people would ever know.

She'd been thrilled at the idea of being special, being different. At being noticed. At no longer being invisible.

Hudson praised her and told her that she was a natural and followed direction better than most of his models. He'd paid her money for taking the pictures. He'd asked her to come to another shoot the following week. She said she couldn't, but then she found she couldn't resist and went. Soon, she participated in weekly shoots with him. After nearly two months, he asked her to change into *Englisher* clothes. She couldn't do that, could she? But she did. And she had enjoyed it. Like being a different person with each new outfit. She wasn't hurting anyone and was earning money for her future.

The clothes were always modest, but sometimes they put makeup on her. At first, she looked strange and felt out of place, but soon got used to her different appearance. None of her Amish community would recognize her when she was dressed and made-up for a shoot. She felt free and no longer invisible. She felt important. She felt like *somebody*.

But now, her absence had been noticed. Amos paid more attention than the others. Part of her liked that someone in her Amish community finally noticed, but he could become a problem if he truly did keep her from leaving for her job. It was her job. An unusual job for an Amish person, true. For her, it was a dangerous job. How ridiculous. She didn't hurt anyone. No one would hurt her. But still, it was a secret. She certainly couldn't tell Amos where she went. But how many times could she claim to go for a walk and have him still believe her? Or worse yet, ask to go with her?

If she *had been* going for a simple walk, she would welcome his company and attention. She smiled at the thought.

She sighed. That could never happen. She needed to figure something out before her next photo shoot.

Chapter Four

When Deborah rolled out of bed Monday morning, she was actually kind of pleased to be able to stay home and not have a photo shoot demanding her attention. Last week had worn her out. Between the sneaking off, traipsing through the lumpy field and posing just so over and over, every muscle in her body had tensed up. Even muscles she hadn't used for any of those tasks. Just the stress made everything taut.

But there was no stress today. She could help out her sisters and *Mutter*, or slip away and relax at the pond. Maybe she would do a little of both.

After breakfast, *Vater* sat in the living room with his leg propped up, and Amos had gone outside to work in the barn. The lumber he'd ordered with *Vater's* permission and gratitude had arrived late on Saturday. Today, he would start his repairs on the hayloft.

Mutter scurried into the kitchen with her coat on. She scanned her daughters. "I'm going to Sister Bethany's Fabric Shoppe. Your *vater* needs a new shirt, and I want to start a new quilt." Her gaze settled solidly on Deborah. "Would you like to come with me?"

Deborah couldn't believe it. As she stood a little taller to speak, she opened her mouth, but before any words could come out, Naomi stepped in front of her.

"I want to go. Can I go with you, *Mutter*?"

"Of course. You can all go. Get your coats."

Hannah and Lydia exchanged glances and identical tilts of their heads.

Sarah clapped her hands. "Yeah. I want to go."

"I'll stay here and start preparations for lunch," Joanna said.

"I'll stay, as well," Lydia said. "Sarah, do you want to help me make a cake? I'll let you lick the bowl."

Sarah clapped her hands again. "Oh, *ja*. I want to lick the bowl."

Mutter had invited Deborah, and now half of her sisters were going.

Hannah, Miriam and Naomi quickly bundled into their coats. Hannah would drive and *Mutter* would sit up front with her. That would leave Deborah to sit in the back with Miriam and Naomi. Miriam was always a pleasure to be with. But Naomi?

Mutter looked directly at Deborah. "You don't have your coat on. Aren't you coming?"

Naomi made a face at Deborah from behind *Mutter's* shoulder.

Lydia put a hand on Deborah's shoulder. "I could use your help with the cake."

Deborah knew her sister didn't, but said, "*Ja*, I'll stay and help."

Mutter smiled at her middlemost daughter. "You are such a *gut* girl."

Deborah smiled back. Her *mutter's* brief attention was somehow worth not going.

Naomi's expression turned smug before she stepped out the kitchen door ahead of everyone. Why her next-to-the-youngest sister insisted on being spiteful didn't make sense to Deborah.

"Mutter?" Deborah asked. "Could you get me some fabric for a quilt, as well?"

"Of course, dear." With that, the foursome left.

Lydia didn't move from Deborah's side but stared out the window at the top of the door. She looked a little troubled, then spoke softly. *"Danki* for not making a fuss about staying. I figured Hannah would have her hands full with Naomi along. Why our sister has chosen you to clash with, I don't know."

It was nice to know that at least one other person in the family noticed Naomi's ill temper toward her. "I do my best to stay out of her way."

"You do it very well. I'm pleased you take the high road."

Maybe that was why no one minded Deborah being gone. Naomi behaved better in her absence. "What do you need me to do?"

Sarah pulled on Lydia's arm. "I wanna lick the cake bowl."

Lydia gave Deborah a helpless look. "See if *Vater* needs anything. We'll start the cake." Her sister allowed their youngest sister to drag her to the cupboard with the mixing bowls.

Deborah liked feeling useful. With her *mutter* and half of her sisters gone, there would be something for her to do. She stopped short in the middle of the living room. *Vater* lay fast asleep, pushed back in the recliner. She returned to the kitchen. *"Vater's* sleeping. What can I do?"

Lydia glanced around. "I think we have it all covered. *Danki* for asking."

Even with half of the women gone, she wasn't needed. "Why don't you read a book or something?"

Deborah didn't want to read a book. She'd been eager to help. Movement outside caught her attention.

Amos helped *Mutter* and her sisters into the big black buggy.

His kindness and thoughtfulness made Deborah want to be near him. "I'm going to take Amos a cup of coffee and a leftover biscuit from breakfast."

Lydia set a large mixing bowl on the table in front of Sarah and handed their youngest sister a wooden spoon. "That would be very nice. I'm sure he would appreciate it."

Deborah hoped so. She snatched her coat, swung it on and fastened it up the front.

Lydia handed Deborah a mug of steaming coffee and the remaining breakfast biscuit. "You're so thoughtful."

If her sister only knew her kindness was an excuse to go see their handsome helper. As she stepped outside, the buggy had just turned onto the road. She hurried to the barn. "Amos?"

He stepped from a horse stall and smiled when he saw her. "*Hallo*, Deborah. What brings you out here?"

His greeting tingled her insides. She held out the offerings. "I brought you coffee and the last biscuit."

He leaned the pitchfork up against the wall and removed his work gloves before he took the biscuit and coffee. "*Danki*. This is quite a treat."

"A treat? It's just a biscuit and coffee."

"Ah, but I come from a farm with all men and one woman. There were never leftovers, so extra food was unheard-of. My brothers and I gobbled up every last crumb our *mutter* prepared." He took a sizable bite. Before long, the beverage and food were gone. "*Danki*. Now that I'm fed, I'll be able to continue my work throughout the morning."

"Are you going to work on the hayloft today?"

"*Ja*. This is a *gut* time, before plowing and planting."

"I'll help you."

His brown eyes stared at her and blinked several times. "I can't allow that. Carpentry is man's work."

She took a deep breath and huffed it out. "Didn't we already go over this? One man, lots of women." She pointed to herself. "Done a little carpentry from time to time. Helped plow and plant. And taken care of the livestock. I even once helped my *vater* fix and grease a buggy wheel."

He shook his head. "I just can't picture you wielding a tool."

Deborah grabbed a framing hammer from where tools hung on the wall. She felt the weight of it in her hand and then rotated her wrist, turning the implement in a circle.

Amos chuckled.

"You think me incapable?"

"*Ne*. I'm thinking you are probably quite capable. I'm grateful for your assistance. While I was waiting for the wood to be delivered, I moved the hay back away from the edge using both the attached ladder and the A-frame one. I removed some of the near boards I could reach from the loft. Your *vater* approved and bought wood for the whole floor to be rebuilt. I could use your help in handing the boards up to me. Do you know where your *vater* keeps his work gloves? I wouldn't want you to get any slivers of wood."

That had been too easy to get him to agree. She'd thought she would have to do a lot more cajoling to get him to consent. She went over to a plastic tub on the floor and popped off the top. After taking out her favorite pale green pair, she snapped the lid closed to keep bugs and critters out of the gloves.

After two and a half hours of hauling up boards and nailing them in place, Deborah was more tired than she'd been in a long time. She was also more satisfied with her work than she'd been in a long time. There was something so gratifying about accomplishing a task like this. Not like modeling, where she sat there and posed this way and that. It wasn't fulfilling. Not like this had been.

Miriam entered the barn. "My goodness, you've made quite a bit of progress."

Amos nodded toward Deborah where she stood on one of the two ladders. "Your sister helped. I wouldn't be nearly as far along without her."

"Deborah can be a very hard worker."

Not a glowing compliment, but at least it wasn't negative.

Deborah felt bad that she was spending time with the man who was interested in Miriam. It reminded Deborah that she often wasn't around to help with the work. She wasn't usually needed anyway, and she shouldn't feel bad working with Amos, because she'd done nothing wrong or inappropriate. Miriam could have offered to help him.

"She's been very helpful." Amos shot Deborah an appreciative glance.

Deborah's insides tingled at his encouraging look.

"We all strive to do our part." Miriam shifted her gaze from Amos to Deborah. "I just came out to let you know that lunch will be ready in about fifteen minutes, if you want to get washed up."

"Danki," Deborah said at the same time Amos did.

"Bitte." Miriam left without so much as a second glance at Amos. So, hopefully her sister wasn't any more interested in him than he seemed to be in her.

Deborah scurried down her ladder as Amos climbed down his. She certainly was hungry and knew a delicious meal awaited. She removed her gloves, as did Amos. Deborah grabbed both pairs and tucked them safely inside the plastic bin.

"Just a second." Amos headed back for the ladder. "I want to bring down the nail pouch, so I don't forget to refill it before we go back up." He climbed up.

We. He'd said *we.* So he *wanted* her to continue to help him. She smiled. She definitely wanted to continue to help him, as well. It gave her a chance to spend time with him and be useful.

"Got it." He backed down the ladder. "Ouch!" He jerked his right hand away from the ladder.

Deborah stepped closer. "What happened?"

"Splinter. I should have been more careful." He jumped the rest of the way to the ground and tossed the nail bag onto the stack of lumber.

"Let me see." Deborah grabbed his hand and turned it palm up. The realization that she was holding a man's hand—a man who wasn't a family member—sent a jolt up her arm. She still wasn't doing anything wrong. She was merely helping someone who was helping her family.

He scratched at his palm with his fingernail. "I can take care of it."

"It's your dominant hand. It'll be easier if I do it."

She released him. "Move over to the brighter light of the doorway." He obeyed.

Deborah took a slow, deep breath to calm her fluttering insides and grabbed the red-and-white first-aid kit off the tool wall. Popping it open, she set the kit on the end of the pile of boards and removed the tweezers.

Once her fickle insides were wrestled under control, she cupped her hand around his and lifted the end of the large sliver with the tip of the tweezers, pinching it. "This is going to hurt."

"Pull it out fast and get it over with."

"Okay." She yanked it free as she spoke the word.

He sucked in a breath through gritted teeth but didn't move his hand, not even a twitch.

It took all her strength to focus on the sliver and not on holding his warm, strong hand in hers. *Keep your breathing natural.* She picked out a couple of more small ones, then dabbed the abrasions with an alcohol wipe. "There. That should do it. Are there any others? I can't see any." When he didn't answer, she looked up.

He stared down at her with a strange expression on his face.

Her question came out a little soft. "Did I get them all?" Leaving her hand cupped around the bottom of his, she continued to stare up at him. That same strange feeling she'd had when he'd knocked her out of the way of the falling board more than a week ago wrapped around her like a gentle hug.

After a moment, he nodded but didn't pull his hand away. "We should go wash up for lunch. We don't want to keep the others waiting."

This time, she nodded but didn't move until a loud motorcycle raced by on the road. She drew in a quick breath, breaking the moment and retrieving her hand. "I'll put the first-aid kit away."

He cleared his throat and dropped his hand to his side. "*Danki.* It feels better already."

His praise caressed her like a long-awaited, warm spring breeze.

Tuesday, again she had another pleasant day helping Amos with the hayloft. But Wednesday was a different matter entirely. She was expected at the studio for a shoot. She needed to slip away undetected by Amos. A part of her wanted to stay and work beside him again even though they had finished the hayloft floor. She'd told Hudson she didn't know if she would be able to make it, but he was counting on her. And if she was going to be honest with herself, she missed modeling and Hudson's praise.

However, slipping away had been easier than she'd thought it would be. Amos drove *Vater* to Dr. Kathleen's to check his leg. *Mutter* went as well, along with Hannah and Naomi, so Deborah had a *gut* excuse not to go. The buggy was full with *Vater's* leg needing to be propped up.

Deborah had been able to stroll at a leisurely pace through the field as she had done before Amos arrived. She caught her ride and reached the studio early. She hurried inside.

Hudson stood with Summer, Tina and Lindsey over what appeared to be concept drawings. Which meant today's shoot wouldn't be for some boring clothing catalog.

Deborah liked these shoots best. She could be more free and have fun. "Am I the first model here?"

Four pairs of eyes turned toward her.

Hudson stepped away from the group. "Yes. You're early." He sounded pleased.

Was that because she was early or just because she showed up after saying she might not? It didn't matter. She was here and glad about it. She joined them at the table to look at the printouts of various period dresses and multiple backgrounds.

Deborah picked up a paper with a royal blue velvet gown. "I call dibs on this one. First come, first serve."

Hudson waved his arm over the table. "You get to wear them all."

"What about the other girls? Are we all going to take turns wearing each dress?"

"Not exactly. You're the only model today."

She set down the paper. "Is everyone else sick?"

"No. I need only one model today. And since I can't call you to cancel, I canceled the others."

So did that mean Deborah had been a last resort? Hudson didn't seem to be upset that she was his model today. She had told Hudson from the beginning she didn't have a telephone number. Though her *vater* did, she technically didn't. She couldn't risk him calling. She would never be able to explain receiving a call from an *Englisher*. And an *Englisher* man, no less.

Deborah would stand in front of either one of the different pull-down backdrops or a green screen in the assorted outfits, and Hudson would put her in various backgrounds, mostly outdoors ones. These shots would likely be for book covers. "So, you're shooting covers today."

"Yes. I have several custom-ordered for specific books. The others I'll put on my website to sell."

She posed in a Victorian dress, a medieval gown and

a gypsy outfit, as well as others. Her favorite was the flowy, gauzy lavender fantasy dress with sparkly accents.

"Gaze off into the distance as though you see someone you're glad to meet." Hudson snapped multiple pictures as he spoke. "Turn on the fan."

A gentle breeze played with her loose hair. What would Amos think if he could see her?

"Good. I like that distressed look."

She was modeling only until she found someone to marry, and that wasn't likely to be anytime soon.

"I'll put you in a meadow, on a high castle wall, and even give you wings."

Amos would think her silly, foolish and worthy to be shunned. Her insides twisted at the thought of him being so disappointed in her.

She spun and faced the camera. "I'm sorry. I need to go."

"But we still have more outfits to shoot."

"Call in one of the other models." She hurried to the dressing room. It had been a mistake to come.

Amos stood in the barn, greasing a buggy wheel. He'd noticed it squeaking a little on the trip to the local Amish doctor's.

He had his usual supervisor—the gray tabby—who watched him work in and around the barn. He'd learned the cat's name was Sissy. Amos had cut out a small section of the tack room door at the bottom for the cat to come and go. By the time he'd gone to bed that first night, Sissy had brought two more kittens, for a total of five. He enjoyed having them as roommates. When Sissy got tired of her kittens, she would curl up on his cot.

Once again, he stepped away from his work on the buggy wheel to go outside and look beyond the barn toward the field Deborah often disappeared through. He'd thought she might help him. She said she'd greased a buggy wheel before, but she'd taken advantage of him being gone to take her *vater* to have his leg checked and had left without permission or telling anyone where she'd gone.

He'd been a bit breathless on Monday when Deborah had removed his wood sliver. Not from the pain but from having a woman holding his hand. Not holding his hand like they were courting, but nonetheless, her touch had affected him. At first, it had briefly reminded him of when his *mutter* had removed slivers from his hands when he was a boy, but it had quickly turned into something different. Something more. Something he wanted to repeat. Could Deborah be different from the other Amish girls who had disappointed him? Part of him hoped so. But why hope for anything when he was leaving? It wouldn't matter.

Today, she wasn't here to tend to any wounds he might incur. She had slipped away while he was gone. He'd become complacent because she'd been helping him the past two days. He should have insisted she come to the doctor's with them. He'd forgotten she *was* different from other Amish girls. Not content to stay around the farm. She had a restlessness about her. What was it that caused her to feel the need to always wander off?

He'd already trekked out to the pond in case she had simply gone there as she said she often did, but she was nowhere in sight. Though he hadn't really expected to find her there, disappointment that she wasn't had stabbed at him. He would have to wait until she returned, and then he would keep an even closer eye on her from now on. He shouldn't allow himself to get tangled up with thoughts of her. Thoughts that would likely lead to heartbreak again.

When he returned inside to the buggy, Jacob was leaning against it. "You are a difficult man to track down."

Amos looked back toward the door opening. None of the Millers were around to take notice of his cousin.

Jacob pushed away from the buggy. "I made sure I wasn't seen."

That was a relief. "It's *gut* to see you. What are you doing here?"

"Looking for you. You weren't easy to find. I was on the road near your family's farm every day for nearly a week and didn't see you once. Then I remembered where you said you were working. Are you staying here?"

"*Ja.* Bartholomew broke his leg. I'm helping out on his farm while he's laid up. It's fairly light work, being winter. I did replace his rotting hayloft floor." He pointed above him. "That's how he injured himself."

"You appear to be enjoying yourself."

"The work is *gut*." And he slept like a contented man because of it.

Jacob's mouth hitched up on one side. "Or is it because you have your eye on one of his daughters? Are you looking for a *frau* while you're here?"

Part of Amos *was* looking for an Amish *frau*. Was it because he wanted one? Or because it was expected of him? Or because he wanted to believe a *gut* Amish woman could fall in love with him? On the other hand, Jacob was here to help Amos leave the Amish. Amos wasn't sure what he wanted anymore. "*Ne.* I don't think I'm ready to marry yet." He needed to figure out where he belonged first. Here, in his plain world, which might include Deborah, or out there, in the fancy one without her.

"Do you still want to leave?"

"*Ja.* I think I do."

Jacob pulled a cell phone and cord from his jacket pocket. "Then I brought this for you. Have you used one before?"

Amos nodded. "On *Rumspringa*." He hesitated before taking the forbidden device. This was a step down a path away from Deborah.

"Make sure to keep it charged. I'll text you with a meeting time and place. I've put it on Silent, so you'll need to check it each day for messages and text back that you received it. I'll contact you with a time and place for next week. Will you still be here or at your parents' farm?"

"Here." Amos shifted his gaze from the phone to his cousin. "But I don't know if next week will work. Bartholomew still needs my help."

"He wouldn't have any trouble finding someone else. Maybe even one of your brothers."

Jacob was right, but Amos didn't want anyone else taking his place here. This was his place. At least for the time being. "I made a promise to him." When he was no longer needed here, it would be easier to leave. Being on the Millers' farm had already been a small step in breaking ties with his family.

Jacob studied him for a moment. "Do you truly want to leave?"

"*Ja, ja.* I do." No sense in getting even more attached to this family.

His cousin narrowed his eyes. "All right. I'll be in

touch to see how things are going." He shuffled his feet. "How are my *mutter* and *vater* and my brothers and sisters?"

"They are doing well. They miss you."

Jacob laughed. "I know they didn't say that. That would be frowned upon."

"I can tell by their guarded speech when they talk about their children and their worried expressions. And you are prayed for at church." When Amos left, he would be included in the unnamed lost members who left the Amish faith, along with Jacob, the bishop's granddaughter and a few others.

Amos walked Jacob to the barn door opening and peered out into the yard to make sure no one was there. The pair stepped outside. He wished his cousin farewell and watched him until he made it to the road.

Rubbing a hand across the back of his neck, he tried to sort out his thoughts. It would be easier to break ties with his community when he wasn't needed here. But for now, he *was* needed. He returned to the barn to finish greasing the buggy wheel.

"Who was that *Englisher*?"

He looked up and saw Deborah strolled toward him. "Who?"

"The man who just left."

Should he make up a story, tell her the *Englisher* was lost and had asked for directions?

"He's the same man you spoke with at the hospital, isn't he?"

She'd seen him then? He'd thought he'd sneaked away unnoticed. Now she would think less of him. He decided to go with the truth. "That was Jacob. My cousin."

"Oh. Is he still on *Rumspringa*?"

"Ne."

Her big, beautiful green eyes widened. "He left the church?"

"Six months ago."

"What was he doing here?"

"Asking about his family."

"But he turned his back on them when he left."

"He still cares about them. Just because someone leaves doesn't mean they no longer believe in *Gott*."

"Is he going to come back?"

"I doubt it." He didn't want to talk about his cousin anymore. "When your parents and I came back from the doctor's, you were gone. Where did you go?"

Her eyes widened again, and she looked away. "For a walk. I went to the—"

"Don't say the pond, because I checked there."

She gave him a steady stare. "Well, I *did* go there first. Then I walked farther. As my family says—" she put on a silly expression "—I'm fanciful with my head full of daydreams and nonsense."

He narrowed his eyes. "You aren't nearly as out of touch with things as you would like your family to believe. I believe you're quite smart and intuitive."

Her facade changed to a mix of shock and…pleasure? "You think I'm…smart?"

"Why wouldn't I? You seem smart to me and quite capable."

She straightened and stood a little taller.

But before she could distract him further, he said, "I told you that you need to tell me where you're going."

She gave him a tight smile. "You weren't here." She turned toward the buggy. "You want me to help you with finishing up?" She was changing the subject.

He should press the issue, but he didn't want to argue with her, didn't want to scare her away. He wanted things to be pleasant between them. "I would like that. Next time, tell someone where you're going. I know you don't understand or believe it, but I do feel responsible for everyone here while your *vater* is recuperating."

"But you're not. I can take care of myself."

"Sometimes your family may not notice you, but I do."

She gifted him with a sweet smile that made his brain a little fuzzy.

Chapter Five

Deborah sat at the kitchen table almost a week and a half later, poking her finger into a flat of potting soil and dropping in vegetable seeds. It would give their kitchen garden a head start. Lots of celery for the impending weddings this fall.

Amos had planted himself firmly in her mind with his declaration that he noticed her. Though his attention to her whereabouts hampered her ability to escape when she needed to leave, it was nice to have someone aware of her. What kind of an excuse could she give to go outside to see him, if only for a minute or two?

Hannah strolled in. "*Mutter* needs thread."

Deborah's ears perked up. "Is she going to Sister Bethany's Fabric Shoppe again?"

Hannah shook her head. "She wants to stay with *Vater*. Lydia, would you mind going for her?"

"I'll go." Deborah jumped to her feet and brushed dirt from her hands. She had missed out on a trip to the fabric shop the last time, and *Mutter* had forgotten to get her fabric for a quilt. Thanks to her modeling job, Deborah had money to buy her own fabric.

Lydia smiled. "That settles it. Deborah and I will go."

Sarah jumped up and down. "I wanna go. I wanna go."

Lydia pulled a stiff smile and tilted her head. Her sister didn't like to make waves. Deborah could tell she was trying to decide whom she was going to disappoint. Deborah or Sarah. Lydia was a peacekeeper.

Deborah took the decision out of her hands. She put her hand on Sarah's shoulder. "We would love for you to come with us."

Lydia gave her an appreciative smile.

Sarah was most generally always a joy to be around, more so than Naomi. Why couldn't Naomi just be nice to her? Deborah had never done anything to her. Maybe she would be better when she grew up a little more.

"I'll get my shopping bag, and then I'll go see about hitching up the buggy." Deborah ran upstairs and grabbed some of her money she had tucked away and her canvas shopping tote. When she came back down, she swung on her coat.

"*Danki*, Deborah," Lydia said. "I'll get Sarah ready."

"It's not a problem." She headed to the barn.

Amos was there, working diligently. Today, mucking out a stall. Deborah never saw him slacking off in his duties. He was always *doing* something. Sissy, one of their barn cats, watched his every move.

"You are such a *gut* Amish."

He faced her with a smile, and her heart soared. "You are *gut*, too."

"I'm not all that *gut*." If he knew about her secret life, he wouldn't say such things.

He leaned on the shovel handle. "Did you need me for something?"

"*Ne.* I'm just getting the buggy ready. Lydia, Sarah and I are going to Sister Bethany's Fabric Shoppe."

"I'll help you."

"You don't have to." But she hoped he did.

"I want to. I'm done here." He pushed the full wheelbarrow out of the way. "I'll get the harness. Would you get Floyd from his stall?"

"Sure."

Floyd was a large gray-and-black draft horse. A gentle giant. He greeted her with a nicker and tucked his head over her shoulder, pulling her close for a hug.

She wrapped her arms around his beefy neck. "I'm glad to see you, too."

"He really likes you."

Deborah turned.

Amos stood with his arms folded, his hip leaning against the stall frame and a crooked smile on his face. "I've never seen a horse so friendly before."

"Floyd has been in our family for a long time. I believe he's special."

With the bridge of his nose, the large draft horse nudged her back, which was equivalent to someone shoving her quite forcefully. Deborah careened forward several steps to try to keep her balance. But it wasn't going to do any *gut.* Momentum and gravity were going to land her face-first on the ground.

Amos jumped forward and caught her in his arms, keeping her from landing in a heap in the straw. "Whoa."

The silly horse did that on purpose. But why?

She stared up at Amos.

And stared.

And stared.

Did he realize he was holding her? She should back

away, but truthfully, her knees had lost their ability to hold her up.

This needed to stop happening—standing so close to him and gazing at him like he could ever mean anything to her. And *touching. Ja*, always innocently, but nevertheless, touching.

He'd come with intentions toward her sister Miriam. Hadn't he? But he never spent any time with her, and Miriam never manipulated events to be near him. She seemed content to wait for him to come to her. Maybe Deborah could help them. That thought caused a dull ache to form in her chest.

She kept staring.

But he was staring, too.

She cleared her throat and forced strength back into her jellied legs. "I'll lead Floyd out."

He cleared his throat, too. "*Ja*, right. I have the harness ready." He released her and backed away, then turned and disappeared.

She spun back to the gray-and-black draft horse, shook her finger at him and spoke in a low voice. "You did that on purpose. Behave yourself."

The big ol' lug whinnied, bobbing his head up and down.

"Are you laughing at me?"

The horse bobbed his head again.

She grabbed his rope from the wall, then tossed the loop over his head and around his neck. "You need to learn some manners."

The big draft horse hooked his chin over her shoulder and pulled her in for another hug.

Poor thing thought she was mad at him. "I forgive you. But if you do it again… I won't mind." She led him out to where Amos stood between the buggy shafts. She maneuvered Floyd around and backed him into place. Whether hitching up a horse or rebuilding a hayloft floor, being near Amos made her insides dance.

Soon the buggy was ready, and Lydia and Sarah came out to where the buggy was parked in front of the house.

Sarah let go of Lydia's hand, ran to Amos and threw her arms around his waist. "Amos!"

He patted her on the back. "*Gut* to see you, Sarah."

Lydia touched Sarah on the shoulder. "Leave Amos alone."

Sarah stepped backward and latched onto his hand.

"Sarah, what were you told about running up to people and hugging them?"

"But I know him. He's not a stranger." She pulled him toward the buggy. "You coming with us."

Lydia put her hands on her hips. "Sarah, let him go."

Sarah's bottom lip pushed out as she released him, and she plopped down on the ground. "I want Amos to come with us!"

Deborah did, too, but couldn't say so. *Please let Sarah get her way.*

This was typical behavior for Sarah. She loved everyone and thought of everyone as her friend. When she got scolded, she often threw a tantrum.

Amos knelt in front of her. "I would love to go with you, but you need to ask nicely, *ja*?"

His patience with her Down syndrome sister warmed Deborah's heart.

"You come with us…please?"

"It would be my pleasure." When Sarah tilted her head, he added, "*Ja*, I will go."

He was going! Deborah's heart skipped a beat.

Sarah jumped to her feet and pulled him toward the buggy door. She climbed in the front. Assuming Amos would drive, that left the back for Deborah and Lydia. Though disappointed at first, it did afford her the vantage point of watching his profile as he drove without it being awkward or anyone noticing what she was doing.

Amos looked back over his shoulder. "Are you two doing all right back there?"

She and Lydia nodded.

Soon they arrived at Sister Bethany's Fabric Shoppe, a small building to the side of the main house on Bethany and her sister's parents' property. Deborah and her two sisters piled out, and Amos took care of Floyd and the buggy.

Lydia stopped Sarah on the porch. "Remember not to touch everything. If you want to look at something, ask me first."

Sarah nodded briskly, and they all went inside.

Besides fabric and sewing notions, Bethany and her sister Rosemary had finished quilts for sale, completed clothes, wooden toys, Amish dolls with clothes and a small variety of jarred canned goods and cooking utensils. A little bit of everything, most of it made by people in their district.

Deborah headed straight for the solid colored fabrics. Bethany and Rosemary had fabric already cut in common lengths. It was time Deborah had a new dress, as well as started a quilt for when she got married—*if* she got married. What color would Amos like? She chose a pink fabric for a nice spring dress and various other colors for a quilt.

Sarah tugged on Deborah's arm.

"What is it, sweetie?"

"Deborah." Sarah pushed an Amish romance novel into her stomach. "Deborah."

Deborah had forgotten about the Amish novels the sisters carried in the store. Though Deborah already had one checked out from the library that she was reading, she took Sarah's offering anyway. *"Danki."* *Amish Identity* by Mary Rosenberg. At least the model on the cover was dressed accurately. She'd seen books where the model actually had the cape dress on backward. This one looked very authentic. In fact, she had a dress this same col— Deborah gasped. *She* was the model on the book's cover!

At the very first photo shoot she'd stumbled upon, Hudson had said he would create book covers with her image. She just never imagined her picture would ever make the cover of any book. Ever! But here she was. Fortunately, it didn't expose her full face. She'd been too shy in the beginning to look at the camera. But the side view of her looking down at a black-eyed Susan was still unmistakably her.

"Deborah," Sarah said again.

Her baby sister wasn't just calling her name, she'd recognized her on the cover.

"Shh." Deborah put her finger to her lips.

Purchased books were often passed around the community. Not this one. Deborah stuffed it into her shopping bag. Then she hurried to the shelf of books and thumbed through the others. Another book by the same author, but no others with Deborah on the cover. She sighed with relief.

Sarah pulled at Deborah's cloth shopping bag. "Deborah."

Deborah crouched and put her finger to her lips again. "Shh. Let's not tell anyone."

"I want the book!" Sarah said in a louder-than-necessary voice.

Deborah glanced around, but no one looked their way. Then she grabbed a carved wooden cat and held it toward her littlest sister. "Would you like me to buy you this kitty?"

Sarah's almond-shaped eyes widened. "*Ja.* I want the kitty." And with that, Sarah was both distracted and pacified.

Bethany rang up her sale, including the fabric, book and wooden cat. She held the novel in her hand. "Have you read this author before?"

Deborah shook her head, hoping Bethany didn't look too closely at the cover.

"I hear this author's more accurate with the Amish details than most of these writers. I don't know that I believe she's actually an Amish woman. No real Amish woman would write a novel."

Well, the cover was more accurate. A little too accurate. If Deborah modeled when no other Amish would, she supposed anything was possible. She wanted to snatch the book from Bethany's hands and stuff it back into her bag.

"You'll have to tell us how you like it." Bethany finally released it.

"You're buying a book." Amos stood right beside her.

Deborah put her hand over her head on the cover. "*Ja.* These can be entertaining. It's fun to pick out the inaccuracies and to get an idea of how *Englishers* view us." She pushed it toward the opening of her cloth shopping bag hanging on her arm, but the corner kept getting caught on the top edge and the handles.

"Careful," Bethany said. "You don't want to damage the cover."

Oh, but she *did* want to damage the cover. She wanted to make it unrecognizable. She couldn't let Amos—or anyone else, for that matter—identify her. Finally, the book cooperated and dropped safely to the bottom. Deborah quickly shoved her fabric on top of it and paid.

Amos frowned at her. "Your face is red. Are you feeling all right?"

She nodded quickly. "It's just a little warm in here. I'll wait in the buggy." She hurried out into the cold and took a deep breath.

That was close.

Chapter Six

At breakfast the next morning, Amos wiped the last of the gravy off his plate with a biscuit. He was going to get fat if he kept eating like this, but the Miller ladies cooked so well, and there was always plenty of food for him to eat until he was full. He wasn't used to there being leftovers, but there generally was.

Bartholomew took a swig of his coffee. "You'll leave right after breakfast."

Amos swallowed hard to get his last bite down around the rising lump in his throat. "I don't think I should go. You're still in a cast." A new cast, in *Ordnung*-approved black. He'd had to color the foot portion of his former bright green one that showed below his pant leg with a black marker.

Bartholomew smiled. "Though you've been a huge help and put my mind at ease, we will survive one day and night without you. Don't get me wrong. I deeply appreciate all you've done around here. My new hayloft floor looks quite sturdy, but it's important for you to visit your family. I'm sure they miss you."

Amos wasn't so sure about that. Work tended to be

light around the Burkholder farm, and even lighter in the wintertime. "I will head off soon." Though he *was* reluctant. He glanced at Deborah.

She piped up. "*Vater?* It's quite a ways and cold out. Maybe one of us could drive him home so it doesn't take him all day."

"Fine idea. Did you have someone in mind?"

Amos liked the idea of a long ride with Deborah.

"What about Miriam?" Deborah seemed pleased with herself.

He was unexpectedly disappointed, even though he supposed a ride with Miriam would be quite pleasant, as well.

Miriam sneezed. "I think I'm coming down with a cold. It wouldn't be a *gut* idea to be in a cold buggy for hours. Why don't you go, Deborah?"

Bartholomew reached for his crutches. His shoulder had healed well enough in the last little while for him to use them on a limited basis. "Then it's settled. Deborah, you go. Take the trap."

The open, two-wheeled buggy would be appropriate, since it would just be the two of them.

"I wanna go," Sarah pleaded.

Teresa patted her youngest daughter's arm. "Not this time, dear. You stay here with me. We can bake some cookies."

"Cookies!"

Amos pushed away from the table. "I'll hitch up the buggy."

Deborah smiled at him. "I'll be out in a few minutes."

He had the buggy hitched by the time Deborah came out lugging a heavy, thick canvas bag. He took it from her. "What's in here?"

"Warmed bricks for our feet and a warm quilt to cover our legs."

He situated the bricks on the floor and helped her in.

"I'm sorry Miriam couldn't go."

He wasn't. But was Deborah truly sorry she had to go?

He put the buggy into motion and pulled up on the road. "When this was your idea, why did you suggest your sister go? Do you not like my company?"

"*Ne*, that's not it at all. I like your company *very* much. I mean, I enjoy time with you. Oh, I don't know what I'm saying."

She was cute when she was flustered. What had caused her to sputter? Him? "So, why your sister?"

"When you first arrived, I thought you were interested in her. Weren't you? Aren't you?"

He shrugged. "Maybe at first."

"But not anymore?"

"Ne." Someone else occupied his thoughts even if he didn't want her to.

The pleasant drive to the other side of the district took over two hours. As Amos drove into the yard, he felt like a foreigner returning home. This was only the third time he'd seen his family since he'd gone to work at the Miller farm. The other two times had been at the biweekly church services.

Bartholomew had talked Amos into this overnight trip home. He hadn't wanted to go. But he could protest only so much before Bartholomew would have suspected he didn't want to go home. This was going to be a long few hours until bed and then again in the morning. Hopefully, his family wouldn't sense his reluctance to be home. He would return to the Millers' with them after church tomorrow.

He parked the buggy out front. "Come in and meet my parents," he suggested as he helped Deborah down.

His *mutter* rushed outside into the cold without a coat. "Amos!" She hugged him, then turned to Deborah. "You must be one of the Miller girls. I'm sorry, but I don't know your family well enough to know which one you are."

"*Mutter*, this is Deborah."

"I'm pleased to meet you." His *mutter* hugged Deborah, as well. "I'm Karen."

"I'm pleased to meet you, too, Karen. Or rather, meet you again."

"I think I remember you have older sisters who are twins, then some other sisters and the sweet baby is Sarah."

"That's right."

From the barn came his *vater* and two brothers, who each shook his hand in greeting.

Amos gritted his teeth. "*Vater*, this is Deborah Miller." He turned to her. "My *vater*, Joseph. This is Daniel and Titus."

Mutter waved her hand in the air. "Come in out of the cold for a slice of pie and a cup of hot tea," his *mutter* said to Deborah. "It will be nice to have some female company."

Daniel elbowed Amos. "I assume you're going to be courting Deborah. But what about the others? Are any of the others being courted?"

His brother's question surprised Amos. He hadn't thought him interested yet. "The two oldest are being courted." He wouldn't say that they would be engaged this fall, as that was the family's business to announce after the engagements were official. "As far as I know Miriam isn't being courted, nor Joanna, but she's still a little young."

Amos wouldn't say that he wasn't courting Deborah, nor did he plan to court her. There were plenty of other young ladies for his brother to consider.

Vater clasped Amos on the shoulder, causing him to tense. "*Mutter*, you and Deborah go on inside. I need to talk to Amos for a minute."

Amos watched Deborah disappear into the house.

"Daniel, Titus, go finish the work in the barn." *Vater* waved his hand for them to leave.

Why couldn't Amos leave, as well? "What do you need to talk to me about?"

"You've had some time to think while at the Millers'. Have you made up your mind what job you want to pursue?"

Ja, Amos had done a lot of thinking, but not about what his *vater* referred to. "It's a big decision." Bigger than his *vater* realized.

"I'm sorry this farm isn't big enough to divide three ways, but don't let that stop you from making this decision. Don't put it off."

Amos wasn't putting off going into the *Englisher* world. Not really. True, he likely could have left by now, but the Millers really did need help. And he'd said he would help. He was a man of his word. When Jacob said to go, Amos would find someone else to help the Millers and be gone. He could do that. Couldn't he? Something twisted inside him.

Vater and Amos joined *Mutter* and Deborah inside. Amos set the bricks on the stove to warm up before Deborah made the drive back home. He supposed he could have driven himself with the Millers' buggy and returned it tomorrow when he went to church. Why hadn't he thought of that before? Maybe because a part of him wanted to spend time with Deborah.

The following morning, Amos's desire to get to church churned inside him like a whirlwind. His family had all said that they had missed him and included him as though he hadn't been gone for a month. As *gut* as it was to visit his family, seeing Deborah—all the Millers—would make him happy. He looked forward to returning home with them.

When his family arrived at the host home, he immediately scanned the crowd outside for the Millers. He didn't find any of them. They must not have arrived yet.

He studied each buggy as it pulled into the Beilers' yard. He and his brothers had shown up early to help set up. Church was due to start in a few minutes. Where were the Millers? He knew he shouldn't have left them. With Bartholomew still recovering, they needed a man around. They needed him.

Then at last, a final buggy rolled down the road with a horse clopping briskly in front of it. Floyd.

He met the buggy where it parked.

Hannah sat at the reins.

"I'm sorry," Amos said. "I should have come by your place to help you all."

Hannah smiled. "That wouldn't have likely gotten us here any faster. Our issues were beyond anyone's control."

He could have at least helped. "You all head inside, and I'll take care of Floyd."

Everyone piled out, and Sarah wrapped her chubby arms around his waist. "I missed you. Don't ever go away again."

He patted the girl's back. "It couldn't be helped, and I won't be able to stay on your farm forever. I'll have to leave sometime." He sought out a glance from Deborah, and she graciously gave him one. Had she missed him? He felt drawn to her. What was it about her? There were things about her he didn't know. There was more to her than the normal Amish-piety exterior. Could she be the forthright Amish woman he'd been looking for?

"I'll help Amos," Deborah said.

His heart cheered.

The others tromped off. Hannah had her arm looped through her *mutter's* and seemed to be whispering in her ear.

Amos worked on unhooking the harness from the buggy. "Where's Miriam?"

Deborah's smile slipped a little. "She's at home. She was too sick to come."

"I'm sorry to hear that." What had changed Deborah's mood? He'd only asked about— "I only asked because she hadn't been feeling well, not because I'm interested in her. You believe me, don't you?"

She gazed at him with that wistful almost smile that made his heart do funny things. *"Ja."*

The rest of the Millers filed inside while Amos and Deborah tended to Floyd and turned him out with the other horses in the field.

He escorted Deborah inside. She went up to sit with her sisters and her *mutter*, and he sat in the back with his brothers. Deborah sat on the outer end, almost as though she didn't belong with the family. He understood the feeling of not quite belonging in one's own family, or in the community.

After the service, Lydia left with Dr. Kathleen to look in on Miriam.

At the end of the afternoon, Amos hitched the horse back up and drove the Millers home.

He found he felt more comfortable with Deborah's family than his own. They had different expectations of him and were grateful for all his work, instead of thinking of him as less capable because he was the youngest.

Later in the evening, Amos dug out the cell phone from where he'd stashed it under his cot.

The kittens, now about five weeks old, climbed out of their box, up the side of the quilt that hung down to the floor and onto the cot. He petted the three that faced him and meowed. They were very cute, and he enjoyed watching them change from day to day. One of the kittens leaped from the cot to his thigh and climbed up.

Once the kitten had settled himself on Amos's shoulder, he pressed a button on the phone to light it up. A text from Jacob waited. He clicked the message open.

How are you doing? Will have a place for you to stay soon.

Amos hit Reply. Doing well. Soon will be fine. Still needed at the Mi—

"Hallo," a female voice said behind him.

Amos fumbled the phone and then shoved it inside the front of his shirt before turning around. "Deborah." He should have closed the door to his small living quarters.

"I wish we had a bigger space for you than this." Deborah stood in the doorway.

"This is fine. It takes less to heat."

"It does seem toasty in there. Maybe a little too toasty. Your face is red."

He didn't doubt his face looked flaming hot, but it wasn't from the heat. He'd almost been caught using an unauthorized device.

"How are the kittens doing?" She plucked one from his shoulder.

"They're getting very energetic and don't want to stay in their box anymore." He sucked in a breath as another kitten suddenly attached itself to his back and proceeded to climb.

When the kitten appeared over his shoulder, Deborah laughed. "Do they do that a lot?"

Her laugh sent a thrill through him, making the needlelike claws worth it.

He thinned his lips and nodded. "I tried to stop them, but…" He shrugged. Like his growing feelings for the girl standing before him.

After Deborah left, Amos pulled the cell phone back out of his shirt. He hoped Deborah hadn't noticed it there. He finished his text to his cousin and pressed Send.

If he was caught using an unapproved cell phone, he could be shunned. Then how would he help the Millers? He stashed the phone back under his cot, farther than he had before. What if someone came in here and found it? No one usually entered his quarters, that he knew of. Everyone respected this as his area.

But still, he needed to be careful.

Deborah would never understand and would be the first one to shun him.

The thought of her never talking to him again made his heart hurt.

Chapter Seven

After a shoot the following week, Deborah headed back across the field to the pond in the stand of trees. Once the fields were planted and growing, she wouldn't be so noticeable tromping across them. She stashed her pack among the sycamore trees and covered it with dry leaves. They were getting pretty shredded and small, more like confetti these days. When she prepared to make a dash for home, she stopped short and gasped. *"Mutter!"*

Busted!

She looked in one direction then the other. No one else was around.

Mutter walked back and forth and in circles at the edge of the pond.

Deborah hurried over to her. "Wh-what are you doing here?" Had *Mutter* seen her stow her change of clothes?

Mutter turned her gaze on Deborah with a confused glaze in her eyes. "I don't know. Where am I?" She had the hem of her apron between her fingers and was pulling at it as though she was trying to pick something off it.

What was wrong with her? Was *Mutter* playing some

sort of game? Had she seen Deborah and wanted her to confess? "Um, the pond? I was just taking a walk."

"A walk." *Mutter* blinked several times, then her face lit up in recognition. "Deborah." She looked around. "What are we doing out here?"

Deborah knew what she was doing, but it was a little scary that *Mutter* didn't know why she was here. Didn't she know why she came? Did she realize Deborah had come from a different direction than from the house?

Mutter rubbed the sleeves of her dress.

That was when Deborah realized *Mutter* wasn't wearing a coat. She took her *mutter's* hands. Ice-cold. She quickly removed her own coat and manipulated her *mutter's* arms into the sleeves. Though she didn't cooperate, Deborah prevailed and fastened the buttons down the front. What had her *mutter* been doing out here in the cold without her coat?

"Thank you, dear. You're so sweet."

Deborah wrapped her arm around her and guided her in the direction of the house. Goose bumps rose on Deborah's arms. The early-spring sun wasn't strong enough to warm the air much.

Halfway between the pond and the house, Amos met up with them. "What are you doing out in the cold without a coat?"

"I gave mine to my *mutter*."

Amos squinted at *Mutter* but didn't comment on the coat. "Let's get you two back where it's warm." He shucked off his coat and put it on Deborah. His warmth enveloped her.

She resisted the urge to release a contented sigh. "What about you? Won't you get cold?"

He shook his head. "I'll be fine. It's not far."

Far enough to get cold. But she didn't argue because she was cold, and his coat was so warm.

The trio walked in silence and entered through the kitchen side door.

"Mutter." Hannah tried to keep her tone light, but Deborah could hear the concern in it. "There you are. I didn't know you went outside."

"She was out by the pond." Deborah rubbed her hands together.

Hannah and Lydia exchanged worried glances.

Then Hannah spoke in a level but firm voice. "Joanna, take Naomi and Sarah into the other room."

Naomi opened her mouth to protest but was silenced with a stern look from Hannah. The three shuffled out.

Miriam swung on her coat, grabbed the milking bucket and crossed to Amos. "Would you walk me out to the barn?"

The late-afternoon milking gave Miriam an excuse to leave the house and take Amos with her. Deborah recognized the chore as an excuse. Why was Miriam deciding now to show an interest in Amos? He wasn't even interested in her anymore. But he hadn't put up a fuss and allowed Miriam to easily take him away. A little too easily. Jealousy reared up inside her. She tamped it down.

Amos glanced back over his shoulder on his way out.

Chores and romance aside, something more important was going on. Something unpleasant. Deborah turned to her older twin sisters. "Why was *Mutter* outside without a coat? She was freezing."

Lydia's weak giggle wasn't convincing. "Oh, *Mutter* is fine. She goes out all the time without her coat. One would think she was an Eskimo. You don't need to worry about her."

Vater hobbled into the kitchen on his crutches. "You found her." He put his arm around *Mutter's* shoulder. "Let's get you warmed up."

Hannah took Deborah's coat off *Mutter* and handed it to Deborah. "You should probably return Amos's coat to him. We wouldn't want him to get sick."

From under the sink, Lydia pulled out the tin washbasin and set it on the floor in front of a chair. They would put *Mutter's* feet in warm water and give her some hot tea.

Vater gave Deborah a pointed look. "*Ja*, Deborah. Amos will be needing his coat."

So many questions festered on her tongue. The three of them obviously knew something about *Mutter*. Deborah didn't know exactly how to phrase those questions, so she left. She would ask later.

When she got out to the barn, the sound of milk swishing into a bucket met her ears. The cow stall blocked her view of Miriam. Was Amos with her? Deborah hoped not. She breathed a sigh of relief when she found him in the tack room, where his cot was. The kittens tumbled around on the floor of the toasty room. "I brought you your coat." She reluctantly took it off and put on her own. His warmth was gone. She missed it.

"*Danki.*" He took it and put it on. "Can I ask you a question?"

Oh, dear. He was going to ask where she'd gone today. "I guess so."

He narrowed his eyes. "What's wrong with your *mutter*?"

Deborah squinted back at him. "Nothing is wrong with her."

"*Ne.* I didn't mean that to sound disrespectful."

"Well, it did."

"What I meant is that she's not like other women. She's different. Forgetful."

"Aren't we all forgetful from time to time? Haven't you ever gone into another room and forgotten why you were there?" Deborah knew she did on occasion.

"This is different. This goes beyond those little things. She's called me Bartholomew at least three times and David a few times. I know Bartholomew is your *vater*. But who's David?"

Her *mutter's* brother. "Haven't you ever accidently called someone by the wrong name? Hasn't your *mutter* called you by one of your brothers' names? Most all *mutters* do."

"This is different. I can tell she thinks I *am* David. Who *is* he?"

"Her brother. He was older than her by ten years. He died when she was fifteen."

"She mistook me for David when I first arrived. She stands in the yard like she doesn't know why she's there. Then one moment she looks at me as though she'd never seen me before, then the next she suddenly remembers me."

Her *mutter* had looked at Deborah like that. Deborah had thought that with so many daughters, her *mutter* got confused about which girls in the community were hers, and that memory challenges came with age.

Amos faced Deborah squarely. "That's not normal."

Her *mutter* wasn't normal? She'd just chalked it up to her *mutter* being a little quirky and ditzy. She felt overlooked and that no one truly cared whether Deborah was around or not. Now that she thought about it, other *mutters* didn't seem that way. With Deborah being gone during the day so much this past year, she hadn't noticed her *mutter* declining.

Amos put a hand on her shoulder. Deborah's concern for her *mutter* numbed her response to his touch. He seemed so sincere, so caring. "I'm afraid she might get hurt or lost or worse. What would have happened if you hadn't found her?"

Her *mutter* did seem worse than usual. Especially since *Vater's* injury.

"Do you think my *vater's* injury could have anything to do with it?"

"It was pretty stressful for her. Would be for anyone to have a loved one injured."

Deborah didn't like to think of her *mutter* as anything less than 100 percent. She hadn't really thought that there was anything seriously wrong with her. Deborah would watch her *mutter* closely and stay at her side for the next couple of days.

What she saw, and the conclusion she came to, caused her stomach to pinch and twist.

Deborah sat with her *vater* on the porch. *"Vater?"*

"Ja."

"Have you noticed that *Mutter* is a bit…forgetful?"

He chuckled. "Aren't we all?"

Just what Deborah had said to Amos when she was defensive. *"Ne.* I mean more so than the rest of us. She… she's not like the rest of us. I think something might be wrong."

"Wrong?" His voice rose. "There is nothing wrong with your *mutter.* Don't say things like that." *Vater* struggled to his feet, one foot still in a cast. He awkwardly jammed the crutches under his arms. It made his show of angry haste almost comical.

Deborah would have laughed if not for the seriousness of her *mutter's*…condition? Did she have a *condition*? She definitely had something.

Deborah watched her *mutter* for two more days, and her concerns grew with each passing day.

She tried to approach her older sisters with her concerns, but they told her to leave it be.

Did everyone know something was off with *Mutter*? No, not all of her sisters. Her three older ones did—and for a lot longer than Deborah had—but no one would talk to her about it. Except Amos, and he wasn't family. Nor did he know any more than she did.

What was she going to do?

Chapter Eight

Amos reread his cousin's text message from last night. Jacob would pick him up on the far edge of the Millers' field away from any houses. He wanted to show Amos where he would be living when he left the community. Make Amos more comfortable with the idea of leaving.

He wasn't comfortable with the thought of leaving at all, but neither was he with staying. He *had* become comfortable at the Millers'.

If he wasn't forced to return to his parents' farm, he would seriously consider remaining Amish as well as single. Amish was what he knew. Leaving had seemed to become necessary to go into the *Englisher* world to work. So why bother returning to the Amish one? No *gut* could come from having a foot in each world. He would end up preferring one and resenting the other.

Amos tucked the cell phone into his coat pocket and peered out the barn door. None of the Miller girls or their parents were in sight. He could escape undetected. He strode briskly across the field, hoping no one came out of the house until he was on the other side of the syca-more trees by the pond. Though they had no leaves yet, their trunks would hide his progress through the other side of the field.

This was the same direction Deborah left by. When she "went to the pond," did she keep on going this way? Did she feel the same guilt he did? Not likely. She was just going for a walk. Unlike him sneaking off.

He'd meant to question her yesterday about where she'd gone, but he'd been distracted by Teresa wandering and Deborah without a coat.

Something was going on with Teresa, and he suspected that Bartholomew and the older girls knew about it. But not being a family member, they weren't likely to confide in him.

He passed by the pond and glanced at the log he'd shared with Deborah. He'd enjoyed their walk and would like to do so again. What beyond the pond drew her away from the house so often? He saw nothing of interest, just more fields. Did she visit a friend? Or meet up with a young man? That unsettled him. It shouldn't. He shouldn't be thinking of taking walks with Deborah at all when he didn't plan to stay in the community. And yet, his mind—or his heart—managed to repeatedly sneak off in that direction.

At the road, Jacob waited, leaning against an old blue pickup truck. He spoke in English. "I thought you might not come."

Amos responded in *Deutsch*. "I texted you that I would."

Jacob continued in English. "Yeah, but I know how things can come up." He patted the side of the truck. "How do you like my ride?"

His cousin sounded like a fancy outsider. After only six months? Would Amos sound like that soon? "It's nice." He supposed it was nice, but didn't know vehicles, or particularly care about them. Sure, he'd driven cars on *Rumspringa*. Driven fast, but knew, for him, they were always temporary. Another thing he had been wrong about.

Jacob shook his head. "Out here, you'll need to speak English."

For some reason, Amos didn't want to. "I will when we get to wherever we're going." He saw no reason to do so now. Jacob understood *Deutsch*.

Jacob pushed away from his truck. "Jump in." He climbed into the driver's seat.

Amos made his way around the other side and got in. A part of him bristled that this was *wrong*. He shouldn't be doing this, but he wasn't actually doing anything *wrong*. There was nothing *wrong* with getting a ride from an outsider. Being with a former Amish would be frowned upon, and if discovered, Amos would be admonished, though being in a vehicle wasn't technically *wrong*. But going against the *Ordnung* and his promise when he joined the church *was* wrong. Where he was going and why—*that* was *wrong*. His actions today would be more than frowned upon. He would be shunned. None of that would matter once he left. Except Deborah. He would miss her. The thought of not seeing her made his chest ache.

His cousin put the truck into motion. "You'll like Donita and Frank. They're a sweet couple. They left the Amish life twenty years ago. Half of their ten children went back, the other half stayed fancy. Now they help other Amish who wish to leave. You'll live with them until you find a job and can get your own apartment."

Amos hadn't given much thought about what he'd

actually be doing once on the outside. He'd pictured it a bit like *Rumspringa*—just hanging out with other people, not putting down permanent roots like a job and an apartment. He was woefully unprepared for this. His instinct had been to leave. "I don't know how to do those things." Would there be any jobs on farms? That was the only work he knew. And carpentry. All Amish knew how to build. But with so many men being forced to work in the *Englisher* world, would there even be any jobs available for him?

"They'll help you with everything. Getting a driver's license, finding a car or truck to buy and locating a place to live. You could stay with me, except there are already five of us in a little two-bedroom apartment. Maybe we could find something together, just the two of us."

Amos liked the idea of rooming with his cousin. It would make the move easier.

"I don't know if I want a car." However, his Pennsylvania driver's license, which he'd gotten on *Rumspringa*, was still valid for a few more months. Leaving the community didn't mean he had to throw the whole *Ordnung* out the window. He just wanted to see if it was the right place for him.

"You'll need one to get around."

"I can walk."

"In the winter?"

His cousin had grown soft.

"I'll manage, and spring's here." Barely. He needed to think about plowing. He needed to make sure the Millers' plow and tractor were in *gut* condition. If they were anything like the rest of the farm, they likely needed some work.

Jacob chuckled. "You'll change once you've been out here for a while."

Did he want to change? A part of him didn't. One of the reasons he was speaking *Deutsch* while Jacob spoke English. At the same time, he didn't want to remain as he was on his *vater's* farm. He didn't feel as though he fit in there. Hadn't *Gott* made it clear the Amish life wasn't for him? Or else Esther would have married him, and he would have stayed in Pennsylvania. He would have land to work.

Before long, Jacob pulled into a driveway on the edge of town. The house was a modest size. Probably had been an Amish home at one time. The sizable yard nestled up to a field.

"Do they have a working farm?" he asked in *Deutsch*. He could work on their farm. That made him smile.

His cousin shook his head and spoke in English. "No, they have only the house. The fields belong to an Amish family." He put the truck into Park, turned off the engine and got out.

Amos hesitated before doing the same.

A man who looked to be about sixty stepped out onto the porch and was dressed in typical *Englisher* clothes—nothing fancy, just a red-plaid flannel shirt and jeans. "Come on in. Donita has some hot chocolate and cookies waiting for you, boys." That must be Frank. He spoke in English with no hint of his former Amish life.

Amos was probably going to like this man. He followed Frank and Jacob inside. The aromas of chocolate and cinnamon wrapped around Amos like a warm blanket. Made him feel comfortable and at home. From the delectable smells, he could mistake this for an Amish home.

The house was similar to an Amish one, but with pictures scattered on the walls and shelves, as well as some useless knickknacks. But for the most part, the interior was simple.

Donita's smile lit her whole face. "Welcome. Please, sit down." She had no accent either.

Had these people actually been Amish?

Amos grumbled inside. He was going to like her, too. What was his problem? Wasn't it *gut* that he liked them? He sat on a glider-rocker and accepted the steaming mug of liquid bliss with marshmallows and a sprinkle of cinnamon.

Donita's eyes twinkled. "This is how Jacob liked his cocoa when he lived with us."

That made sense as to why she'd made it perfectly. Amos had loved his aunt's made-from-scratch hot chocolate. The cinnamon had been the perfect touch.

Amos spoke English out of respect for his host and hostess. "Thank you." He took an offered chocolate chip cookie. His favorite.

After the hot chocolate and cookies, Frank stood. "Let me show you the room you'll be in when you come to stay with us."

Amos stood, as did Jacob. Frank climbed the stairs first, followed by Amos, and Jacob tagged on at the end.

Frank knocked on the first door on the left. "Jesse's at work, but I like to knock anyway." He opened the door to a small room with a twin bed, nightstand, dresser and small desk.

Simple. Functional. Inviting.

Frank stepped aside. "This will be your room when you come. It may be small but you'll have it to yourself. Jesse will be moving out at the end of the week. We found a family at church who will rent him a room."

"Why doesn't he just stay here and rent from you?"

"We provide the first landing, so to speak. We feel led to assist with the transition and prepare you for a life on your own. We'll help you learn how the world outside the Amish community works."

Jacob jumped in. "On the surface, it seems like it would be simple to just move to the *Englisher* world, but when you've grown up having all your decisions made for you, like we have, it's not as simple as moving into town. It's a huge adjustment."

Frank nodded. "Donita and I are here to make your transition easier. We have a weekly Bible study here for any former Amish who want to come. We have quite a crowd on Tuesday nights."

Amos liked the idea of having people to guide him. "This is very nice. I'm sure living here will be *gut*."

Frank motioned down the hall. "This is the bathroom. You'll be sharing it with five to eight others. All depending on how many we have at any one time. If you decide to come before Jesse leaves or even stay right now, we have a cot we can set up in one of the rooms."

The thought of staying right now and not seeing Deborah again made his stomach tighten. "I can't stay right now. I'm helping out an injured farmer. He has all daughters. He doesn't have anyone to do his farmwork while he heals."

"All daughters?" Frank smiled. "I understand."

It wasn't like that, but it didn't matter if he thought Amos was angling to court one of them. Because he wasn't.

Jacob led the way back downstairs and shook Frank's hand. "It was good seeing you. I'll keep you posted about this one." He squeezed Amos's shoulder. "We need to get going."

Amos shook the older man's hand. "Thank you for showing me around and explaining things." He turned to Donita, who sat, typing on her laptop computer. "Thank you for the hot chocolate and cookies. They were very *gut*."

"You're welcome. I look forward to seeing you again."

Unfortunately, he was definitely going to like these people. He hadn't realized until now that he'd secretly hoped to not like them, because it would have given him a reason *not* to live in the outside world. He'd thought he *wanted* to like them. Was afraid he wouldn't, which would mean his transition to the *Englisher* world would be harder. But he did like this nice couple. They were eager to make his transition trouble-free, so it would be easy for him to leave one life for another. Nothing to stop him now.

Deborah popped into his head. Would she understand why he was doing this? Of all people, he thought she might, but he couldn't tell her.

Amos headed outside with his cousin. He needed to get back before he was missed. He got into his cousin's truck.

Jacob pulled out of the driveway. "So, did you like them?"

For some reason, he was loathe to answer, but did so honestly. "*Ja*, I did. I really did."

"You sound surprised."

He was. He had anticipated *not* liking them. How could he like people who'd turned their backs on their Amish faith? But wasn't that exactly what he was planning? "I know why you brought me here."

Jacob turned onto the country road leading to the drop-off spot. "Why?"

"You wanted me to get to know Frank and Donita so I'll be more comfortable leaving."

"It's human nature to resist new things. I sense you're changing your mind. Ever since you started working on the Millers' farm, you've been weakening in your resolve."

"Not true. It's just that I'm needed there. As soon as Bartholomew's back on his feet and strong enough, I'll leave."

"Are you sure?"

"Ja." But that wasn't true. If his cousin had been pushing this the week before Bartholomew got injured, Amos would have already been gone, and the bishop would have asked someone else to help the Millers. Who would it have been? His brother Daniel? Daniel certainly was keen on finding out if any of the Miller girls were available to be courted. Would he be interested in Deborah? *Ne.* Daniel wasn't right for Deborah. Maybe Miriam.

His cousin pulled to the side of the road, where he'd picked up Amos. Amos climbed out of Jacob's truck.

"I'll text you next week to let you know how things are going. We don't want to put this off too long, or you'll come up with all sorts of reasons not to do it."

Amos nodded and shut the door. He could sense reasons already forming in the deep corners of his mind, and that was where he would keep them. He *needed* to leave his Amish life.

Jacob drove off, and Amos headed across the field.

Halfway between the pond and the house, a girl ran toward him. Sarah. Her arms flailed as she stumbled over the uneven ground. Her almond-shaped eyes were wider than normal. "Amos! Amos!"

He quickened his pace. When he reached her, he lowered onto one knee. "What is it, Sarah? What's wrong?" Was it Bartholomew? Teresa? Deborah?

Sarah hugged him. "You were gone. I got scared of you."

Was that all? He was gone? He looked beyond the girl to Deborah sauntering toward them. "Sarah. Let Amos go."

Sarah shook her head against his shoulder. "*Ne.* I don't ever want him to leave again."

Deborah knelt next to her little sister and patted her back. "It's all right. He's here now. Let him go."

Sarah pulled back but kept a grip on his shoulders. "You not go away again!"

Deborah took a deep breath.

He sensed she was going to admonish her sister, so he spoke up. "I already told you that I can't promise to never go away. This isn't my farm. When your *vater* is all healed up, he won't need me any longer. I'll have to leave then."

"*Ne, ne, ne!* You have to stay. I won't like you if you leave."

"I'm sorry. I'll come visit." But he couldn't very well do that if he was shunned. This little one might be the most upset of all when he was gone. Would Deborah be upset at all?

Sarah slapped her hands on the top of his shoulders. "I don't like you!" She ran for the house.

"Sarah! Come back here and apologize," Deborah called.

But the girl wouldn't be stopped.

Amos stood and held out his hand for Deborah. Interesting that Sarah was upset that he'd left but hadn't made a fuss when Deborah went missing for most of a day.

Deborah took his offered assistance and stood.

Her bare hand in his warmed him all over. He didn't want to let go, and she didn't seem eager to retrieve her hand even after holding it was no longer necessary. He stared down at her. He should let her go.

And not just her hand.

She stared up at him. "I— We missed you. Where did you go? No one knew where you went or knew anything about you being gone."

That spoiled the moment. He pulled his hand away and started walking again toward the house. "Um... I went for a walk." Wasn't that what Deborah always told him?

Deborah fell into step beside him. "A walk? To the pond, no doubt."

Her tone told him she suspected he went farther than just the pond. "I wanted to see what was in that direction that fascinates you so much. You take a lot of walks that way." *Gut.* He could turn this back to her being missing yesterday. He hadn't gotten to ask her where *she* went. His questions for her had been preempted by her *mutter* wandering in the field. "I didn't get to ask you yesterday, where you had gone. You forgot to tell me before you left."

"Oh, yeah. Oops. Sorry."

He waited, but she didn't say anything more. "So, where *did* you go?"

"Does it really matter now? I'm back."

"*Ja*, it does." Mostly because he was curious.

"I went for a walk." She picked up her pace.

At the edge of the yard, he did something he shouldn't.

He took hold of her arm. "We need to talk about this." He guided her toward the barn.

Once inside, she turned and folded her arms. She looked upset. Upset with him.

He wanted to let this go. He wanted to make her happy. Make her smile. But he couldn't drop this. "I need to know where you went yesterday." She opened her mouth, but before she spoke he continued, "And don't say for a walk. I need to know specifically where you were."

"Why can you go for a 'walk' and not report to anyone, but I can't?"

"Because I'm a m—"

"A man. That's not a reason. It's an excuse. You tell me where you went today on your 'walk,' and I'll tell you where I went on mine."

He couldn't do that. She wouldn't understand. He took a slow breath. "What if something happened to you?"

"I'm here. I'm safe. End of story."

"If I thought it was the end of you disappearing, I would drop this, but I'm not confident you won't wander off unannounced. If something happened to you, no one would know where you were."

She stared at him a long while before answering. "Nothing happened to me. What if something had happened to you?"

"Why do you keep turning everything back on me?"

"Am I? Maybe *I* was worried that you disappeared without telling anyone. You saw how upset Sarah was."

"Sarah? Is she the only one who was upset?" He hoped Deborah had missed him.

She straightened. "Well…we were all concerned for you."

Why did he get the feeling she was hiding something?

Because he was? Did all of his suspicions about Deborah stem from his own guilt? No wonder she didn't want to tell him when he treated her not much better than a criminal. What should he do? He didn't want to make her feel bad, but he felt responsible for her.

One word popped into his mind. *Trust.*

He supposed he did trust Deborah. He really hadn't thought about it one way or the other. Why would he? He didn't *not* trust her, but he'd been treating her as though he didn't.

"I fear I've been treating you like a child, like I don't trust you. I want you to know that I do trust you. From now on, you don't have to tell me *where* you're going, but I do need to know you're safe. Though I would appreciate knowing where you are." He waited, but she didn't say anything. "Don't you have something to say?"

"Like what?"

Seriously? She was supposed to be so impressed that she confessed her secret to him.

That didn't happen.

"Like where you go all the time."

She chewed on her bottom lip, then spoke. "I go... into town. To visit a friend...in need."

Finally. "That wasn't so hard, was it?"

"So where did you escape to?"

He was a man and didn't owe a woman an explanation of his whereabouts. Even so, he wanted to tell Deborah the truth but couldn't. She wouldn't understand what it was like for a man. Now that she'd told him where she went, he couldn't turn the questioning back on her. "I had hoped to ascertain where you went all the time." He'd tried to figure that out while he walked across the field to meet Jacob.

Of course, *she* would have a noble reason for leaving all the time. He should have guessed. Now that he knew she was helping someone, what excuse could he have for singling her out to talk to her so often?

Living on a farm with all women and girls except Bartholomew Miller was vastly different than home with all men and boys except his *mutter*.

There, it had been sensible, ordered and predictable.

Here, chaos reigned. Unbeknownst to him *how* it was possible, this bedlam worked.

Deborah lay in bed in the dark, staring up at the ceiling. She felt like a heel. She hadn't lied directly to Amos. Not really. She had just omitted what kind of "need" Hudson had. He *needed* models. Could he do a shoot without her? Of course, but he was technically still in need.

She'd kept trying to get Amos to talk about where he had gone, as benign as it probably was, to distract him from where she'd been. But he was like the squirrels who kept going after the food in the bird feeder. They never gave up, and Amos wouldn't give up asking her.

She needed to be more careful about returning. She had focused on getting away and hadn't worried about when she came back home. How could she return without him seeing her? The problem was, after she'd been gone all day, he was probably on the lookout for her.

Maybe she could have her ride drop her off at a different place so she could look as though she was coming from somewhere else. But how many different places could she be picked up from and dropped off at?

Across the room, her sister breathed slow and deep.

Too bad Amos wasn't still interested in Miriam, then

he would be too distracted by her to notice whether Deborah was around or not.

Her heart tightened at the thought of all of the attention he would pay to her sister.

Ne. Miriam wasn't the answer.

As Amos had said, it was only until *Vater* was healed, and then Amos would leave their farm. She didn't like thinking about him no longer being here. Not seeing him every day.

Maybe she wouldn't need to sneak away many more times while he was here. She had a shoot next week, but maybe after that, she could tell Hudson that she couldn't make any other shoots for a while.

That was a better solution.

She rolled over and tried to force sleep to come.

Chapter Nine

Deborah waited until everyone was busy elsewhere to use the telephone in the house by the front door. Even though they had one, no one could use it without *Vater's* permission. The chances he would grant permission for this call didn't exist. She never had much cause to use the phone. Whom would she call that she couldn't visit in person?

She picked up the slim gold-colored phone from the small table and slipped out onto the front porch with it, closing the door against the cord but not latching it. Glancing around the yard for any signs of Amos, she carefully removed the receiver as though someone might hear the nonexistent sound. She pressed the numbers for Dr. Kathleen's clinic, hoping the beeps of the buttons didn't carry inside, and leaned toward the door to listen for anyone coming.

Nine months ago, Kathleen Yoder had returned after being gone from the community for fourteen years. She'd done what no other Amish person had. She had gone to college and become a doctor. Then she'd returned and was now the community's doctor.

She didn't call herself Dr. Yoder, as an *Englisher* would have. Or now that she was married, she didn't go by Dr. Lambright. She went by Dr. Kathleen. Some people simply just called her Kathleen. She didn't seem to mind. The community had been slow to accept her as a doctor, but most people had come around.

One ring, then a second came through the line.

"*Hallo.* Dr. Kathleen's medical clinic. Jessica speaking. How may I help you?"

"*Hallo,* Jessica. This is Deborah Miller."

Jessica's voice brightened. "Hi, Deborah. How are you and your family?"

"We're all fine. Well, mostly. That's why I'm calling."

"Are you ill? The doctor has an opening after lunch if you would like to come in then."

"That would be great."

"I'll just write your name in her appointment book."

"Oh. It's not for me. It's for my *mutter.*"

After a pause, Jessica said in her same cheerful tone, "All right. I've got her name written down. What does she need to see the doctor about?"

How was Deborah supposed to answer that? "I don't really know. That's why I want Dr. Kathleen to see her."

"What are her symptoms?"

"Um. Forgetfulness. She gets confused sometimes. But only sometimes."

"Have her come in after lunch, and Dr. Kathleen will see her." No need for a specific time, as with outside doctors. Everyone had lunch right at noon, so after that, the travel distance determined the approximate time. And no need to worry if you were a little—or a lot—late. The doctor worked in everyone.

Deborah hung up, hoping she was doing the right

thing. If no one in the family would talk to her about what was going on with *Mutter*, then she needed a professional's opinion. What if *Mutter* wandered off and got hurt?

Now the question was how to get her *mutter* to Dr. Kathleen without anyone stopping her. Or asking her what she was doing.

She slipped back inside, but before she could set the telephone back on the small table, it rang.

Deborah jumped, sucked in a breath and looked around. Their phone rarely rang. Dare she answer it? Of course, there wasn't anything wrong with that. She picked up the receiver.

It was Jessica. "Dr. Kathleen said that she would like to check on your *vater*, so she'll come out to your place after lunch."

"Ne!" No one else could know about taking her *mutter* to see the doctor. They would try to stop her. "Never mind. We're fine." She clunked the receiver into the cradle.

"Who was that?"

Deborah swung around to face her *vater* leaning on his crutches. "Um." She glanced at the phone. "Jessica… at Dr. Kathleen's clinic. She…wanted to know how *you* were doing."

"Did you tell her I'm doing well?"

She gave a noncommittal nod.

Vater hobbled away.

She slumped against the door. That was close.

After lunch, a buggy pulled into the driveway. When Dr. Kathleen stepped out, Deborah's stomach lurched. *Ne, ne, ne!*

She'd told Jessica *not* to have the doctor come. Oh,

this was terrible. Bad, very bad. She needed to stop Dr. Kathleen before she spoke to anyone.

She ran outside to intercept the doctor, but Hannah and *Mutter* got to her first.

And *Vater* called out from his place on the porch. "*Hallo*, Kathleen."

Too late now. Her *vater* was one of those who called the doctor by her first name alone.

How was Deborah going to keep Dr. Kathleen from saying anything about her call regarding her *mutter*?

Amos approached and took hold of the horse's bridle. "Do you want me to unharness him?"

"*Ne,*" Dr. Kathleen said. "I won't be very long."

He gave a quick nod. "I'll take him to the water trough and secure him there."

"*Danki.*"

Amos's attention shifted away from everyone and everything else and turned to Deborah.

She bit her bottom lip to control the smile that threatened to bubble over. How could she feel so silly just because he looked at her?

He tilted his head toward the barn. "You want to help me?"

Ja, but she couldn't. "I want to hear what the doctor has to say." *And keep her from saying something she shouldn't.*

Dr. Kathleen climbed the steps onto the porch. "*Hallo*, Bartholomew. How are you doing today?"

"I'm doing well. What brings you here?"

Deborah dragged her attention from Amos and willed the doctor not to say. "Oh, she was probably just driving by and decided to stop in, for a visit, all by chance, no planning, just happened."

Her *vater* and sister stared at her.

Dr. Kathleen smiled, then looked at *Vater*. "I came to see how you're doing. I wanted to check your leg and that shoulder to see how they're healing."

Deborah sighed, but the doctor could still let it slip that Deborah had called.

Vater glanced at Deborah. "Deborah said you'd called. You didn't have to come all this way."

Mutter opened the screen door. "Why don't we all go inside? I'll make some hot tea." She seemed normal today.

Maybe Deborah had acted rashly. Maybe there was nothing wrong with *Mutter*. Maybe Deborah had imagined the whole thing.

Everyone trudged inside. Everyone except Deborah.

The doctor hadn't said anything. Yet. But when she was through examining *Vater*, she would certainly turn her attention to *Mutter*.

Deborah better get inside to keep that from happening. The rest of the family had gathered in the living room, as well. A crowd would make it harder to steer the conversation, or to stop Dr. Kathleen from saying something Deborah hoped she wouldn't. Deborah stuck the tip of her index fingernail between her teeth.

Mutter and Hannah brought out two plates of old-time cinnamon jumbo cookies to feed everyone, as well as a tray full of steaming mugs.

When *Mutter* sat, she waved a hand toward Deborah. "Don't bite your nails."

Deborah lowered her hand into her lap. Her being repeatedly missing from the family went unnoticed, but this, her *mutter* noticed. She snatched a mug of tea and a cookie from the coffee table and slouched back into the straight-backed chair.

Sure enough, once Dr. Kathleen said *Vater* was recovering well with no unforeseen problems, she turned to *Mutter* and struck up a conversation.

To most people, it probably sounded like two Amish women having a typical conversation. But Deborah could hear the small hesitations from her *mutter* and little things that were wrong in what she said. But to the unaware person who didn't know *Mutter* well and didn't live with her, she sounded like any other Amish woman. But she wasn't.

Dr. Kathleen held up her half-eaten cookie. "These are delicious. Did you make them?"

Mutter said *ja* at the same time Hannah said that she'd made them. Then her sister corrected her statement to say they both had.

Mutter shifted on the sofa to face Hannah, who was next to her. "Martha, I made these myself."

Oh, dear. That was *Mutter's* sister's name. *Mutter* wasn't all right. What would happen now?

Not realizing her mistake, *Mutter* continued, "You were never *gut* at making these. They always turn out flat. But you make the best cakes. Mine never turn out very *gut*."

Vater struggled to his feet. "Well, we won't keep you, Kathleen."

Had the doctor noticed that *Mutter* had called Hannah by the wrong name? Would she say anything? Maybe the doctor didn't know them well enough to have realized the wrong name was used. *Vater* had noticed and was eager to have the doctor leave.

Thankfully, the doctor hadn't said anything about

Deborah calling her clinic to try to make an appointment for her *mutter*. Maybe Jessica hadn't told Dr. Kathleen about it. *Ne*. Jessica had said the doctor would look at *Vater* while she was here checking out *Mutter*.

Dr. Kathleen stood. "Thank you for the tea and cookies," she said to *Mutter*, then turned to *Vater*. "Though your shoulder is better, I don't want you using those crutches much yet. It still needs to heal, and I don't want you to reinjure it. Next week, I'll come back and start you on some exercises to strengthen it." Dr. Kathleen picked up her backpack of medical supplies and headed for the door. "Deborah, would you walk me out?"

Deborah rushed to her side and held the door open. "Of course." She followed her out, down the steps and across the yard to where Amos had parked the horse and buggy. Because this wasn't expected to be a long visit, the horse hadn't been unhitched.

Kathleen stopped next to her buggy. "Bring your *mutter* to my clinic tomorrow afternoon. I'll make sure I don't have any other appointments."

"You want to see her?"

Had she noticed? Or was the doctor simply granting Deborah the appointment she'd asked for?

"I didn't really see or hear anything out of the ordinary—except calling your sister by the wrong name— but there's something that seems off that I can't put my finger on. Add that with your concern, and it makes me want to see her in my clinic."

"I'll bring her. *Danki* for not saying anything about my calling about her."

"No one else knows?"

"Knows there's something wrong with *Mutter*? I think my *vater* and older sisters do, but no one will talk to me about it. I tried, but they brushed it aside or changed the subject. Do they know I called for an appointment? *Ne.* I think they would try to stop me. They seem to be ignoring the issues."

"People don't like to think that a loved one has problems. Especially in Amish communities. We think we should be able to pray *all* our problems away, but *Gott* never said we would be free of troubles. Look at the Apostles. They all had more troubles after Christ was crucified than before. I don't believe it's whether or not we have troubles that tests and shows our faith, but how we deal with them that can glorify *Gott.* Bring your *mutter*, and we'll see what's going on." Dr. Kathleen climbed into her buggy and drove away.

Deborah stared after her. So, the doctor *had* come to check on *Mutter* as well as *Vater.* Her relief was palpable.

From inside the barn, Amos watched Deborah, who was standing in the yard. The doctor had left, but she didn't retreat into the house or look as though she was going to move anytime soon. What was she doing? This could be a *gut* opportunity to talk with her.

He exited the barn and his heart rate increased the closer he got to where she still stood. "Is everything all right?"

She jerked around to face him. "What? What do you mean by that?"

"Your *vater*? I assume that's why the doctor stopped by."

"Oh, *ja, Vater*, he's doing well, Dr. Kathleen doesn't want him to use his arm much yet, she's going to start him on some exercises next week. That's all. Nothing more."

"Gut." He squinted a little. Why was she talking so fast? "Is something wrong?"

"Wrong? Why would you ask that?"

"You're frowning, asked why I asked and you're talking faster than normal."

"Talking fast? That's just because I'm cold." She rubbed her upper arms as though to prove her point.

Did she have another secret? "Maybe you should go back into the house." But he didn't want her to. He could fetch his coat for her to get her to stay.

"Oh, yeah. I should do that." She turned and walked away.

He wished he could call her back, but he didn't have a reason to do so.

She paused at the bottom of the steps to the front porch. Instead of going inside, she headed out across the field. Without her coat.

Going for a walk? Certainly she wouldn't head into Goshen to visit her friend this late in the afternoon. It would get dark before she could return.

He ran back inside the barn and grabbed his own coat, then trotted after her.

He caught up to her by the pond and sat on the log next to her. "I thought you might be going to visit your friend."

She scrunched up her face. "What? What friend?"

"The one in need you go to all the time."

Her eyes widened. "Oh. *That* friend. *Ne.* I just came out here to think. Did you come to check up on me?"

He held out his coat, which was still in his hand. "I thought you might get cold. You said you were cold before coming."

"Danki. That was very thoughtful. Won't you get cold?"

"Ne." He wrapped it around her shoulders. "Do you want to be alone? I can leave."

"Ne, please stay." She shifted to face him better. "May I ask you a question?"

"Of course." He settled himself on the log.

"What if there was something you felt you should do—felt it was the *right* thing to do—but you knew your parents wouldn't approve if you asked them?"

Like leaving the Amish community? Her words could be describing his own dilemma. "If it truly is the right thing, wouldn't your parents tell you to do it?"

"Not if *they* thought it was wrong."

"Then how could it be right?"

"Sometimes, one person can view something as right and another view it as wrong."

Exactly. Like him leaving his Amish community to figure out where he belonged.

She continued, "So, what if there's a hungry child. The right thing to do is to give the child food, but the only food belongs to someone else. Is it wrong to take what belongs to someone else to feed the child? It wouldn't be right to let the child go hungry. No Amish person would deny a child food. So, it's like you have permission in advance."

Did her "friend in need" require food?

"That's a bad example." She waved her hand in the air. "Just forget it."

"Ne. I understand what you're trying to say. Do you truly want to know what I think?"

"Ja."

"I think you need to decide if doing the right thing is…not more important, but more *right* than the wrong thing is wrong. If that makes sense."

"So, the right thing needs to be more right than it is wrong?"

"Something like that." Some of the church leaders wouldn't say so. Something was either right or wrong, it couldn't be a little of both. But some things weren't as clear.

"*Danki.* That's helpful."

He was glad he could help. Now he just needed to figure out for himself if his right thing was more right than the wrong part of it was wrong.

At this moment, sitting with Deborah seemed very right, but this moment couldn't last. Bartholomew would heal and not need help, and Amos would be expected to return to his parents' farm, which his brothers would split, leaving Amos to fend for himself. He wasn't a very *gut* Amish if he thought only of himself. He glanced over at Deborah. She deserved a better Amish man than he was turning out to be.

Chapter Ten

Deborah escorted her *mutter* into the barn. She glanced around for Amos but didn't see him. She was both grateful and disappointed. "Could you sit right there on that barrel until I get Floyd hitched up?" She didn't want her *mutter* wandering off.

Mutter complied. She seemed to be in a bit of a confused state but amenable.

Deborah retrieved the buggy harness from the wall outside the tack room. Though she tried to see Amos whenever she came out to the barn, it was *gut* he wasn't here right now. She wouldn't have to explain where she was going or what she was doing or why.

All the leather and metal in the harness weighed heavy in her arms. She hung the various parts on the pegs designed to hold the harness in preparation for putting it on the horse.

Then she walked Floyd out of his stall and tied his lead rope to a post. One of the kittens lay undisturbed upon the horse's back, and another stood on his withers and mane.

Amos's voice came from behind her. "Let me help with that."

She spun around, spooking the horse, who double-stepped in place.

Amos rushed over, reached around her with one arm and took hold of the rope. His other arm, which was on the other side of her, stroked the horse's neck. "Whoa, boy."

The horse settled with a snort.

Deborah's breath caught at him being so close.

Amos stared at Deborah for a moment, then cleared his throat. "I obviously startled you. You weren't expecting me to come in here—the place I spend the most time." He squinted mischievously. "Which makes me wonder what you're up to."

From his crooked grin, she knew he was teasing her. He liked to joke about where she went during the day and various other things. She would like nothing better than to stand there and look at him, but she didn't have time for his shenanigans today. "I'm not up to anything." She couldn't allow her serious mission to be thwarted.

He looked from her to her *mutter* and back. "You are up to something. You're taking her to see the doctor, aren't you?"

The temptation to lie tickled her tongue, but that would be wrong. She ducked under his arm instead. *"Ja."*

"Alone?"

She set a step stool next to Floyd's front legs. The horse was too tall for her to reach without it, even at five-nine. *"Ja."* Then she took the breast collar and climbed on the step.

Amos took hold of the collar, keeping her from putting it on the horse. "Does your *vater* know about this?"

She tried to pull the apparatus free. *Vater* couldn't know until after Deborah found out what was wrong with *Mutter*. "He ignores her condition. Even you noticed something was off with her."

He wrestled the collar from her hands. "You need to tell your *vater*."

"He'll say *ne*." She stepped down from the stool.

"He's the head of your family. It's *his* decision."

Mutter appeared beside them. "Amos, introduce me to your young lady."

Deborah squinted at *Mutter*. How could her *mutter* not recognize her? Deborah's heart sank. She knew *Mutter* rarely noticed when she was gone, but to not even recognize her caused her heart to physically hurt. Lately, *Mutter* had been getting worse. "*Mutter!* I'm Deborah. Your daughter."

Mutter squinted and studied her middlemost daughter. Then recognition broke on her face. "Deborah!"

Pushing the stool aside with his foot, Amos wrapped the collar around the horse's neck, causing the kitten on Floyd's withers to jump off and scamper away.

"Now you're helping me?" She picked up the kitten still lying on the draft horse's back and sent him off with his sibling.

"I think your *vater* should know." Amos made short work of harnessing Floyd and attaching the buggy. "But if he isn't willing to get her the help she needs—" he glanced at her *mutter*, who appeared to not realize she was being talked about "—I think just this once, it will be all right. See what the doctor has to say. As long as no decisions are made without his consent."

Mutter jerked away from Deborah. "*Ne!* I'm not going to a doctor. Doctors are bad. They hurt people."

Had it just now registered to her *mutter* that they were

going to the doctor's? "*Mutter*, you need to. The doctor's not going to hurt you. She's going to help you."

Mutter shook her head.

Hannah entered the barn.

Uh-oh. What would her sister do? This was getting more and more complicated by the minute. Could Deborah talk her sister in to leaving them be and allowing Deborah to take their *mutter*?

But before Deborah could do or say anything, *Mutter* rushed to Hannah's side. "Hannah won't let you."

Hannah took *Mutter's* hand in one of hers and patted it with the other. "*Ne, Mutter.* You misunderstood. You remember the Yoders."

"*Ja.*"

What was her sister doing?

"You remember Kathleen Yoder."

"*Ja.* She was such a sweet girl, but she left and never came back. We still pray for her."

"She *did* come back. Last year."

Mutter's eyes widened. "She did?"

"*Ja.* She's invited us for tea. You would like to visit with Kathleen, wouldn't you?"

"*Ja.*" The fear melted from *Mutter's* expression, and she climbed into the buggy without another word of protest. Hannah followed, settling herself in the back beside *Mutter.*

Deborah peered in the back. "You're coming with us?"

"You obviously need someone who knows how to handle *Mutter.*"

She couldn't believe her sister was helping after brushing Deborah's concerns aside. She climbed in front.

Amos led the horse out of the barn, then fed the reins

through the rein slits at the bottom of the windshield. He climbed in.

Deborah cocked her head. "You're coming, too?"

He nodded and then set Floyd into motion.

She was grateful to have her sister and Amos along for support, as well as to help her make the best decision possible for *Mutter*.

Deborah's feelings tangled together. How could her *mutter* not remember her own daughter when she could recall two people outside of the family? One from fourteen years ago and the other she'd only known for two months.

Amos kept his voice low. "As soon as we return, you are going to tell your *vater* that we took her to the…to visit Kathleen and what she had to say."

Deborah nodded and kept her voice low as well. "If my *vater* knows that my *mutter* has a problem, why hasn't he done anything about it?"

"He's probably afraid."

She couldn't imagine. "My *vater* has never been afraid of anything."

"This is his *frau*. No one wants to think something is wrong with a family member."

"Ignoring it won't make it go away or make her suddenly better. I think she's getting worse."

From the back seat, Hannah said, "She is."

Deborah turned to face her sister. "What caused your change of heart? When she was out wandering, you acted like nothing was wrong. Now you're helping me?"

Mutter stared out the window with a contented smile on her face.

Hannah continued. "As you realized, *Mutter's* getting worse. She'd been quite manageable for years."

"She's been like this for years?" Deborah couldn't believe it. How had she not seen it?

"Not like she is now. Just the occasional lapse. Certain words and places set her off."

"Words like *doc*—"

"Don't. Let's not upset her needlessly. *Ja*. Words like that. Since *Vater's* accident she's gotten worse, and I never know what will set her off. As I said, she was manageable. I had hopes to marry Nehemiah Zook this fall, but I can't if *Mutter* is like this. She needs constant supervision lately."

Deborah had had no idea what her sisters had been dealing with all these years. "When did you first notice something about her?"

"When Lydia and I were ten or so, *Vater* told us to keep an eye on her. She had disappeared a couple of times, and *Vater* had to go find her. He told us she'd just taken a walk and gone farther than she meant to."

"I like taking walks," *Mutter* said, still gazing out the window.

Was that where Deborah got her affinity for taking walks? Was she going to end up like her?

Hannah continued, "By the time we were twelve, we knew something wasn't right."

"So if Lydia knows about *Mutter*, why didn't she come, too?"

"She's going to keep *Vater* occupied so he doesn't question where *Mutter* has gone and keep Naomi and Sarah under control."

Her oldest sisters were helping her. "What about Miriam? Does she know?"

"*Ja*. She's afraid of never marrying, as well."

"Is that why she's never agreed to have a boy court

her?" So, it was just as well that Amos wasn't interested in her.

Hannah nodded. "None of us see how we can. *Vater*
can't run the farm and keep an eye on *Mutter.*"

Was *Mutter* really that bad off that her daughters felt
as though they could never marry? Because of *Mutter's*
condition, she probably hadn't noticed when any of her
daughters went missing, let alone Deborah. With her
older sisters busy keeping an eye on *Mutter*, they either
didn't notice Deborah's frequent absences, or they just
didn't have the energy to keep track of their *mutter* and
watch over an eight-year-old Down syndrome sister *and*
a sister who could take care of herself. Not to mention
Naomi's neediness.

This was a lot to digest. She would let it all sit and
simmer until after the visit to the doctor. She didn't want
to think about it all right now, so she turned her thoughts
to more pleasant things. Like the handsome man seated
next to her—a man who was both kind and helpful. Gratitude filled her at his presence.

When Amos pulled the buggy to a stop in front of the
clinic, Hannah said in a light friendly voice, "Deborah,
go tell *Kathleen* we're here for *tea* and a *visit.*"

Deborah understood to forewarn the doctor about the
state of their *mutter.* She got out of the buggy and hurried
inside. Jessica Yoder, the doctor's sister and receptionist, sat at a desk just inside the door. Deborah stopped
short. Jessica smiled and greeted her warmly. "*Hallo.*
Dr. Kathleen is expecting you. We thought you were
bringing your *mutter.*"

"She's coming right behind me. I need to—"

Dr. Kathleen came out of her office. "You made it. Is
your *mutter* with you?"

"Right behind me. She thinks we're here for tea and a visit. She became very upset when she learned we were coming to see a doctor."

Dr. Kathleen smiled. "Then today I'm simply Kathleen." She gave her sister a pointed look. Her sister nodded back in understanding. "And we shall have a nice visit."

Jessica jumped to her feet. "I'll get the tea started. We have half of a cake. I'll slice it."

Amos opened the door for Hannah and *Mutter*. Then he came in and closed it behind them.

Dr. Kathleen greeted *Mutter* and had her sit on the sofa in the waiting room, which used to be a living room and still resembled one. At least well enough that *Mutter* wouldn't notice the difference. Hannah sat next to her.

Dr. Kathleen looked at Amos. "Normally, only family members are present at something like this."

Hannah spoke up. "He knows. It's fine if he stays."

"Very well, then." Dr. Kathleen sat in a chair nearest to *Mutter*.

Jessica brought them each a slice of cake and a cup of tea.

Deborah sat in a chair across from the sofa, next to Jessica.

Amos separated himself from the group of women and sat in the chair behind the small desk that Jessica had occupied. He looked like a man at a quilting party. He fidgeted as though uncomfortable, but he stayed. He could have excused himself and kept occupied outside, or even gone to find Noah Lambright, Dr. Kathleen's husband, but Amos chose to stay. That said a lot about him.

But just what did it say about him? Did it say he was interested in what was wrong with her *mutter*? Did it say he cared? Or did it just say that he was nosy? Whatever the reason, his being here calmed Deborah. When it came time to talk to her *vater* about all this and tell him that she, Hannah, Lydia and Amos had gone behind his back to take her *mutter* to see a doctor, Amos could be an advocate on their side. Maybe her *vater* would be more likely to listen to another man.

Amos studied Deborah as the women talked. He wasn't sure staying was the best choice. He just knew he wanted to be here for Deborah. If she needed him. If her *mutter* forgot who she was again. How terrible for her own *mutter* to not recognize her. He couldn't imagine.

Dr. Kathleen skillfully questioned Teresa Miller, not once letting the older woman know that she was being examined. She asked questions about her daughters and husband, about the farm, about when she was married. He couldn't tell how the answers gave anything away that might be wrong. She seemed perfectly normal, but he knew she wasn't.

When Deborah glanced his way, which seemed to be often, he gave her a smile. Most of the time she returned his offer of encouragement in kind.

Dr. Kathleen leaned forward. "Teresa, would you help Jessica in the kitchen make a fresh pot of tea?"

Jessica rose.

When Teresa stood and had her back to the doctor, Kathleen mouthed to her sister, *Keep her in there.* She took a pad of paper from the end table next to her.

Jessica nodded. The two crossed the large room and went through the open doorway into the kitchen.

Amos moved from his place at the desk and sat in the chair Jessica had vacated, right next to Deborah. Though he liked sitting near to her, it was harder to watch her from this vantage point.

Dr. Kathleen spoke in a soft voice. "Tell me what you've noticed that concerns you."

"Hannah, you've known about her condition the longest, maybe you should start," Deborah said.

Dr. Kathleen looked at Hannah. "That sounds like a *gut* idea." Then she glanced at Deborah and Amos in turn. "But I want to hear from each of you. One person may notice something the others don't."

Hannah cleared her throat. "*Mutter* has always been a little different from the other *mutters*, but nothing concerning. I guess I was eight or so when I realized other *mutters* weren't the same as mine. Lydia and I would whisper about it in bed at night. When we were ten, *Vater* asked us to keep an eye on *Mutter*. We didn't understand why, but we did as we were told. Each night, *Vater* would ask us what *Mutter* did that day. He would ask specific questions, like if she ever just stood and stared. We thought it was some sort of game."

No wonder one of the twins always gave him directions instead of their *mutter* when their *vater* wasn't around. They were shielding Teresa and making sure no one knew she had a problem.

Kathleen wrote on her paper. "What were the repeated things you told him?"

"She would stare off into space like she saw something interesting someplace else. She would call my twin and me by each other's names, which we thought was fun. For a long time, we thought we were *gut* at fooling her. Now we feel bad for doing it. She would wander off and not know where she was."

"What were the most unusual things she did?"

"She put the bowl of cake batter in the oven, and the oven wasn't even on. She hung the dirty clothes on the clothesline. She would forget one of us was her daughter. She would cry for no reason."

Kathleen turned to Amos. "You've been at the Miller farm for only a short time. Have you noticed anything?"

He shifted in his chair. It felt wrong to talk about her this way. He turned toward Deborah, and she nodded for him to go ahead. Knowing she was all right with him talking about her *mutter* made him feel better about this. If it would ultimately help Teresa, he needed to report his observations. "She recognized me before Deborah. When we were hitching up the horse to come here, she asked me to introduce her to my young lady." Remembering the hurt look on Deborah's face made his chest ache all over again. "She forgets things. I found her wandering in the road. She didn't know why she was out there. She's called me by other people's names. I thought it was because I was new on the farm and she couldn't remember my name."

Kathleen asked Deborah, "Does your *mutter* often forget who you are?"

"*Ja.*"

"More so than your sisters?"

"I used to think I was the *only* one she forgot, but now I wonder if everyone isn't forgotten." Deborah stared at her oldest sister.

A sheepish expression crossed Hannah's face. "She seems to forget Deborah more than anyone else. She's gotten worse since our *vater* broke his leg. Instead of the occasional slipup, it's happening most days. We used to be able to manage her so others wouldn't notice. It's become more and more difficult."

Kathleen wrote some more. "I remember when your *vater* got hurt. She was quite upset. I thought it was just because she feared losing him. I gave her something to calm her on the ride to the hospital, but now I'm afraid that just masked her condition."

Hannah nodded. "I wondered why she seemed calmer at the hospital and around doctors than we expected her to be."

"Has she had any serious accidents with head trauma?"

"Not that I can remember," Hannah said.

"Has she had any serious illnesses with a high fever?"

"I don't know," Hannah answered again.

Kathleen nodded. "I'm going to need access to her medical records." She excused herself for a moment. When she returned, she held out a piece of paper. "This form needs to be filled out and signed."

Hannah took the form. "I can do that."

Dr. Kathleen shook her head. "You can fill it out, but we need either your *mutter's* signature or your *vater's* on her behalf."

Hannah stared at the form. "I'll fill it out, and then I'll have our *mutter* sign it."

Kathleen glanced at their *mutter's* back through the kitchen doorway, then returned her gaze to Hannah. "She needs to understand what she's signing, or I can't submit it in good conscience."

Hannah nodded. "I can make her understand well enough."

"I would prefer your *vater* be apprised of this. He should give his consent, as well."

"Does he have to?" Hannah said.

"Legally? *Ne.* But because your *mutter* is Amish and her husband is head of the household, he should be involved, or we could all be shunned for going behind his back."

Deborah and Hannah nodded.

Amos broke his silence. "Do you suspect that Teresa might have fallen and hit her head or had some illness that caused her problems?"

"Those are two possibilities. If she has had either, it will give us a direction to look in. If not, that, too, will give us other avenues to search."

Amos hesitated but felt the subject no one seemed to want to bring up needed to be. "You haven't mentioned it, but could she have Alzheimer's disease?"

"Let's not use that label yet. It could be any number of things. I need to order more tests before I go there."

Deborah spoke up. "What if we can't get our *vater's* permission? What do we do then? Leave our *mutter* like this?"

"Let's see what he says first. I'm sure he wants what's best for her."

What the doctor thought was best might not be the same as what Bartholomew Miller thought.

Deborah had a pinched expression and looked like she might cry.

He wanted to wrap his arms around her and comfort her. Not only would that be inappropriate, but he also didn't know how to do it without others seeing.

But since he couldn't do that, maybe he could find a way to convince Bartholomew that there was no shame in seeking counsel from the doctor.

Chapter Eleven

After the visit to the doctor's, Deborah sat on the porch with her *vater*. She and her sisters agreed she might have the best chance to convince him to release *Mutter's* medical records and get her diagnosed. She could give a fresh perspective. The twins had been *Vater's* confidantes and helpers for years. Maybe he would listen to someone else, but she wished Amos was beside her for moral support. "*Vater?* May I talk to you?" Her twin sisters were right inside, listening, ready to step forward if necessary.

"Of course. Any of you girls can always come to me. I think I know what this is about."

"You do?"

But he didn't seem upset. Instead, he looked almost happy. "Amos?"

"Amos?" Just the mention of his name made something happy swirl around inside her despite the current circumstances. "*Ne.* Why would you say that?" Did her *vater* know she had feelings for him? How embarrassing.

"I see the way you look at him, and the way he looks at you."

Amos looked at her in a certain way? The same way

she tried *not* to look at him? She mentally shook her head. Before the conversation had even started, *Vater* had derailed her. "I don't want to talk about Amos." Not that she didn't enjoy talking about him, but now wasn't the time. She tamped down her feelings for the kind farmhand. "I want to talk about *Mutter*."

Vater's congenial attitude fell away as he stood and tucked his crutches under his arms. "*Mutter* is well." He hobbled down the steps and across the yard.

He obviously didn't want to talk about the painful subject. He'd shut her down before she'd even started. Should she go after him?

The front door opened. Hannah, Lydia and Miriam stepped out onto the porch.

Deborah faced them. "I'll go after him and try again."

Miriam heaved a sigh as though defeated.

Lydia shook her head. "*Vater* doesn't want to hear about *Mutter*." She sounded defeated, as well.

Hannah planted her hands on her hips.. "Well, he's going to. He can't ignore this any longer. Come on. We'll *all* talk to him. He can't ignore four of us at once." Hannah headed toward the barn, where *Vater* had gone, with Lydia and Miriam on her heels.

Deborah trailed after her three older sisters. Amos had said it wasn't a *gut* idea to have them all gang up on *Vater* at once. "But what about *Mutter*, Naomi and Sarah?"

"I told Joanna to keep them all in the house." Hannah strode with determination in her steps.

How much did seventeen-year-old Joanna know? She knew enough to obey Hannah.

Deborah stood shoulder-to-shoulder with her sisters as they entered the barn, having automatically lined up from oldest to youngest. They would be able to speak freely with him out here, where neither the younger girls nor *Mutter* would hear.

Though they'd told Amos that they would deal with their *vater* themselves, he was in the barn as normal. Hannah and Lydia didn't want him involved because *Vater* had tried to keep this within the family and didn't want to embarrass him by bringing in an outsider. Maybe that was why *Vater* had come out here, to keep them from broaching a subject he didn't want to talk about.

Deborah had wanted Amos in on the discussion. He'd been a big help in taking *Mutter* to see the doctor, and she treasured his support.

Hannah drew in a deep breath. "*Vater*, we need to talk about *Mutter.*"

He shook his head. "Is this why you girls followed me out here?" He glanced toward Amos, who stood in the doorway of the cow's stall. "This is not the place."

Amos leaned the mucking shovel against the wall and strode past them all. "I'll be outside if anyone needs me." He gave Deborah a pointed look and a nod.

Her insides danced, and she nodded back out of appreciation, both because he was giving the family privacy, and because he would be available should they need him. What she wanted to do was hold on to him to stop her world from tipping out of control, and right now, he felt like the only solid thing in her life, but she let him leave without a word.

Hannah took a step forward. "*Vater*, Lydia and I want to get married, but we can't leave *Mutter* without someone to look after her. I think Miriam has settled on never marrying, because she thinks she can't. She'll take on the responsibility of *Mutter* and become an old maid, but I know she would like to marry and have a family of her own. We hate to saddle her with this job. We need to do something about *Mutter*."

Vater glared at his eldest, then shifted his gaze to Deborah. "Deborah, go in the house."

Deborah wasn't sure what to do. Obey her *vater*? Or stay put? She was the one who had taken their *mutter* to Dr. Kathleen.

Miriam gripped Deborah's wrist and said in a quiet voice, "Stay."

Lydia spoke up. "*Vater*, Deborah knows all about *Mutter's*…issues."

His gaze darted from daughter to daughter to daughter. "She doesn't know. She doesn't understand."

Hannah spoke up this time. "She does know. Deborah and I took *Mutter* to see Dr. Kathleen."

"You did what? You told the doctor? Behind my back? This is a private family matter."

Lydia, the peacemaker, took *Vater* by the arm. "We all know that *Mutter* needs special help and guidance. If we deny that, we can't help her. We want to do what's best for her."

Hannah added, "And for the whole family."

Deborah shifted her feet. "And for you, too."

Vater glared at each of his daughters in turn. Then the fight went out of his eyes, and he seemed as though he was giving in, just a little bit. "Your *mutter* is just fine. We've always been able to take care of her."

"*Ne*, she's not fine." Deborah didn't know where that burst of courage had come from, but for some strange reason, she sensed it might be that Amos was nearby.

"Things can't continue this way," Hannah said. "We can only take care of her if none of us ever marries or leaves."

Lydia jumped back in. "*Mutter* is getting worse."

"*Ne*, she's not. I won't listen to any more of this non-sense." *Vater* glanced toward the barn opening. "This isn't the place to discuss this."

Hannah squared her shoulders. "This is precisely the place. Amos went with us to see the doctor."

Vater's eyes widened. "You told him our family's problems?"

Deborah took a step forward. "We didn't have to. He's seen *Mutter's* odd behavior and figured it out." Amos knowing and being understanding about it strengthened her resolve. None of them could excuse this away now that an outsider knew.

Vater clenched his jaw and hobbled around in a circle. He looked as though he'd wanted to storm away again, but his crutches made that difficult. He stopped and faced the open doorway. "Amos! Come back in here!" He had spoken loud enough for someone to hear if they'd been right outside but didn't quite yell. He obviously thought Amos stood close by, listening.

Amos didn't appear.

Vater huffed out a breath. "Deborah, go get the boy. I'll see what he has to say for himself."

Deborah froze in place. Would *Vater* scold Amos? Send him away from the farm?

Hannah stepped forward. "*Vater*, he's done nothing wrong."

"This is my *frau* we are talking about. My family. I will speak to him if I wish." He turned back to Deborah. "Get the boy."

Amos was hardly a boy, but Deborah backed out of the barn. Had *Vater* sent her away to once again exclude her from a conversation with her older sisters? She would ask them later. She refused to be shut out again.

Amos stood by the woodpile, swinging the ax. Definitely *not* a boy. He hadn't been listening. She thought more highly of him for that and wanted to run into his arms.

The tool came down on a log, and the two halves toppled in opposite directions. He leaned to pick up the larger one.

"Amos?"

With the log in hand, he turned and smiled. *"Ja?"*

Her mouth momentarily responded in kind, then she remembered why she'd been sent out here. "My *vater* wishes you to come back in. We told him you know about our *mutter*. He isn't happy."

He tossed the hunk of wood on the ground with several others. "I'm sure he isn't. All of this can't be easy for him."

Her sisters hadn't wanted Amos involved for *Vater's* sake, but Deborah believed he could help. Show *Vater* that people outside the family could be kind to *Mutter*, as well. *Vater* might not have wanted Amos to know, but he already did. Deborah wanted him at her side to draw from his strength. She walked with him back inside the barn.

Her sisters and *Vater* stood in silence.

Amos approached slowly.

Vater became stiff and set his jaw. "Girls, leave us."

Oh, dear. Deborah hoped *Vater* didn't blame Amos and reprimand him. She wanted to stay at his side to lend support. *"Vater*, I don't think we can keep this a secret from the community any longer. I'm sure some people already suspect something is wrong with *Mutter*. The way Hannah or Lydia are always close beside her and shield her from others. How they talk for her."

Vater took a slow breath. "Go inside the house and wait for me there. Let us men talk."

Deborah glanced from *Vater* to Amos. Amos nodded that he would be fine and gave her a reassuring smile that calmed her inside.

With reluctance, she and her sisters moved toward the door. Defying *Vater* wouldn't help Amos.

She sent up a quick prayer for Amos.

Amos faced Bartholomew Miller, bracing himself for the man's ire. He had volunteered to speak to Bartholomew, but now he wasn't so sure of the wisdom in that. This was a family matter. Amos wasn't family. Bartholomew would likely send him away from the farm entirely. If that was the case, he would take his belongings and text Jacob to come get him. He would sleep in the back of his cousin's pickup if he had to.

The older man shifted on his crutches. His expression was weary and haggard. The poor man looked worn-out. Not only had he been saddled with all daughters—not one son to help shoulder the workload of a farm—but he also had a child with Down syndrome and a *frau* with medical problems. So many burdens for one man to bear.

Amos wished Bartholomew would sit down but knew he likely wouldn't. That would be a sign of weakness. "I want to help you, your *frau* and your family in any way I can." He'd grown to care a great deal about this family. In fact, he felt more comfortable with them than his own. He had a useful place here, unlike on his *vater's* farm.

Bartholomew nodded. "Anything we say here needs to stay between the two of us."

"I understand."

"We'll talk man-to-man. Women can be too emotional. Tell me what you've noticed about my *frau*."

Unusual for an Amish man to talk to another about so personal a subject. Maybe to the bishop or one of the elders, but not a young man such as himself. He hoped the older man didn't think him disrespectful. After all, what kind of counsel could a young, single man give a married one old enough to be his father? But the unique position Amos found himself in—working on their farm for weeks and living in the barn—gave him an advantage others in the community didn't have. He would adhere to Bartholomew's wishes and not speak to anyone about this, and he would proceed with the utmost respect. "I can tell your *frau* loves all of you a lot."

"But?"

"But…" Speaking of this made him uncomfortable. He wished he could just listen, but silence wouldn't help Teresa Miller or her family. "She forgets things and gets confused. When we were hitching up the buggy to take her to the doctor's, she asked me to introduce the girl with me. It was Deborah. Her own daughter. She remembered me but not her." Poor Deborah. The ache for her welled anew. He couldn't imagine his own *mutter* forgetting him. "She forgets other things, too, and wanders sometimes like she doesn't know where she is. Your daughters do a *gut* job of shielding her, but they can't always. I found her on the road a week after I arrived here. I didn't think much of it, but now I know better. What if she wanders off and gets hurt or lost?"

Bartholomew stared at Amos for a long minute before he spoke. "I appreciate your candor and compassion for my *frau* and daughters." He paused. "What would you do if you were me?"

Gott, guard my words and help me say the right things. Was Amos prepared to give an older man advice about his *frau*? "I think… I would try to figure out what's causing her to forget and be confused. Dr. Kathleen needs her medical history and records to diagnose her properly. She requires your permission. Maybe there's a treatment that can help your *frau* remember."

"And if there's not?"

So he feared there would be no help or hope for his *frau*.

"Then I guess we'll deal with it at that point. We can't help her properly until we know what's wrong."

"We?"

"*Ja*. The more people who can look out for her, the safer she'll be."

"You aren't suggesting I tell the rest of the community, are you?"

"Wouldn't that be better than keeping secrets and something bad happening to her?"

Bartholomew backed up and sat on an upturned log that served as a stool. "I do want her to be safe."

"I can tell. That's why you've had your daughters keeping such a close watch on her for so long. It can't hurt to speak to Dr. Kathleen. She's compassionate and discreet."

"I wish to say *ne*, but you—" he waved a crutch in the general direction of the house "—and my daughters make sense. I can't ignore the Lord's prodding any longer. I don't want any of my daughters to remain single when they want to marry. I just wanted to keep Teresa close and protect her."

"I think the best way to protect her is to let others—

not a lot of people, but a few who can help—know what's going on with her."

"I do want to protect her. Take me to the doctor's."

This conversation went better and easier than Amos imagined. The older man must have been ready. "Right now?"

"*Ja*, right now. I shouldn't wait." Bartholomew had been ready for this step. He'd just needed a little nudge.

"Do you want me to tell your daughters where we're going and what you're doing?"

Bartholomew heaved a sigh. "They'll want to come with us. I'll go inside and tell them and call the doctor to let her know we're coming."

Amos figured at least one of his daughters would want to come, if not several of them. Would that be such a bad thing? He set to work on hitching the larger buggy while Bartholomew crutched inside.

Soon, Amos had the buggy ready and parked in front of the house.

Bartholomew, Deborah, Hannah and Lydia came out onto the porch. *Ah*. Deborah was coming. *Gut*.

The girls climbed into the back. Before Amos could help Bartholomew into the front, the door opened again, and Teresa came out. "I'm not ready yet. Let me get my coat."

Bartholomew took his *frau's* arm and spoke gently to her. "I need you to stay here with the younger children."

Teresa's eyebrows scrunched down. "Stay? But… I…"

Miriam joined them on the porch. "*Mutter*, I need your help hemming my dress."

Teresa's eyes brightened. "*Ja*, I can help you." She turned back to her husband. "I'm needed here, so I won't be able to go with you."

Bartholomew smiled at his daughter, then at his *frau*. "That's all right. Maybe next time."

The pair of women went back inside, and Amos helped Bartholomew maneuver his casted leg and his crutches into the buggy.

Tension filled the buggy during the slow ride.

Finally, they arrived at the doctor's. It sure was nice to have one right in their community, and that she was one of their own, who understood so much more than an outsider could. Amos helped everyone out, and Noah Lambright, the doctor's husband, took over the care of the horse and buggy so Amos could go inside the *dawdy haus* clinic with the others.

With no other patients there, Dr. Kathleen offered them seats in the waiting room to accommodate their large group, which was too big to fit in the exam room comfortably. Since her sister had gone for the day, the doctor brought them each a cup of tea or coffee. "How are you doing, Bartholomew? Are you having any trouble with your shoulder or getting around on your crutches?"

"*Ne*. I'm doing well."

"Are the physical-therapy exercises helping?"

"*Ja*. We didn't come for me."

Dr. Kathleen nodded. "Teresa?"

Bartholomew took a slow breath. "*Ja*. She's not doing well, as my daughters have already told you."

"I saw for myself. I'd like to do some tests, but I need your permission and to have access to her medical records."

"You have my permission."

"I'll need it in writing." Dr. Kathleen brought out the required documents, filled in the needed information and had Bartholomew sign them. "Now, tell me a bit about your *frau's* medical history. When did you first notice something wasn't quite right with her?"

"When she was carrying Hannah and Lydia. I thought it was just part of being pregnant. But she continued after they were born for a few months and slowly returned to her normal self. She got worse with each successive pregnancy."

"Has she had any operations?"

"She had one tonsil removed when she was six and again when she was ten, and her appendix out six months later."

Dr. Kathleen made notes. "Any accidents?"

"She was in a buggy accident when she was three. Two of her siblings and her *mutter* didn't survive, and she was in the hospital for a couple of weeks. She had a dizzy spell and fell while she was carrying Deborah, and when Deborah was born, Teresa lost a lot of blood."

Amos couldn't imagine all that happening to one person.

No wonder she forgot Deborah most. She'd had quite a bit of trauma with her. Amos glanced at Deborah. Her eyes glistened. Was she about to cry? He wanted to wipe away her tears.

Bartholomew chuckled. "Not surprising that she doesn't like doctors. She's never had *gut* experiences with them."

Dr. Kathleen smiled. "I noticed. I hope to be as much her friend as her doctor. Childhood diseases?"

"All the normal ones, chicken pox and the like."

Dr. Kathleen listed off a multitude of childhood diseases that Bartholomew answered affirmative to. "Chronic problems?"

"Like what? Being forgetful and confused?"

"Other things like a cough that won't go away, regular headaches, persistent rash?"

Bartholomew shook his head.

Hannah jumped in. "She does get quite a few headaches, and her hands shake."

Lydia nodded her agreement.

"Shake? How?"

"Her hands are usually at her sides, and they twitch, sort of." Hannah stood and demonstrated.

"And the headaches? Is there anything different going on when she gets those? Same time of day? Certain situations?"

Lydia answered this time, "When she's stressed, which happens after she's been confused. That's when her hands shake most, too."

This time, Hannah nodded.

Bartholomew stared at his twin daughters. "I had no idea."

Both gave him identical tight smiles, but Hannah spoke. "We handled it so you could take care of the farm."

Lydia spoke up. "But her episodes are getting more frequent."

"And lasting longer," Hannah added. "We need to keep a constant watch on her."

From the stunned looks, neither Bartholomew nor Deborah knew any of this last part. Deborah swiped a tear from her cheek. Amos wished he could comfort her. Tell her everything would be all right.

After all the questions were answered, Dr. Kathleen made arrangements to go to their house to draw blood for tests.

Would Amos be invited to the *appointment*? What

would the doctor ask all the others, and what would her diagnosis be? He would have to wait and see.

He glanced at Deborah. She held her jaw stiff as though she had something important caught between her teeth. He wished there was something he could do for her.

Deborah struggled to hold her tears at bay the whole ride home from their visit to Dr. Kathleen's. She had no idea her *mutter* had been through so much. Instead of going into the house with the others, she headed across the field to the pond. She plopped down on the fallen log and let the tears come.

How could she not have known what her own *mutter* was going through? She had been selfish and thinking of only herself while her *mutter* suffered. Running off whenever she could. Behaving like a spoiled child. Parading in front of a camera. Should she quit modeling? How could she continue and help look after her *mutter*?

"Deborah?"

She jumped at her name, stood and turned to face Amos, slapping away her tears. "I...um..."

"Are you all right?"

"Of course. Why wouldn't I be?" She didn't want him, of all people, to see her as an emotional mess.

"You heard some pretty upsetting things at the doctor's. I suspect you didn't know all that about your *mutter*."

Her emotions welled up and threatened to douse her in another wave of tears. Blinking several times, she swallowed hard. "I know now."

"Don't cry."

"I'm not crying."

He stepped forward and rubbed his thumb across her cheek. "Then what's this?" On his thumb sat a fledgling tear.

His touch sent a shiver through her.

"A raindrop?"

He looked up at the cloudless sky. "Okay. A raindrop."

His sweetness opened the floodgates, and she covered her face with her hands and sobbed.

Strong arms wrapped around her. "It's going to be all right. Your *mutter's* going to get the help she needs."

He shouldn't be holding her. Though not forbidden, it was frowned upon, but she didn't care. She needed the comfort. She needed the comfort from *him.* "I never knew she went through so much. I was too busy feeling sorry for myself to notice."

"It sounded like they all did a *gut* job of hiding her condition from you and everyone."

She pulled back but not out of his embrace. "I'm her *daughter.* I should have noticed."

"You did notice. You just interpreted the information inaccurately."

She considered that. She had noticed *Mutter's* forgetfulness and took it as a personal affront. She'd noticed her *mutter* acting out of touch and assumed that was where Deborah had gotten her flights of fancy. And she'd noticed *Mutter* wandering off and thought she just liked walks alone, as Deborah did.

She gritted her teeth to keep the tears at bay. No use. They came anyway. "I'm sorry. I'm a blubbering idiot."

"You're not an idiot. You're a caring daughter."

His kindness overwhelmed her.

Amos brushed away her tears again with his thumbs. She shouldn't let him do that but reveled in his attention. It felt *gut* to have someone notice her and care about her. She gazed up into his sturdy brown eyes.

He gazed back.

Her insides wiggled. A pleasant yet scary feeling.

She should move.

But didn't.

She should look away.

But didn't.

She should…

"Deborah," he whispered, inches from her face.

His warm breath fanned her cheek.

"Ja."

He leaned closer.

Then she heard her name again as though from a far-away dream, but Amos hadn't opened his mouth.

She heard it again, shrill this time.

Amos jerked away from her.

Deborah stepped back.

Naomi tromped toward them. *"Vater* wants you in the house."

Of course, Naomi would spoil the moment, but it was just as well. She had no right standing here with Amos. No right staring at him as though there was something between them.

Her sister maneuvered between them to walk next to Amos.

Deborah's moment of being noticed had been crushed once again by Naomi.

When she went inside the house, she found Hannah, Lydia and Miriam working in the kitchen. Joanna and Sarah's voices came from the living room, as well as *Mutter's* and *Vater's.*

Perfect, Amos and Naomi were still outside. Though

Deborah would rather be with Amos, she would take this opportunity to speak to her three older sisters without anyone else around. "I'm glad you three are here."

"You are?" Miriam said. "Why us?"

Deborah kept her voice low. "Because you three seemed to know all about *Mutter's* problem. Why didn't any of you ever say anything or tell me? I could have helped."

Lydia opened her mouth but didn't say anything when Hannah held up her hand. Hannah, always in charge. "That was my decision, and I came to regret it. It was easier in the beginning for Lydia and me to handle *Mutter*. We worked well as a team and reported back to *Vater*. But when Sarah came along and was so needy and Naomi became jealous of all the time she demanded, it became harder to manage it all. Miriam partially figured things out and started pitching in and helping. So, we three worked together to manage *Mutter*, placate Naomi, deal with Sarah and take care of the house. You and Joanna always took care of yourselves, which was a huge help. We didn't have to worry about you."

"But if you had told me, I could have helped instead of just 'not being a bother.'"

"You're right. We should have."

Miriam finally spoke up. "Hannah and Lydia want to marry in the fall, so I'm going to take over everything they've been doing. I sure could use your help."

"What about you? Don't you want to get married?"

Miriam's words came out flat. "I'm praying the Lord won't have me fall in love." Her shoulders bowed forward.

Deborah had never heard of any woman in their community not *wanting* to get married.

Miriam's eyes watered. "That's a sacrifice I can make."

"*Ne.* You don't have to. Dr. Kathleen will figure out what's wrong with *Mutter* and make her better."

"And if she can't make *Mutter* better?" Lydia said.

Deborah didn't want to think that way, but she must consider it. "Teach me everything about taking care of her before you two marry. Then Miriam and I will teach Joanna."

Hannah spoke. "Then when Miriam marries and you marry and Joanna marries, do you honestly think Naomi will pick up the slack?"

Lydia's expression held both hope and defeat. "Let's wait and see what Dr. Kathleen says."

The strangest feeling engulfed Deborah. Like she actually belonged in her own family. Finally. She'd felt like a stranger for so long, she hadn't known *how* to belong. But now she knew *why* she'd felt like an outsider. She *had been* an outsider.

Her *vater* and her older sisters had been so caught up in surrounding *Mutter* to protect her that they hadn't realized they were cutting off the rest of the family. Deborah liked this new camaraderie with her sisters.

Now Deborah was in on the horrible secret.

Now she was included and would be there to help.

Now she wouldn't be left out.

She belonged.

Chapter Twelve

Deborah hated waiting. Yesterday, Dr. Kathleen and her sister, Jessica, arrived at the house just after breakfast and amazingly drew blood from everyone, including Amos, without a fuss from *Mutter* when it was her turn. True to her word, Dr. Kathleen had kept the visit friendly, like a neighbor dropping by.

Now they all had to wait for the results. Deborah couldn't pretend to be busy around the house but actually do nothing. She needed to get out. Get away. She was scheduled for a photo shoot today that she *had* planned to skip, but it offered the perfect distraction.

She peered out the kitchen window. Amos still puttered around the yard. Why did he have to pick today to work outside, cutting wood for the small potbellied stove in his little room? She'd interrupted this chore the other day. How much wood did he need? The room wasn't that big.

Before that he'd inspected the outside of the barn and repaired the chicken coop, which wasn't even broken. Granted, it did need help, but it wasn't quite broken yet. It just leaned slightly. And he ambled around doing other busywork in the yard. A lot of things needed some TLC.

Being the only man on the farm, *Vater* could never quite get to everything that needed attention.

If she didn't leave soon, she would be late and miss meeting her ride into town. Her sisters were easy to get away from, but Amos proved to be difficult. He kept a vigilant watch over the entire farm and its inhabitants.

She could tell him she was going to meet her "friend in need," but she didn't want to be questioned about that. She needed to devise a plan. If she went out the front door, he wouldn't be able to see her leave the house.

After slipping out, she went the long way around the house, away from where he worked. The chopping had ceased. Where was he now?

She peered around the house and directly into his broad chest.

"Where are you off to?" He smiled down at her. "Sneaking off?"

Why did he have to be so observant?

She forced a smile. "Just heading to the pond."

"*Wunderbar.* I'll go with you."

Ne! she wanted to say but held her tongue. If she protested, he might get suspicious. Hopefully, he would get bored quickly and want to return. She trudged slowly in the direction of the pond, hoping he would give up before they reached it.

He didn't.

She sat in her favorite spot on a log. The once fully frozen pond had half melted. Spring warmth was just around the corner. Some ducks walked on the frozen edge while others paddled around in the slushy center.

Amos sat on the log a couple of feet away from her. Even though she needed to be somewhere else, she liked having him here with her. Liked sharing her special spot, but as much as she wanted to, today was not the day to enjoy this. "I'm sure you have to get back to work."

"It can wait awhile. I can see why you like to come here a lot. It's nice. Peaceful."

And usually, she was all alone. The way she liked it. She stood. "I feel bad about keeping you. Let's head back."

He stood, as well. "I *should* get back. The corral needs some work."

She walked at a brisker pace than she'd walked out to the pond to get him off her tracks. Once he got busy with the corral, she would be able to hustle away.

While he was in the barn gathering tools, Deborah ran through the field, making sure to keep the barn between her and the corral to hide her escape. She tramped as quickly as possible through the bumpy field. She needed this shoot today. Needed to forget about her family's problems for a little while.

Out of breath, she reached her rendezvous spot, but the car wasn't there. She'd missed her ride. Now what was she going to do? Should she call Hudson from one of the Amish phone boxes near the road and tell him she couldn't make it today? Or start walking into town and be even later? She headed off along the road. She didn't want to go back home. Not after all the trouble she'd taken to escape.

After five minutes, a car drove past and pulled off to the side of the rode. The driver rolled down the window and waved for Deborah to come over.

She approached the vehicle and recognized the driver. "*Hallo*, Mrs. Carpenter." She had received rides from her before.

"Deborah, right?"

She nodded.

"Do you need a ride into town?"

"I would love a ride. I can pay for the gas."

"No need. I'm going that way anyway."

Deborah got in. "I was late for meeting my ride and missed it."

"Well, it's a good thing the Lord had me driving on this road today." Mrs. Carpenter dropped off Deborah at the gas station a couple of blocks from the photography studio.

Deborah never had anyone drop her off right at the studio. She didn't need to be questioned about what she was doing or telling other Amish exactly where she went. Amos wanted to know her whereabouts, but he was the last person she wanted to know, aside from the church leaders.

After all, she wasn't doing anything wrong. She never wore revealing clothes, and she wasn't hurting anyone.

Not really.

She had planned to model until she found a husband then quit. She figured she'd have a nice bit of money to help her husband buy a farm. In fact, she was doing a *gut* thing. But with *Mutter's* troubles, she'd decided she would quit after this photo shoot. Hudson would be in an agreeable mood from a successful session.

She pulled open the door to the studio, and as she strode inside, her stomach tightened.

Hudson stood behind his camera, snapping pictures of a model wearing a slim knit dress. Another catalog shoot. These were her least favorite.

Summer turned to her a moment before Hudson did. He scowled. "Debo, you're late. I was beginning to think you weren't going to show."

"I'm sorry. I had a hard time getting away, and I

missed my ride." It wouldn't matter anymore. She knew that after today she wouldn't be coming back.

Hudson stomped over to her and gripped her shoulders. "You need to decide what's more important. I count on you being here. When you leave me in the lurch, you hurt all of us." He swept his arm toward his assistants and the other models.

"I'm sorry. Do you want me to leave?"

"No. You're finally here. Go with Tina and Lindsey, and they'll get you ready. And, Debo, be ready when you come back." With his fingers pinched together, he drew his fingertips down in front of him from his head to his waist. "In here."

Hudson could be a little overdramatic.

She followed in Tina and Lindsey's wake.

Deborah sat uncomfortably as Tina brushed and worked with her hair. Was Tina being purposefully rough today? Or did Deborah just not want to be here today so every little thing bothered her?

Amos would have a fit if he knew where she was. The ache inside her chest wrenched tighter. She took a deep breath to clear it away. She needed this distraction. She was earning money for her future. She was doing nothing wrong.

Once transformed from head to toe and back out in the studio, she stood off to the side for Hudson to need her and give her instructions. She didn't have to wait long.

"Okay, Angela. Get into your next outfit." Hudson turned to Deborah, then motioned with a sweep of his hand for her to step in front of the white backdrop.

She obeyed and faced the camera.

Hudson looked through his camera on the tripod. "I

want a neutral, content expression. Neither happy nor sad. Think of your face as a blank canvas, waiting for the right emotion to descend upon it."

A blank canvas? How was she supposed to achieve that? She tried to appear neither happy nor sad. Was she succeeding?

"No, no, no." Hudson stepped out from behind his camera. "Not distressed. Let's try something else." He moved back behind his camera and pointed over his head. "Pick a point behind me and think of something happy. Like ropes of diamonds."

Diamonds didn't make her happy.

"Or ice cream."

That was better, but it was still cold outside. Now, if it was the middle of summer, ice cream would make her happy.

"Or a new fur coat."

Hudson really had no clue what made Deborah happy, so she pictured the kittens in the barn. They were so adorable.

The camera lens clicked repeatedly. "Good. Keep that up."

Then she pictured the kittens scampering about. Suddenly, Amos was there, being the man about the farm. Doing all the chores a man normally did, with the kittens climbing on him.

"Perfect," Hudson said.

Hay had showered down around her, and Amos swooped her out of harm's way, and they tumbled into a pile of hay. He stared at her. Instead of him pulling away this time, her heart took control, and Amos inched closer and closer until he was a breath away—

"Debo!"

Deborah blinked and focused on Hudson standing in front of her.

His hand on her arm. "I got the shots. I don't know where you went, but it was absolutely perfect, beyond what I had hoped for."

Her face warmed at having allowed herself to think of Amos in such a way. It was a silly dream. Wasn't it?

"From that blush, I'll guess that there was a handsome guy in your daydream." Hudson gave her a knowing smile, winked and walked off.

She put her hands to her hot cheeks. He couldn't possibly know. He didn't even know about Amos.

When the session concluded, Deborah chickened out telling Hudson this was her last shoot. She slipped away unnoticed. She would have to figure another way to tell him.

She couldn't go on like this much longer.

The following week, when their house telephone rang, Deborah picked up the slim-line phone and took it to her *vater* in the living room.

"Hallo?" Vater paused, then said, *"Hallo,* Kathleen… Teresa would do better if you came here… Just me?" His features settled into a grim expression. "When?… I will come… *Danki. Auf wiedersehen."* He hung up the phone.

Deborah released her breath. "What is it?"

"The doctor wishes to see me. Not your *mutter."*

Deborah's insides tightened. Had the doctor found something wrong with *Vater* in his blood? "When must you go?"

"She can see me now. Would you tell Hannah and Lydia to come with me? And then ask Amos to hitch up the buggy?"

"I want to come, too."

Vater stared at her for a moment, then nodded. "I've kept things to myself for too long. I thought I could ignore this, but I can't."

In the buggy, Amos drove, and *Vater* sat up front with him. Deborah sat in back with her two oldest sisters.

At the Amish clinic, Jessica Yoder welcomed them and asked them to take a seat in the waiting area.

The emptiness in the pit of Deborah's stomach kept her on her feet. She wanted to run out of there. She didn't want to hear whatever bad news the doctor had, but she *needed* to know. Or how else could she help *Mutter*?

Dr. Kathleen came out with Rebecca Beiler and her three-year-old son. "Make a follow-up appointment with Jessica."

Amos, standing beside Deborah, took her hand. "Everything will be all right."

Though startling at first, his warm, strong hand around hers comforted Deborah. She never wanted him to let go. "How can it be? *Mutter* is… There's something wrong with her. What if she has Alzheimer's disease?"

"Let's not invite trouble. Trust *Gott*." He gave her hand a squeeze and let go before anyone saw.

Deborah had thrilled at his touch, but now her hand felt oddly empty.

Dr. Kathleen faced the crowd and smiled. "Oh, my. I didn't expect so many of you. Come into my office. I'll grab a few more chairs."

Amos picked up one of the vacated chairs. "How many do you need?"

"If everyone is coming in, three—wait—four. And one to prop up Bartholomew's leg."

He hefted two straight-backed chairs.

Deborah grabbed one herself, and Dr. Kathleen carried the fourth.

Once everyone sat, Dr. Kathleen turned to *Vater.* "Are you sure you want so many present for your *frau's* diagnosis?"

Vater looked at each of his daughters and Amos. "My daughters help their *mutter* all the time. They should know what is going on with her. They'll help me remember what you say. Amos has been helpful, as well."

"All right."

Hannah cleared her throat. "Is it Alzheimer's disease?"

"Ne."

Dr. Kathleen looked directly at *Vater.* "I don't have enough information yet to make a final diagnosis, but I'm fairly certain it's not Alzheimer's. We do need to do more tests, but I'll give you my preliminary findings. As far as I can tell, Teresa has two issues. One is complicating the other."

Deborah shifted to the edge of her seat. If she scooted any closer, she'd land on the floor. She held her breath.

The doctor went on. "I believe Teresa might have what's known as Graves' disease. It's an immune system disorder that results in the overproduction of the thyroid hormone, known as hyperthyroidism." She put her hand on her throat. "The thyroid is located here. Hers doesn't seem enlarged. With more tests, we can know for certain."

"Is there a cure for it?" *Vater* asked.

"Not a cure, but it can be managed. There are a few medications, but I'm reluctant to recommend any of them."

"Because you aren't sure yet?"

"*Ne.* Because of Teresa's other condition. She's pregnant."

No one spoke. No one moved. It seemed as though no one dared to breathe lest it make this unbelievable news real.

Pregnant? *Mutter* was going to have another baby?

Hannah and Lydia exchanged knowing glances.

"Her pregnancy is heightening the Graves' disease, causing the thyroid to produce more hormones than normal. This is why she seems worse when she's pregnant, because she is. Graves' can be the cause of the anxiety, shaking hands, forgetfulness, insomnia, as well as a host of other things. Many of the things in her medical history could be adding to her memory issues, as well."

Vater frowned. "Pregnant?"

"*Ja.* That's why I don't want to give her any medications just yet. Whatever she ingests, the baby receives. The only one I might be comfortable giving her while she's pregnant would be a beta-blocker, but I believe we can achieve similar results with natural methods. Graves' is hereditary. Mostly occurring in women under forty."

Mutter had turned forty not more than three months ago.

"I would like to draw more blood from all of you to test for Graves' specifically." Dr. Kathleen handed *Vater* a sheet of paper. "This is a list of natural things to do to help manage Teresa's condition. Because we are Amish, we already do most of the things they suggest—minimize stress, eat fresh fruits and vegetables, don't eat processed foods, as well as others. They are listed on that paper. Her natural diet and low-stress environment have been managing her Graves' without even knowing it, but she'll need to cut out all caffeine."

"Is *Mutter* going to be all right?" Deborah asked.

"I think so, with a little extra care and attention. I'd like to come by the house to give her the news myself and draw more blood from each of you to test for Graves'."

"What about the baby? Will it be all right? Will it have Down syndrome like Sarah?" Not that that would change anything. The baby would still be born, but the family could be better prepared.

"That's one of the tests I'll request to have them run at the hospital. We want to keep *mutter* and baby as healthy as we can."

The following day, Dr. Kathleen dropped by the house to give her diagnosis to *Mutter*. The whole family, as well as Amos, gathered in the living room.

Dr. Kathleen went around the room telling each person their blood type. She saved *Mutter* for last. "Your blood type is O positive. You might possibly have Graves' disease. It's not life-threatening. We just need to adjust some of your meals and habits. Also…you are pregnant, Teresa. Congratulations."

Mutter beamed, unaware of the emotional turmoil this was causing her and would continue to cause. Not just for herself, but for the whole family.

Miriam's voice held less enthusiasm than one normally would have. "I am so happy for you, *Mutter* and *Vater*."

Joanna expressed her pleasure, too.

Sarah clapped her hands, but she didn't likely understand she would have a baby sister or brother in a few months.

Naomi folded her arms and pouted. She would be receiving less attention in the future and wasn't happy about it.

Kathleen continued, "I'm ordering further tests at the hospital."

Mutter's broad smile disappeared in a flash, and she shook her head. "*Ne.* I'm not going to the hospital. I don't like doctors." Fear etched the lines of her face.

Before anyone could think to stop her, Naomi said, "Kathleen's a doctor. *Doctor* Kathleen."

Mutter stared at Kathleen. Her eyebrows furrowed, and her lips twitched. "*Ne.* Kathleen is a friend and neighbor." Her face relaxed, and her whole demeanor calmed.

Several relieved breaths exhaled around the room, including Deborah's.

"That's right," Kathleen said. "I'm your friend, but because you're older, your pregnancy needs to be monitored more closely to keep the baby healthy and safe."

Mutter shook her head. "I won't go to the hospital."

Kathleen put a reassuring hand on *Mutter's* arm. "I can go and be with you every step of the way."

"*Ne.* I'm not going. I don't like doctors." *Mutter* stood and rushed into the kitchen.

Vater trailed after her on his crutches, followed by Hannah and Lydia.

Deborah had been excluded from too much of the family's goings-on. She would not be left out again and joined them. Amos came as well and stood in the doorway.

It took cajoling and comforting from *Vater*, Hannah, Lydia and even Amos to calm *Mutter* and convince her to go to the hospital for tests.

Deborah knew so little about *Mutter* and her condition to be of any use. That would not be the case next time. She would learn all she could about her *mutter's* condition to help her.

Chapter Thirteen

Deborah's sisters and *Mutter* bustled around the kitchen, preparing lunch. Deborah took the opportunity to sneak into the living room, where her *vater* sat with his leg up.

He spoke before she could. "I have had enough of sitting around." He rubbed his shoulder, the reason why he shouldn't use his crutches too much. The use of them had already slowed his shoulder healing.

"I'm sure you have." Deborah sat next to him and cast a glance toward the kitchen to make sure no one had decided to wander this way. She needed to speak quickly while she had him to herself. "*Vater*, I want to find natural alternatives to the prescription medications to keep *Mutter's* anxiety under control when she goes to the hospital. I would like your permission to go to the library in town after lunch and do some research. I won't use the computer myself. I'll have one of the *Englishers* do it for me. I'll see if I can check out a book about natural remedies, too."

Vater put on his thinking face of thinned lips and squinted eyes and remained quiet for a moment. "*Ja*. That would be *gut*. Also, go to the bookstore and purchase a book on natural remedies so we always have something here. I'll give you money. Amos will go with you. He can pick up my planting seeds and a few other things. Have Hannah make a list, as well. Don't tell *Mutter* or the younger ones. Send Amos in here so I can tell him."

A trip into town with just Amos. In spite of her worries about *Mutter's* conditions, Deborah's insides danced.

After lunch, she slipped outside unnoticed. Even with finally being included in the family secret, everyone overlooked her. This time she didn't mind.

Amos had Floyd partially harnessed to the wagon.

Deborah set her shopping bag with *Vater's* money and some of her own, along with a few more empty cloth shopping bags, on the floor of the wagon and helped. Soon, she sat on the seat next to Amos as they headed into town.

As the wagon lumbered down the road, she studied the man sitting next to her out of the corner of her eye. He seemed so comfortable at the reins. And why shouldn't he be? He had been born and bred Amish. He'd grown up at the reins. It wasn't that he looked comfortable so much as content. *Ja*, that was it. Content. Something Deborah had never been. Even from a young age, a restlessness had been inside her. She'd always yearned for more in life than rising early, working hard from sunup to sundown and going to bed at the end of the day. Though all *gut*, she sensed a different purpose for herself.

Dr. Kathleen had felt that pull, too. She'd gone out into the world, then had returned to help others. Deborah wanted that, too. But what purpose could she have? She didn't want to be a doctor, or go to school for years.

She shifted on the seat. "Do you think Dr. Kathleen was wrong to go into the *Englisher* world and become a doctor?"

"She is doing great *gut* for our community, so I don't see how that can be bad."

"But she left for so long. Our people believe that when a child of the Amish goes out into the world, they are turned over to the devil. That if they died out there, they wouldn't go to Heaven. Is that true?"

"I hope not."

"Because of your cousin Jacob?"

He hesitated before he answered. "Him and others. I'm not sure I see where living here or out there or any-where changes what's in your heart. If you love *Gott*, you love *Gott*. He is not limited to one place or another but is everywhere."

"I like that. *Gott* is not limited."

"*Ja*. I like that, too. We shouldn't put restrictions on *Gott*." Amos pulled up in front of the library. "I'll leave you here while I go to the feed and seed stores."

Deborah climbed down. "About an hour?"

"Maybe a bit more."

"*Gut*. That should be plenty of time." She wanted to stay at his side and go everywhere he did. If she did that, there wouldn't be enough time to get everything done and return before supper, so she headed inside the library.

Deborah had lost track of time, and over an hour later, she peered out the front window of the library. She'd searched through many natural-remedy books and checked out three. One of the librarians had searched on the computer and printed off several pages of informa-tion for her.

Amos stood on the sidewalk, talking with a man, and walked away from him. His cousin. The cousin who had been at the hospital the day *Vater* had gotten injured. The cousin who had come to the farm to talk to Amos. The cousin who had left the community. Deborah pushed open the door and trotted down the front walk to him. "Jacob, isn't it?"

He turned with a start, guilt contorting his face. Like a child caught taking a cookie before supper. *"Ja."* He glanced around.

"I'm Deborah. I live on the farm your cousin Amos is working on."

He swallowed hard. "It's nice to meet you. I'm Jacob—but you already know that. You know you could be shunned for speaking to me."

"Only if someone sees and tells one of the church leaders. Then I will confess my wrongdoing, be forgiven and not be shunned."

Chuckling, his body relaxed. "You like to live dangerously."

"I wouldn't call talking to you *dangerous*. Even if it were, I wouldn't say I *like* danger."

He smirked. "I'd say you like danger just a little bit."

How had this conversation gotten off the topic of why she'd come over here to talk to Jacob in the first place? She best get it out before things got off track again. "Is Amos planning to leave the community?"

He froze in midbreath, and his words squeaked out. "What? Why do you ask that?"

"Because *you* left, and I keep seeing you talking to him."

He hesitated. "We're still cousins. He lets me know how my family's doing."

Though she believed him, she felt there was more to this. "Don't make him leave."

"I can't *make* anyone do anything. It was nice talking to you." He walked around an old blue pickup truck and climbed in. He waved as he drove off.

An uneasiness coiled around Deborah's heart. Was Amos truly thinking about leaving? Was this why he'd said he hoped *Gott* was everywhere? Because he hoped *Gott* would be with him when he left?

The clomping of a horse's hooves brought her back to the present. Amos smiled at her from inside the buggy.

Ne, he wouldn't leave. Would he?

She climbed in.

"Discount store now?" Amos clicked out the side of his mouth and gave the reins a snap. Floyd plodded forward.

"Um." She shook away the thought of his potential leaving. For now. "I think there's a health-food store on the way. Can we stop? I want to get some things to try with *Mutter*." At the store, she spoke to a helpful employee and bought a homeopathic book. She also purchased some natural remedies for *Mutter*. Afterward, she completed Hannah's list at the discount store.

On the way out of town, Deborah pulled out the homeopathic book she purchased and flipped through the pages. How would she get *Mutter* to agree to take the remedies she'd purchased? Hannah would probably have a *gut* idea how best to approach the topic with her.

Amos leaned over and looked at the book. "Is all that safe for the baby?"

"Why wouldn't it be?"

"I don't know. I just know there are some foods we don't feed to young babies because their bodies can't digest them until they're older."

Amos posed a *gut* question. "You're right. Can we stop in at Dr. Kathleen's, and I'll ask her? I don't want to risk *Mutter* or the baby."

Once at the doctor's office, the doctor scrutinized

each of the remedies and searched in her own texts as well as thumbing through Deborah's books. "You've chosen well. These remedies all seem safe."

"*Danki*. I wanted to make sure before I gave *Mutter* anything."

"It is always *gut* to be safe. Let me know how she does on each of these. Start them one at a time to make sure she doesn't have a reaction. If she does, you'll know it's the newest one."

"*Danki.*" Deborah tucked the remedies back into her cloth shopping bag with the books.

Dr. Kathleen gave Deborah a pointed look. "Have you thought about studying homeopathy? Natural remedies."

"I don't want to be away to learn such things. My family needs me to help with *Mutter*."

"You wouldn't have to leave. More and more studies are available online from home. I think you have a natural gift for it."

Deborah had enjoyed the research and learning. "Do you think the church leaders would allow that?"

"Times are changing. Our Amish needs have changed. Amish don't want to rely on *Englishers*, but we have to more and more. If we don't want to be dependent on the outside world, then some of us need to get more education than eighth grade, for the *gut* of the whole community. We must become self-reliant in some of these higher education areas. Just think about it, Deborah."

She would. She liked the idea of learning more about natural remedies and learning at home. She left with Amos. The encounter with Jacob niggled in her mind. Should she ask Amos outright if he was going to leave? She wasn't sure she would like the answer. "Why do people abandon their Amish ways and go live in the *Englisher* world?"

"Um, uh… Why do you ask?"

"Oh, never mind." She shouldn't have said anything. She didn't want to know.

He turned sideways in the seat. "You asked earlier about Dr. Kathleen's actions. Now this. You aren't thinking of leaving, are you? Because that would be a bad idea."

Bad idea, indeed.

"Me? *Ne.* But people do it. Like your cousin and the bishop's granddaughter. Why do they turn their backs on all the beliefs they were raised with? Do they not believe in *Gott* anymore?"

He faced forward again. "I suppose they must have reasons they think are important enough. Maybe they are disillusioned with this life. That Amish aren't who they pretend to be. But as I said before, I believe *Gott* is everywhere."

That hit her square in her guilty heart. She had been pretending to be both Amish and an *Englisher* for a year, and felt torn between the two. But would she ever seriously consider leaving? She doubted it. "Why did your cousin leave?"

"He felt the *Englisher* world held more opportunities for him."

Was that what Amos was looking for? More opportunities? "What opportunities would be better than our Amish life?"

"I don't know. I guess they're just different."

So far, he hadn't given her an indication one way or the other if he planned to leave. "What about you? Is there anything that would draw you to escape into the *Englisher* world permanently?"

"I don't know. I suppose if a person searched long enough, they could come up with something that made sense to them."

Her heart sank. How much more noncommittal could he be? He was searching for a reason to leave. Why couldn't he have said that *nothing* could ever make him leave? *Nothing*.

At the farm, she left Amos in the barn to finish unhitching and caring for Floyd. She had returned in time to help prepare supper. The task had never appealed to her before, but now that her family included her, she liked the camaraderie and connection with her sisters and *Mutter*.

She pulled Hannah aside. "I checked out three books from the library and bought one at the health-food store on natural remedies."

"We should ask Dr. Kathleen if these will be safe for the baby and for *Mutter*."

"I stopped in on the way home. She said the ones I got would be fine."

Hannah hugged her. "*Danki*. You have done such a *gut* job. I'm sorry I ever doubted you could be of help."

Her sister's praise wrapped around Deborah like a prewarmed quilt. "How could you have known when I was never here?"

Dr. Kathleen's suggestion of learning more about natural remedies intrigued her and took root. She could not only help her *mutter*, but also others in her community. And somehow, she needed to convince Amos to stay.

The task of helping Sarah make biscuits fell to Deborah. And she had fun doing it. Sarah enjoyed most everything, unless she wanted her way and wasn't getting it, but in general, her baby sister was a joy. Soon they would have another little one running around the house.

At the kitchen sink, Deborah washed flour off her hands and glanced out the window. When she saw a shiny black Porsche pull into the driveway, her heart seized. *"Ne. Ne. Ne."* Hudson couldn't be here. She'd never told him where she lived.

"What's wrong?" *Mutter* sat at the table, turning pages of a cookbook.

"Nothing." Deborah shook water from her hands and grabbed a kitchen towel. "I'll be right back."

All of her sisters stared at her, but Hannah spoke. "Where are you going?"

"Outside. Be right back." Deborah raced out of the house in hopes of stopping Hudson before he got out of his car. She needed him to turn around and leave before anyone saw him.

But Hudson did get out and had closed his car door by the time Deborah reached him. She opened the door. "How did you find me? Get back in. You have to leave right now."

"It wasn't easy." Hudson closed the door again, leaned against it and pulled an envelope out of his inside jacket pocket. "Your latest wages. You never came to collect it."

Deborah took it. "Thank you. Bye."

He didn't budge. "You've missed a couple of photo shoots. I had to come to see if you were all right. You've put me in quite a bind, Debo."

She cringed at her modeling alias. It all seemed so silly now. How could she have ever thought that life was so *wunderbar*? This was as *gut* a time as any to tell him. "I'm fine. But I can't model for you anymore. Please go."

Hudson straightened, pushing away from the car. "You're quitting?"

"*Ja*. My *mutter* is ill. I'm needed here. Now, please go before anyone sees you."

He took her hand. "Debo, I can't let you go."

She pulled on her hand, but he held fast. "Don't call me that. You have to let me go. You have plenty of other models."

"No one like you."

She shook her head. "I know your other models get you the shots you need. I liked believing I was special, but I know now that I'm not."

He squeezed her hand. "You *are* special. You're special to me. I didn't keep using you on shoots just because you're beautiful and a good model. I didn't keep excusing your tardiness or not showing up because you're irreplaceable as a model. I did those things because you're irreplaceable to me. I care a lot about you. I hoped to come here to convince you to leave this simple life and be with me."

Two months ago, she might have considered his offer, but now it just sounded ridiculous, and not just because of her *mutter's* conditions. There was Amos, too. "Leave? I can't leave."

"Yes, you can. You could be so much more than this. You could be a star. I can make you a star. I know you love modeling. I've seen it in your eyes."

He was right. Modeling *had* sparked something inside her. Partly because his attention had made her feel special and partly because she was doing something forbidden. She felt sort of a thrill getting away with it, but it had been wrong.

"I did love it, but I can't do it anymore. My family needs me." And she needed her family. Modeling had been hollow. She could see that now. She'd welcomed her family into that empty space, and they brought her joy.

"Please consider my offer. I'll take care of you. I have a large apartment. There's plenty of room for you."

"Are you asking me to marry you?" That didn't sound like Hudson. He was not the commitment type.

"Not right away. Maybe in time."

Which most likely meant never.

"You expect me to leave my family, whom I could never come back to, to live with you? You don't know me at all." She hadn't known herself either, but now she did, at least a little better. And what she knew was that she was Amish and would always be Amish. Her family needed her, and she would be here for them. For a change.

"I thought you cared about me, too."

Deborah had basked in his praise, but she held no fondness for Hudson outside of modeling. She'd thought she did. She had even had a crush on him in the beginning. She could see now how shallow all that had been. "I'm not modeling ever again, and I'm not going to leave with you. My family needs me. I belong here. Goodbye, Hudson." She tossed the envelope back at him and walked away.

"Debo. Debo? Debo!"

At the name of her model persona, Deborah ran and didn't stop until she was back inside. She would never be Debo again.

"Who was that man?" *Mutter* asked.

Oh, dear. Her *mutter* had seen, and likely her sisters, too. Had *Vater* seen? *Gott* willing, he had not. Hopefully, her *mutter* would forget as easily as she forgot Deborah. "No one. He lost his way." Both those statements were true. Hudson was no one to her anymore, and he'd lost his way because he never should have come out here.

* * *

Amos had watched Deborah run inside. What had that *Englisher* said to her to make her so upset? He strode over to the man in the dark suit who still stood beside his car. "What business do you have with Deborah?"

The man leveled his gaze at Amos and gave a sardonic laugh. "*Deborah?* You have no idea who she is. To me, she's Debo, the model. *My* model."

"Model?"

"That's having your picture taken with a purpose."

Why did *Englishers* think Amish didn't know anything about the outside world just because they chose not to get caught up in all those meaningless activities and collecting useless possessions? Sometimes *Englishers* were more ignorant than the Amish. But soon, *Amos* would be an *Englisher.*

The man went on. "In this case, catalogs and book covers. She's been modeling for me for over a year." He made his fingers do a walking motion. "Ever wonder where she sneaks off to? To see me." He poked his own chest with his index finger.

That couldn't be. Deborah couldn't be a model. She went to help a friend. Not to model. Deborah wouldn't do that. He studied the *Englisher. This* was the "friend in need" she slipped away to help so often?

"I asked her to come live with me. She's considering it."

Ne, Amos would *not* believe that. He wouldn't believe anything this *Englisher* said. "You need to leave." He narrowed his eyes.

"Admit it, you don't know your little Amish girl as well as you thought you did."

Anger rose up inside Amos. "Now."

The man opened his car door. "Tell Debo she hasn't seen the last of me." He got in and drove away, kicking up dirt and gravel. Once on the blacktop of the road, the car sped up and raced away with a thundering roar.

Amos picked up the envelope Deborah had tossed back at the man. The outside simply read "Debo." What was in it? Should he open it? Should he give it to her *vater*? He flipped it over. The flap hadn't been sealed down, just tucked inside. Deborah would never know if he peeked at the contents. He stared at it for a long time before he retreated into the barn and stowed it under his cot.

He would ask Deborah about this. She would tell him who that man was and what was really going on.

He strode to the house and entered through the kitchen door. All the women stood or sat, busy at tasks. "Deborah, may I speak with you?"

Sarah came over and hugged him around the waist.

Lydia put her hand on the little girl's shoulder. "Let him go."

Sarah did and smiled up at him.

He smiled back at her, then looked at Deborah.

She stared, unmoving, as though she might deny his simple request.

"Go on." Teresa waved for Deborah to comply.

She released the dishcloth in her hand and followed him outside. "What is it? I need to help with supper."

"Let's talk in the barn." He led the way, and once inside, he faced her. "Who was that man?"

Her gaze darted around as though she didn't know who he was talking about, but then she asked, "Who, the man in the black Porsche?"

She knew the kind of car? Had she ridden in it, as well? He held up his hand. "Before you say anything else, wait here." He didn't want her to be tempted to lie. He went into his small room, returned with the envelope and held it up. "He told me you've been modeling for him."

Her face paled. "You spoke to him?"

"I did, but I didn't believe anything he told me. He called you Debo. I want to hear what you have to say about this."

She stared at him for a long time, then took a deep breath. "*Ja*. I did some modeling, but it wasn't anything bad. It was for high-end catalogs and book covers."

He stared back. That wasn't the answer he'd expected. He'd thought she would explain this whole thing away and paint a completely different picture. "Having your picture taken willingly like that is bad. He's the *friend* in need you've been helping?"

She bit her bottom lip. "Sort of."

Then it was true. "You know consenting to have your picture taken is forbidden."

Her voice came out small and frail. "I know."

"I can't believe you would do something so blatantly wrong." Just another Amish girl being duplicitous. Were there any who were trustworthy? What should he do now? "He said he asked you to go away with him and that you are considering it."

"*Ne!* He asked, but I would never do that. Never consider it."

Dare he believe her? Either she told the truth now and lied before, or she lied now and told the truth before. Either way, she'd lied to him. She had participated in an activity she knew went against their Amish beliefs. He held out the envelope. "What's this?"

She looked from him to the envelope and back to him before taking it. "Did you open it?"

"*Ne.* I thought about it, but it's yours."

"It's money for the work I did." Her voice sounded defeated. "I'm sorry I ever did it. I quit. I'm not modeling for him anymore. It's over." She stared at Amos a moment. "What are you going to do?"

The proper Amish thing to do would be to tell her *vater*. To tell the church leaders. But then a proper Amish wouldn't be making plans to leave. "I don't know."

"I promise I'm not going to model anymore. Ever again. I want to help take care of my *mutter*. And now with a new little one on the way, there will be a lot to do."

No wonder she was a mystery to him—she'd been harboring a secret. A huge secret. Maybe more. "Any more secrets I should know about?"

"Ne." She chewed on her bottom lip.

He wanted to believe her but didn't know how with all her secrets and lies.

"Let me know what you decide to do." She walked away.

Part of him wanted to tell on her as quickly as possible to hurt her the way she'd hurt him, and then leave this farm to get away from her. Get away from this community. But another part of him wanted to keep her secret and protect her.

He cared about her more than he realized, and that made her betrayal of trust hurt that much more. How could he ever trust her again? He couldn't. He needed to leave as soon as possible. But could he leave her? His heart didn't want to.

Tears coursed down Deborah's cheeks as she ran through the field to the pond. The ducks squawked and flapped their wings to get out of her way. "Sorry." She plopped down on her sitting log.

How could she have been so stupid? The attention

and praise Hudson had given her had been empty and worthless.

The look of disappointment and disapproval in Amos's eyes wrenched at her heart. What had she done? He would never trust her again. That hurt more than she thought it could. If she'd walked in a different direction, she never would have met Hudson. Never modeled. Never fallen into that temptation.

She tilted her head heavenward. "*Gott*, I am so sorry for what I have done. What do I do now?"

The image of banding together with her sisters, helping their *mutter*, flashed in her mind.

A peace washed over her soul, and a contentment she'd never felt before swirled inside her. A smile pulled at her mouth. She sensed the Lord calling her to care for her *mutter*. Deborah had a purpose now.

She stared at the crumpled envelope fisted in her hand. She'd forgotten about it. She didn't want this money or any of the money she'd earned. It was all tainted.

Standing, she wadded up the envelope with the enclosed money into a ball and prepared to throw it into the water. She stopped with her hand over her head, getting the impression to hold on to it. But why?

She flattened the rumpled envelope and folded it in half. She would need to figure out what *Gott* wanted her to do with this money.

Chapter Fourteen

Amos stewed for two days over Deborah's misdeeds. He should tell Bartholomew what she'd done. But that would hurt Deborah. But to not tell her *vater* would be a betrayal of the trust he'd placed in Amos, and a betrayal of the trust the bishop had placed in him. But Deborah would hate him if he told. But then, he'd betrayed them all by plotting his escape from the community.

He wanted to be away from her, but at the same time, not let her out of his sight. Even now that he knew her secret, he sensed there was so much more to learn about her. He didn't need to get tangled up with a duplicitous girl and her secrets. This twisting inside rattled him. Though he knew what he should do, he didn't want to do it.

He'd thought life on a farm with females would be easy, simpler. He couldn't have been more wrong. He should just get his departure over with instead of continuing to delay. He could see no other way out of this mess except to leave the community now. Before any of this mattered.

He headed to his little room in the barn. The kittens lay curled up in a huddle on his cot. He pulled out the cell phone. He'd thought he wanted to leave but now a part of him wasn't sure anymore.

Had it only been a week or two before Bartholomew's accident that he'd run into Jacob in town? His cousin had understood Amos's angst and betrayals. Had told him that *Rumspringa* wasn't a *gut* representation of actually *living* in the *Englisher* world. That he needed to try it. So, why not? The Amish world hadn't treated him very well, had ended up not having anything to offer him. No land to work or a trustworthy wife.

Amos sat on the other end of the cot from the kitten pile with the cell phone in his hands, weighing it as he weighed his options. He liked working on the Miller farm, felt at home here, but he couldn't stay indefinitely. Bartholomew would get his cast off soon. Amos couldn't return to his family's farm. What had he told Deborah? The *Englisher* world held different opportunities. He wouldn't know what those opportunities were until he tried. Right?

He pressed the button to turn on the phone. Nothing happened. He held down the button. Still nothing. Dead battery. He'd forgotten to plug it in all this time. He could charge it in the electrical outlet in the main part of the barn, normally used to plug in a heater to keep young or sick livestock warm on bitter winter nights. He dug the cord out from under the cot. Dare he charge it now?

The sound of female humming drifted into the barn.

He tossed the phone and cord under the cot. It hit the back wall with a thump. He cringed.

The humming grew louder, as one of the girls entered the barn. "Great Is Thy Faithfulness" floated through the air.

Deborah?

He stepped out of his room.

Miriam sucked in a breath, interrupting her tune.

Not Deborah. Just as well. "I'm sorry. I didn't mean to startle you."

She smiled. "My fault. I was deep in thought. Not paying attention."

Miriam *was* a sweet girl. No secrets. No disguise. No subterfuge.

Maybe he was drawn to enigmatic girls for a reason. But if he didn't want to be surprised or disappointed, he should find a girl who didn't hide behind a mask. But how would he know? "What brings you out here?"

She held up the shiny galvanized pail. "I'm on my way to milk Sybil."

Of course. He should have known. Quiet, dependable Miriam. Always doing her work without complaint. No mystery about her. Just what he needed.

But nothing about her appealed to him. Nothing drew him in. Nothing made him want to know more. Was there anything more to know?

Not like Deborah, who had an alluring mystique about her.

And secrets.

The following week, Deborah helped her *mutter* on with her coat. *Mutter* had scheduled tests at the hospital today, and *Vater* was taking her, accompanied by Hannah and Lydia, who had been the most involved in *Mutter's* management.

The anxiety remedies Deborah had purchased in conjunction with avoiding caffeine seemed to keep *Mutter* amenable. Deborah prayed the calm lasted. Mostly for *Mutter's* sake so she wouldn't be frightened, but also for the others looking after her.

The foursome headed out the door, followed by Deborah and Miriam.

Amos stood out front with his hand on Floyd's bridle. Her emotions fluttered about from one to another and back. First happy to see him, then guilty for her secret, then dread that he would tell someone mixed with relief he hadn't. Maybe she needed some of those remedies to calm her nerves.

He had avoided Deborah since the Hudson incident, showing up only at mealtimes and leaving shortly afterward. As far as she could tell, he hadn't told her *vater* about her having modeled. She was afraid to ask what he decided to do with the information, fearful it would push him into telling *Vater* and others what she'd done.

Right now, she couldn't brood over what he *might* do.

Amos held open the buggy door and spoke to *Vater*. "I can drive if you like."

"*Danki*, but I will feel better to have a man on the farm while I'm in town. We will probably be there most of the day."

Deborah stepped forward. "I could go and help out."

"I think too many people going might make *Mutter* more nervous than she already is. Even though the herbs you purchased seem to be helping. We'll tell you everything we learn."

She ached to go, but agreed it was probably best if she didn't. "Are you picking up Dr. Kathleen on the way?"

"*Ne*. She's meeting us at the hospital."

"Don't forget to tell her how the remedies are working so far."

"I will, little *mutter* hen." *Vater* patted Deborah's hand and climbed in the back with *Mutter* and situated his crutches.

Hannah, at the reins, drove away.

As they left, Deborah's heart weighed heavy.

Amos came up beside her. "Your *mutter* is going to be all right."

Surprised, she turned to him. The first words he'd spoken to her in days. Words of comfort, no less. "You're speaking to me again?"

He gave her a weak smile but didn't answer her question. "Your *vater* and sisters will take *gut* care of her."

That was part of the problem. They *always* took care of *everything*, unintentionally excluding Deborah to the point she wasn't needed. But *she* had been the one to find the natural remedies, and that made her feel better. "*Danki* for being here to help us in all of this."

"I'm glad I could, but I haven't done very much."

"Oh, but you have. Just being here to support us and keeping our secret. At least for now." Deborah knew how to keep secrets. And now Amos knew hers. How long would he keep it? "Unless the doctors can figure out exactly what's wrong with her and make her better, I think a lot more people are going to find out about her conditions."

"That won't be so bad, will it?"

His concern touched her, especially after so long a silence. Was his talking to her a sign that he'd made a decision?

"It depends on how they react."

He nodded. "True. Even in our community people can be unkind without realizing it."

"Especially children. They may not mean to be, but words could be out of their mouths before anyone can stop them." Deborah hoped no one spoke cruelly to, or about, *Mutter*.

In the late afternoon, Amos tinkered with the tractor, making sure it was in *gut* working order to plow soon. The kittens climbed all over the tractor and him, investigating his work.

Deborah lingered in the barn with him so she would know as soon as her parents and twin sisters returned. Several clip-clopping false alarms had sent her rushing outside. Still no sign of them. "Sooo…you haven't said anything to my *vater* about my modeling. Does that mean you've decided not to?" Her fear of pushing him into an action that would have repercussions for her still coiled inside her, ready to strike. Why had she asked now? Because the tension between them needed something to defuse it. That *something* could be nothing other than his decision. Also, his not speaking to her bunched up her insides even more. Besides, not knowing what he would do weighed on her.

"And here I thought you liked my winning company."

Well, she did, but she couldn't tell him that. His words had held a hint of hurt and bitterness. "Never mind. I shouldn't have asked."

He stared at her a moment as though he wanted to say something, then turned back to the tractor, and then back to her. "I'm still having a hard time believing you modeled. You aren't the person I thought you were. I thought I knew you, but I was wrong."

That stabbed her heart. She was disappointed in herself, as well. Should she let the topic drop? Or explain herself? She hated having Amos think poorly of her. "I didn't know who I was. I thought I was an Amish girl waiting for the rest of her life to begin. I thought my family didn't understand me or care. I thought I needed someone to tell me nice things to feel worthy." Was she only making it worse with her self-centered selfish words?

"And now?"

"You don't want to hear me ramble on."

"I actually do. You thought you needed someone to make you feel worthy. And now?"

"I'm not sure, but I know modeling will never make me feel worthy. That's not the kind of worth I need or want. I was an Amish girl living outside my own life. Instead of including myself as a part of my family, I waited for my family to include me. I excluded myself and blamed them. That probably sounds foolish to you."

"Needing to feel like you matter is important."

The quality in his voice made her wonder. "You understand needing to feel like you matter, don't you?"

"I've had my share of disappointments."

Was that why he was going to turn his back on his whole way of life? Dare she ask him? "Disappointments? Here or back in Pennsylvania?"

"Both."

So he was including her.

He pointed with a wrench he'd been using on the tractor toward the large open doorway.

"What disappointments?"

"I think I hear them coming back."

She listened and heard the faint clomping of a horse's hooves. How had he heard that so much sooner than her? She dashed out as the buggy turned into the driveway.

Lydia, at the reins, drove the buggy to the front of the house and stopped.

Hannah jumped out with her finger to her lips. "Shhh. *Mutter* and *Vater* fell asleep on the ride home."

Deborah peered through the window into the back.

Vater's arm encircled *Mutter's* shoulders. Her head lay on his shoulder, and his head rested on hers. He loved *Mutter* so much, regardless of what was happening and all that had happened with her.

Would Deborah ever find an unconditional love like that? Not with Amos. She'd disappointed him. Her parents had something rare. 'Twas true that Amish always took care of their own, but sometimes grudgingly. Not so with *Vater*. He happily cared for *Mutter*.

Miriam came out of the house.

Lydia stepped down from the buggy. "Hannah, I'll make sure the others stay inside while you tell Miriam and Deborah what we learned."

Hannah kept her voice low and pointed toward the horse. "I'll talk while we unhitch Floyd."

Amos helped Deborah on one side while Hannah and Miriam worked the harness on the other side.

Deborah rose up on tiptoe and peered over Floyd's back at Hannah. "What did you find out?"

"First, *danki* for finding those remedies. They helped *Mutter* a lot. She remained calm most of the time. She had a few nervous episodes, but *Vater* was able to assuage her fears. She's indeed pregnant. We spoke to many, *many* doctors, including a psychiatrist. They confirmed that she has Graves' disease. They all believe that her pregnancy is aggravating it. They also discovered scar tissue on her brain, likely from the buggy accident when she was three. It traumatized her, and that, compounded by multiple surgeries when she was young, is causing some of her memory issues and other problems."

"Poor *Mutter*."

"The psychiatrist thinks that some of her memory

issues are actually her regressing to a younger age as a way of coping. He would like to see her weekly."

"Is she going to go?"

"I don't know. No one in our community has ever gone to a psychiatrist. *Vater* would need to get permission from the bishop. I doubt he would give it. Plus, I don't think *Vater* wants to have her going to an *Englisher* doctor every week."

"Why doesn't she just go to Dr. Kathleen? Bishop Bontrager would approve that."

"Dr. Kathleen is a different kind of doctor."

"Did they give her medications to help her symptoms?" Deborah asked.

"*Mutter* and *Vater* agreed that they didn't want to expose the baby to medications if they didn't have to. Dr. Kathleen is going to monitor *Mutter* closely."

"Is the baby all right? Does it have Down syndrome like Sarah?"

"We don't know. When *Mutter* found out that the amniocentesis test had any risk at all, she refused. She became very agitated, and we had a hard time calming her back down. Whatever we found out wouldn't matter. The baby is already who she's going to be with a strong heartbeat. We'll love her no matter what."

"She? Is it a girl?"

"We don't know for sure, but chances are it will be. We all got to see the new little one on an ultrasound."

"When's the baby due?"

"August. From the ultrasound, they think she's around sixteen weeks."

If Deborah and her sisters could manage *Mutter* for the next five months, through her pregnancy, then once the baby was born, she would naturally improve. In the meantime, Deborah would hire an *Englisher* to do more research on the computer. She would find whatever natural treatments would help *Mutter* best, and use her modeling money for that.

That evening, Deborah sat at the kitchen table with her *vater* and three older sisters. *Vater* devised a rotating schedule among the five of them to keep an eye on *Mutter*. *Vater* would take charge of her in the evenings and through the night. Hannah would oversee *Mutter* first in the morning, then Lydia, then Miriam and then finally Deborah up to and through supper.

Deborah pointed to her twin sisters. "But what about in the fall when Hannah and Lydia marry?"

Lydia piped up. "I won't marry. I'll always stay here and take care of *Mutter*."

Mutter would likely need close supervision the rest of her life.

"I'll stay, too," Hannah said.

Then Miriam spoke. "No need for the two of you to give up on marrying. You both have *gut* men who want to marry you. I'll stay with *Mutter*."

"Don't *you* want to marry?" Hannah asked.

"Knowing *Mutter* needed supervision, I've never truly believed I could. I've tried to keep boys from being interested in me so I could remain single."

Deborah's spirit lifted, then fell. "*Ne*, Miriam. I'll take care of *Mutter*. You—as well as Hannah and Lydia—have already done your fair shares. It's my turn to care for her."

"It would be *gut* if you all marry. Your *mutter* is going to need a lot of medical care in the next few months. It's going to be expensive. I may need to sell the farm. My mind will rest easier knowing you each have a home."

Deborah gasped in unison with her sisters. "*Ne, Vater.* Say it isn't so."

Vater let out a dejected sigh. "I will speak to the bishop, but I don't have much hope."

Before anything more could be said, *Mutter* entered the kitchen, and the conversation stopped.

Mutter looked around the table. "Bartholomew, you didn't tell me we had company. You ladies must think me a terrible hostess."

Deborah and her sisters exchanged glances with each other, then with *Vater.*

Vater spoke up. "We're all fine. No need to fuss. Sit."

Mutter sat. "I don't normally take a nap." She'd fallen asleep in the living room rocking chair right after supper. "But…" She leaned forward with a twinkle in her eyes. "We're expecting our first child."

Deborah's jaw went limp. First?

"If it's a girl, we're going to name her Hannah, and Micah for a boy."

Deborah glanced at her oldest twin as tears stung her eyes. Poor Hannah. It was so hard watching *Mutter* like this. Deborah preferred it when she had been blissfully ignorant. But there was no going back. She couldn't un-learn everything she knew now.

Vater gave *Mutter* a sad, weary smile. "These ladies already know. They came to see how they could help you. They are each going to take turns coming over and doing what they can."

Mutter smiled. "*Danki.* You are all so kind."

Each of her sisters said that they were glad to help, but there must be something more that Deborah could do. But what?

Chapter Fifteen

In the Millers' living room sat a pile of books. The one on the top caught Amos's attention. An Amish romance novel. Such silly books. Why did women like to read that nonsense? Especially practical Amish women. Didn't the Amish pride themselves on being separate from the world? Not to be just like them but without conveniences?

He picked it up and read the back cover. He still couldn't see the appeal. He turned it over and studied the profile image of an Amish woman looking down at a yellow flower with a dark center. He scrutinized the cover. Not just an Amish woman—Deborah! He wouldn't have believed it to be her if not for her confession to him.

Multiple footsteps thunked on the kitchen floor. The women had returned from visiting a neighbor.

He tucked the book under his arm and slipped out the front door. He took charge of the horse and buggy and walked the pair to the barn. Leaving Floyd hitched, he hurried to the safety of his room and stared at the cover again. Definitely Deborah. What should he do with this?

He knew Deborah had been modeling, but she said

she'd quit. She could get in trouble for this. He hadn't told Bartholomew or anyone else about her modeling and had no plans to at this point. To do so would be duplicitous, considering his own plans, as well as hurt Deborah. She would be angry with him. That bothered him more than her breaking the rules of the *Ordnung*.

He had work to get done before it was time to eat.

At supper that night, Amos ate with a guilty conscience. He knew he should give the book to Bartholomew and tell him what he knew about Deborah's modeling. But what about himself? He, too, harbored a secret. Guilt on top of guilt. Even after the hurt she'd caused him with her subterfuge, he still wanted to protect her. He was attempting to get away from duplicity in others, so he wouldn't stoop to it himself.

Miriam took a drink of milk. "Has anyone seen the novel I was reading? I left it in the living room, but it's gone."

"What's your book about?" *Mutter* asked.

"It's an Amish romance. *Amish Identity*. It's not really mine." Miriam turned to Deborah. "I hope you don't mind that I borrowed it."

Deborah's face turned ashen, and a slight tremor laced her words. "Um… I actually haven't finished with it myself."

Amos should probably say something, but he wanted to talk to Deborah first.

Vater swallowed his bite and pointed with his table knife. "I'm not so sure I like you girls reading those. They give you false ideals. Then you expect this romance nonsense that isn't practical in everyday life."

Mutter giggled. "*Ne*. They don't. The stories are all made-up. They're just *gut* fun. It's nice to take a break once in a while. Let the girls have their little escapes. They always get their work done. Our girls are too smart to be swayed by stories."

Amos imagined that Deborah wished that her *vater* would forbid romance novels.

Bartholomew nodded. "Very well. Just be sure to get your work done."

All the girls around the table smiled except Deborah. Her ashen complexion had paled even more.

After supper, Amos came up beside Deborah and whispered, "May I talk to you?"

"I can't. I need to find my book Miriam *borrowed*."

"It's in the barn." He walked away, knowing she would come.

She snagged her coat and followed him out. "You have my book?"

"I saw it in the living room. I took it out to the barn."

She fell into step with him. "I can't picture you reading Amish romances."

He stopped. "*Ne.* I took it because *you* are on the cover."

Her eyes widened. "You recognized me?"

He proceeded to walk again. "It wasn't hard."

She trotted to catch up. "Do you think Miriam recognized me?"

"She didn't act as though she did." He went into his room and reached underneath his cot. He grabbed the novel but could feel the cell phone on top of it. He tried to shake the device off as he pulled the book out, but they both came. He dumped the phone onto the floor. In a single motion, he stood, kicked the phone back under the cot, turned and thrust out the paperback. "Here it is." Hopefully, she hadn't noticed the phone.

She stared at the floor near the cot for a moment longer before looking up at him. "*Danki*. I appreciate you not telling anyone about this."

If he exposed her secret, he would need to confess his own. "I thought you said you didn't have any more secrets."

"This isn't a different secret. It's part of the same one. I said I had modeled for catalogs *and* book covers." She tapped the front. "Book cover."

True. It had just been such a shock to see her like that. "You know that there are more copies of this out there? What happens when one of your sisters or someone else in the community picks one up and realizes that's you on the cover?"

"I don't know. Hudson took these shots on the very first photo shoot I did. I never imagined seeing myself on the cover of a book. It's so strange." She tilted her head. "You look as though you're the one who should feel guilty. I really have quit."

Keeping her secret wasn't the root of his guilt—keeping his own was. He couldn't risk anyone trying to talk him out of his decision.

Now that Bartholomew's cast was off, Amos wouldn't be needed for much longer. He would stay on until Bartholomew regained the strength in his injured leg. The young man, Jesse, who was supposed to have left by now had lost the place he was to move to. Whether he was gone or not, when it was time to leave the Millers', Amos wouldn't be returning to his parents' farm. It would be too hard to leave if he did.

Having spent the previous week making sure the fields were properly planted had given Amos a sense of great accomplishment. Not being around to reap the harvest of his labor caused sorrow and disappointment to roll through him. He would be leaving soon, but surprisingly, a part of him didn't want to anymore. He didn't want to leave the Millers' farm or Deborah. He felt at home here and wanted to stay.

Surprising revelation.

"Since you haven't said anything yet, does that mean you've decided not to tell anyone my secret?"

Ja, but it might be best not to let her know that yet. "I'm not sure." Once he was gone, she would know her secret was safe.

"My resolve to not model is solid. I won't ever do it again."

He believed her, but was it because he truly did or only because he *wanted* to. If he could, he would wrap her in his arms and protect her.

Alone in the room she shared with Miriam, Deborah tucked the book between the mattress and box springs and sat on her bed. She wished Miriam hadn't discovered her book. She would no doubt ask about it again. Deborah had almost forgotten about the damaging evidence, having tucked it away *under* her bed. Obviously, not a *gut* place. She should have set it afire in the burn barrel, then Miriam wouldn't have discovered it. She and her sisters often borrowed things from each other, many times without asking. Deborah would figure out a time when she could dispose of this copy.

Amos had been right. Numerous copies of this novel undoubtedly floated around out in the *Englisher* world, and likely, a few in their community. Who else held a copy? Then there were the other books that could potentially have a picture of her, as well. It would be only a matter of time before someone else discovered her secret. Should she ask Hudson to not sell any more of her pictures for covers? To destroy all the pictures he took of her? The thought of talking to him again gave her shivers. That he thought she would go with him to New York had been preposterous. *Ne.* Talking to Hudson would be a bad idea. A clean break was best.

Then what could she do? How long before someone else recognized her?

She would sleep on it.

But sleep evaded her, so she lifted her troubling situation to the Lord.

Gott, what should I do? I could confess to my family, but that would hurt everyone, and they would be disappointed in me. There's a gut *chance no one will ever find out, and then no one would get hurt. But the not knowing if someone will discover my secret is agitating. Tell me what to do.*

Vater had told the bishop and church leaders about *Mutter's* conditions. They in turn brought the concern before the congregation. Several families had recently experienced hardships, some with crops, others with medical expenses, and one family's house and barn had burned to the ground. There wasn't extra money in the community right now to cover so many needs. Maybe in a year or two things would be different, but *Mutter* and her family needed help now. The women did offer to take turns sitting with Teresa for a few hours each day to ease the burdens on her daughters.

But the future of the Miller farm was in jeopardy. They couldn't lose their livelihood. There must be something more Deborah could do to help.

The book cover flashed in her mind, and she thought of Hudson. That was it. She could continue to model, earning money to pay the doctor bills. But her declaration to Amos about never modeling again played in her head. Taunting her. This was the path she'd set herself on over a year ago. This was how she could help her family. Apparently, her desire to be the one to stay with *Mutter*, and also learn about homeopathy, so her sisters could marry would have to wait. Her family needed money now, but not for her to dally with natural remedies and sit with her *mutter* when there were others who could do that.

Deborah grabbed the telephone from the small table by the front door and slipped out onto the porch, pulling the door most of the way shut on the cord. She called for a ride from an *Englisher*. It took only a couple of calls before she found someone willing to pick her up within a half an hour.

Thankfully, Amos wasn't on watch at the moment, and she slipped away and across the field without any trouble. Once in town, she changed into jeans and a sweatshirt, let down her hair and walked to her destination.

She opened the door to the photography studio. The excited—and frustrated—voices of Hudson and Summer collided with each other and bounced off the cement walls. Deborah strolled inside to the sight of Hudson packing his camera gear in their hard-shell cases. Now that the weather was getting nicer, he must be preparing for a shoot outside in lieu of using one of his nature backdrops. She would take any job. Work six days a week if that was what it took to save the farm.

"Hallo?" Deborah called.

Hudson swung around toward her and frowned. "You? What do you want?"

She wouldn't be deterred by his foul mood. "I was hoping you had a modeling job for me."

He folded his arms. "I thought you quit. Never going to model again."

"I changed my mind."

"Why? You and that man on your farm were both pretty adamant."

She'd hoped he wouldn't ask, just be happy she was back. "My *mutter* needs some medical treatments. It's going to cost a lot. I need to earn money to help pay for it."

Summer pointed over her shoulder. "I'll see what needs to be packed in the back."

Hudson unfolded his arms and crossed the room to Deborah. "So, you're desperate."

She hadn't wanted to use that word, but it fitted. "In a way."

"The only job I have, you won't be interested in." He held out his hands. "Sorry."

"Why not? I'll take anything."

"Really? It's in New York City." He tapped his chest with the fingertips of both hands. "I finally got my break. I'm going to be famous."

"New York?"

He narrowed his eyes. "You desperate enough to come? You could be famous, too. It'll easily pay two or three times what any of us were making here."

She didn't care about being famous, but she needed the money. Two or three times more? Her family wouldn't have to worry about the medical bills. But leave Indiana? Leave her family? New York would mean no more running across the field to a photo shoot during the days and spending the evenings with her family. She would have to choose between the two.

"You said you'd take *anything*."

"I don't know." This was a much bigger decision than simply modeling. She'd have to leave behind her whole life and take up a new one. There would be no coming back. Could she sacrifice everything for her family, who never noticed if she was there? They certainly wouldn't miss her. "Give me time to think about it."

"No time. I'm leaving in the morning, and I need to know if I'm to save room for you in the van."

If she didn't go, her family would lose everything. If she went, *she* would lose everything. To choose modeling *was* to choose her family and vice versa. She'd thought Hudson had been ridiculous for suggesting she go with him the day he'd come out to the farm, and now that was exactly what she was contemplating. Her short-lived dream of learning homeopathy would die today. She'd been raised to think of others before herself, to be self-less. She hadn't been doing either of those lately. Her life would change one way or another. She might as well make the change count for something. "I'll go to New York."

His eyes widened. "Seriously? I didn't think you would, but I'm *really* glad you are. You don't need to take anything from your Amish life. We'll get you all new clothes and anything else you need. We need to pack up all my photography gear."

Tears blurred her vision. "I need to go say goodbye to my family."

"Don't cry. It's not like you can't come back and visit."

But she couldn't. She would never see her family

again. She would miss her family, and the community, too. A large part of her would miss Amos. But wasn't he going to leave anyway? Leave her behind? So, whether she stayed or not, he would be gone. "I'll be back in the morning."

Amos stood on the corner, waiting for Jacob in Goshen. He'd texted his cousin that he was ready. Just when he'd thought that there might be *one* Amish girl who wouldn't disappoint him, he'd been wrong. How could he have allowed himself to get emotionally tangled up with another female? Women caused chaos wherever they went. Life had been simpler on a farm with all males. Except his *mutter*.

Deborah, in *Englisher* clothes, strolled out of a building. Star Photography Studio.

She'd promised she quit. Promised to never go back. Just like a woman to go back on her word.

Not this time.

She headed off in the opposite direction from him.

He hustled after her and almost caught up to her and was about to call out when she entered a gas station/convenience store. He went inside but couldn't see her. Where had she disappeared to?

"Hey, Mr. Amish man?"

Amos swung around to the cashier behind the counter. Was he talking to Amos?

The young man inclined his head toward the back. "She's in the restroom, changing."

Amos stepped over to the counter. "Who?"

"That Amish girl. She comes in sometimes when I'm working. She goes in dressed like an Amish and comes out looking normal, then later in the day, she goes in normal and comes out Amish. But this time was weird. She was only gone for twenty minutes or so. Usually, it's hours."

So, she changed her clothes here. "Thank you." He went outside to wait and sat on the curb.

Ten minutes later, she exited and walked right past him.

He stood. "Deborah."

She spun around.

"Or should I call you Debo?"

"What are you doing here?"

Even now, with her new betrayal, he wanted to take her into his arms. Instead, he closed his hands into fists to keep himself from reaching out for her. "I could ask you the same thing, but I already know. I saw you come out of the photography place. You promised you'd quit modeling and never go back."

"I have no choice. My *mutter's* medical expenses will cost too much. My *vater* will have to sell the farm to get her the help she needs."

Excuses. "I was foolish enough to think you were different. I was going to ask you to leave with me, but didn't because of your emphatic declaration of quitting."

"Leave? So, you're in town to meet up with your cousin, never to return home. This whole time on our farm, you've been plotting your departure. I'm leaving to help my family. What's your excuse?"

Because he couldn't trust her or anyone, but that wasn't exactly true. He didn't want to risk trusting for fear he'd be hurt again. Was that a *gut* reason to leave?

Tears filled her eyes. "I'll miss you, Amos Burkholder." She turned and walked away.

He wanted to call her back. Shake some sense into her.

Wrap her in his arms. He did none of those. Instead, he strolled back to the corner, where Jacob waited.

Deborah walked the whole way home from town. Two hours gave her a lot of time to think. Though she'd wanted to be the one to stay at home and take care of her *mutter*, it seemed as though the only way she could take care of her *mutter* and family was to leave them. She could make *gut* money modeling and pay for the medical bills that were already mounting up.

She ran into the house and up the stairs. She knew what needed to be done. She grabbed her tin of money and the novel with her on the cover. Back downstairs, she hurried outside. She'd seen her *vater* in the barn. She headed inside the shadows of the yawning opening. *"Vater?"*

He limped out of Floyd's stall. "Ah, Deborah. Sad news. Amos has left us. It was time for him to go home."

Home? Hardly. But that wasn't why she had come. *"Vater*, I have some *gut* news." She opened her tin. "This is for *Mutter's* medical expenses. I'm going to be able to pay for the rest of them, too."

He took her offered tin. "How? Where did this money come from?" He shifted his gaze back up to her. "There's so much."

"I earned it." She bit her bottom lip.

"Doing what? You don't have a job."

She swallowed down her guilt and fear. "I actually do. I've been working in town. That's where I would go all the time when I went for a walk."

"Why did you keep it a secret?"

She held out the Amish novel. "I've been modeling. This is me on the cover of this book."

He took it. "This is wrong, Deborah. It's forbidden to have your picture taken. This is a graven image. You must stop at once."

"I know. I did stop, but…"

"But you continue?" The hurt in his eyes stabbed at her heart.

"I have to. I can pay for *Mutter's* medical bills."

"*Ne.* I forbid it."

Tears blurred her vision. "I don't want our family to lose the farm."

"We will survive this. *Gott* will take care of us."

"*Ja.* And He's going to use me to do it. I'm leaving in the morning for New York City. I'll send all the money I make."

He shook his head. "*Ne.* I won't accept it."

Then she would pay the hospital directly.

"You must stay."

"*Ne.* If I go, I can help the family."

"You're just going to leave us?"

She nodded, afraid her voice would fail her.

Tears rimmed his eyes. "What am I supposed to tell the rest of the family?"

It touched her that he cared so much. She'd never seen him this emotional. "Tell them whatever you want. Tell them I've lost my way." She choked on every untrue word. "Tell them I've chosen the world over them."

"What about your *mutter*?"

"Don't you understand? I'm doing this for her. For all of you."

"If she could understand all that was going on with herself, do you think she would want you to do this for her?"

Ne. "This is the way I can help. Help her. Help you. Help the whole family."

"Where do I tell her you've gone?"

"She probably won't even notice. She'll forget she ever had a daughter named Deborah. It's best that way."

"Is that why you're doing this? You feel overlooked?"

Being overlooked was the reason it had been so easy for her to start modeling. She did it now because she loved her family too much to see them suffer.

If she'd paid more attention, maybe she would have realized something had been amiss. Words poured out that she couldn't stop. "When I was younger, I felt as though I was getting away with something and to get out of work." There had been a thrill in that. "Then, well… because no one noticed me, whether I was here or not. Naomi claimed as much of everyone's attention as she could. It didn't seem worth it to compete with her. If I wasn't here, I wasn't as hurt that no one paid attention to me. You all *couldn't* notice me if I was absent, then it wouldn't be because no one cared. I felt…"

Vater's voice came out sad and full of compassion. "Alone and unwanted?"

How had he known? *"Ja."*

Vater looked sad. "I'm sorry I made you feel that way. You are neither alone nor unwanted. Each of my girls is a precious gift from *Gott*."

Deborah didn't feel like a gift. "Do you ever wish one of us had been a son who could help you more with the farmwork?"

"I always hoped to have a son, but I would never trade one of you girls for a son."

"Not even Naomi?" She shouldn't have said that. It popped out on its own accord.

He smiled. "Not even Naomi."

She suddenly realized that Naomi probably acted out for the same reason Deborah had withdrawn from the family—lack of attention. If either of them had known *Mutter* had problems, maybe neither would have taken the paths they did. But Deborah's path was set. She took her *vater's* hand. "I need to do this. I'll be able to pay the medical bills. You can keep the farm."

"I would rather have my whole family than the farm."

"You need the farm to support the family. Without it, what would become of everyone?"

"*Gott* will take care of us."

"Maybe *Gott* sent me to that first photo shoot as a way to take care of my family."

"Don't do this."

"It's already done."

"Then undo it."

She wanted to, but that wouldn't help anyone. "I'll leave first thing. Don't tell anyone until I'm gone."

"The morning? Then I still have time to pray for you."

It wouldn't do any *gut*.

She'd once looked forward to modeling. Not anymore. It was a burden she must bear.

Chapter Sixteen

In the predawn light, Amos drove his cousin's pickup along the country roads. He still had a current driver's license from when he was on *Rumspringa*. Granted, it was from Pennsylvania, but still *gut* for another six months. And he had liked cars—fast cars—as a lot of Amish boys did, but gave them up when he joined church.

The truck's engine suddenly chugged to a stop, and he lost the power steering. He cranked the wheel hard and coasted the vehicle to the shoulder. After several failed attempts to restart it, he jumped out and walked. Still a *gut* three miles to the Millers', he hoped he got there before Deborah left for New York City.

He'd joined church back in Pennsylvania so he could ask Esther to marry him. After courting for two years, she'd turned him down and married someone else that same year.

Now history was repeating itself. He'd become Amish for a girl, and now he would stay Amish for a girl.

Something pricked his heart. Was he only Amish to please this girl or that? His parents? The church leaders? Were any of those *gut* reasons?

As he approached the Millers' house, the sun peeked over the eastern horizon.

Teresa Miller stood at the end of the driveway, looking back and forth.

He hurried up to her. "Teresa, what are you doing out here?"

She twisted one hand in the other and shook her head. "Why am I here?"

She must be having a bad day.

He took her hands in his. "Why don't we go up to the house?"

"I forget things." Teresa blinked several time in rapid succession. "I'm not well. I know that. But I'm not *un*-well. Does that make sense?"

"*Ja.* But you're doing much better."

Her eyes brightened. "Am I?"

"*Ja.*" All the natural treatments and changes in her diet had improved Teresa's Graves' symptoms. She would never be like everyone else, but she would be functional. She would always need someone to watch over her. And she would always have loved ones to do that.

"You are a *gut* boy." She squeezed his hands. "Promise me something."

He wasn't really in a position to promise anyone anything. "If I can."

"Don't ever leave us."

His heart ached for her. He'd already done just that. "I wish I could promise you that." He truly did. "But I can't. The bishop has told me to return to my parents' farm." He felt bad for telling her that when he had already left the community. True, no one knew yet. The Millers thought he'd gone home, and his family thought he was still at the Millers'.

"Oh, but you can't. You must stay. Here. With us. I'll have my husband talk to the bishop. I feel better because you're here. You help Bartholomew. He needs another man here. Too many women. We need you. He needs you. I need you."

What could he say to that? His heart cried out, *Ja, I'll stay.* Then he could continue to see Deborah every day—*if* he could convince *her* to stay.

"You're the one who found me on the road that day, aren't you?"

She remembered that? *"Ja."* He wished he knew then what he knew now. He could have helped her better, taken care of her.

"Don't tell my husband or daughters that there's something wrong with me. They depend on me. It'll be our little secret."

Should he tell her they knew? "Don't you think they might already know?"

"Do you think so?"

"Ja." He motioned toward the house. "Let me walk you to the house."

"All right. I still don't know why I came out here."

"To make my day." Seeing her had made him happy.

"You are a sweet one." She hooked her arm in his.

Halfway across the yard, Teresa stopped and pointed. "See those trees that edge our property?"

He nodded. A line of windbreak vegetation stood to the north.

"I want my *dawdy haus* right next to the highbush cranberry bushes."

A nice spot. "Why are you telling me?"

"So you know where to build it when the time comes." She must be confused again.

"You want *me* to build your *dawdy haus*?"

"Of course. Who else?"

He didn't know what to say. Should he tell her he couldn't build it for her? Or hope this conversation was one she'd forget? If Deborah didn't stay, then he would leave, as well.

He cared deeply for this family.

And for a certain young woman.

Hannah came out of the house. *"Mutter?"*

"Over here." Amos guided Teresa toward her daughter. "Let's get you back inside."

Hannah rushed over. *"Mutter.* Don't go outside without telling anyone." She turned to Amos. *"Danki.* We thought you'd gone back home."

Not home, but she didn't need to know that. "I came back to talk to your *vater.* It's urgent."

"He's in the barn."

"Danki." As Amos crossed to the barn, he looked around the yard and at the newly sowed fields. He stared at the patch where Teresa Miller wanted her *dawdy haus.* He missed this place and its people—one most of all—even though he'd been gone for only one night.

Deborah's father pitched hay from the loft Amos had built. "Bartholomew."

Hay showered down, and he rested the pitchfork on the loft floor. "Amos. I thought you went back home."

Amos didn't want to take the time to explain just where he'd been. "We need to hurry. Deborah's leaving. We need to stop her."

"Ne. She's not."

"Ja. She is. There's… It's hard to explain, but if we both go, maybe we can talk her out of this foolishness."

Kittens scampered from the room Amos had occupied at the sound of his voice, meowing.

Bartholomew chuckled. "Someone was missed." He climbed down the ladder and gripped Amos's shoulders. "I know about the modeling. She was going to leave, but she's come to her senses."

"She has?" Amos gritted his teeth as two kittens climbed up his trouser legs, one in the front and one in the back. He plucked off the one in front. The other made it up on his shoulder. "She's staying?"

"*Ja.* She's staying."

Relief swept through Amos.

The older man stared up at the hayloft. "You did *gut* work. I won't be getting injured again." He waved an arm to include the surroundings. "It's back to me doing all the work around here. I appreciate all your hard work. You've done an excellent job with everything. I don't know how we would have managed without you."

"Danki." Teresa's words came back to him. What had she said? *He needs another man here.* That was the answer teasing him as he walked. "I'd like to stay on and continue to help you."

"What about going back to your family's farm? I'm sure they've missed you."

"The farm will go to my brothers. I believe this is where I'm supposed to be." This was where *Gott* had been preparing him for.

"Then you're welcome to stay. I'm not about to turn away help."

That pleased Amos. "But first, I have a confession."

"Bishop Bontrager is the one to hear confessions."

Telling Bartholomew Miller might not be necessary, but Amos *needed* to do it if his plans were going to work out. "I have wronged you and need to ask your forgiveness."

"I can't think of anything you've done wrong. Whatever you think you've done, I forgive you."

That was nice, but Amos hadn't told him yet. "The whole time I was working here, I plotted to leave our community."

Bartholomew's eyebrows pulled down. "Leave the community?"

"I've changed my mind. I thought *Gott* was calling me away. I'd been hurt by…people. I figured if I was going to have to work in the *Englisher* world, I might as well live there, too."

"And?"

"I know I belong here." And not just in the community, but here on this farm. "Do you forgive me?"

Bartholomew rubbed his hand across his mouth. "It seems my farm has been harboring all kinds of secrets. *Ja*. I forgive you."

"Danki." Now for the hard part. Amos cleared his throat.

"Speak, boy. You obviously have something else to say. More secrets?"

Amos shook his head. "I would like…your permission to court—"

"Ja." A smile broke on the older man's face. "You have it."

Amos stood mute with his mouth hanging open, then found his voice. "But I haven't said which daughter."

"Deborah, of course."

How had he known? "Why not Miriam or Joanna?"

"Because you're not in love with either of them. You weren't thinking of asking for Miriam or Joanna, were you? Because that would have to be a different answer altogether."

"You would've said *ne*?"

"Of course."

"Why?"

"Because you're not in love with either of them. But you are with Deborah."

"Well, I wouldn't say I *love* her. Not yet. But I believe I'm on my way. And that's why I want to court her."

Bartholomew shook his head. "Young people can't see what's right in front of them, or know their own hearts."

Amos didn't know what the older man meant.

Bartholomew clasped Amos on the shoulder. "Trust me. This strange cacophony of emotions churning inside you that you're trying to sort out—that's love, boy."

Amos did have a myriad of emotions when it came to Deborah. But did they equal love? He didn't know.

But he aimed to find out.

Deborah stood on the shore of the pond with a heavy heart, watching the ducks and ducklings paddle around in the water.

Gott had wrestled with her most of the night. *Vater's* prayers had made her thrash about instead of sleeping, until she'd made the decision to stay. The right decision. She knew that in her soul. Though she hadn't gotten very much sleep, she felt surprisingly *gut*. Lighter.

She'd called Hudson early this morning to tell him to leave without her. He'd hung up on her.

Gott wanted her to stay with her family, which had been a great relief to her. What they were going to do about the medical bills, none of them knew, but if they could bring in a *gut* crop this year, they might scrape by. Thanks to Amos plowing and planting their crops for them, they had a chance to keep the farm, but it wouldn't be easy.

Oh, Amos. Why did he have to leave? She might never see him again. Her nose stuffed up with unshed tears, and she swallowed the lump in her throat. Was there anything she could say to convince him to return?

As though her thoughts caused him to appear, Amos approached. "*Hallo*, Deborah."

Was he really here? "Amos?"

"*Ja*. It's me."

His smile melted her heart, and she wanted to run to him but didn't. "What are you doing here? I thought you left."

"That's funny. I was going to say the same to you. I came to talk you out of leaving."

"I'm not leaving."

"Me either."

"But you were in town yesterday. I thought you'd already left. My *vater* said so."

"I had, but I couldn't sleep."

Just like Deborah. *Vater* must have been praying for him, too.

"I realized I didn't want to leave. I have been hurt a few times by girls I thought I wanted to marry. I decided that I couldn't trust any Amish girls. That's why I left."

And Deborah had fueled his mistrust by modeling and threatening to leave, as well.

He went on. "But *Gott* made me see that my trust was misplaced. I need to trust Him. I thought I wanted to leave, but I don't. I'm staying."

Dare she believe it. "You're staying? Really?"

"Really." He took her hand. "I've asked your *vater* permission to court you. He gave it."

Had she heard correctly? "You want to court *me*?"

"Ja."

Part of her wanted to throw herself into his arms— something a *gut* Amish would *never* do. She'd definitely spent too much time in the *Englisher* world. Another part of her didn't believe his declaration could be true. Or at least, the declaration she'd imagined he'd said and dreamed he'd said.

"Are you going to give me your answer or continue to make me suffer?"

"I… I want to say *ja*, but I'm finding it hard to believe you would choose *me*. I haven't exactly been a model Amish."

"Who of us are perfect? None. And…"

"What?"

He chuckled. "I just realized your *vater* was right."

His laughter soothed her. "About what?"

"When I asked his permission to court you, he told me something. Something I didn't believe."

"What?"

"I don't know that I should say right now."

"Please." She wanted to know what her *vater* had said to make him smile like that. A smile that made her want to get lost in it.

"He told me that I was in love with you. I thought he'd gone daft."

Her heart soared. Loved? Dare she hope? "Go back. Say that again."

"I thought your *vater* was daft?"

"Ne. Before that."

His mouth pulled up on one side. "I asked his perm—"

"After that."

Mischievousness played at the corners of his mouth. He'd been teasing her.

He caressed the back of her hand with his thumb. "I love you, Deborah. I want to court you and marry you one day."

"I want that, too."

"Our own house and lots of children."

She sucked in a breath and pulled her hand away. "Oh, but I can't. I'm so sorry."

His smile slipped away. "If you're not ready, I'll wait."

The tears she'd held at bay before sprang to her eyes and blurred her vision. "It's not that." He was her dream come true. "I believe *Gott* wants me to remain here on my parents' farm the rest of my life to care for *Mutter*. So I can't marry."

"I want that, too. To stay on this farm. I've been trying to figure out where I belong. I felt *Gott* leading me away from my family's farm. I thought I was supposed to go out into the *Englisher* world. But that's not where He was leading me. He was preparing to send me here. Your *mutter* asked—*ne*—told me to build her a *dawdy haus* by the windbreak. I want to do that. Your *vater* has already given his permission for me to stay here. I want to live here and help take care of her. With you, of course."

Deborah had believed she needed to give up on the dream of marrying one day. Believed that was her penance for modeling. In spite of her poor choices in the past, *Gott* was giving her the desire of her heart.

"What do you say? Deborah Miller, will you marry me and be my wife?"

She did throw herself into his arms this time, and he

caught her. "*Ja.* I want to be your wife." He lifted her off the ground and swung her around.

When he set her back down, he stared at her a moment with a huge grin, then he pressed his lips to hers.

A thrill tingled through her. "Well, now you'll have to marry me."

"Gladly." He kissed her again.

* * * * *

HIS AMISH CHOICE

Leigh Bale

Thank you to Janet Pulleyn for infecting me with the soap-making bug. I have had a blast learning and consulting with you on new colors and fragrances. And thanks to Paul for letting me invade your home on more than one occasion. You are dear friends. Now, where shall we go out to dinner next time?

The Spirit itself beareth witness with our spirit,
that we are the children of God.
—*Romans* 8:16

Chapter One

Elizabeth Beiler set her last crate of honeycrisp apples into the back of the buggy-wagon and took a deep breath. Picking the fruit was hard work but she could never get enough of its fresh, earthy-sweet smell.

Brushing the dust off her rose-colored skirts and black apron, she adjusted the blue kerchief tied beneath her chin. Because she was working outside, she'd left her white organza *kapp* at home. She arched her back, her gaze scanning the rows of apple trees.

Finally, they were finished. Not that Lizzie begrudged the work. It brought her a sense of accomplishment and security. She was just tired and feeling jittery with Eli Stoltzfus's constant presence.

At that moment, he emerged from the orchard, carrying two heavy crates of fruit in his strong arms. His blue chambray shirt stretched taut across his muscular chest and arms. His plain broadfall trousers and work boots had dust on them. Wearing a straw hat and black suspenders, he looked unmistakably Amish. His clean-shaven face attested that he was unmarried. Lizzie was dying to ask if he'd had any girlfriends during the four years he'd been living among the *Englisch*, but kept her questions to herself. It wasn't her business after all. Not anymore.

His high cheekbones and blunt chin gave him a slightly stubborn look. With hair black as a raven's wing and gentle brown eyes, he was ruggedly handsome. Not that Lizzie also was interested. Not in this man. Not ever again.

As he approached, she turned away, conscious of his quiet gaze following her. She often found him watching her, his intelligent eyes warning that there was an active, gifted mind hidden beneath his calm exterior.

"Come on, Marty and Annie. It's time to go home," she called to her two sisters in *Deitsch*, the German dialect her Amish people used among themselves.

The girls came running, the long ribbons on their prayer *kapps* dangling in the wind. At the ages of ten and seven, neither girl was big or strong, but they were sturdy and a tremendous help on the farm. Their happy chatter also alleviated *Daed*'s quiet moods. He hadn't been the same since *Mamm* died almost five years earlier. The union of Lizzie's parents had been one of love. The perfect kind of marriage she had once dreamed of having with Eli.

"What are we having for *nachtesse*?" seven-year-old Annie asked, slightly breathless from her run.

"*Ja*, I'm starved." Marty was right behind her, biting into a crisp, juicy apple from the orchard.

"I'm going to make slumgullion," Lizzie said, thinking the meat and pasta dish was easy to make and very filling. "And we've also got leftover apple crisp from yesterday."

She was conscious of Eli adjusting the crates of apples in the back of their buggy-wagon, no doubt listening to their conversation. He must be ravenous too, but he would eat at home with his parents.

"Yum! I'm so hungry I could eat Billie." Annie leaned toward the bay gelding and made gobbling sounds. The gentle animal snorted and waved his head. Everyone except Marty laughed.

"You couldn't eat Billie. He's a horse. Don't be *dumm*," Marty said.

"No calling names, please. Be nice to your sister," Lizzie reprimanded in a kind voice. "As soon as *Daed* gets here, we'll go home."

They didn't have long to wait. Jeremiah Beiler emerged from the orchard, walking with their *Englisch* truck driver. *Daed*'s straw hat was pushed back on his head. Sweat-dampened tendrils of salt-and-pepper hair stuck to his high forehead. Dressed almost identically to Eli, *Daed*'s long beard was a light reddish shade with no moustache, signifying that he was a married man, now a widower.

The truck driver nodded, said something Lizzie couldn't hear, then climbed into the cab of his tractor trailer and started up the noisy engine. A rush of relief swept over her. The back of the 18-wheeler was loaded with crates of apples from their orchard and the driver would deliver them safely to the processing plant in Longmont. Their harvest was secure.

Because of Eli.

As the truck pulled away, *Daed* turned and smiled at them, but frowned when his gaze met Eli's. Lizzie knew her father didn't approve of Eli. He feared the younger man's worldly influence on his children and had hired him only at the bishop's urging.

"You all did *gut* work," Jeremiah said.

Eli gave a slight nod, then went to hitch his horse to his buggy. Lizzie watched him for a moment. Out of the blue, he had returned just over three weeks ago, asking to be reinstated in the *Gmay,* their Amish community.

If he had been a full member of the church before his decision to live among the *Englisch,* his choice to leave them would have been seen as a breaking of his faith and he would have been shunned. But because he'd never been baptized into their faith, he'd been welcomed back with open arms, no questions asked. Just a blind acceptance that he really wanted to be here. But Lizzie wasn't convinced. Eli had broken her heart. Leaving her the day before they were to be baptized together.

When they'd been only fourteen, he'd proposed marriage and she'd accepted. But long before then, he'd whispered about attending college to learn more about science and biology. Their eighth-grade education had never been enough for Eli, yet she had thought he'd made peace with the life they had. The life they'd intended to share. Lizzie hadn't believed he'd really leave. At least not without saying goodbye.

Annie and Marty beamed at their father's praise. They all felt a great weight lifted from their shoulders. The warm weather was an illusion. When they'd first settled in Colorado eight years earlier, they hadn't realized the growing season was much shorter than their previous home in Ohio. A killing frost could strike at any time. With their apples picked, they could now turn their efforts to other pressing matters.

To the south, the alfalfa was ready for cutting. The last of the season. They would store the hay in their barn to feed their own livestock through the long winter. *Daed* would mow it tomorrow. The weather should hold long enough for the hay to dry, then Lizzie would assist with the baling. Between now and then, she planned to bottle applesauce. They no longer needed Eli's help and she wouldn't have to see him every day. Though it wasn't charitable of her, she counted that as a blessing.

"*Komm*, my girls. Let's go," *Daed* called.

Annie giggled as her father swung her into the buggy. Marty scrambled inside with Lizzie. *Daed* gathered the leather leads into his hands and slapped them against Billie's back, giving a stiff nod of parting to Eli.

"*Sehn dich schpeeder,*" Eli called as he lifted one hand.

See you later? Lizzie hoped not, then felt guilty for being mean-spirited. The little girls waved goodbye, but not Lizzie. It still hurt her deeply to think that Eli had loved worldly pursuits more than he'd loved their faith and *Gott*. More than he'd loved her.

"*Heemet!*" *Daed* called.

Home! With a cozy barn and hay awaiting him, Billie had plenty of incentive to take off at a brisk walk. The buggy-wagon wobbled as they traveled along the narrow dirt road leading out of the orchard.

Glancing over her shoulder, Lizzie noticed that Eli had his horse hitched up to his buggy and wasn't far behind them.

When they reached the paved county road, *Daed* pulled the horse up and looked both ways. A couple of cars whizzed past, spraying them through their open windows with a fine mist of grit. Once it was clear, he proceeded forward, setting the horse into a comfortable trot along the far-right shoulder. Within minutes, they would be home. Marty and Annie leaned against Lizzie and yawned. The gentle rocking of the buggy and the rhythmic beat of hooves lulled Lizzie to close her eyes.

She awoke with a start as the buggy-wagon jerked forward. A sickening crash filled her ears. Apples went flying, peppering the road. Lizzie reached for Marty, but found herself airborne. Bloodcurdling screams split the air. The hard ground slammed up to meet her. Pain burst through her entire body, a lance of agony spearing her head. She cried out, then choked, the air knocked from her lungs. Her brain was spinning, her limbs frozen with stinging shock. One thought filled her mind. Her *familye*! She had to help them.

Lifting her head, she stared at the remnants of the wood and fiberglass buggy-wagon, strewn across the county road. The fluorescent slow-moving-vehicle symbol that had been affixed to the back of their wagon now lay broken beside her. In a glance, she saw a blue sedan parked nearby, the right front fender smashed in. She blinked as a teenage boy got out of the car, his eyes wide with panic. In his hand, he held his cell phone. Had he been texting while driving?

Lying below Lizzie in the ditch, Billie snorted and thrashed in his harness. Giving a shrill whinny, the horse lunged to his feet, the laces hanging limp from his back. The poor beast. At least he didn't appear to have a broken leg.

Lizzie wiped moisture from her forehead, then gasped when she discovered it was blood. She scanned the road, looking for *Daed* and her sisters. From her vantage point, she couldn't see any of them. Her vision swam before her. She couldn't focus. Falling back, she lay there for a moment, trying to fight off the woozy darkness, but despite her best efforts, it crowded in on her.

When she came to, Lizzie realized she must have fainted. She had no idea how long she'd been out. A rush of memory made her jerk upright, then cry out with anguish. Her entire body hurt, a searing pain in her head. She must get up. Must find her father, Annie and Marty.

"*Schtopp!* Just rest." A soft, masculine voice came from above her.

Blinking her eyes, she saw Eli kneeling over her. In a glance, she took in his somber expression filled with concern. He must have come upon them right after the crash.

"*Vie gehts?*" he asked in a soothing tone roughened by emotion.

"*Ja*, I'm fine. Marty and Annie. *Daed*. Help them," she said.

"They're all alive. The *Englischer* has called for help on his cell phone. An ambulance is coming from the hospital in town," he said.

"Where…where is my *familye*?" She sat up slowly to look for them, her head whirling from another dizzy spell.

"I didn't want the girls to see you until I was certain you were all right. They're very frightened as it is. I'll bring them to you now." He stood, looked both ways, then hurried across the road.

He soon returned, holding the hands of her sisters as he crossed the busy road. He hesitated as a car and truck whipped past, swerving to avoid the debris scattered across the asphalt. One of the vehicles stopped and asked if they needed help. The *Englisch* boy went to speak with the driver.

"Lizzie!" Annie cried.

Both little girls fell into her arms, sobbing and hugging her tight. Cupping their faces with her hands, she looked them over, kissing their scratched cheeks, assuring herself that they were safe. Their faces and arms were covered with abrasions, their dresses soiled, but they otherwise seemed fine.

"There, my *liebchen*. All will be well," Lizzie soothed the girls for a moment. Then, she looked at Eli. "But where is my *vadder*?"

"He cannot be moved just now. He has a serious compound fracture to his lower left leg. I believe his tibia is all that is broken. I have splinted the leg and stopped the bleeding, then wrapped him in a warm blanket I had in my buggy."

A broken leg! But how did Eli know what to do? A blaze of panic scorched her. They'd already lost *Mamm*. What would they do if they lost *Daed* too?

"I must go to him." She tried to stand.

"*Ne*, just sit still a moment. There's too much traffic on the road and you are also hurt. I believe you have a concussion." Eli held out a hand to stop her.

Lizzie recoiled, fearing he might touch her. How could he know she had a concussion? He wasn't a doctor. Or was he? She no longer knew much about this man. Was four years long enough for him to go to medical school? She had no knowledge of such things.

She reached up and touched her forehead. A wave of nausea forced her to sit back. When she drew away her hand, fresh blood stained her fingers. No wonder a horrible pain throbbed behind her eyes and her brain felt foggy. Maybe Eli was right.

"May I…may I wrap a cloth around your head? It's important that we stop the bleeding. I've already done all I can for Jeremiah," Eli said, his voice tentative.

"*Ja*," she consented, giving in to common sense.

She sat perfectly still as he removed her blood-soaked kerchief. Her waist-length hair had come undone from the bun at the nape of her neck and she felt embarrassed to have him see its length. It was something special she was keeping for her husband on their wedding night. Thankfully, he politely averted his gaze as he opened the first aid kit.

"Where did that come from?" She pointed at the box.

He answered without looking up. "My buggy."

"How do you know so much about medical care?"

He shrugged, his gaze briefly meeting hers. "I went through the training and am a certified paramedic. I'm specially trained to help in critical situations like this."

So, he wasn't a doctor, but he might as well be. Although she'd heard about Amish paramedics and firefighters working back east in Lancaster County and Pennsylvania, she'd never met one before and was fairly certain her church elders wouldn't approve. Higher learning was shunned by her people because it often led to *Hochmut*, the pride of men.

"Is…is that what you've been doing among the *Englisch*?" she asked.

He nodded. "*Ja*, it's how I earned my living."

So now she knew. He must have worked hard in school to learn such a skill. She couldn't blame him for wanting to know things, but neither did she approve of him casting aside his faith for such worldly pursuits.

Eli cleansed her wound with an antiseptic towelette. His touch was warm and gentle as he wrapped her head with soft, white gauze.

"You will need three or four stitches in the gash." He gave her a soulful look, as if he could see deep inside her heart and knew all the hurt and longings she kept hidden there.

She looked away.

Sirens heralded the arrival of two ambulances and some police cars. Lizzie lost track of time as the officers set up a roadblock with flares and took their statements. She watched Eli untangle the harness and lead Billie out of the ditch. Speaking to the distressed horse in a low murmur, he smoothed his hands over the animal's trembling legs. He then salvaged the bruised apples and put the filled crates into his own buggy.

When the medics loaded them into the two ambulances, Annie leaned close against Lizzie's side, her eyes red from crying. "Is *Daedi* going to be all right?"

Lizzie reached over and took the child's hand. "The Lord's will be done, *boppli*. We must trust in Him to get us through."

As she spoke these words, she tried to believe them. If *Daed* died, could she forgive the boy who had caused the accident? Christ had forgiven all and she must do likewise, but she wasn't sure her faith was that strong.

"I'll look after Billie." Eli stood at the foot of the ambulance, holding the lead lines to the horse's halter. His expressive eyes were filled with a haunting unease, as though he were anxious to leave.

"Danke." Lizzie gave a brisk nod.

He stepped back and the medics closed the double doors. Lizzie laid her head back and closed her eyes. And in her heart, she carried a silent prayer that they would be all right.

The following day, Eli tugged on the leather leads as he veered Jeremiah Beiler's three draft horses slightly to the left. The big Percherons did as he asked, plodding steadily down the row of alfalfa as they pulled the hay mower. The low rumble of the gas-powered engine filled the air. Eli glanced at the position of the sun, unable to believe it was afternoon already. Another hour and he would finish this chore. Jeremiah's hay would be secure. It would take a few more days for the hay to dry, and then he would gather it into bales.

"Gee!" he called, turning the team to the right.

A movement brought his eye toward the red log house where Lizzie and her *familye* lived. Turning slightly, he saw her and two men heading toward him, stepping high as they crossed the rutted field. Even from this distance, Eli recognized the slant of Bishop Yoder's black felt hat. His companion was Darrin Albrecht, the deacon of their congregation. Both men were dressed identically in black frock coats and broadfall pants. Eli had gotten word of the Beilers' accident to the bishop late last night. No doubt the elders had come to check on Jeremiah's *familye*.

Lizzie accompanied them, wearing a blue dress and crisp black apron. As they drew near, Eli saw a fresh gauze bandage had been taped to her forehead, no doubt hiding several stitches from her visit to the hospital. She and the little girls must have just gotten home. He'd seen the *Englisch* midwife's car pull in the driveway an hour earlier. She must have given them a ride from town.

Sunlight glinted against Lizzie's golden hair, the length of it pinned into a bun beneath her starched prayer *kapp*. One rebellious strand framed her delicate oval face and she quickly tucked it back behind her ear. Her blue eyes flashed with unease, her stern expression and brisk stride belying her injuries. Eli was eager to hear how she was feeling and also receive news of her father's condition.

Pulling the giant horses to a standstill, he killed the engine and hopped down off his seat. As he walked the short distance to meet them, he rolled his long sleeves down his forearms.

"Hallo," he called.

He glanced at Lizzie, trying to assess her mood. Their gazes clashed, then locked for several moments. As always, he blinked at the startling blue of her eyes. Her expression showed a fierce emotion he didn't understand. A mingling of repugnance and determination.

"Guder nummidaag," Bishop Yoder said.

"It looks like you've been busy today." Deacon Albrecht surveyed the cut field, as though evaluating the quality of Eli's work.

After being gone four years, Eli was surprised at how easily farming came back to him. It felt good to work the land again. It felt good to be needed. Holding the lead lines in his hands as the powerful horses pulled the mower had given him a sense of purpose he hadn't felt since Shannon's death seven months earlier.

Thinking of his sweet fiancée made his heart squeeze painfully and a gloomy emptiness filled his chest.

"You have done *gut* work for the Beilers," Bishop Yoder said. "They will need the strength of a man on this place for a few more months, until Jeremiah is back on his feet. He will have surgery today and will be in the hospital awhile longer, until the swelling goes down so they can cast the leg."

Eli nodded, wondering what the bishop was getting at.

Bishop Yoder placed his hand on Eli's shoulder, his gray eyes filled with kindness, but also an intensity that couldn't be ignored. "I've spoken with your father. He agrees that you should work here for the time being, caring for Jeremiah's farm as if it were your own. But with this request comes a great responsibility and commitment to your faith. I know you have told me you are recommitted to *Gott*. Are you certain our way of life is what you want?"

Eli hesitated. With Shannon gone and his confidence shattered, he had needed to get away from Denver and all the reminders of her death. Here in Riverton, he hoped to find the peace he so desperately longed for and a way to forgive himself for what had happened.

His heart still felt unsure, but he was determined to stay the course and wait for certainty to come. He couldn't go back, so he'd have to find a way for himself here.

"I am." Eli nodded, his throat dry as sandpaper. Speaking the words out loud helped solidify his commitment.

"I just spoke with your *mudder*. She is inside the house, almost finished bottling applesauce for Lizzie," the bishop said.

Eli nodded, forcing himself to meet the man's gaze. "*Ja*, and my *vadder* was here earlier this morning, helping with the milking."

"You all have been most kind." Lizzie stared at the ground, her words low and uncertain.

Eli felt a wave of compassion. "It's our pleasure to help. You would do the same for us."

Or at least, he hoped she would. Her manner was so offish toward him that he wasn't sure. When he'd left four years earlier, he'd written to her often, at first. Not once had she replied. That alone told him she wanted nothing to do with him. After a year and a half of trying, he'd finally moved on with his life, meeting and falling in love with Shannon.

"Gut," the bishop continued. "Tomorrow at church, I will announce your plans to be baptized, so you can participate in the instruction classes again. They've already begun, but since you took them once before, I think we can catch you up. Then you'll be prepared for your baptism in a few months."

Lizzie looked at him and a rush of doubt speared Eli's chest. The last time he'd attended the classes, he'd been a rebellious kid and hadn't paid much attention. In those days, all he could think about was getting out of here. Was he ready for such a commitment now? Once he was baptized, there would be no turning back. But he had the next few months to decide.

"I'm happy to assist the Beilers," he said.

A sudden hesitation struck him. A quick glance in Lizzie's direction told him that she didn't want him here. Her expression held a heavy dose of disapproval. As if she thought he was tainted now, because he'd been living among the *Englisch.*

He'd loved her so much when they were teenagers, but he'd had to leave. Had to find out what the world could offer. He'd desperately wanted a *rumspringa*—that rite of passage during adolescence when Amish teenagers experienced freedom of choice without the rules of the *Ordnung* to hold them back. But he'd never meant to hurt Lizzie. In fact, he'd tried to get her to come join him. If only she had responded to his letters. Instead, each one had been returned unopened.

The bishop smiled. *"Ach,* we'll see you tomorrow then. *Willkomm* back, my brother."

Eli nodded, but didn't speak. A hard lump had lodged

in his throat. He felt grateful to be here, but the reasons for the gratitude were murky. Was he truly glad to be back among his people, or was he just relieved to be away from reminders of Shannon? He'd talked to other paramedics who had lost a patient in their care, but it hadn't prepared him for the shock. And to make matters worse, the first patient he'd lost had been someone he dearly loved. Someone who was counting on him to keep her safe. And he'd failed miserably. That's when he realized how much he missed his *familye*. Seeking respite from the world, he'd come home. But thus far, peace of mind had continued to elude him.

Reaching up, he tugged on the brim of his straw hat where a letter from Tom Caldwell was safely tucked away. Tom had been Eli's former boss at the hospital in Denver. His letter was a silent reminder of the *Englisch* life Eli had left behind. And though it felt good to be back in Riverton, whenever Eli thought of never being a paramedic again, a sick feeling settled in his gut.

"If you have faith, all will be well with your *familye*. Never forget that," the bishop spoke kindly to Lizzie.

"*Ja. Danke*, Bishop," Lizzie said, her voice holding a note of respect.

The church elders walked away, leaving Eli and Lizzie alone. A horrible, swelling silence followed. Lizzie looked at the ground, looked at the mountains surrounding the valley, looked anywhere but at Eli.

"You are truly all right?" Eli finally asked, peering at Lizzie's forehead.

"*Ja*, I'm fine," she said, briefly touching the bandage as if it embarrassed her.

"I didn't expect this." He gestured toward the retreating men.

"Neither did I." Her voice wobbled.

"Are you sure you're okay with me working here?" he asked.

She glanced at him. "I don't have much choice."

True. With her *daed* in the hospital and the bishop's stamp of approval, she would have to accept Eli's aid.

"I never meant to hurt you, Lizzie. I know I left rather suddenly," he said.

She snorted and stepped back in exasperation. "*Ja*, you sure did."

"I know I should have spoken to you about it first, but I feared you might tell my *eldre* or the bishop and they would have tried to make me stay."

"*Ach*, so you ran away. You took the coward's route and fled."

He stared in confusion. He'd been gone four years. Why was Lizzie still so angry at him?

"We were only fourteen when I first proposed to you," he said. "I'm sure you agree that was way too young for marriage. When I left, neither of us was ready to start a *familye*. If only you had come and joined me."

"To Denver?" she asked with incredulity.

He nodded.

"*Ne*, I would never leave my people. You knew that."

"But I had to go. I wanted a *rumspringa*."

"So, nothing has changed. You still seek the world." Her voice sounded bitter.

He snorted, feeling frustrated, but unwilling to explain about Shannon and all that he had recently lost. "Believe me, a lot has changed. I'm not the same person anymore."

"And neither am I, Eli. You're homesick for your *familye*, that's all. But before long, you'll get homesick for the world out there that you left behind. We don't drive cars, use electricity, or swim the inner net. You'll get tired of us and leave again."

Swim the inner net?

He tilted his head in confusion, wondering what she meant. Then, he chuckled as he understood her words. "I think you mean *surf the internet.*"

She shrugged, her voice thick with conviction. "Whatever. We don't do that. Pretty soon, you'll become weary of our quaint, boring ways and leave again."

Oh, that hurt. More than he could say. Never had he considered his Amish people to be quaint or boring. In fact, quite the opposite. The science of farming tantalized his intellect. The hard work and life here was definitely far from mundane. It was always a challenge to fight the weather, improve their machinery and produce a better crop...especially in Colorado. He also loved the solitude of fertile fields and the camaraderie of belonging to the *Gmay*. He always had.

"*Ne*, I'm here to stay, Lizzie-bee." But his words lacked the conviction hers had held. After all, his memories of Shannon were in Denver. When she'd died, he'd wanted to leave, but now he missed going to their old haunts where they'd fallen in love. He missed her.

"Don't call me that." Her lips pursed with disapproval and tears shimmered in her eyes.

Lizzie-bee.

He held perfectly still, wishing he hadn't used his old pet name for her. It had slipped out. How he wished he could go back in time and mend the rift between them. That they could be friends again. He could use the comfort of a good friend to help him deal with his broken heart, still full of love for Shannon.

"For the help you will give, you are welcome here on

our farm, Eli Stoltzfus, but don't expect anything else. I don't trust you anymore and that's that." She whirled around and headed toward the house, plodding over the wide furrows of alfalfa with singular purpose.

I don't trust you anymore.

Her words rang in his ears like the tolling of a bell. He watched her go, his heart plummeting. More than anything, he longed for a friend to confide in. Someone to talk with about Shannon and his loss. But it obviously wouldn't be Lizzie. Not only had he lost her friendship, but he'd also lost her confidence and there was no going back.

Chapter Two

"I like Eli. He's so nice," Annie said later that night.

Lizzie jerked, her fingers losing their grasp on the tiny rubber band she was using to tie off the end of Annie's braided hair.

The little girls had both had their baths and Lizzie was finishing their hair before going to bed. Each child sat on the wooden bench in the kitchen, the gas lamp above the table shining down upon their heads. Their bare feet peeked out from beneath the hems of their simple flannel nightgowns. The air carried a slight fruity smell from the detangler she'd used on their hair to get the snarls out.

"Eli is nice, but you can't like him," Marty said. She tugged the comb through a particularly stubborn knot in her own damp hair.

"Why not?" Annie asked, her forehead crinkled in a frown.

"Because he hurt Lizzie's feelings, that's why."

Both girls turned and looked at Lizzie, as if waiting for a confirmation.

"Of course you can like him." Lizzie laughed it off, not wanting to explain how much she'd loved the man and how he'd broken her heart. Everyone in the *Gmay* had known they'd been going together and planned to marry one day.

"We can? You're okay with it?" Marty asked.

"*Ja*, it's not our place to judge," Lizzie reiterated, trying to believe her own words.

"But you were gonna get married to him. Emily Hostetler said he left you to become an *Englischer* instead," Marty said.

"You were gonna marry Eli?" Annie asked.

Lizzie inhaled a sharp breath and held it for several moments before letting it go. Hearing Eli's betrayal put so bluntly made her mind scatter and she had to regather her thoughts before responding. As he had pointed out, they'd only been fourteen when he'd proposed. Way too young to marry. Because they'd been so young, he hadn't taken it seriously, but Lizzie had. When he left, they were seventeen and she'd thought they would wed the following year. It's what they had talked about. But he'd obviously changed his mind—and hadn't felt the need to tell her.

"That was a long time ago. It was Eli's choice to leave. When the time comes, we each must make that decision for ourselves, but I dearly hope both of you will stay." She placed Annie's *kapp* on her head, then hugged the girl tight.

"I'll never leave," Marty said.

When Lizzie released her, Annie stood, her inquisitive gaze resting on Lizzie. "Is that true, Lizzie-*bee*? Eli really left you to become *Englisch*?"

Lizzie-bee. The nickname Eli had given her when she'd been barely thirteen years old because he thought she was always as busy as a bee. Back then, Lizzie had loved Eli to call her that name. Now, it was a reminder of all that she'd lost.

"Where did you hear that name?" Lizzie asked a bit too brusquely.

"It's what Eli called you when he came into the house to take Fannie home after she bottled our applesauce. You were upstairs," Annie said.

Fannie was Eli's mother and a dear friend. She was as generous as the day was long. It had hurt her deeply when Eli left.

Lizzie sat very still, looking at her two sisters. Marty had been six when Eli had left, so she undoubtedly remembered him. Annie had been only three. Lizzie didn't want to discuss what had happened, but neither would she lie. Nor did she have a right to speak ill of Eli.

"Is it true?" the girl persisted.

"*Ja*, it's true," she said, tucking an errant strand of hair beneath Annie's *kapp*.

The child's eyes crinkled with sadness. "But everyone loves you. Why would Eli leave?"

She said the words as if she couldn't understand why Eli couldn't love her too.

"He…he wanted other things, that's all," Lizzie said.

"Did he hurt your feelings when he left?" Annie persisted.

"Of course he did." Marty flipped her long hair over her shoulder.

"*Ja*, he did," Lizzie admitted. She didn't look at the girls as she parted Marty's tresses and quickly began to braid the lengthy strands. Perhaps it was good for her sisters to learn early that a man could break your heart.

"But he's back now. You don't need to have hurt feelings anymore. You can forgive him and all will be well. Maybe he'll even want to still marry you now," Annie said.

If only it were that simple. Right now, Lizzie didn't want to marry Eli. And she certainly couldn't believe Eli wanted to marry her—not after the way he'd abandoned her. But sweet little Annie had always had such a calm, quiet spirit. Honest and trusting, the girl always exemplified a childlike faith in the good of others. Lizzie never wanted to see that faith shattered. But more than that, Lizzie had to set a good example for her sisters. With *Mamm* gone, they deserved to feel safe and loved. They were both looking to her for guidance and she didn't want to let them down.

"The Lord wants us to forgive everyone. We should never judge others, because we don't know what's truly in their heart or what their circumstances are. Plus we each have our own faults to repent from," Lizzie spoke in a measured tone, believing what she said, though she still struggled to apply it to Eli.

Annie nudged Marty with her elbow. "See? I told ya so."

Marty accepted this without question and Lizzie breathed with relief. She quickly finished her chore. Upstairs, she tucked the girls into bed, feeling like a hypocrite. She told her sisters to forgive, yet she hadn't done so herself. But honestly, she didn't know how. Saying and doing it were two different things. Forgiveness wasn't as easy as it seemed. Especially when she'd been hurt so badly.

She secured the house for the night and turned out the kerosene lights. Alone in her room, she prayed for help, but received no answers. Lying in the darkness, she closed her eyes and tried to sleep, but her mind kept racing. If Eli hadn't left, they'd likely be married now. They would probably have one or two children too. How different their lives might have been. They could have been happy and in love and working for the good of their *familye*. Instead, she felt disillusioned and distrustful. But it did no good to dwell on such things. It would not change the present. Her *familye* needed her and that was enough.

Punching her pillow, she turned on her side and closed her eyes, gritty with fatigue. She tried to rest, but it was a long time coming.

In the morning, she felt drowsy and grouchy. Determined not to be cross with the girls, she kissed each one on the forehead to wake them up. She ensured they were dressed and sitting at the table eating a bowl of scrapple—a mixture of corn meal, sausage and eggs— before she lit the kerosene lamp and stepped out onto the back porch.

Crisp darkness filled the air as she crossed the yard. The chilling breeze hinted that winter was not far away. In the waning shadows, she tossed grain to the chickens, then gathered the eggs into a wire basket. When she went to feed the pigs, she found the chore already done, the trough filled with fresh water.

Oh, no. This could only mean one thing.

Turning, she went to the barn. A faint light gleamed from beneath the double doors as she stepped inside. A lamp sat on the railing of Ginger's stall. The chestnut palomino was old, but *Daed* still used her to pull the buggy when Billie was lame. Thinking Billie needed a few more days of rest, Lizzie planned to use Ginger today, to get to church. It was too bad they'd lost their larger buggy-wagon in the accident. Now, they'd have to use their older, smaller buggy.

"Easy, girl." Eli stood bent over the mare's left back hoof. He wore a plain white shirt and black suspenders, his nice Sunday frock jacket hanging on a peg nearby.

Releasing the animal's leg, he patted her rump as he stood up straight. Then, he flinched. "Lizzie-bee! You startled me."

She bit her tongue, forcing herself not to reprimand him. It would do no good. The name *Lizzie-bee* was too embedded in their past history.

"I came to feed the animals. I didn't expect you to be here today," she said.

He shrugged. "I figured you would still need help even on the Sabbath."

Leading Ginger out of her stall, he directed the mare over to the buggy. Glancing at the other stalls, Lizzie saw that Eli had already fed Billie and *Daed*'s six Percheron draft horses. And judging from the two tall canisters sitting near the door, he'd already done the milking too. It appeared he was taking his promise to the bishop very seriously.

"Have you eaten?" she asked, feeling obligated to use good manners.

"*Ja*, my *mudder* fixed a big meal for *Daed* and me. I'll have the horse hitched up in just a few minutes, then I'll drive you to church," he said.

He didn't look at her while he put the collar on the horse. Ginger stood perfectly still, knowing this routine by heart.

"That won't be necessary. You're very kind, but I can drive the *maed* myself," Lizzie said.

He paused, holding the saddle lacings in his big hands. "I… I don't think that's a good idea. You were nearly killed just a few days ago and I… I assured the bishop that I'd look after all of you."

His voice caught on the words and he turned away, but not before Lizzie saw his trembling hands. Or had she imagined that? Why did he seem so upset by the accident?

"*Ne*, you told him you'd look after the farm. That's not the same as driving us to church," she said.

He nodded, accepting her logic. "Still, I feel responsible for you. I don't want to have to tell Jeremiah that I was derelict in my duty."

Hmm. Maybe he was right. The horror of the accident came rushing back and she realized she wasn't eager to climb into a buggy again. If her fear distracted her while she was driving, it could put her sisters in danger. Perhaps it would be better to let Eli drive them for a time. But she hated feeling like a burden almost as much as she hated to depend on him.

"You needn't feel obligated. I've driven a buggy many times before," she argued half-heartedly.

"I know that. You're a capable, strong-minded woman, but I'd feel better if you'd let me drive today. Just until Jeremiah is out of the hospital." His gaze brushed over the clean gauze she had taped over her forehead. She hated wearing a bandage and would be glad when the wound healed enough to remove the three tiny stitches. No doubt, they'd leave a small scar to remind her that *Gott* had saved her *familye*'s lives.

"*Komm* on, let me drive you," he said, his voice coaxing.

Oh, she knew that look of his. The calm demeanor. The slightly narrowed eyes. The softly spoken words and stubborn tilt that said he was going to do what he wanted one way or the other. Some things never changed.

But *she* had changed. Those soft feelings for Eli had been put away, and she wouldn't fall back into old habits, like smiling at him when he behaved this way. It was time for this conversation to end.

"All right, you can drive today. I'll go get the *kinder*." She picked up a canister of milk and lugged it across the yard toward the well house. Fed by a cold mountain stream coming out of the Sangre de Cristo Mountains, the stone bath had been built by *Daed* when the *familye* first moved to Colorado.

Once inside, Lizzie set the heavy can into the chilled water and realized her hands were shaking from her exertions. When she turned, she found Eli right behind her with the second can.

"They're too heavy for you to carry," he said.

Yes, they were, but she could manage. With her father gone, she'd do whatever she must. Feeling suddenly awkward, she scooted out of Eli's way as he placed the second canister into the water bath.

"Danke," she said before hurrying to the house.

The girls were standing on the front porch waiting, their *kapps*, dresses and aprons neatly in place. They smiled, looking so sweet and innocent that a feeling of overwhelming love filled Lizzie's chest.

"We even washed the breakfast dishes," Annie said with a big smile, handing Lizzie the basket they would take with them.

"You did? You're so helpful." Lizzie smiled back, wiping a smudge of strawberry jam away from the girl's upper lip.

The clatter of hooves caused them all to turn. Eli

drove the buggy toward them, his straw hat, vest and jacket now in place. Inwardly, Lizzie took a deep, startled breath. He looked more handsome than a man had a right to be and it pierced her to the core.

As he pulled Ginger to a halt and hopped out of the buggy, Annie scurried behind Lizzie, as if to hide.

"*Ne*, I don't want to ride in the buggy. Can't we walk today?" the child asked, gripping folds of Lizzie's dress as she peeked around her legs with caution.

"*Ja*, I would rather walk today too." Marty's eyes were also creased with fear as she sidled up against Lizzie.

Taking both girls' hands in her own, Lizzie knelt in front of them to meet their eyes. "It's too far to walk, *bopplin*. We'll have to ride. But I will be with you and the Lord will make sure we are safe."

Annie shook her head, her breathing coming fast, as though she'd been running. Lizzie knew a panic attack when she saw one. She pulled both girls into her arms and gave them a reassuring hug.

Eli stepped up onto the porch, removed his straw hat and crouched down so he could meet Annie's gaze. "Ginger is an old, gentle horse and she can't go very fast. You like her, don't you?"

"*Ja.*" Annie nodded.

"And you trust me, right?"

A pause, then another nod.

"Then I promise to pull far over onto the shoulder of the road and drive extra careful so we don't have another accident. If I hear a car coming up fast behind us, I'll pull completely off the road until they have passed us by. I'll take good care of all of us, this I promise," he said.

A long silence followed as Annie drew her eyebrows together, signaling that she was thinking it over. Lizzie didn't know what she'd do if her sisters refused to get into the buggy. It was eight miles to the Geingeriches' farm—and eight miles they'd have to travel back. If they walked, they would arrive late, sweaty and tired. And the evenings were too chilly to walk home late at night. But she hated Eli's word choice. There had been a time not so long ago when she had trusted him and he had made promises to her too. Promises she'd naively believed with all her heart...until he'd broken them.

"All right. We will ride," Annie finally said in a tone of resignation.

Eli smiled wide, placed his hat back on his head, then picked the girl up. Taking Marty's hand, he walked with them to the buggy and set them gently inside. Lizzie was right behind them. Watching his tenderness with her sisters brought a poignant ache to her heart. Without Lizzie asking, he helped her into the carriage too, holding on to her forearm a bit longer than necessary. The warmth of his hand tingled over her skin and she pulled away as quickly as possible.

When he was settled in the driver's seat, he took the leather reins and slapped them against the palomino's back.

"Schritt," he called.

The horse walked forward, settling into an easy trot.

Sitting stiffly in her seat, Lizzie adjusted her long skirts and scrunched her knees as far away from Eli's as possible. She thought about her discussion with him the day before. He'd said he wanted to stay in Riverton. That he wanted to live the Amish way of life. But what if he changed his mind? She told herself she didn't care. He meant nothing to her now except that he was a member of the *Gmay*. So why did the thought of him leaving again make her feel so sad and empty inside?

Eli turned off the pavement and headed down the dirt road leading to the Geingeriches' farm. Another buggy and horse were right in front of them, with several more following behind in a short convoy. Eli followed their pace. Each *familye* waved and greeted one another like the best of friends. A faint mist had settled across the valley, but he knew the morning sun would soon burn it off and all would be clear by late afternoon when they began their journey home.

His parents should already be here. Joining them for meetings made him feel almost normal again. They were so happy to have him home that he felt good to be here. But he still couldn't help wondering if he'd made a wrong choice by returning to Riverton. He wanted to be here. He really did. But he couldn't seem to get Shannon off his mind. Her smile. Her scent. The way she'd begged him to save her life the night of the drunk driving accident. And then the stricken look on her parents' faces at the cemetery when they had buried their only child.

When the white frame house came into view, Eli breathed a sigh of relief. He'd promised the girls they'd be safe on their journey to church and he was grateful that he'd been able to keep his word. Too many automobiles flew way too fast down the roads. With drivers talking on their cell phones or texting, he could understand why the Amish were nervous as they drove their horse-drawn buggies and wagons. What was so important on the phone that it was worth risking someone's life? He'd had a cell phone when he'd lived among the *Englisch*, but he'd only used it when absolutely necessary. He'd found them a poor substitute for building relationships face-to-face. He was just grateful that a worse tragedy hadn't struck the Beiler *familye* and Jeremiah would recover from the accident.

Turning the horse into the main yard, he pulled up where two teenage boys were directing traffic. A long row of black buggies had already been parked along the fence line. Eli waited his turn, then pulled up as instructed.

"I can unhitch your horse," one of the boys offered.

"Danke." Eli handed the lines over, watching as the two teenagers removed the harness in preparation of leading the mare over to a field where she could graze and water with other horses.

Eli helped the girls out of the buggy. He noticed how Lizzie avoided his hand by gripping the edge of the carriage. She didn't meet his eyes as she smoothed her apron, then reached back into the buggy for a basket that was neatly covered with a clean dish towel. He had no idea what was hidden beneath, but surmised it was something tasty for their noon meal later on. The thought of spending the day with Lizzie made him feel warm. If he hadn't gone to Denver, they probably would have married. They'd be taking their *familye* to church like any other couple. But then he wouldn't have met and loved Shannon, and he couldn't forget that she had meant the world to him.

"Lizzie!"

A young woman with golden hair was busy spreading a cloth over one of the long tables set up outside. Eli didn't recognize her and wondered if she was a newcomer to the *Gmay*. She stood beneath the tall spread of a maple tree laden with leaves of bright yellow. The autumn air had a distinct crispness to it, but was still pleasant enough to eat outside.

As she approached, the woman arched her back, displaying an obvious rounding of her abdomen. Eli figured she must be about six months pregnant.

"*Guder mariye*, Abby. How are you feeling today?" Lizzie asked as the woman waddled toward them.

Ach, so this was Abby! Eli had heard all about her from his parents.

She rested a hand on her belly as Jakob Fisher joined them, taking her arm in a protective gesture. Before he'd left Riverton, Eli had known Jakob and his first wife, Susan, and their two small children, Reuben and Ruby. Jakob was older than Eli and they'd never been close friends, but Eli was sad to learn that Susan had died in childbirth while he was gone. Jakob had married Abby a year earlier and now they were expecting their first child together.

"I am well. The doctor has told me I'm perfectly healthy and should deliver just after the New Year," Abby said.

"*Ach*, you may deliver early. Wouldn't it be fun to have a Christmas baby?" Lizzie asked, her voice filled with jubilation.

Jakob smiled wide. "*Ja*, that would be the best Christmas gift ever."

Abby just beamed, her face glowing with an ethereal beauty that seemed to accompany every new mother as she worked hand in hand with *Gott* to create a new life.

"*Hallo*, Eli." Jakob nodded to him. "I would like to introduce you to my wife, Abby."

Eli smiled and nodded at the pretty woman. "I'm so glad to meet you."

"Likewise," she said. "I heard you are looking out for the Beilers while Jeremiah is laid up."

"*Ja*, the bishop thought it would be best," Eli replied with a half smile.

"Because of the accident, I heard in town that they're planning to put up more Amish buggy signs along the roads," Jakob said.

"*Ach*, it's about time," Abby said.

"*Ja*, that would be *gut*. I just hope it gets the drivers to slow down," Lizzie murmured.

Eli hoped so too. He hated the thought of any other members of their *Gmay* getting hurt.

The women stepped ahead of the men, moving off toward the kitchen. Marty and Annie joined Jakob's two children, racing across the front lawn in carefree abandon. Church Sunday was a time to worship *Gott*, but it was also a time to socialize and relax from daily labors. Both adults and children alike usually looked forward to this day with happiness. But not Eli. Not when he glanced over and saw several older women watching him, their heads bent close as they chatted together. He couldn't help wondering if he was the topic of their conversation, especially when Marva Geingerich eyed him with a look of revulsion.

"Don't mind old Mrs. Geingerich. She doesn't approve of anyone," Jakob whispered.

Eli jerked, realizing that Jakob had stopped walking and was watching him closely. "Does my nervousness show that much?"

Jakob nodded, his mouth turned up in a generous smile. "I'm afraid so. When my Susan died, Marva didn't approve of me either, simply because I was alone with two young *kinder* to raise. It didn't matter that I had no control over my wife's death or that I was grieving. Marva seems to be able to find anything and everything to disapprove of."

When Jakob put it like that, it sounded rather silly, but Eli didn't laugh.

"You must have been brokenhearted to lose Susan. How did you recover?" Eli asked, eager to know how to ease the gnawing pain he felt deep inside for Shannon.

"I'll let you know if I ever do. Right now, I doubt a person can fully heal from losing someone they have loved. But you have to keep living. And the Lord blessed me with a second chance at happiness. I never thought it possible, but I'm so deeply in love with Abby and I can't imagine living life without her." Jakob's gaze rested on Abby, his eyes filled with such wonder and devotion that Eli felt a lance of jealousy pierce his heart. Surely there would be no third chance for him.

Turning toward him, Jakob lifted a hand and rested it on Eli's shoulder before squeezing gently. "I know it couldn't have been easy for you to walk away from your *familye* when you left us, nor any easier for you to return. It took a lot of courage to come back and face your *eldre*. Now you have a second chance with Lizzie too."

Eli blinked, not quite understanding. For the first time since his return, Eli wondered if everyone believed he still wanted to marry Lizzie. After all, none of them knew anything about Shannon. But Lizzie didn't want him. Her words to him yesterday had indicated loud and clear that she didn't love him anymore.

"Facing my *eldre* was easier than you might think," Eli said. "They're both relieved I'm back. But Lizzie is a different story. I think I've burned a bridge with her that can never be rebuilt."

Jakob nodded. "No doubt she is still angry and hurt that you left, but she's refused to look at any other man since then. She has a *gut*, forgiving heart. With time, I'm sure both of you will be able to let go of the past, just as I did."

That was just it. Eli didn't want to let go of Shannon. How could he forget what she had meant to him and the part he'd played in her death? It was his fault she had died, but he didn't mention that to Jakob.

With one last smile of encouragement, Jakob turned and joined the other men as they lined up to go inside the spacious barn for their meetings. Eli followed, standing behind Martin Hostetler, who was three years older than him. With auburn hair, a smattering of freckles across his nose and blue eyes that gleamed with merriment, Martin was hardworking and filled with energy. Eli was surprised the man was still single.

Martin nodded and asked him several questions, but was cut off when they went inside, much to Eli's relief. His thoughts were filled with turmoil. As they trailed into the barn and took their place opposite the women, he considered Jakob's words. Yes, it had taken courage to return, and yet it hadn't been so difficult. Not when he'd been yearning for home—and everything in Denver had reminded him of Shannon, filling him with grief and guilt. But now that he was here, he feared he'd made a mistake. People in his *Gmay* would expect him to marry. And he couldn't do that right now. Maybe never. Perhaps he didn't belong in this world anymore.

He glanced at Bishop Yoder's pretty daughters sitting with Lizzie. The young women smiled shyly, then ducked their heads close together in a whispered conversation. Though he'd known most of them before he left, they all looked alike to Eli. Modest, chaste and pretty.

With her creamy complexion and stunning eyes, Lizzie stood out among them, like a beacon of light in a sea of fog. Eli knew the Hostetlers and Geingeriches each had a daughter of marriageable age too, but he wasn't interested. Not in any of them.

He glanced at Lizzie, who stared straight ahead at the bishop. As the *vorsinger* called out the first note of the opening song, she opened her mouth and sang in German from the *Ausbund*, their church hymnal. How ironic that she was the only woman in the room who didn't seem to be looking at him.

Someone cleared their throat nearby and he glanced over to find his father's disapproving frown aimed at him. It didn't matter that Eli was a grown man. He was unmarried and still living in his father's household. Trying to refocus his thoughts, Eli joined in with the slow harmony, the words returning to his memory like a dear old friend.

Almost immediately, the bishop and deacon stood, then disappeared into the tack room to hold the *Abrot*, a leadership council meeting to discuss church business. While they were gone, the congregation kept singing, with no musical accompaniment. Eli stared at the closed door, trying to clear his mind and relax. Forcing himself not to look at Lizzie again. Attempting to push her from his mind. But it did no good. Again and again, he glanced her way, his thoughts returning to her wounded gaze. She'd made her position perfectly clear when the bishop had asked him to work on her farm. They needn't discuss the matter further. And yet, Eli couldn't fight the feeling that they still had unfinished business between them.

Chapter Three

The congregation knelt in silent prayer until Bishop Yoder released a discreet sigh. As a body, they each rose to their feet, turned and sat on the hard, backless benches. Once they were all seated, Lizzie watched as Bishop Yoder stood at the front of the room. With such a small *Gmay*, they had only one minister... Lizzie's father. And with him still in the hospital, the bishop would probably preach to them.

"What is in your heart today?" he asked the worshippers.

The question took Lizzie off guard. Tilting her head, she listened intently as the bishop spoke, his voice soft but powerful, like the sound of rolling thunder off in the distance. He met the eyes of each person in the room as though he were speaking to every single one of them. When he met Lizzie's eyes, she looked down, feeling suddenly embarrassed.

"Do you carry peace and charity within you, or do you harbor anger and malice toward someone?" the bishop asked, pausing to give them each time to search their hearts.

Lizzie squirmed on her seat. She glanced at Eli, but

found him gazing straight forward, his expression one of thoughtful introspection.

Bishop Yoder lifted a book of scriptures. "But whosoever shall smite thee on thy right cheek, turn to him the other also."

Lizzie had heard this passage numerous times and thought she understood it clearly...until now. She had no desire to be hurt again and again, especially where her heart was concerned. But wasn't that what the Lord expected? For her to humble herself and cast aside her harsh feelings.

"Over the next weeks, I hope each of you will resolve any hard feelings you might carry toward others," the bishop continued. "Examine your own thoughts and actions and bring them into line with how the Lord would have you live. I beseech each of you to hand Him your anger and pain, your shortcomings and flaws. Then, once we all are in accord with each other, we will hold our Council Services in preparation for Communion."

Communion! A sacred time when the entire congregation must be in complete harmony with one another. With all that had happened recently, Lizzie had forgotten it was nearly that time of year.

As the bishop continued speaking about the rules of their *Ordnung* and the responsibility of each member of their community, she clenched her eyes tightly closed and gripped her hands together in her lap. Surely the bishop wasn't speaking directly to her. He couldn't know the resentment she still harbored toward Eli. Could he? Yet whether he could or not, she was the minister's daughter, after all, and she knew she should set a good example of love, tolerance and forgiveness. But how could she forgive Eli after what he'd done? He had soured her toward all men. She would probably never marry now. Never have a *familye* of her own. Never live in her own house. Over time, several men had asked her out. Martin Hostetler had pursued her doggedly, but seemed to have finally given up after the first year. Now it appeared she would become an old maid. Pitied by the other members of her community.

She took a slow breath, trying to settle her nerves. Her thoughts were selfish, she knew that. She was so worried about herself and what others might think about her that she hadn't stopped to consider Eli and his well-being. Why had he returned? What had happened to him after all this time? After he'd left, she'd been worried for him, fearing that he was lost forever. But here he was, seeking a second chance. And who was she to refuse him?

She had to find a way to let go of her anger. To forgive him. But how? All her life, she'd been taught the principles of repentance and forgiveness. So, why was it so difficult to exercise those virtues now?

Puzzling over her dilemma, Lizzie was surprised at how quickly time passed before they broke for the noon meal.

"*Komm* on. You can help me serve my potato soup." Abby spoke cheerfully as she took Lizzie's arm and pulled her toward the barn door.

"Potato soup?" Lizzie said, her mind still focused on the sermon.

Abby laughed. "I know it's a bit fancier than our normal fare of bread and peanut butter, but I'm feeling extra domestic lately. All I want to do is cook and clean. Jakob says I'm *nesting*. He says it's normal for a woman in my condition to act this way."

Laughing at Abby's enthusiasm, Lizzie let herself be

pulled along. She could just imagine how fun it must be to anticipate her first child. But that thought brought her another bout of confusion, sadness and guilt.

Inside the kitchen, a dozen women crowded around, helping prepare the food. Their identical dresses were simple but pretty in assorted colors of blue, burgundy, purple and green. Each woman wore a pair of black, sensible hard-soled shoes, and a starched organdy *kapp*. Lizzie thought there was something lovely and serene about their simplistic dress.

Naomi Fisher stood slicing loaves of homemade bread in front of the counter while Sarah Yoder laid dill and sweet pickles on a plate. Abby stirred an enormous silver pot on the stove as Lizzie reached for a large serving bowl.

"I'll ladle the soup into the bowl and you can serve it hot to the men." Abby picked up a long ladle and dipped it into the frothy, white soup.

Lizzie nodded, sliding on a pair of oven mitts to protect her hands from the heat. Lifting the bowl, she held it steady while Abby ladled it full. The warm, tantalizing aroma made Lizzie's mouth water.

"Um, it smells delicious," Lizzie said.

"*Danke*. I crumbled bits of bacon and shredded cheese into it. It's one of Jakob's favorite dishes. It'll go well with Naomi's crusty homemade bread," Abby said.

"Did you see Eli Stoltzfus listening to the bishop's sermon? I hope it sank in. That boy needs to mend his ways, that's for sure."

Lizzie looked up and saw elderly Marva Geingerich standing next to Linda Hostetler. The two women were unwrapping trenchers of sliced cheese and ham. Slightly deaf at the age of eighty-nine, Marva's rasping attempt at a whisper carried like a shout across the kitchen and everyone paused in their work. Especially Fannie, Eli's mother.

"*Ja*, I saw him. He's trying hard to fit back into the *Gmay* and doing a good job of it from what I can see," Linda said.

Marva's thin lips curved in disapproval. "*Ach*, I don't know why he ever came back. Once they leave and get a taste of the *Englisch* world, they never can get rid of it. I've seen it happen several times."

Something hardened inside of Lizzie. Though she was angry at Eli, she didn't like what she was hearing. It wasn't fair and it wasn't right.

"Marva! What are you saying?" Naomi paused in her slicing, her forehead creased with a frown.

"He won't stay long, you mark my words," Marva said. "As soon as that boy gets tired of living our humble way of life, he'll be off again to live among the *Englisch*."

"You don't know that. Eli returned of his own choosing. He wants to be here with us." Sarah Yoder, the bishop's wife, set a casserole dish on the wooden counter with a thump.

Marva jerked her head up, the wrinkles around her gray eyes deepening with her scowl. "*Ach*, he's been gone too long. Who knows what wickedness he's been up to? I don't know how he'll ever fit in with the *Gmay* now. No doubt he's got plenty to repent of. Mark my words, he'll leave again and that will be that."

An audible gasp filled the room and Lizzie flinched.

Turning, she saw the reason why. Eli stood in the doorway, holding an empty glass in one hand. His expression looked peaceful as a summer's morning, but Lizzie knew he'd overheard the conversation and must be upset. It was there in the subtle narrowing of his eyes and the tensing of his shoulders. Other people might not notice, but Lizzie knew him too well. For just a moment, she saw a flash of anger in his eyes, then it was gone and she thought perhaps she'd imagined it.

He cleared his voice, speaking in a composed tone. "I'm sorry to intrude, but Ezekiel has a cough. Could I trouble someone for a glass of water?"

Ezekiel, or *Dawdi* Zeke as most everyone called him, was the eldest member of the *Gmay*. Having just turned ninety-four years, he still had an active mind and was as kind and compassionate as Marva was harsh and unforgiving.

"Of course you can." Naomi, who was *Dawdi* Zeke's daughter, took the glass from Eli's hand, filled it with tap water, then handed it back to him.

"Danke." He ducked his head and left without another word.

Everyone stared in mortified confusion, not knowing what to say. A part of Lizzie felt compassion for Eli and the urge to run after him. But another part thought it was just what he deserved. That made her feel worse because it wasn't charitable to think that way.

"How could you say those things? It wasn't very nice. We should be more compassionate." Naomi shook her head, her expression showing her dismay as she gazed intently at Marva.

"I don't know what you mean. I only spoke the truth." Marva drew back her shoulders, pursed her lips and lifted her chin a little higher.

The hackles rose at the back of Lizzie's neck. Even if it was the truth, it wasn't kind. She would never consider belittling Eli to other members of the congregation on Church Sunday. It wasn't their place to judge him or anyone. Especially right after the bishop had preached to them about forgiveness and their upcoming Communion. But she couldn't help feeling like a hypocrite since Marva had voiced aloud her very same concerns.

Lizzie's gaze shifted to Fannie, Eli's mother. She had been cutting thick pieces of Schnitz apple pie but had dropped the knife onto the table when Marva had begun speaking. Looking at her now, Lizzie saw that her face had gone white as a sun-bleached sheet, her chin quivering.

"He's *mein sohn*. Do you really think he'll leave again?" she cried with naked fear.

Naomi quickly set her bread knife on the table before wrapping her arms around the other woman in a comforting hug. "*Ne*, it's nonsense! Don't you listen to such talk, Fannie. Eli fits in here with all of us just fine. He's one of our own and a welcome addition to our community. We love him and we're blessed to have him back. Look at all the *gut* he's done already for the Beiler *familye*. Isn't that right, Lizzie?"

Naomi looked at her and Lizzie blinked in stunned silence before stuttering over a reply. "*Ja*, he…he's been very kind."

"And who are we to judge others? We all have our faults. We are all happy that Eli has returned to his faith." Sarah nodded her approval.

"*Danke.*" Fannie wiped one eye, showing a tremulous smile of appreciation.

"Humph! We'll see." Marva huffed as she carried a tray of sliced homemade bread outside.

Swallowing hard, Lizzie realized she was staring. Her

mind whirled in confusion. Seeing the hurt on Fannie's face, she hurried over to comfort the woman.

"Don't listen to such talk. Eli loves you and Leroy. He wants to be here with you," Lizzie said, trying to believe her own words.

"But what if Marva is right? What if Eli leaves again? I don't know what I'd do. He's our only *sohn*," Fannie whispered.

A tremor ran down Lizzie's spine, but she fought off her own fears and tried to be brave. "If he leaves, we'll do as Christ taught and turn the other cheek. We'll exercise faith and face whatever comes our way and pray that he'll come back again. We can never give up on anyone."

Speaking these words aloud brought Lizzie a bit of courage. She meant what she said, yet her heart thumped with trepidation.

"I just don't think I can stand to lose him again." Tears shimmered in Fannie's eyes.

"We'll all be here for you, no matter what happens," Lizzie said.

Fannie nodded, but her sad expression still showed her unease as she returned to her chore of slicing pie.

Lizzie watched her, her own hands shaking.

Abby laid a hand on her arm. "Lizzie, are you all right?"

She gave a stuttering laugh. "*Ja*, I'm fine."

What else could she say? Only Eli knew if he would stay or go. Any member of their community could leave at any time, including her. Lizzie just wished she could be certain she wouldn't be hurt by his decisions.

"Don't worry," Abby said to her. "It'll be all right. *Komm* on. Let's get out of here. I need some fresh air."

Lizzie followed her friend outside, the screen door

clapping closed behind them. They paused beneath the shade of the back porch. Children raced across the yard in a game of chase. Teenaged boys stood in a group, watching the teenaged girls. The afternoon sun sparkled in an azure sky. Lizzie wanted to cherish such a day…one of the last warm ones before the cooler weather rolled in. As she gazed at the rows of men sitting at the long tables, she let their subdued laughter soothe her ruffled feelings.

"I can't believe Marva said those horrible things. What was she thinking? She has such a waspish tongue," Abby whispered, her hands gripping the soup ladle like a hammer. "She's never been happy since her son brought the *familye* here from Ohio after his *vadder* died. She understands about repentance and forgiveness and should know better than to speak that way."

"Marva is rather stern," Lizzie agreed in a vague tone, once again feeling like a hypocrite.

"Jakob told me you and Eli were engaged once. I hope her words didn't upset you too badly," Abby said.

Lizzie shrugged as she gripped the serving bowl tighter, letting the soup warm her chilled hands. "That was a long time ago."

"Are you still friends with him now that he's returned?" Abby peered at her, as though looking deep inside her heart.

Biting her bottom lip, Lizzie couldn't meet Abby's gaze.

"Oh, Lizzie. I'm so sorry." Abby squeezed her arm. "His return must be difficult for you. And to have him working at your farm every day… But don't forget to keep an open heart and have faith. *Gott* will care for you both and all will work out fine. I know it will."

Lizzie couldn't manage to muster a smile in return. "I'm not so sure."

Resting her palm against her baby bump, Abby rubbed gently. "With my past history, I never would have believed *Gott* could make my life turn out so well. I thought I could never trust men and would never marry. But I soon learned that I was wrong. Give *Gott* a chance and He'll work so many blessings in your life, just as He did mine."

Lizzie understood. Since her marriage to Jakob, Abby had confided that she'd been physically and verbally abused by her father and elder brother. Abby was so happy now and Lizzie was glad. But she almost dropped the serving bowl when Abby turned and headed straight over to the table where Eli was sitting.

Breathing a sigh of resignation, Lizzie followed her friend, but couldn't help wondering if this day could get any worse. She wanted to turn the other cheek. To forget her pain and humiliation and believe that Eli truly was back for good. But she couldn't help thinking that Marva was right about one thing. Eli wouldn't stay.

"When did you cut your leg on the hay baler?"

Eli sat at the table next to Darrin Albrecht, their deacon. The autumn sun beat down on the men, but they'd each removed their black felt hats for their noon meal. They spoke in companionable friendship, waiting as the women set the food before them.

A rather hefty and somber man, Darrin was middle-aged with a thick head of salt-and-pepper hair and a long beard to match. As the deacon, it was his job to assist the bishop in disciplinary issues, to ensure that all members of the *Gmay* were following the rules of the *Ordnung* and to announce upcoming marriages.

"It's been two months since it happened and it wasn't even a bad cut. I can't understand why it's taking so long to heal," Darrin said.

Out of his peripheral vision, Eli caught sight of Lizzie standing just behind his left shoulder. She held a large, steaming dish, the aroma tantalizing. He leaned back, giving her and Abby room to scoop soup into his bowl. Along with the other women, they worked in silence, seeing to everyone's needs before their own. Glancing up, he saw Lizzie's face looked pale. She'd been in the kitchen earlier and he couldn't help wondering if she agreed with Marva Geingerich's opinion of him.

He clamped a hard will on his anger. When he'd returned, he'd known he might face disapproval from some of his people. It didn't change anything. He wanted to be here. And that meant he must exercise self-discipline, control his feelings and remain passive in the face of adversity. It's what the Lord would want him to do.

"Are you all right?" he asked Lizzie, worried that she and his mother were both overly upset by what had transpired.

"*Ja*, of course. Why wouldn't I be?" Before he could answer, she ducked her head and moved on to Deacon Albrecht's bowl.

Turning, Eli faced Darrin. "May I see your wound?"

He was conscious of Lizzie moving to the other side of the table as she served the other men, still close enough to overhear his conversation.

Beneath the table, Darrin hiked up his homemade pant leg to the knee. A gauze bandage had been affixed to the side of his lower calf with white tape. Eli ducked down and Darrin lifted the gauze to reveal a thin, jagged cut no more than an inch long. Though it didn't look deep, the wound was swollen and angry red.

"*Ach*, I have no doubt it's infected." Eli wasn't a medical doctor, but he recognized a septic injury when he saw one.

"Norma cleans it for me every day with hydrogen peroxide and ointment, but it doesn't seem to make any difference." Darrin pressed the bandage back in place and pulled his pant leg down.

Sitting up straight, Eli considered the man for a moment. "Have you seen a doctor about it?"

"*Ne*! There's no need for that. I don't trust those *Englisch* doctors." Darrin waved a hand in the air, then buttered a thick slice of bread.

Eli watched the man as he lifted his glass and smiled at Lizzie. Setting the serving bowl of soup down, she picked up a pitcher of water and refilled his glass...which Darrin had emptied for the third time since they'd sat down twenty minutes earlier. Several women from the congregation hovered nearby to keep the men's plates and glasses filled.

"You seem overly thirsty today," Eli said as he lifted a spoonful of soup to his mouth.

"*Ja*, he's always thirsty lately, even when he's not working in the fields." Linda Albrecht set a plate of sliced ham in front of them. She must have come outside while they were engaged in conversation.

"What about fatigue? Are you feeling more tired than usual?" Eli asked.

Darrin inclined his head. "Now that you mention it, I am more tired, even when I've had a full night's sleep. And sometimes, my feet feel numb too. Do you think the cut could be causing that?"

Eli took a deep inhale and let it go. This didn't sound good. "I'd feel better if you saw the doctor as soon as possible."

"That's what I suggested, but he won't go," Linda said, resting her hands on her hips as she tossed her husband an *I told you so* look.

"*Ach*, I'm fine. I'm sure the wound will heal eventually," Darrin insisted.

Eli met the man's eyes and touched his arm to make his point clear. "I think you're wrong, Deacon Albrecht. Please, go see the doctor. I don't want to alarm you, but you should ask him to test you for diabetes. If you've got diabetes, chances are it's probably keeping your wound from healing, which could cause other serious problems down the road. Don't take chances with your health. You want to be around to take care of your *familye* for many years to come."

Linda widened her eyes and pressed a hand to her chest. "Oh, my! Diabetes?"

Eli nodded. "He has some of the symptoms, but don't take my word for it. Let the doctor diagnose it for you. He'll be able to run some blood tests and let you know for sure. If the test is positive, he'll prescribe medication to control the problem. At the very least, he can ensure that wound on your leg doesn't turn gangrenous."

Linda gasped. "Gangrene?"

Darrin pursed his mouth, looking doubtful. Because Eli believed the man had a serious health problem, he pressed the issue further. "I'm dead serious about this, Deacon Albrecht. Go to the doctor first thing tomorrow morning. Please, do as I ask."

Darrin must have heard the urgency in his voice because his mouth dropped open. "You really mean it, don't you, Eli?"

Eli nodded emphatically. "I absolutely do. I want you to get some proper medical help."

"*Ja*, don't you worry. We will go first thing after our morning chores," Linda said. She was looking at her husband with a stern, wifely expression that would tolerate no refusals.

Knowing Linda would make Darrin go to the doctor, Eli felt relieved. He smiled and switched topics to the price of hay. When he reached for his empty glass, he caught Lizzie standing nearby. A disapproving expression drew her eyebrows together, but she hurried to fill his glass.

"*Danke*," he said.

"*Gaern gscheh.*" She seemed both surprised and critical of what he'd told Deacon Albrecht. No doubt she disapproved.

She walked away and Eli longed to call her back. To tell her of the extensive training he'd received in order to become a paramedic and that he knew what he was talking about. But these people would not be impressed. Nor did he want to sound boastful. After all, his training was from the Lord so he could serve others. It wasn't a matter of pride.

And he was glad he had it—and could use it to help the deacon. Though Eli wasn't positive Darrin Albrecht had diabetes, he was absolutely certain of one thing. If the man didn't get quality medical care soon, his wound could fester into gangrene and he'd lose his leg and possibly his life. But how could he tell Lizzie that? How could he explain that he only had the Deacon Albrecht's best interests at heart?

"Eli, if you're finished eating, will you help us out?"

Jarred from his thoughts, Eli turned to find Martin Hostetler standing next to him, a wide smile on his face.

"Come play volleyball with us. We need another player to complete two teams and, as I recall, you are good at it." Martin tossed a white ball high into the air, then caught it.

Deacon Albrecht smiled. "Go on, Eli. You'll have more fun with your young friends than sitting here with me."

Eli stood and turned toward the lawn. A net was tied across the grass, affixed to two long poles that had been cemented into old tires. Lizzie stood in front of the net. Seeing her, a feeling of anticipation zipped through Eli. Obviously she'd been recruited too. It had been years since he'd played volleyball…back when he and Lizzie were kids and still crazy in love with each other.

Walking over to the net with Martin, Eli glanced at the other unmarried people surrounding him. They seemed to be paired up on two sides. Some were as young as eleven years, while a few were as old as him and Martin.

Lizzie stood gripping her hands together, looking suddenly shy.

"Which side am I on?" Eli asked.

"You'll be on this side." Martin pointed to Lizzie's team and Eli saw her immediate frown.

She turned away, stepping to the back row, but Martin placed Eli right beside her. From where he stood beneath the shade of a tall elm tree, Bishop Yoder showed a satisfied smile. Eli couldn't help wondering if the man had rigged this to get him near Lizzie. Everyone knew they'd been engaged once. No doubt some of the congregation was trying to pair them back together. One look at Lizzie's wary gaze told him it wouldn't work.

She turned aside, seeming to focus on the other team

as they served. She jumped gracefully, her hands fisted together as she struck the ball. From there, Eli knocked it easily over the net, scoring a point for their team.

Several of their teammates clapped their hands and cheered, but Lizzie stood silent. The ball was served again and volleyed back and forth for several minutes, then it zipped directly toward Eli. He hit the ball lightly, offering a layup to Lizzie, just like he'd done when they were teenagers. Instead of spiking the ball over the net, Lizzie jumped back and let the ball hit the ground. It rolled onto the graveled driveway and one of the younger children chased after it.

The other team cheered.

"Tied points," Martin called from in front of the net. Facing Eli, the redheaded man smiled wide, but there was no malice in his expression. He was merely having fun.

"I thought you would spike the ball, like you used to do," Eli spoke low for Lizzie's ears alone.

"I… I didn't see it soon enough," she returned, sounding slightly irritated.

Eli didn't know if she was flustered by his presence, or if dropping the ball was her way of rejecting him. He couldn't help thinking about what Jakob had said earlier. Did Lizzie still harbor resentment toward him for breaking off their engagement when he left all those years ago?

"Are you sure you're all right?" he asked her while the other team readjusted their positions so they could serve the ball.

"Of course, why?"

Yes, he definitely caught a note of exasperation in her tone.

He shrugged. "No reason, really. I just noticed that

you seemed annoyed when I was speaking with Deacon Albrecht and now again."

Her slim jaw hardened. "You're not a doctor, Eli. But I can see you gained plenty of *Hochmut* from going to college. You seem to think you know what is good for everyone."

So that was it. Like many of their people, she didn't approve of higher learning. She thought he was too prideful.

"I don't think that at all. I only want to help, Lizzie-bee. That's why I told Deacon Albrecht to go see a doctor as soon as possible…so he can get an accurate diagnosis," he said.

Releasing a heavy sigh, she turned away and focused on the game. She did an admirable job of ignoring him. No doubt she agreed with Marva Geingerich, that he would leave again. And how could he persuade her that he really wanted to stay in Riverton when he hadn't yet convinced himself?

They won the game, but Lizzie hurried off to help in the kitchen before a second match began. Karen Hostetler, who was Martin's eighteen-year-old sister, and Ellen Yoder, the bishop's daughter, both smiled prettily at him. In between serving the ball, they engaged Eli in conversation. He tried to show interest, but his gaze kept roaming over to the house where he sought some sight of Lizzie. After the second game ended, the teams broke up. Eli was glad. He had no interest in playing volleyball. At least, not without Lizzie.

He didn't see her again until it was time to drive her and the little girls home that evening. Though he wanted to head back before it got too late, he had to stay a little longer so he could attend the instruction class with the two others who were planning to be baptized in a few months. As Eli listened to the lesson from Bishop Yoder, he liked what he heard, but felt a bit nervous when he considered its importance. Once he was baptized into the Amish faith, his life would change forever. He would not take the vows unless he was absolutely confident that he intended to live them for the rest of his life.

On their way home, Marty and Annie were eager to chat about their day. As the buggy moved along at a rapid pace, Lizzie sat quietly with her hands in her lap. Eli longed to talk with her about his class, to get her opinion on several issues, but whenever he tried to engage her in conversation, her response was rather abrupt. Finally, he gave up trying.

As they pulled into the farmyard, dusk was settling over the western sky with clouds of pink, orange and gray. He looked up at the tall Sangre de Cristo Mountains and thought he'd never seen anything so beautiful in all his life. He had just enough time to milk the cows and head home to his parents before it turned dark.

"*Danke* for driving us safely," little Annie said.

"*Ja, danke* for keeping your promise," Marty agreed.

The girls both smiled and hugged him, but Lizzie simply nodded, then went inside the house.

Watching her go, a feeling of melancholy blanketed Eli and he wondered what he could do to improve her opinion of him. It seemed that she'd lost all faith in him, and he couldn't really blame her. But that's when he made a promise to himself. No matter how long it took, he was determined to regain her trust. He just wasn't certain how.

Chapter Four

By noon the following morning, Eli had almost finished raking the alfalfa. Dust sifted through the air as the two-horse hitch plodded along with the patience of Job. The tines connecting to the four horizontal bars of the side rake moved in a circular motion as they rolled the hay into straight, tidy windrows. The action also fluffed and turned the hay, so it would dry well before they baled it tomorrow. Eli was eager to get the hay in as quickly as possible. The unseasonable warmth wouldn't hold much longer. He figured they had one or two more days before the clouds rolled in and brought rain to the valley.

Glancing toward the farmhouse, he saw Lizzie outside hanging clothes on the line. They hadn't spoken since church and he felt the tension between them reaching clear across the field.

Annie was helping her older sister, lifting damp clothes out of the white laundry basket to hand over to Lizzie. Marty stood nearby, gathering seeds from the dried marigolds that had grown all summer long in the flowerbeds surrounding the house. Above the rattling noise of the hay rake, Eli could catch hints of the happy sound of their laughter.

The rake gave a little bump and he turned to face forward, focusing on his work. When he finished twenty minutes later, he pulled the draft horses to a halt, lifted the horizontal bars, then drove the Percherons toward the barn. Lizzie was no longer in the yard and he figured she'd gone into the house with the girls.

He deposited the rake in the barn, then cared for the horses. After watering the Percherons, he checked each of their hooves, bodies and heads. If one of them picked up a stone or had a wound of some kind, they wouldn't be much use in baling tomorrow morning. It'd take all six draft horses to pull the heavy baler and hay wagon.

Satisfied the animals were in good condition, he turned them loose in the pasture. Before he went up to the house for some lunch, he entered the cool shadows of the barn. Removing his straw hat, he wiped his forehead on his shirtsleeve and sat on a tall stool.

Another letter had arrived from Tom Caldwell, his old boss at the hospital in Denver. Pulling the short letter from the envelope, Eli read it one more time. Tom knew about Shannon's death and understood that Eli had been badly shaken by the accident. Tom had encouraged him to take and break and go home for a visit. But now, Tom was shorthanded and badly needed qualified paramedics. In his letter, he'd offered Eli a raise if he would return to work by the end of October. Eli had already sent his regrets. He was not at all certain he'd ever return to Denver—but he definitely wouldn't be going back that soon. After all, Jeremiah wouldn't be healed enough to work by that time and Eli had given his word to the bishop that he would care for the farm until then.

"Eli?"

He jerked around, dropping the letter in the process. The paper wafted to the ground and he scooped it up, shoving it into his hat.

"What's that you're reading?" Lizzie stood in front of the double doors, holding a tray with a plate of food and tall glass of milk. A shaft of sunlight glimmered behind her, highlighting her in beams of gold.

"Nothing of consequence."

A flush of heat rose in his face. It was bad enough that his parents knew he was receiving letters and were worried his *Englisch* friends might draw him back to Denver. If only he didn't feel so conflicted. Helping Deacon Albrecht yesterday had felt so good and familiar, but he couldn't tell Lizzie that, nor his parents either. Not after what Marva Geingerich had said. They might judge him harshly. If only Shannon were here. She would advise him in that soft, understanding manner of hers. But if she were still alive, he would never have come home.

"Is it a letter?" Lizzie stepped closer, setting the tray on a low ledge of timber.

He placed the hat on his head. "*Ja*, a letter."

Her eyes crinkled with concern. "A letter from whom?"

"An old friend in Denver," he said, trying to sound unruffled.

She tilted her head to one side, her eyes narrowing. "An *Englisch* friend?"

He nodded, unwilling to lie. Except for his love for Shannon, it seemed he couldn't keep any secrets from this woman. When they'd been young, she was the only one who had known of his desire to go to college. She hadn't told a soul and, because of that, he'd thought she'd understand when he left. That she might even join him. But he had been dead wrong.

She took a deep breath, then let it go in a slow sigh. "What do they want?"

The moment she asked the question, she blinked and flushed with embarrassment. She lifted a hand to nervously adjust her white *kapp*. He almost laughed at the feminine gesture, unable to keep from admiring her graceful fingers, or the way her blue eyes darkened.

"I'm sorry. I shouldn't have asked that. It's none of my business. I brought you something to eat." She turned and gestured to the tray.

He cleared his throat, feeling like he'd swallowed sandpaper. "Was there…was there something else you wanted?"

She nodded, meeting his eyes again. "*Ja*, I was waiting until you finished raking the hay. I know that's the priority right now. But I was wondering if you might have time to drive the *maed* and me into town to visit our *vadder* at the hospital this afternoon."

Ah, so she still wasn't over the shock of the accident and still didn't feel confident enough to drive herself. He thought about teasing her, but sensed it was difficult for her to confide this weakness to him. Besides, he liked having something normal and mundane to distract him from the conflict waging a war inside his mind.

"Of course. I'd be happy to drive you and the *kinder*," he said.

"*Gut*. We'll be ready to leave as soon as you've eaten. I also wanted to stop off at Ruth Lapp's house. She wasn't at church because she has bronchitis, so I thought I'd take a meal to her *familye*. Nothing fancy. Just a casserole and some pumpkin muffins."

Yum! Pumpkin muffins. His mouth watered at the thought. He glanced at the plate she'd brought him, noticing she'd included a muffin with thick cream cheese icing for him too. "That's very kind of you."

In fact, her generosity reminded him of why he'd returned. Because he loved this way of life. The way his people looked after one another. Their generosity and devotion to what they believed was right. He realized that even old Marva Geingerich's biting comments were made out of fear that he might leave again, which would hurt those he left behind. A part of him wanted to stay, just to prove her wrong. To show the *Gmay* how much he loved it here.

"But I'll need to leave early tonight," he said.

"Oh?" She cocked an eyebrow.

"I need to drive to Bishop Yoder's house. He's helping me make up for lost time, so I can catch up with the other students planning to be baptized in a few months. I still need to read the articles of the Dordrecht Confession."

"*Ach*, you didn't read them the last time you took the classes, before you left?"

"*Ne*, I'm afraid not."

"Then of course you must go. That's very important. You won't want to be late. We'll only be gone long enough to pay a quick visit to *Daed* and drop off the meal," she said.

"*Gut.*"

They gazed at each other and the silence lengthened. In the past, they'd never had a lack of things to say to each other. Even silences had been comfortable between them. But not anymore.

Putting her hands behind her back, Lizzie scuffed the

toe of her shoe against the ground. "*Ach*, I guess I'd better get back to the house and get the *kinder* ready to leave."

"*Ja*, I'll bring the buggy out in a few minutes."

With one final nod, she whirled around and was gone, leaving him feeling suddenly very empty inside.

As Lizzie hurried to the house, she thought it might have been a mistake to ask Eli to drive her and the girls into town. It seemed silly that she couldn't drive herself. And yet, she still felt too nervous. But more than that, she hated to admit that Eli's presence brought her a great deal of comfort. She liked having him here and that was dangerous on so many levels. More than anything, she had to protect her heart. Because she couldn't stand the pain of loving and losing him again.

Within ten minutes, she had the kitchen tidied and the children ready to leave. Standing on the front porch with Marty, she held a large basket containing the promised meal for the Lapps inside. She'd also tucked a couple of pumpkin muffins in for her father, although she wasn't sure if he had any diet restrictions. If so, she'd give them to the nurses.

The rattle of the buggy brought her head up and she saw Eli driving Ginger toward them from the barn.

"*Komm* on, Annie. We're going to see *Daed*," Marty called excitedly.

Annie came running, a huge smile on her face. In her excitement, she slammed the front door behind her. "*Ach*, I can't wait. It's been forever since we saw *Daed*."

Lizzie smiled at her exuberance and tugged playfully on one of the ribbons to her *kapp*. "It's only been a few days, *bensel*."

The child hopped on one foot with excitement. "It feels like forever. I can't wait for *Daed* to come home."

Neither could Lizzie. For some reason, she felt more vulnerable with him gone. More dependent upon Eli. She'd have to correct that problem soon. She couldn't rely on Eli forever.

They settled into the buggy with Eli holding the lead lines in his strong hands. There was something restive in watching him work with the horse. Though he displayed self-confidence, he was quiet and respectful, seeming lost in his own thoughts.

"When do you think Billie will be ready to drive again?" she asked.

He stared straight ahead as he responded. "Physically, I think he's ready now, but I'm not sure how he'll respond up on the county road. Tomorrow, I'll take him out alone, to make sure he doesn't panic when cars and trucks whiz by us."

How insightful. It hadn't occurred to Lizzie that the horse might also be skittish around motorized vehicles now. It figured that Eli was perceptive enough to realize this and considerate enough to drive the horse alone, so no one else would get hurt if the animal bolted.

"I appreciate that," she said.

He shrugged one shoulder. "It's no problem. I'm happy to help out."

Yes, that was just the problem. His kindness and generosity to her *familye* made it difficult to be angry with him. Yet, she didn't dare forget.

Marty scooted forward from the back seat and leaned against Lizzie's shoulder. "Do you think *Daed* will be able to come home with us today?"

"I don't know, *boppli*. I doubt it. We'll have to see what the doctor says."

Not to be left out, Annie nudged her way in and leaned against Eli. "How long will *Daed* have to stay in the hospital? I miss him."

Lizzie reached up and squeezed Annie's hand. "Like I said, we won't know until we talk to the doctor. I know we all miss *Daed*, but he's going to be all right and we'll see him soon. Now, sit back and give Eli room to drive."

Satisfied with this reassurance, the girls smiled and sat back. Eli glanced Lizzie's way and his soft smile made her heart skip a couple of beats in spite of herself.

Along their way, they stopped off at the Lapps' modest farmhouse to deliver the food. As Eli pulled up out front, Lizzie faced him.

"Since Ruth is so sick, will you keep the *kinder* out here with you, please? I don't want them to catch her illness. I'll only be a minute," she said.

Marty and Annie frowned, but didn't say anything. No doubt they were hoping to play with Ruth's children.

Eli ducked his head in assent. "Of course."

Lizzie nodded and hopped out of the buggy. When she reached back, Eli handed her the basket.

Moments later, Ruth answered the door. She was fully dressed, but her apron was stained and slightly crooked. There were dark circles beneath her eyes, her hair coming loose from her *kapp*, and her nose was bright red. In one hand, she clutched several tissues. With her other hand, she bounced her toddler on her hip, the little boy holding a full bottle of milk.

"Lizzie! It's nice of you to visit." Ruth covered her mouth as she gave a hacking cough that sounded like it rattled something deep down in her lungs. "I don't dare let you in. I fear I'd only give you my cold and then you'd pass it on to your entire *familye*."

"You should try a humidifier. That might help you to breathe easier," Lizzie suggested.

Trying not to be obvious, she glanced behind Ruth, noting that everything inside the house looked in fairly good order. Two older children sat on the sofa, quietly reading books. The baby seemed well cared for too. Except that she didn't feel well, Ruth seemed to be coping and seeing to the needs of her *familye*.

"*Ja*, I have one running now," Ruth said.

"*Gut*. I won't stay, but I wanted to help in some way. At least you won't have to cook *nachtesse* tonight." Lizzie handed over the basket.

"*Ach*, that's so kind of you. You're a *gut* friend." Ruth took the basket with her free hand and smiled as she jutted her chin toward the buggy. "Is that Eli Stoltzfus I see in the buggy?"

Lizzie nodded, her senses flaring. "*Ja*, it is."

"You're back together then?"

Lizzie automatically stiffened. "*Ne*, he's just helping out at the farm while my *vadder* is laid up."

"*Ja*, I heard something about Jeremiah being injured. I'm so glad you and the girls are safe and hope Jeremiah is better soon." Ruth set the basket on a table before shifting the baby to her other hip. "It'd be so nice if you and Eli got back together, though."

Lizzie didn't know what to say, so she chose to ignore the comment by smiling brilliantly. "If you need anything at all, you just let me know."

"I will." Ruth nodded.

"I'll check on you again in a few days," Lizzie promised, stepping down off the porch.

"*Danke* so much." Ruth waved to the occupants of the buggy before going inside and shutting the door.

Whew! Thankfully, Ruth didn't push the issue. Lizzie wasn't prepared to answer questions about her and Eli. They weren't getting back together, but it poked at old wounds to go around telling everyone that.

As she climbed into the buggy, Eli reached out and pulled her up. The grip of his hand around hers felt strong yet gentle. She quickly sat and smoothed her skirts before he clicked his tongue and the horse took off again.

"What you just did was very *gut*. You're a kind example for your *schweschdere*." He glanced back at the two little girls.

"*Danke*." Lizzie didn't know what else to say. She hadn't sought his approval and yet she couldn't help feeling suddenly very happy inside. She told herself it was because she'd just done an act of service to someone in need, but she knew it was something more. Something she didn't understand.

They didn't speak for most of the remaining journey into town. Following the traffic light on Main Street, Eli pulled up in front of the hospital and climbed out.

As he took Lizzie's arm to help her down, he looked rather stoic. "I'll let you go inside to visit your *vadder* while I tie the horse."

Hmm. Obviously he wasn't eager to see Jeremiah. That suited Lizzie just fine.

"*Danke*." She beckoned to her sisters.

As they hurried up the steps, the automatic double doors whooshed open. Lizzie glanced over her shoulder and saw Eli back inside the buggy and pulling away.

Inside the small hospital, the air smelled of overdone meatloaf and antiseptic. Several people sat in the reception area, gawking at Lizzie and the girls. No doubt they found their Amish clothing a bit strange. Lizzie was used to such stares and ignored them as she approached the front reception desk.

"We're here to visit our father," she spoke in perfect English.

A nurse wearing a blue smock and pants smiled pleasantly. "Oh, I'll guess you're Jeremiah Beiler's daughters."

"Yes, that's right," Lizzie said.

"The doctor is with him right now. Room eighteen just down the hallway." The nurse pointed the way.

Taking Annie's and Marty's hands, Lizzie led them down the hall, the click of her shoes echoing behind. A man wearing a white smock stood just inside the room, a stethoscope hanging from his neck.

"*Ach*, here are my girls now."

Jeremiah lay in a hospital bed covered with a white sheet. His broken leg lay flat on the mattress, but cradled by pillows and a blanket.

"*Daedi!*" Both Annie and Marty ran to their father, hugging his neck tight.

He chuckled and kissed them each on the forehead. "I'm so glad to see you *maed*. Have you missed me?"

"*Ja*, something fierce, *Daed*," Marty said.

"And have you been *gut* for Lizzie?"

"*Ja, Daed*. We're helping her all we can," Annie said.

He laughed again and glanced at the doctor, who grinned at the two little imps. Lizzie smiled and nodded respectfully as her father introduced her to Dr. McGann. She'd heard good things about the man from other members of the Amish community. He wasn't pushy and seemed genuinely concerned for their welfare. Just the kind of man she wanted to care for her father.

"When can you come home?" Marty asked, her voice anxious.

Jeremiah looked at the doctor and lifted one hand. "You see? I told you I have a lot of support at home. Can't I go there to recuperate?"

Dr. McGann shook his head. "I'm afraid not yet. The swelling needs to go down before we can cast your leg. The orthopedic surgeon did a fine job in aligning the broken bones, but it was a serious break and you mustn't put any weight on the leg yet."

"How long will he need to stay here, Doctor?" Lizzie asked, wanting to do what was best for her father, but anxious for him to be where she could care for him.

"We'll have to see. Let's give it a few more days and go from there. Otherwise, your father is doing well and I see no reason why we shouldn't be able to rehabilitate his leg. But he won't be able to put any weight on the broken bones for at least six more weeks."

"Six weeks! So long?" she asked with amazement, thinking of all the chores awaiting them at home and how difficult it would be to keep her father down. Perhaps it was best for him to remain here at the hospital awhile longer.

Dr. McGann nodded. "I'm afraid so."

"Danke." Lizzie reminded herself that the results of the accident could have been much more serious.

Dr. McGann smiled at Marty and Annie. "Now, if it's all right with your sister, how would you two like a nice lollipop? I happen to know that Nurse Carter keeps a jar of them by her desk just for pretty girls like you."

The children looked at their elder sister, their eyes round and hopeful. "Can we have one, Lizzie? Please?" Annie said.

"*Ja*, I think that would be all right. But be sure to say thank you," Lizzie said.

The girls hurried toward the door and Dr. McGann accompanied them out of the room. "I'll bring them right back," he called over his shoulder.

"Thank you." Lizzie smiled her gratitude, then faced her father, grateful to have a few moments alone with him.

She moved in close to his bed and took his hand. He squeezed her fingers affectionately.

"How are you doing, really?" he asked.

She released a pensive sigh. "*Gut*. All is well, *vadder*. You needn't worry."

She quickly told him that the bishop had asked Eli to work their farm and all that the Stoltzfus *familye* had done for them.

"*Ja*, Bishop Yoder came to see me. He thinks having Eli work at the farm is the best thing for us right now."

"Eli and his *familye* have all been very kind."

Jeremiah listened quietly, his brows furrowed in a subtle frown. "I'm grateful to them, but I'm worried too."

"About what?"

He met her gaze, his expression austere. "You. Eli was always much too ambitious and prideful. He wants too much of the world. Don't forget that he left us once. He could do so again. Be wary of him."

Hearing these words, a dark foreboding settled over Lizzie.

"But he's returned now. He says he wants to stay this time. He's even taking the baptism lessons." She didn't know why she defended Eli, but it seemed an automatic response.

"I hope he does stay. But I've seen this happen before.

Once members of our faith leave the first time, it's easier to leave a second and third time. Just be careful. I don't want to lose you or see you get hurt again, Elizabeth."

Elizabeth. That alone told her that her father was quite serious. With good reason. Lizzie agreed that her father's concerns were legitimate, but his words sounded too much like Marva Geingerich's. Lizzie couldn't help thinking that everyone deserved a fair, ungrudging second chance. Even Eli. Of course, that didn't mean she loved him and wanted to marry him now. Both of them had grown far apart over the past four years. But she did hope that he found happiness and peace in service to the Lord.

"Has Eli raked the hay yet?" Jeremiah asked.

Lizzie nodded, relieved to change the topic. "He raked it just this morning, before we came into town. Even Deacon Albrecht complimented his work."

Jeremiah nodded. "*Gut.* I'm glad Eli hasn't forgotten how to farm."

They talked for several minutes more, then the girls returned with red-and-green lollipops. They stuck out their tongues, to show how they'd changed colors and they all laughed.

Remembering that Eli had to meet the bishop, Lizzie kept their visit short. They kissed their father goodbye, then walked out into the hall. Eli stood leaning against the wall, holding his black felt hat, his ankles crossed as he stared at the floor. When Lizzie and the girls appeared, he stood up fast, his brows drawn together in a thoughtful frown. Lizzie couldn't help wondering how long he'd been standing there and if he'd overheard her conversation with her father.

"Are you ready to go?" he asked, his voice subdued as he put his hat on his head.

"Ja, danke." She headed toward the outer door.

The two girls skipped along happily beside her as they licked their lollipops.

As always, Eli helped them into the buggy before walking around to the other side. Once they were all settled, he released the brake and called to the horse. As they lurched forward, they each seemed lost in their own thoughts. For the first time since the accident, the girls seemed comfortable riding in a buggy. They finally dozed off, a compliment to Eli and his safe driving. Lizzie felt drowsy too, but couldn't let down her guard enough to sleep. She wasn't really worried they might get hit by another car, but rather she couldn't stop thinking about what her father had said.

Be wary of Eli. It's easier to leave a second and third time.

Would Eli stay or go? Lizzie would never know for certain. Which was exactly why she intended to keep her distance from him.

Chapter Five

As planned, Lizzie and Eli baled hay the following morning, just as soon as the sun had evaporated the glistening dew from the earth. Standing on the baler, she tugged hard on the leather leads to turn the six-hitch team to the right.

"Gee!" she called.

The wagon lurched as the horses stepped forward. The baler trembled. Lizzie widened her stance on the platform to keep from tumbling over the thin railing onto the hard-packed earth.

She was thankful for Tubs and Chubs. As the two strongest horses, Lizzie had hitched them in the middle, providing an anchor and stability to the other four Percherons. The powerful animals leaned into their collars and plodded along without complaint. The soft jingle of their harness mingled with the dull thuds of their heavy hooves as they pulled the baler and hay wagon behind them.

The rattling hum of the gas-powered engine filled Lizzie's ears. The smell of freshly mowed hay was mingled with dust and chaff. She inhaled a slow breath and promptly sneezed. As she reached with one hand for the tissue she kept tucked inside the waist of her black apron, her hip bumped against the guardrail. Not a lot of protection, but it helped steady her on the baler.

She looked over her shoulder. With his legs planted firmly beneath him, Eli swayed easily on the flatbed hay wagon. Taking advantage of the brief lull while they turned the corner, he'd popped up the spout of a blue jug and drank deeply. Water droplets ran down his chin and corded throat before he wiped them away with the back of his hand. As he closed the spout, he looked up and met her gaze. She spun around, embarrassed to be caught staring. But honestly, she just couldn't help herself.

Straightening the horses out to pick up the cut alfalfa, she looked back at the baler. It started up again, churning and spitting out tidy square bales tied together with two strands of heavy twine. She stole a quick glance at Eli again, noticing how he pulled each bundle with ease, the muscles in his shoulders and arms flexing as he tossed the hefty bales onto the quickly expanding stack behind him.

Down one row and up the next, the hay bales piled up and soon filled the wagon. Only a few more rows to go and the hay would be in. No more worries about storm clouds. No more fears of not having the necessary feed for their livestock when the winter snows came deep and cold. No more fretting over…

"Ready to halt!" Eli called above the rumbling of the engine.

"Whoa!" Caught off guard, Lizzie tugged on the leads and the solid horses came to a smooth stop. They seemed unconcerned by this brief interlude, their docked tails swishing back and forth.

The baler and wagon jerked slightly and she looked back to make sure Eli was all right. He had no railing to keep him from falling off the wagon. If he couldn't keep up with the baler, it was her job to slow the horses. But Eli never seemed to have any problems and she couldn't believe how easily he had stepped back into the role of a farmer. If not for the constant ache in her heart, she could almost pretend that he'd never left at all.

He jumped down from the wagon and sauntered over to turn off the baler. "*Ach*, we've done fine work today. Another couple of hours and we'll be finished with the baling."

He flashed a dazzling smile that made his dark eyes sparkle and showed a dimple in his left cheek. Lizzie blinked and turned away, ignoring the swirl of butterflies in her stomach. She was not going to renew her feelings for this man. No, she was not.

She breathed steadily, trying to settle her nerves and enjoying the quiet break for a few moments. By nightfall, they'd be finished with the baling and she could relax. Almost. She wished she had a quiet heart, but worries about her father and all the work still needing to be done weighed heavily on her mind…not to mention her riotous feelings about Eli. In spite of her upbringing and learning to maintain a constant trust in the Lord, her mind felt burdened by doubts. Of course, she would never confess any of that out loud. She didn't want to worry her father or the bishop…or anyone else in the *Gmay*. She must have faith. All would be well. The Lord would care for them. Wouldn't He?

Eli hopped up onto the platform, standing shoulder-to-shoulder with her. She tried not to notice the warmth of his tall frame against her side, but found herself scrunching her arms so she didn't have to feel his sleeve brushing against her.

"May I?" he asked, reaching in front of her to take the lead lines.

She didn't argue as she handed them over. He flashed another smile and her heart gave an odd little thump.

"Schritt!" he called, slapping the leathers lightly against the horses' rumps.

The Percherons stepped forward and the baler gave a sudden wobble. Gripping the guardrail, Lizzie held on with whitened knuckles until they were moving at an even pace. For several moments, she stared at Eli's hands. His fingers were long, graceful and steady, the kind a surgeon would have in a medical office.

Mentally shaking herself, she adjusted the kerchief tied around her head. Because of their grimy work, she'd left her delicate prayer *kapp* in her room earlier that morning.

Within minutes, Eli pulled the horses up in front of the barn. He'd already opened the double doors in the top of the loft and the gas-powered hay elevator sat waiting for them. Marty and Annie came running from the house, but knew to stay out of the way. They watched from a safe distance, sitting on the rail fence in the shade by one of the corrals.

Looping the lead lines over the guardrail, Eli hopped off the baler platform. Lizzie went to join him, but was returning Annie's wave and not paying attention. She lost her balance and felt herself fall. Reaching out, her hands clasped at something, anything to break her fall.

"Oof!" She gasped as she dropped right into Eli's outstretched arms.

She felt the solid wall of his chest against her cheek

and heard his steady heartbeat in her ear. Her legs were twisted and she struggled for a moment to regain her footing.

"Are you all right?" he asked, the sound of his deep voice echoing through her entire body.

"I...*ja*, I'm fine."

She looked up and found his face no more than a breath away. Her gaze locked with his and she felt held there by a force she didn't understand. Nothing else existed but them.

Gradually, the farm sounds invaded her dazed brain. The mooing of a cow, the cluck of chickens scratching in the yard. She became aware of the horses and her sisters watching with avid interest. She was also highly conscious of Eli's solid arms clasped around her in a most improper display.

"Are you okay?" Marty called.

"*Ja*, I just lost my balance, that's all."

Lizzie pulled away from Eli and readjusted her apron and kerchief, trying to gather her composure. Trying to pretend she wasn't shocked to discover that she was still highly attracted to this man she could neither forgive nor forget.

Eli stepped back, but she caught the glint of hesitation in his eyes. His startled expression told her that he'd felt the physical attraction between them too. So. He wasn't as unaffected as he portrayed. Which gave her even more reason to keep her distance from him.

Turning aside, he tightened his leather gloves on his finger, then moved over to the hay elevator and started it up. The rattling sound jangled Lizzie's nerves even more. She longed to run to the house and seek sanctuary in her room until her body stopped quaking. But she couldn't leave. There was still work to be done.

That's when she realized why she was in such a foul mood. For some reason, she couldn't bring herself to remain detached from Eli. She told herself it was simply because of what they'd once meant to each other, but somehow she knew it was something more. Something she was having difficulty fighting. And she couldn't help thinking it would be a very long autumn working beside Eli until her father recuperated.

The following morning, Eli scooted the three-legged stool closer to the black-and-white Holstein and sat down. Hunching forward, he applied disinfectant, then set a sterilized silver bucket beneath the cow. With firm squeezes of his fingers, he shot darts of smooth white milk into the bucket. He soon set up an easy rhythm, the metallic whooshing sounds of milk hitting the pail easing the tension in his mind.

Lizzie sat adjacent to him, milking another cow. Marty and Annie were nearby, waiting to assist with pouring the full buckets into the tall canisters. Eli kind of enjoyed the little girls' incessant chatter and spurts of giggles. In the coziness of the barn, it was almost a tranquil moment, except that Lizzie had barely said two words to him.

"Meowww."

The lazy call of a gray barn cat drew his attention. Without changing his pace, Eli glanced over as the feline slinked its way into the barn. It moved languidly before sidling up against Eli's legs and rubbing its furry head against him in a cajoling manner. When Eli didn't acknowledge the cat, the feline lifted a paw and clawed several times at the hem of his broadfall pants.

Eli chuckled. "Look here, *maed*. Milo is trying to sweet-talk me into giving him some milk."

"Shoo, Milo! This milk isn't for you." Marty rushed at the cat, clapping her hands loudly.

Milo darted over to Lizzie, who had paused long enough to look up. She spared the cat barely a glance before returning to her milking. Milo stayed close by, watching them intently with green eyes.

Luna, a yellow tabby cat, came quickly into the barn with her tail high in the air. She nudged Milo, who greeted her by swatting at her face. Obviously, he didn't want competition in his quest for milk.

Undeterred, Luna sat close by, licking her chops and giving a disgruntled *yowl*. Both cats eyed the milk greedily. Eli smiled, but continued with his work. It soon became difficult to ignore the impatient squalls and growling coming from deep in the back of Milo's throat.

"Meow!"

"What a mournful cry. So pathetic. You'd think they were starving." Lizzie spoke without looking up.

"*Ach*, go away, Luna. You too, Milo. Scat, both of you!" Little Annie copied her sister by clapping her hands, but the felines barely spared the child a glance.

Neither cat was prepared to budge. When both animals started crying repeatedly, Eli finally took pity on them. With perfect aim, he shot a stream of milk, striking Milo directly in the face. The cat sat up on his hind legs and lapped milk off his whiskers. Eli was soon shooting jets of milk into both cats' mouths, one after the other.

Annie squealed with glee. "Look what Eli's doing."

Marty laughed openly at the sight. "How do you do that?"

Eli paused in feeding the two cats and noticed that

Lizzie had stopped her milking and was watching him quietly.

"I've had a lot of practice over the years. Doesn't your *vadder* spray milk at the cats?" Eli asked.

"*Ne*, he doesn't," Annie said.

"He'd probably say it was a waste of good milk," Marty said.

Eli shrugged as he shot another gush at the felines, catching them perfectly in the mouth. "The cats have to eat too."

"But they eat mice. That's their job and why they live out here in the barn," Marty said, placing one hand on her hip in a perfect mimic of Lizzie.

Eli laughed out loud. Both children glanced at Lizzie, as if seeking her opinion on the subject.

Lizzie blinked for a couple of moments, then showed a half smile. "It won't do any harm. Milo and Luna won't take enough milk to keep us from making our cheese and cream. And Eli is right. They have to eat too."

Eli was relieved. Though he knew she didn't approve of him, he didn't want to antagonize Lizzie.

He offered a bit more milk. The cats held their front paws aloft and greedily lapped up the treasure. The liquid dripped down the fronts of both animals and dampened their fur, but they didn't seem to mind. One shot caught Milo on the side of his face. He shook his head and made a funny expression before using his paws to wipe and lick off the milk.

Lizzie chuckled out loud. "I think Milo may have had too much already."

Her bright laughter caught Eli off guard. It did something to him inside…a reminder of what they'd once meant to each other and how much he'd loved her. But that was when they were little more than children. He hesitated, feeling mesmerized by her quiet beauty. Loose wisps of hair had come undone from beneath her prayer *kapp* and framed her delicate face. Her blue eyes danced with amusement, her soft lips curved in a smile.

This was the Lizzie he remembered from his childhood. This was the Lizzie he'd fallen in love with all those years earlier. And for just a moment, it was as if he'd never left. She was his Lizzie-bee, who laughed easily and had a warm sense of humor that exposed her intelligence and kindness. He couldn't help thinking of Shannon, who rarely laughed, but had a dry wit that could leave him in stitches. With her short chestnut curls and heavy features, she was so different from Lizzie. And yet, he'd loved them both at separate times in his life. But his feelings for Shannon had been more mature. More lasting. His love for Lizzie had been only a childish infatuation. Hadn't it?

"Do it again, Eli. Do it again," Annie encouraged.

Awakened from his mindless wandering, Eli took careful aim and shot more milk at the cats. When Luna started licking Milo's furry coat, they all laughed. Eli's attention was drawn to Lizzie's beaming face again. Her eyes were bright, her expression vibrant as she watched the barn cats' funny antics. She glanced up and her gaze locked with his. Then, she frowned, as if she'd remembered all the sadness that still lay between them.

"*Ach*, I think that's enough. We need to get back to work." Lizzie turned on her stool and returned to her milking.

Eli did likewise, noticing that the two cats had started licking themselves to clean every drop of milk off their fur.

Marty and Annie didn't complain as he handed off his

filled milk pail to them. He waited patiently as the girls carried it over to the tall container, lifted it and poured the contents in. While they were occupied with that chore, he glanced over at Lizzie and found her watching him. She jerked, looking embarrassed. Her bucket was also full and she hesitated, not seeming to know what to do with herself until the girls returned for her milk.

"It's good to hear you laugh again," Eli spoke low.

She swallowed and looked down at her shoes. "I laugh all the time."

No, she didn't. Not anymore. Not the deep, hearty laughter that exposed the joy she felt inside. In fact, the absence of her laughter was very telling. Very rarely did her eyes sparkle, or her lips curve up with amusement. Eli knew she wasn't happy. Not anymore. And he wasn't certain if it was because of him or because of the added responsibilities resting on her slender shoulders.

Maybe both.

"You used to laugh all the time," he said. "Remember when we went fishing together? We had a lot of fun then."

Her frown deepened. "That was a long time ago."

"It's just been four short years."

"It's been four long years," she said.

She looked away, her expression wistful and sad. He didn't need to ask why. It had been only four years, and yet it had been a lifetime. But more than that, his reminder had crushed the tenuous humor between them. Even the two cats frolicking in the hay couldn't get a smile out of Lizzie now.

Marty returned with his empty bucket and he ducked his head, resuming his milking. Out of his peripheral vision, he watched as the little girls emptied Lizzie's bucket and she moved on to the next cow. He longed to chat about inconsequential things as he worked, but didn't know what to say anymore. Lizzie seemed to feel the same way. She was overly quiet, as if she wished she were with anyone but him. They used to be so comfortable with each other. So natural and relaxed. Their discussions and laughter were spontaneous. And he felt suddenly very sorry that he and Lizzie had lost the camaraderie between them.

While the girls remained behind to feed the pigs and collect eggs, Lizzie finished her chores, then hurried to the house. Watching her go, Eli felt an emptiness inside his chest. It reminded him of how alone he really was and he missed Shannon more than ever before. His ruined relationship with Lizzie seemed to make his solitude even worse.

Chapter Six

A number of days later, Lizzie shook out a damp sheet and hung it over the clothesline. She quickly attached it at each end and put a couple of pins in the middle, to keep it from sagging to the ground. In spite of the chill in the air, morning sunlight gleamed across the yard, a mild breeze coming from the east. Red, gold and brown leaves fluttered to the ground. Maybe later that afternoon, she could get the girls to rake the front yard.

By noon, the laundry should be dry and ready to be ironed and put away. She took a deep inhale, enjoying the momentarily peaceful interlude and the beauty of the autumn leaves. Once the weather turned, she'd have to hang their clothes on racks inside the house to dry.

The rattle of a buggy caught her attention and she lifted her head toward the dirt road. Mervin Schwartz pulled into the front yard. Wiping her hands on her apron, Lizzie went to greet him. She held the horse steady while Mervin heaved himself off the buggy seat. A portly man of perhaps forty-five years, he winced as he tried to step down.

"Let me help you." Lizzie took his arm, noticing he

wore a work boot on his right foot and only a heavy wool sock on his left.

"Danke," he spoke in a breathless wheeze once he stood on the ground. He favored the shoeless foot as he hobbled toward the front porch.

"Do you have an injury?" she asked, helping him climb the steps to the front door. Instead of going inside, he dropped down into one of the low Adirondack chairs *Daed* had made with his own hands.

"Ne, but I've got the gout something terrible." He groaned, easing himself back as he gripped the arm-rests of the chair.

"I'm so sorry. What can I do? Can I get you something?" she asked, feeling a bit helpless and wondering why he'd come all the way out here to their farm when he should be home, resting.

Mervin shook his head, his face flushed with sweat in spite of the cool day. "I came to see Eli Stoltzfus. He helped Deacon Albrecht with his leg wound and I'm hoping he'll know what I can do to ease the pain in my foot."

Lizzie blinked, thinking Mervin had lost his mind. "But Eli isn't a doctor."

"I don't want a doctor. Eli is one of us and yet he's had schooling and will know what to do for me."

His obvious faith in Eli astonished Lizzie. A number of her people served one another according to their specialties. Amos Yoder was the best blacksmith in their community. Linda Hostetler dried plants to make special teas, ointments, tonics, salves and liniments. Everyone valued their contributions. But their skills had been learned at home, as part of the community. Not through a fancy education in the *Englisch* world. To have a member of their congregation ask for Eli's help specifically because he'd received a college education seemed odd to Lizzie, especially since her people shunned higher learning.

"I... I'll see if I can find Eli," she said.

Stepping down from the porch, she rounded the house and hurried toward the barn. Inside, the musty scent of clean straw filled her nose as she blinked to let her eyes become accustomed to the dim interior. Eli sat on the top of an old barrel, a harness spread across his lap as he mended the leather straps. Lizzie wasn't surprised to find Marty and Annie helping him. The girls both liked Eli and he was kind to them. Wherever he was, they were usually there too. Just now, her sisters were pulling the lead lines out of the way, holding them straight so he could make sense of the melee of straps, hooks and buckles.

"*Ach*, that's good. Hold it steady now."

Eli bent his dark head over the mess, his long, graceful fingers pulling apart a particularly stubborn knot. His black felt hat hung from a hook on the wall, his short hair curling against the nape of his neck.

In the quiet of the barn, no one seemed to notice Lizzie. For a few moments, she stood watching from the shadows, enjoying the serenity of the scene. Then, she cleared her throat.

"Eli?"

He looked up, his handsome mouth curved in a ready smile, his sharp gaze seeming to nail her to the wall.

"Lizzie-bee." He said her name softly, like a caress, and she couldn't help shivering.

She folded her arms. "Um, Mervin Schwartz is up at the house. He's hoping you can help him with his gout."

Eli's forehead crinkled as he stood and laid the harness on the ground before looking at the little girls. "Well then, my two good assistants, it seems we will have to mend the harness later on. Right now, someone needs our help."

He smiled and tugged playfully on the ribbons of their prayer *kapps* before whisking his hat off the hook and heading toward Lizzie. He paused at the door, pushing it wide while he waited for her to precede him outside. She did so, feeling suddenly flustered by his good manners. The little girls exited as well, and then raced ahead of them. As Lizzie walked toward the house, she was more than conscious of Eli following behind. She could almost feel his steely eyes boring a hole in her back.

The girls greeted Mervin and initially watched with curiosity as the two men discussed the problem, but the girls soon disappeared when Mervin removed his sock and revealed a rather hairy foot with a large, red bump on the side of his big toe. Even Lizzie could tell it was inflamed. The skin looked red and dry, with an odor like Limburger cheese emanating from his toes. Trying to hide her grimace, Lizzie stood back, feeling a bit repulsed. But not Eli.

With infinite gentleness, he knelt before Mervin and cupped the front of the man's foot in both hands. When Eli lightly touched the bump with his fingertips, Mervin inhaled a sharp breath through his teeth.

"It hurts, huh?" Eli asked without looking up.

"*Ja*, a lot. I can hardly stand to walk on it and I've got chores needing to be done. Can you do something to help me?" Mervin asked.

Lizzie could hardly believe Eli didn't draw back in disgust. A vision of the Savior washing the feet of His disciples suddenly flashed inside her mind and she couldn't help respecting Eli for not shying away.

Looking up, Eli met Lizzie's gaze. "Do you have a bag of frozen peas and a clean dish towel I can use?"

She nodded, thinking of all the foods they had stuffed inside their propane-powered refrigerator. She wasn't naive enough to ask why he needed the peas.

Whirling around, she hurried inside and opened the small freezer box. She rummaged around until she found what she was after, snapped up a dish towel, then raced back outside.

The screen door clapped closed behind her as she handed the items to Eli. After scooting another chair close in front of Mervin, Eli wrapped the cloth around the bag of frozen peas. With gentle precision, he lifted Mervin's foot to the chair and laid the cold compress across his big toe.

Mervin laid his head back and groaned, closing his eyes for several moments.

Sitting next to Mervin, Eli met his gaze. "You know I'm not a doctor, right?"

"*Ja*, but you know what I need, don't you?" Mervin responded in a half-desperate voice.

"*Ja*, you need a qualified doctor," Eli said. "Someone like Dr. McGann can prescribe some medicine to help reduce the uric acid in your joints. All I can suggest is that you take an anti-inflammatory medication, drink lots of water and eat a handful of cherries every day."

Mervin blinked, taking in every word. "Cherries?"

"*Ja*, they're a natural way to reduce the uric acid. But a doctor can give you a complete list of other foods to eat or avoid eating."

Tilting his head to one side, Mervin's jowls bobbed. "Like what kinds of foods to avoid?"

Eli shrugged. "Things like bacon, fish, liver, beef, corn syrup…"

Mervin's eyes widened. "Liver? Bacon?"

"*Ja*, they're high in purine, which contributes to the uric acid in your blood. They'll make the gout worse."

"*Ach!*" Mervin lifted a hand to his face as he shook his head. "I eat liver almost every morning. I love it covered with fried onions."

"I'd recommend you no longer eat it. I'd also recommend you lose twenty pounds."

Mervin frowned.

Eli rested a consoling hand on the man's arm. "You may need to give up a few foods and watch your portion sizes, but I guarantee it'll help you feel better. But more than anything, it's important for you to go see Dr. McGann as soon as possible."

Mervin pursed his lips, his face slightly flushed with repugnance. "But he's an *Englischer.*"

He said it as if it were a dirty word. Although they all lived among the *Englisch* and did business with them, some of their people didn't like to mingle with them any more than absolutely necessary.

"*Ja*, Dr. McGann is *Englisch*. But he's also experienced, capable and kind. He won't force you to do what you don't want to do, but he can ease a lot of your pain. Go see him. I wouldn't send you to him if I didn't believe he could help."

A deep frown settled across Mervin's forehead. "All right. I'll go. But only because you trust him."

"I do. Explicitly," Eli said.

His concession seemed to ease the tension in Mervin's shoulders. Lizzie quickly made a pitcher of lemonade for them to enjoy and they talked about inconsequential things for a short time. When Eli removed the bag of peas, Mervin announced that his big toe felt a bit better.

"It's just a dull throb. I believe I can even stand the drive home now," Mervin said with delight.

"Good. But I fear it won't last long. The pain will return," Eli said.

"That's all right. I'll go see Doc McGann tomorrow and buy some cherries at the grocery store on my way home. And I'll ask Hannah to fix something else for breakfast besides fried liver."

Eli chuckled and Lizzie couldn't help smiling too. They assisted the man to his buggy and she couldn't help noticing Eli's caring compassion. He ensured the man was seated comfortably before handing him the lead lines.

"You drive safely. And I'll check back with you at church on Sunday," Eli said.

"*Danke.* You've been a lot of help, my friend. It's *gut* to have you back home where you belong." Mervin tipped his hat, then clicked to the horse.

As the buggy pulled away, Lizzie couldn't help shooting a sideways glance at Eli. She studied him for just a moment, then flinched when he turned abruptly and caught her watching him.

"*Ach,* look how the time has flown," she said. "I've still got so much work to do. I shouldn't have visited so long."

Turning, she hurried toward the house, trying to ignore the weight of his gaze following her. Her brain churned with confusion. Though she disapproved of Eli's worldly knowledge, she could see how it could benefit their people. That was good, wasn't it? But such knowledge often led to *Hochmut.* And pride was never a good thing. It kept a person from being humble and receptive to *Gott*'s will. And the fact that Eli had gotten his education prior to committing to their faith seemed a bit like cheating to Lizzie. He'd known all along that he could make peace with his people as long as he got his education before being baptized. It seemed he'd gotten what he wanted from the *Englisch* world, which meant it likely cost him little to return. So, how could she accept Eli and his higher learning now? She couldn't. It was that simple.

An hour after Mervin left, Eli had finished repairing the harness and taken Billie out for a drive with the buggy. He wanted to see if the horse was skittish around passing cars and trucks. He was delighted when the animal didn't even flinch.

Now, Eli stood at the side of the barn chopping wood. Wielding an ax, he split the last piece of kindling, then sank the blade of the tool into the top of the chopping block. Arching his back, Eli wiped his forehead with his shirtsleeve, thinking he'd have this cord of wood split by the middle of next week. As he eyed the neatly stacked pile of kindling, he felt satisfied that the Beilers wouldn't run out of fuel for their cookstove this winter.

"Oh, no you don't. Get out of here. Shoo!"

Eli jerked around, wondering what had caused such a frenzy of shouts. Wielding a broom, Lizzie chased two fat pigs across the backyard. Her laundry basket sat on its side beneath the clothesline. Obviously, she had dropped it there when she came out to collect the laundry…and found pigs in the yard. One of the swine raced toward the garden just beyond the clothesline.

"Ne!" Lizzie tore after the animal, swatting its hindquarters with the broom.

The pig squealed and veered right, barely missing the clean sheet. Understanding how the animals could ruin Lizzie's hard work if they tangled with the laundry, Eli raced forward to help her.

"Haw! Haw!" he yelled, waving his arms to direct the swine back toward their pen.

The pigs snorted and oinked as they pattered in the right direction, their short legs moving fast.

Flanking them on the right, Lizzie helped Eli herd them into the pen.

Victory!

Before the animals could escape again, Eli shut the gate. In the process, his boots slipped in the mud and down he went, landing on his backside.

Lizzie gasped. "Eli! Are you hurt?"

Standing just inside the gate, she gripped her broom like a savage warrior. She looked so fierce and endearing that he couldn't contain a chuckle.

Sitting in the mud, he bit his tongue. The cold muck seeped through his pants, soaking him to the skin. Lifting his hands, he flung great dollops of black sludge off his fingers. Now what would he do? He had an afternoon of chores left to complete with no clean change of clothes.

A chortling sound caused him to look up. Lizzie stood in front of him, trying—and failing—to hide her laughter behind her hand.

Eli tilted his head. "May I ask what is so funny?"

She hunched her shoulders, no longer laughing, but her smile stayed firmly in place. "You are. I think you are a bit too old to play in the *dreck*."

He looked down at himself, noting how long it would take to get the mud off, then looked back at her. "*Ja*, I agree. When you can quit laughing, would you mind helping me up?"

He held out his arm and waited. Leaning her broom against the pen, she took firm hold of his hand, braced her feet and pulled hard.

A heavy sucking sound heralded his freedom from the mud. As he stood before her, he felt absolutely dismayed by his predicament...until he heard her laughter again. When he glanced up, her laughter cut off, but her eyes twinkled with mirth. Being near her made his heart rate trip into double time. In spite of her frequent looks of disapproval, he felt happy being around her and figured it must be because they'd been so close once.

"You have *dreck* on your face." He reached his free hand up to wipe a streak of mud off the tip of her nose.

She gave an embarrassed giggle. "At least I'm not wearing it all over my clothes."

He chuckled helplessly and indicated her nose. "I'm sorry, but I just made it worse."

She wiped at her face, removing most of the muck.

Looking into her sparkling blue eyes, he felt thoroughly enchanted. She stared back at him, her lips slightly parted. Then he remembered that Shannon's eyes were a dark amber color and his heart gave a painful squeeze.

He stepped back, feeling flushed with shame. It was disloyal for him to flirt with another woman, wasn't it? Shannon was gone, but his heart was still tied to her. He couldn't seem to let go of the pain or the guilt. It was on the tip of his tongue to tell Lizzie about his fiancée. To confide his heartache over Shannon's death. But Lizzie's expression changed to a doubtful scowl.

She turned toward the house. "I'd better get the laundry gathered in and finish making sandwiches. I'll lay out some of *Daed*'s clothing on the back porch if you'd like to get cleaned up. Then you can join us for lunch."

Without waiting for his reply, she walked fast toward the clothesline. He watched as she rinsed her hands with the garden hose, then jerked the pins from the clean sheets and haphazardly folded them and the other clothing before dropping each piece into the laundry basket. Without a backward glance, she went inside. Only when the door closed behind her did he realize he was still staring.

Swallowing heavily, he shivered as a cool breeze swept over him. He headed toward the house, eager to get out of his damp clothes. When he'd stared into Lizzie's eyes, he'd felt the attraction between them. But it wasn't right. Shannon should be here with him, not Lizzie. He'd been Shannon's fiancé and would have soon been her husband. It had been his job to look after her, to protect her, but he'd failed miserably. And it occurred to him that he'd failed Lizzie too. Twice, he'd lost the opportunity to marry the woman he loved. And both times, it had been his own fault. Though he longed to have a *familye* of his own, maybe he'd let the chance for happiness pass him by.

Pushing his morose thoughts aside, he went to the outside faucet and rinsed himself off. He gasped and trembled in the frigid water. After he'd rinsed the muck off his work boots, he stepped up onto the back porch in his bare feet and found a pile of clean clothing waiting for him along with a fluffy towel. He quickly retired to the barn where he got cleaned up. When he returned to the kitchen, Marty and Annie were already seated at the table. The spicy aroma of allspice and cloves filled his senses.

"We waited for you, Eli. Lizzie made pumpkin bread," little Annie chirped in a happy tone.

"First, you must eat a sandwich." Lizzie stood in front of the counter, slicing homemade bread. She didn't spare him a glance as she set a plate of bologna and cheese on the table beside a bowl of sliced melon.

"We're real hungry and you took a long time," Marty added, her forehead creased with impatience.

He smiled, noticing that Annie's *kapp* was crooked. As he took his seat, he straightened it, then brushed his finger against the tip of her nose. "*Ach*, I'm famished too. Let's eat."

Once Lizzie sat down, they each bowed their head for a silent prayer. After a few moments, Eli breathed a quiet sigh and they all dug in.

"Lizzie says she's gonna cook a turkey for Thanksgiving," Marty said.

"But I want ham," Annie said. She swiveled around to look at Eli. "What's your favorite? Ham or turkey?"

He hesitated before answering truthfully. "I think I prefer stuffed turkey for Thanksgiving and ham for Christmas dinner. Now, what's your favorite pie?"

Annie tilted her head and looked up at the ceiling, as if contemplating this deep subject. "Hmm, I think I like pumpkin the best. But Lizzie always makes pecan and apple too."

"Yum! I'd like a giant slice of each kind," Annie said.

Eli chuckled, enjoying this light conversation. If not for Lizzie being overly quiet, he would have felt completely relaxed. He had to remind himself that this wasn't his *familye* and his visit here was temporary. "That's a lot of pie for such a little *maedel*. Are you sure you can eat all of that?"

"Sure I can. I could eat it all day long." Annie nodded as she took a big bite of her sandwich to make her point.

"How come you left and didn't marry Lizzie?" Marty asked the question so abruptly that Eli choked on a bite of buttered bread. He coughed to clear his throat and took several deep swallows from his glass of chilled milk.

"Didn't you love her no more?" Annie asked before he could reply.

"Anymore," Lizzie corrected in a stern voice. "And it's none of your business."

"Well," Eli began, speaking slowly so he could gather his scattered thoughts. "We were both very young at the time and I wanted to know more about the world before I committed to our faith and settled down to raise a *familye*."

There, that was good. He'd rehearsed the explanation more than once, not wanting to admit that he'd been too frightened to marry so young. He'd wanted to go to school instead. To see and learn more about this world he lived in before he settled down for the rest of his life.

He was about to enlarge on his explanation when Lizzie set her fork down and rose slowly to her feet. Her eyes were narrowed and flashed with an emotion he couldn't name...a mixture of despair and anger.

When she spoke, her voice sounded hoarse with suppressed emotion. "It would have been nice if you had explained all of that to me instead of disappearing without a single word."

Eli stared at her, his mind a riot of thoughts he didn't know how to express. How could she say he hadn't explained? He'd told her everything in his letters. Why hadn't she replied? Why had she ignored his efforts to reach out to her? She could have written back to him.

Before he could think of a satisfactory response, Lizzie walked out to the backyard, pulling the door closed quietly behind her.

The little girls stared after their sister, their gazes round with uncertainty.

"Is Lizzie mad at us?" Annie's lip quivered, her eyes welling up with tears.

"*Ne*, she's not angry at you. Please don't cry." Eli set his sandwich on his plate.

Lizzie wasn't mad at her sisters. She was mad at him.

"I'll go check on her and see if I can get her to come back inside." He stood and smiled, speaking in a light tone he hoped would soothe them. "You two finish your lunch and I'll smooth everything over. Okay?"

They both nodded. He went outside, wondering if he should simply take his muddy clothes and go home. It had been a difficult day and he wasn't sure what to expect when he found Lizzie.

She stood leaning against the tool shed, staring out at the stubbled fields. Tomorrow, he planned to harrow and smooth out the small ruts in preparation for spring planting. When he approached, she quickly wiped her eyes. *Ach*, did she have to cry?

"Lizzie?" He spoke gently, not sure what to say. He didn't want to create more friction between them.

She faced him, her eyes damp and filled with such misery that it nearly broke his heart.

"Why did you have to go away to school? And why are so many people asking for your help?" she asked.

Taken off guard by her questions, he shrugged. "You know why I went to school. And I suppose people come to me because they think I can make their ailments better."

"Can't you stop it?"

"Would you rather I sent them away?"

She looked down at her feet. "*Ne*, that wouldn't be right. You have to help them if you can."

"I don't *have* to help them, but I *want* to, Lizzie. I believe it's what the Savior would have me to do."

"*Ja*, you're right. It's just that…just that…"

She didn't finish her statement, but she didn't have to. Finally they were getting at the crux of the problem.

"It's the fact that I went to college that bothers you, isn't it? That I lived among the *Englisch* and became a paramedic. Right?"

She nodded. "On the one hand, your skills are so beneficial. But on the other hand, it was wrong for you to leave. Higher learning can cause too much *Hochmut*."

"Is that what you think? That I'm filled with pride?"

"*Ja*, *ne*… *Ach*, I don't know anymore. When you left so suddenly, I didn't know what to think. I can't even tell you how badly you hurt me. I thought we were going to marry."

He sighed and looked away. "We were too young, Lizzie. At the time, I truly loved you. But we both needed time to become adults. You know that."

Her mouth dropped open. "So you just forgot about your promises to me? You didn't even have the common courtesy to say goodbye."

Confusion fogged his brain. "I… I left you a long letter explaining everything. And I wrote to you many times afterward. Not once did you respond to me."

Her forehead furrowed in bewilderment. "You wrote your *eldre*, Eli. Your *mudder* shared some of your letters with me, but you never wrote directly to me. Not once."

Taking a step closer, he lifted a hand, forcing himself to be slow to anger. His faith had taught him to be a better man than to yell and say things he'd regret later on. His father had also taught him that a soft answer turned away wrath. So, he spoke in a gentle voice, hoping it worked.

"I wrote to you dozens of times, Lizzie. I... I didn't dare say goodbye to anyone in person because I feared you and my *eldre* would stop me from going. It's hard to explain, but I wanted to know more about the world. I couldn't stay. But I am wondering why you never responded to my letters. Why would you pretend they never existed?"

She shook her head, looking miserable. "I never received any letters from you. Not ever."

Doubt clogged his brain. He'd never known her to lie, so why would she do so now? There had to be another explanation.

"I don't know what to say," he said. "I wrote you many times, but every letter was returned unopened. I told you that I loved you and asked you to join me in Denver, but I never heard back from you."

She snorted. "Even if I had received these letters from you, it would have made no difference in my decisions. I would never have abandoned my faith to become an *Englisch* woman."

Though she spoke softly, he caught the contempt in her voice. The disdain. To her, the *Englisch* were worldly and ungodly...everything she didn't want to be.

"I know that now," he said. "But it took a long time for me to realize you would not agree to come to me. After a year, when I didn't hear from you, I finally accepted that I had lost you for good and moved on with my life."

But he didn't tell her about Shannon. If Lizzie knew

he'd fallen in love with an *Englisch* girl, it might deepen her disgust for him.

"You moved on without me the moment you left," she said. "You loved worldly pursuits more than you loved me. More than you loved *Gott*. And that is because you had too much *Hochmut*. I don't know what has brought you back home, but it doesn't change anything between us. And now, I have work to do."

Lifting her chin, she brushed past him and headed toward the house, her spine stiff and unapproachable. Watching her go, he couldn't help wondering what had happened to all of his letters. They'd been returned, they were now in his possession, but who had sent them back to him? Perhaps Jeremiah? He didn't know for sure.

It didn't matter. He and Lizzie no longer loved one another. Time had drawn them apart and they'd found other lives and other loves. There could be nothing else between them. Not now, not ever.

Chapter Seven

Lizzie slid a canister of freshly made cheese curd into the chilled water of the well house. Vague sunlight gleamed through the open doorway, the air filled with the pungent scent of rain. Higher up in the mountains, it had snowed last night. Just a light dusting, but enough to lower the temperature substantially.

Brr! Lizzie snuggled deeper into her heavy black coat and tightened the blue hand knitted scarf around her neck. The chores were finished and it was time to go inside for the evening. Eli should be leaving to go home soon. For two days, she'd purposefully avoided him after their last discussion. Tomorrow, they'd pay another visit to *Daed* in town. Maybe the doctor would even let him come home. While they would still need Eli to continue on the farm during *Daed*'s recovery, she'd feel more secure with her father's presence.

Stepping outside, she secured the door, then crossed the yard. She glanced toward the barn, noticing a light gleaming beneath the double doors. Eli was still working. She thought about going to see what was keeping him so late, but decided against it. After all that had happened between them, she needed to keep her distance.

A few days earlier, during Church Sunday, he'd been surrounded by several members of their congregation. They each sought guidance on how to cure their various ailments...everything from a persistent cough to shingles. Eli had insisted he wasn't a doctor, but offered his best advice. He then encouraged each person to go into town and visit Dr. McGann as soon as possible.

"Eli! Eli Stoltzfus!"

Lizzie whirled around and saw David Hostetler driving his horse and buggy at a breakneck speed along the dirt road. Gravel flew into the air as the horse pulled into the main yard. The animal was breathing hard and Lizzie ran to see what was the matter.

In a rush, David jumped out of the buggy, then reached back to lift out his seven-year-old son, Timothy. The boy was wrapped tightly in a quilt with only his face visible. He groaned and Lizzie instantly noticed the child's rasping breath, his eyes fluttering open and closed, and his lips a bluish color.

"What is wrong?" she asked.

"Can I help?" Eli startled her when he reached to press a hand to his forehead. Dressed in his warm winter coat and black felt hat, Eli must have just been preparing to go home when he heard David's cries and came running from the barn.

Standing back, Lizzie gave Eli room as David headed toward the front porch.

"He...he breathed in pesticide. He spilled it down his front," David said, his voice sharp and slightly breathless from his exertions.

"Bring him inside," Eli said, his voice and manner urgent.

Without a backward glance, he opened the door and they hurried into the front room. Lizzie followed, anticipating they might need her help. Eli led David straight through to the kitchen.

Startled by the commotion, Annie and Marty hopped up from the couch where they had been reading by lamplight. Standing barefoot in their warm flannel nightgowns, they gazed at the group with a mixture of alarm and shock.

"Lizzie?" Always sensitive to other people's troubles, Annie took her hand.

Lizzie wrapped one arm around the girl's shoulders and pulled her close. "It's all right, *boppli*. Timmy is sick, but we're going to help him get better."

They followed the men into the kitchen.

"Lay him on the table," Eli ordered.

David did so. The boy moaned, his voice a scratchy gurgle.

Eli glanced her way. "Do you have some rubber gloves I can use?"

She nodded, opened the cupboard door beneath the sink and handed him the items. Eli quickly tugged them on, then pulled the quilt aside. Timmy was still dressed in his work clothes. Lizzie's nose twitched as the heavy odor of pesticide struck her. She crinkled her forehead, understanding why her father rarely used such volatile chemicals on his farm. If they were dangerous to bugs, they were dangerous to humans.

Eli looked up at her. "Lizzie, please have the *maed* leave the room immediately. I don't want anyone to touch Timmy or his clothes except me. Not until we can get the poison off him. The quilt and Timmy's clothes should be burned. I doubt anyone can get them clean enough to use again. Don't handle them except with rubber gloves. I don't want you to get hurt. Do you understand?"

She nodded, realizing the gravity of the situation. But for him to say he didn't want her to get hurt made her heart thud. She told herself it meant nothing. That he was only looking out for her the same as he would do for anyone. But for just a moment, she secretly wished it meant a bit more. Then, she reminded herself that they were barely even friends.

"David needs to wash his hands and arms with soap and hot water. He's been holding Timmy and probably has poison on his skin. Lizzie, you'll need to clean the sink afterward with cleanser. Be sure to wear rubber gloves."

She nodded stoically. Without a word, she ushered her sisters out of the room. David followed, leaving his son in Eli's care.

"But I wanna stay," Marty complained.

Understanding the problem very well, Lizzie didn't back down. Just breathing in pesticides or getting them on the skin could do grave damage. Besides, the girls would only be in the way if they stayed.

"*Ne*, my *liebchen*. The poison could hurt you too. In fact, it's time for you and Annie to go to bed." Taking each girl's hand, Lizzie pulled them along.

"*Ach!* I don't wanna go to bed," Annie whined.

Without a word, Lizzie pointed toward the bathroom and spoke to David. "There are clean towels in the cupboard and plenty of soap by the sink. You can borrow one of *Daed*'s clean shirts too. Remember not to touch anything you don't need to as it will spread the poison."

He nodded and headed that way.

Lizzie walked up the stairs with her sisters. "I'm sorry, but it's time to sleep and I need to help the men with Timmy."

"But what if Timmy di-dies?" Annie's voice trembled.

"No one is going to die. We must trust in *Gott* and Eli is going to do everything he can to help." Lizzie tried to make her voice sound calm and soothing, but her pulse pounded with trepidation. Even she could see that Timmy was having difficulty breathing. He obviously needed serious medical care and she wondered what Eli could do with their limited resources.

"Don't worry," Marty said. "Eli will make Timmy better. He knows what to do."

Her sister's confidence in Eli surprised Lizzie. And in her heart of hearts, she said a silent prayer, hoping her sister was right.

When Lizzie returned to the kitchen a few minutes later, David was just coming out of the bathroom. He rolled the sleeves of one of *Daed*'s shirts down his damp arms as he walked swiftly with her to the kitchen.

"I cleaned everything I touched, so we wouldn't have poison spread around your bathroom," he said.

Eli looked up as they entered the room. He held Timmy's wrist, taking his pulse with his bare hand. As soon as he finished, he pulled the rubber glove back on. "Lizzie, would you fill the bathtub with warm water? Timmy still has poison on him and we've got to wash it all off. He'll need some warm, clean clothes to wear too."

"Of course," she said, racing into the bathroom.

Over the next twenty minutes, they did what they could for Timmy. Lizzie found some fresh though rather large clothes for him to wear. By the time he was cleaned up, his breathing came a little easier, but he still had a dry, hacking cough. Eli doffed the rubber gloves, which he'd washed off. When he handed them to Lizzie, his warm fingers touched hers. She looked up and their eyes met for a few brief moments.

"It'll be all right," he whispered for her ears alone, then turned back to the boy.

Lizzie shivered, trying to ignore how Eli's kind words impacted her. He was worried about Timmy, that was all.

She put on the rubber gloves, then carefully folded Timmy's contaminated clothes inside the quilt. As she carried them outside to burn later on, she turned her face away from the heavy stench of poison.

Back inside, she provided a clean quilt and helped Eli wrap it around the boy to alleviate his trembling.

"Daedi," Timmy called in a weak voice, his eyes closed. In spite of the chill air, he was sweating profusely.

"I'm here, *sohn.*" David smoothed his fingers through the boy's slightly damp hair, his big hands trembling.

"I'm sorry. I didn't mean to spill the poison. Are you *bees* at me?"

David gave a laughing scoff, which sounded more like a low sob. *"Ne,* I'm not angry with you. Don't worry, *sohn.* I just want you to get better."

Eli checked the boy's eyes again, then checked his pulse. With pursed lips, he looked at David. "He's breathing better, but not good enough. This *kind* needs a hospital right now. His heart rate is too slow and his pupils are still contracted."

David lifted his hands. "But can't you make him better? I don't want to take him to the hospital if we can avoid it. They're all *Englisch* there and don't understand our ways."

Eli shook his head emphatically. "I've done all I can for him. The hospital has antidotes and respirators to help Timmy. If you want him to live, we need to take him there immediately."

Lizzie hated to admit it, but she thought Eli was right. If they didn't take Timmy to the hospital, he would die. But were it not for Eli, he would be dead already. The quick, capable care Eli provided had eased the symptoms. Hopefully that would be enough to give them time to get Timothy to the hospital. In all these years, she'd condemned Eli for leaving her to seek higher learning. But now, watching him trying to save Timmy's life, she realized his profession was a great benefit.

"What pesticide were you using?" Eli asked.

"Malathion. I sprayed my cornfield, hoping to kill the earworms so I'll have a bigger crop next year. When my back was turned, Timmy tried to mix some of the concentrated poison himself. He was only trying to help, but he spilled it down his shirtfront and breathed in a lot of fumes. I've got the container outside in my buggy."

"*Gut.* That was smart to bring it with you. The hospital will need to know exactly what chemicals we're dealing with. *Komm,* let's go." Taking for granted that David would follow, Eli picked up Timmy and carried him through to the living room.

Lizzie followed, grasping the handle of a gas lamp and holding it high as David opened the front door and they all stepped out onto the porch. A brisk wind made Lizzie gasp. Night had fallen, the frosty air thick with the promise of snow. At some point during the melee, she'd doffed her warm coat and now wrapped an arm around herself. Darkness shrouded the farm in shadows and she hated to let the men leave without her. Hated not knowing the outcome of this frenzied night. But she would have to remain behind with her sisters.

She held the lamp high as the men climbed into the buggy and settled Timmy comfortably. With a frantic yell, David slapped the lead lines against the horse's back and they took off at a swift trot. Before the buggy turned onto the main road, Eli threw a quick look back at Lizzie. In the vague moonlight, she saw him lift one hand in farewell and mouth the word *danke*. Or at least, she thought that's what he said. She wasn't certain.

She waved, but felt haunted by Eli's gaze. In his eyes, she saw something that she'd never seen there before. Complete and utter fear. But what did it mean? Was he afraid Timmy might die? Or was his fear connected to something else? She had no idea, but sensed it had a deeper meaning than just the possibility of losing Timmy.

Lizzie hurried into the waiting warmth of the house. Thankfully, it wasn't snowing yet. It would normally take thirty precious minutes for the men to make it to the hospital in town…twenty minutes at the swift speed they were traveling. She only hoped and prayed the horse could stand the rapid pace.

Timmy trembled and Eli tucked the quilt tighter around him. Gazing at the boy's ashen cheeks, Eli feared the worst. A vision of Shannon's pale face filled his mind. Her weak voice as she begged him to save her life chimed in his ears. Her cries of fear as he tried to stop the bleeding seemed to haunt him. Her brown eyes as they closed for the last time never left his mind for long. He'd failed her. He couldn't save her life. And what if he lost Timmy too? He loved being a paramedic. Loved helping others. But he couldn't lose another patient. He just couldn't!

"Can't we go any faster?" he asked.

David slapped the leads hard against the horse's back. The animal plunged onward at a breakneck speed. "I don't dare push Ben any harder for fear he'll collapse and leave us afoot. I'm also worried a car might come up from behind and crash into the back of us."

Of course. What was Eli thinking? This was a horse and buggy, not an automobile. He'd grown too used to the *Englisch* world where he'd ridden everywhere in cars, trucks and buses. The rapid speed had spoiled him for this slower pace. He had to remember that he was in the Amish world now, where he should rely on faith and *Gott*'s will to get them through. Above all else, they needed to arrive safely. It'd do Timmy no good if the horse dropped dead of exhaustion, or if they collided with a car. Then they'd have to carry the boy into town on foot and they might arrive too late.

Minutes passed slowly until they finally crested a hill and the lights of Riverton came into view. A fresh pulse of anxiousness swept over Eli. Just a few more minutes now.

"Timmy, *vie gehts*?" he asked the boy, trying to keep him awake…to ensure he was still alive.

"Uh-huh." The child's voice sounded vague and his eyes barely fluttered.

"We're almost there now. You're doing fine. Soon, you'll be up and running around your farm with your *brieder* and *schweschder*."

Eli spoke to Timmy over and over again, trying to encourage the boy. Trying to encourage himself. He mustn't give up hope. He must exercise faith. And for the first time since Shannon's death, he offered a silent prayer for help.

When David pulled the buggy in front of the small emergency room, no orderly came out to greet them like they did at the large hospital where Eli had worked in Denver. Overhead lights gleamed brightly in the covered driveway with very few cars in the dark parking lot… not surprising in this small community. As he climbed out of the buggy, Eli figured they'd have one doctor on duty tonight. He just hoped he was inside and not at home waiting for a call.

"I've got Timmy. You should see to your horse, then come inside." Eli spoke quickly to David as he held the little boy in his arms.

David looked panicked. Eli knew the man didn't want to leave his son's side for even a moment. But reason won out over instinct. Since Eli was already turning with Timmy toward the doors and the horse's sides were lathered and heaving from exertion, David nodded his assent.

Without a word, David directed the buggy out of the way of possible traffic. Eli felt the power of David's trust like a heavy mantle resting across his shoulders. A flash of memory swept over him and he remembered the trust in Shannon's eyes too.

He hurried inside, the wide double doors whooshing open then closing behind him.

"I've got a code blue pediatric case here. We need a rapid response team. Now!" Eli called loud and urgently to the receptionist.

A plump, older woman rushed around the reception counter and reached to look at Timmy's face. She didn't seem to notice Eli's Amish clothing, but a few other people sitting in the waiting room stared with open curiosity. Eli ignored them.

"He's a poison victim. Malathion," Eli spoke to the nurse.

Seeing the urgency of Timmy's condition, the woman waved a hand. "This way."

As Eli followed her, a man wearing a white doctor's coat and a name badge that read *Dr. Graham* ran toward them.

"He's got a shallow pulse, contracted pupils and is breathing with difficulty." Without being asked, Eli rattled off the information, just as he would have done as a paramedic in Denver.

They entered a treatment room and a nurse reached for an oxygen mask. Eli laid Timmy on the bed and opened the quilt so the doctor could get a better look at him.

"What poison are we dealing with here?" Dr. Graham asked in a serious tone, flashing a small handheld light into Timmy's eyes to see how his pupils reacted.

"Malathion," Eli said. "We changed his clothing since it was spattered with pesticide and bathed him to get the poison off. After that, he started breathing a bit easier."

With a nod, the doctor ordered an antidote while the nurse hooked up an IV. Even being poked by a needle, Timmy didn't move, remaining as still as death. The slow rise and fall of his chest was the only indication that he was still alive.

Eli stepped back, letting the hospital staff take over. Though he was certified, they didn't know him and now wasn't the time to explain. Bracing his back against the wall, he prayed he wasn't too late. As he listened to the doctor giving instructions for the boy's care, Eli had mixed feelings. A part of him missed this action. The thrill of being able to use his expertise to help others. The joy of saving a life. But another part of him was terrified. He might have done something wrong. It had taken so long to get Timmy here.

"Has your son had any convulsions?" Dr. Graham asked, glancing at Eli from over his shoulder.

"He's not my son, but I'm not aware of any convulsions."

The nurse touched Eli's shoulder. "Why don't you wait outside? I'll bring word to you as soon as I can."

He got the message loud and clear. He was in the way.

Stepping out into the reception room, he saw David standing in front of the desk holding his black felt hat in his hands. He looked helpless and confused, glancing around for some sign of his son. When he saw Eli, he showed a relieved expression and hurried over to him. Eli quickly told him what he knew, which wasn't much.

They sat down to wait. Time passed slowly and Eli had too much time to think about his regrets. Leaving Lizzie four years ago was at the top of the list, followed by losing Shannon. But if he hadn't left Lizzie, he never would have met and fallen in love with Shannon. He wouldn't have had his paramedic training or be sitting in this emergency room now.

He wouldn't have known what to do to save Timmy's life.

"I don't know what I'll do if I lose my *sohn*." David leaned forward and covered his face with his hands.

Eli laid a comforting hand on the man's shoulder. He considered the unconditional love of a father and wondered if he would ever have a child of his own. First, he would have to find a wife—and he'd already ruined both of his chances at that. Even though he'd lost both of the women he'd wanted to marry, he could never regret loving them. And that realization surprised him. Loving someone else was deeply personal. Something to be cherished and protected. It was a conscious decision to hold them in your heart for always. And recognizing this gave Eli hope that he might find love a third time. But when he tried to imagine taking a wife, the only one he could picture by his side in the Amish life he'd chosen was Lizzie—and he held very little hope that Lizzie might love him again.

Chapter Eight

Lizzie pulled Ginger into the parking lot of the town park and headed toward a hitching post where a sign read Buggy Parking Only. With the number of Amish families increasing in the area, the town had accommodated them by providing a safe and convenient place with a carport cover for their horses.

Eli had tested Billie and deemed the animal ready for buggy driving again, but Lizzie still felt unsure of the horse. Ginger was older and calmer, so that's the animal she chose for this journey.

Bundled in her heavy winter coat, she hopped out of the buggy. As she tightened the scarf around her neck, she could see puffs of her breath on the chilly air. A skiff of snow that morning hadn't stopped her from coming into Riverton to visit her father and see how Timmy was doing. She'd also stopped off at Ruth Lapp's house for a short visit, happy to find that the woman was over her bronchitis and feeling much better.

Lizzie tied the horse securely, then stepped over to the sidewalk skirting the street. She had just dropped the girls off at school. It hadn't been easy to coax them out of the buggy. They hadn't heard any word on Timmy's condition and were eager to know if the boy was all right. They also were missing their father and wanted to see him. Lizzie couldn't blame them. She also wanted her dad safely at home.

As she walked up the steps to the front of the white brick building, the double doors swished open and she stepped inside. The doors closed and the welcoming warmth enveloped her. She doffed her coat and wiped her damp feet on the large floor mat and looked up.

"Lizzie!"

Linda Albrecht stood in front of the reception counter with her husband, Darrin. He was deep in conversation with the receptionist.

"Have you heard about little Timmy Hostetler?" Linda rushed over to her.

Lizzie nodded eagerly as she removed her gloves. "*Ja*, David brought him to our house last night for Eli's help before coming to the hospital. Is Timmy all right?"

Linda released a deep breath and placed a hand over her heart. "*Ja*, thank the dear Lord. But Eli told us a moment ago that it was a close call."

Darrin Albrecht joined them, folding some papers before tucking them inside the front of his coat.

"Eli is still here?" Lizzie asked.

"He is." The deacon smiled. "He refused to leave Timmy's side until he was sure the boy was okay."

Lizzie wasn't surprised. Eli would undoubtedly want to stay and offer comfort to David if little Timmy had taken a turn for the worse.

"Were you here to visit Timmy?" Lizzie asked.

"*Ne*, we came for a follow-up visit with Dr. McGann," Linda said. "It turns out that Eli was right and Darrin has diabetes. Dr. McGann also prescribed an antibiotic for the wound on Darrin's leg."

Deacon Albrecht nodded. "That's right. Thanks to Eli, the cut is almost completely healed now. Linda has changed our diet, and between that and my diabetes medication, I feel better than I have in months."

Lizzie blinked at this news, remembering that day at church when Eli had advised Deacon Albrecht to go see a doctor soon. Apparently Darrin had accepted Eli's advice and was doing much better because of it.

"I'm so glad the *gut* Lord has blessed you," she said, feeling reluctant to give the credit to Eli. After all, *Gott* provided everything, including Eli's education and knowledge.

"*Ach*, we'd best get moving. We're supposed to have more snow this afternoon and we still have shopping to do. Don't you stay in town too long," Linda admonished.

"*Ne*, I won't," Lizzie promised.

She waved as they hurried outside, both surprised and pleased that Deacon Albrecht was feeling better and Timmy was going to be okay. Thanks to Eli and the schooling *Gott* had provided him with.

She stopped at the reception counter long enough to inquire if Timmy could see visitors, then headed down the hall to his room. She'd stop in briefly before visiting her father.

"It's a good thing you were around or I doubt Timmy would have made it. But I must admit I'm surprised to discover you're a certified paramedic. We don't see many Amish paramedics."

Lizzie turned a corner and came to a dead stop. Standing in the hallway were Eli, David and Dr. McGann. The doctor lifted a hand and rested it on Eli's shoulder.

"I heard from Dr. Graham that you saved Timmy's life," Dr. McGann continued.

Eli flushed beet red and cast a sheepish glance at the doctor. "The Lord blessed him. I just did what anyone would have done."

"No," David said, speaking in perfect English. "I didn't know what to do. If you hadn't been there, my son might have…"

David didn't finish the statement. His normally stoic expression showed both gratitude and bewilderment as he considered what might have happened to Timmy.

"Thanks to you, a number of the Amish have been coming in to receive medical help. You're a good paramedic and a credit to your people," Dr. McGann said.

"Yes, the Lord has truly blessed us all." Eli turned aside, looking uncomfortable with the praise. His gaze landed on Lizzie and he showed a big smile.

"Lizzie!" he called, looking relieved by the distraction.

She hurried forward, not knowing what to make of all that she'd overheard. Also, being near Eli caused a buzz of excitement to course through her body.

"I'm sorry I wasn't there to milk the cows this morning, but I didn't have a ride home," Eli said.

She shook her head. "Don't worry about it. You had more important things to do here. I understand that Timmy is going to be all right."

She couldn't prevent a note of cheerfulness from filling her voice. All that mattered right now was that the boy was going to live.

"Ja." David nodded happily. "He'll have to stay here a couple of more days, just to make sure he's breathing okay on his own, but he reacted well to the antidote."

"Dr. McGann, this is Lizzie Beiler, a member of our congregation." Eli made the introductions.

"Yes, Ms. Beiler and I know each other already. I've been treating her father." The doctor showed a kind smile.

"That's right. How is he doing?" she asked.

"Very good. The swelling has gone down and I think we'll be able to cast his leg tomorrow morning. He can go home the day after that. But he'll need several more weeks of bed rest before resuming his usual activities. If you want to drive in on Thursday morning, he should be ready to go home then."

"Oh, that's *wundervoll*!" Lizzie exclaimed.

Two more days and her father would be home. What a relief!

"And now, I'd better get back to work." With a gesture of farewell, Dr. McGann headed down the hall.

"And I'm going to go back in with Timmy. Thanks again, my dear friend. And thanks to Lizzie as well." David reached out and shook Eli's hand as he winked at Lizzie, then he turned and entered a room.

Lizzie peered inside and saw Timmy lying on the hospital bed, his eyes closed in sleep. Covered by a thin blanket, he wore an oxygen mask, but she could see the easy rising and falling of his tiny chest.

"And I had better go see my *vadder*." Lizzie stepped around Eli, but paused when he briefly touched her arm.

"Would you mind giving me a ride back to your farm when you're finished? I used David's cell phone last night to call my *vadder* and tell him where I am, but I came into town with David and my horse and buggy are still at your place," he said.

"Of course. I won't be long. I heard that a snowstorm

is headed our way and I need to pick the girls up from school before we go home."

He nodded and she hurried on her way, still feeling the warmth of his fingers on her arm.

Jeremiah was sitting up eating lunch when she stepped into his room. He set a carton of milk on his tray and reached out a hand to her.

"Lizzie! Did you bring me any homemade bread? I'm half-starved for your cooking," he said.

She laughed. "I'm afraid not, but it looks like you'll be home in a couple of days, so you can eat all the bread you want soon." She leaned over and hugged him tight, his words pleasing her enormously. A quick glance at his filled plate told her why he wasn't happy with the hospital food. She had to admit, she wouldn't be interested, either.

"How are the *maed*?" he asked after her sisters.

"*Gut*. They wanted to come with, to see you and how Timmy is doing, but I insisted they go to school." She quickly told him about the close call last night and all that Dr. McGann had said about Eli saving the child's life.

"*Ja*, Deacon Albrecht visited me earlier and told me Timmy will be all right."

"The doctor credits Eli with helping Deacon Albrecht get on top of his diabetes too," she said.

"Hmm." Jeremiah looked skeptical.

"The Lord moves in mysterious ways. Perhaps He used Eli to do His *gut* work here on earth," she suggested.

And if that was the case, wasn't it also possible that the Lord had provided the opportunity for Eli to gain higher learning, so that he could serve others in such a manner? Lizzie didn't pose the question to her father. She knew better than to push the issue, even if Eli's education had saved Timmy's life and helped other members of their *Gmay*.

"*Ja*, it is possible." Jeremiah's voice sounded rather gruff and disapproving.

Sitting in a chair next to her father's bed, she chatted with him about the farm. Finally, Lizzie asked a question that had been weighing heavily on her mind of late.

"When he first went to Denver, Eli said he left me a letter of goodbye. He also said he sent many other letters to me, yet I've never received any. Do you know something about this?" she asked.

Jeremiah's eyes widened and he took a deep breath, taking time to choose his words carefully. A sick feeling settled inside Lizzie's stomach and she dreaded his answer.

"*Ja*, I know about the letters." Lifting his head, Jeremiah met her gaze, his forehead set in a stubborn frown. "I feared Eli might entice you to join him in the *Englisch* world, so I sent all the letters back to him unopened."

So. Eli had told her the truth. He'd tried to say goodbye to her after all. A part of her was relieved that he hadn't lied. That he hadn't abandoned her without a single word. And yet, another part of her was angry that she'd been denied the truth for all this time. Eli had his reasons for leaving, but her father's deception hurt her deeply. A feeling of righteous indignation clogged her throat and she gripped her hands together in her lap, trying not to be angry.

"You had no right to hide my letters," she said.

"I know. Please don't think harshly of me, *dochder*. As your *vadder*, I did what I thought was best, because I love you and didn't want to lose you."

Her heart softened. She couldn't really fault her father's actions. By hiding Eli's letters, he'd only been trying to protect her. To keep her in their faith, with their family.

"You should have trusted me more. I'm a grown woman and the choice to stay or go be with Eli was mine alone to make," she said.

He looked away, licking his dried lips. "I couldn't take that chance. Knowing how much you loved Eli, I feared you might go."

She shook her head. "You might have been surprised. I love my *familye* and my faith dearly too."

He looked at her, his gruff face lined with fatigue. "If I had given you Eli's letters, would you have left?"

She shrugged. "It doesn't matter now. It's in the past."

Yet, she didn't really know the answer. Four years was a long time and yet it was no time at all. She had only been seventeen. She had felt so grown up, and yet since that time, she had changed so much. Her heart had been broken, but her faith had grown. Her *familye* had come to mean more than anything to her, and she knew now that their community was where she belonged. Yet, she wasn't sure if she would have stayed back then. And knowing about the letters changed nothing between her and Eli. He had left. They'd grown apart. Now, their priorities were different. But she had to be honest with herself. She might have gone with Eli. Her love for him had been so strong that she might have put aside her faith and become *Englisch* in order to be with him. But it didn't matter now because she would never know.

The buggy bounced through a mud puddle in the rutted road leading to the schoolhouse. Eli gripped the lead lines tighter and breathed a thankful sigh that they were nearly there. With everything that had happened last night, he hadn't slept at all. He'd been too worried about Timmy. Fatigue hadn't set it until this morning, when he was assured the boy would recover. Now, Eli felt a mixture of lethargy and relief. A few more hours and he'd be able to rest. But first, he had to make sure Lizzie and the girls arrived home safe and all was well on their farm.

"There's Marty." Lizzie pointed as they rode into the school yard.

Eli pulled the buggy to a stop in front of the one-room red log building. Constructed by the men of their *Gmay*, the schoolhouse had come from a kit they'd ordered a number of years earlier. Surrounded by a chain-link fence, the property included a small baseball field and sat in the farthest corner of Bishop Yoder's hayfield.

"Lizzie!" The girl waved.

Taking Annie's hand, both children ran toward them. Several other kids followed along with Rebecca Geingerich, their teacher. No doubt they'd all heard from Marty and Annie about Timmy's accident and were eager to know if he was all right.

"Have you just come from town? Any news of Timmy?" Rebecca asked in an anxious tone, holding her shawl tightly around her shoulders.

Eli nodded. "*Ja*, and he is going to be just fine."

The children listened eagerly as Eli and Lizzie related all that had happened. A few parents who were picking up their kids also paused, seeking the news.

"It was *gut* you were there when David needed you," one man exclaimed.

"*Ja*, little Timmy might not have made it without you," Rebecca said.

Eli waved a hand, feeling embarrassed by the praise.

"The *gut* Lord saw us through. It was *Gott*'s will that Timmy survive."

"*Ja*, it was *Gott*'s will." They all nodded in agreement.

As Eli helped Marty and Annie into the buggy, he knew word would soon spread across the entire *Gmay* about what had happened. Eli really believed what he said. Truly, the Lord had blessed them. This time.

He could take no credit for the child's recovery. In fact, he'd believed Timmy would die. At the very least, the boy should have suffered permanent damage to his lungs. Yet he was thriving and even breathing on his own. Eli never should have doubted the Lord's power. But why hadn't *Gott* saved Shannon? Why did she have to die?

Pondering the inequality, Eli slapped the leads against Ginger's back. He glanced at the gray sky overhead, which mirrored his doubtful feelings.

Marty smiled brightly. "I'm so happy Timmy is gonna be okay."

"Me too," Annie spoke with a contented sigh.

As the buggy sped along the county road, it started to snow. Big, heavy flakes laden with moisture. Reaching out a hand to wipe off the front storm window so he could see out, Eli was eager to get Lizzie and her sisters home safely. He was grateful the buggy had thin glass to protect them from the elements, but he sure missed the windshield wipers of a car.

In the back seat, the two little girls exclaimed about the snow. Cocooned by the sheltering walls of the buggy, they nestled beneath a warm blanket. Soon, their eyelids drooped and they dozed off.

Casting a quick glance over her shoulder, Lizzie smiled with satisfaction. "They didn't sleep well last night. I'm afraid everyone in the *Gmay* has been worried about Timmy."

"*Ja*, his condition was pretty serious," Eli agreed.

"My *vadder* should be able to come home on Thursday," she said, then related what the doctor had told her.

"*Gut*. The storm will have passed by then, but the roads may still be slick. I'd feel better if you let me drive you into town to pick him up from the hospital."

She nodded. "I would appreciate that. I'm not sure I can lift him in and out of the buggy by myself. He won't be able to walk for several weeks."

"It's no problem. I'll help you."

She nodded and a long, swelling silence followed.

"You seem deep in thought today. Is everything all right at the farm?" he finally asked.

"*Ja*, all is well." Her voice sounded small and she tugged her black traveling bonnet closer around her face.

They rode in quiet for several more minutes before Eli couldn't take it any longer.

"Is something troubling you?" he asked.

Finally, she glanced his way. "I... I spoke to my *vadder* about your letters."

A leaden weight settled in Eli's chest. "And?"

"And he confessed that he sent them all back to you." She hurried on. "I hope you won't think unkindly of him. He's very sorry for not telling me about them, but he feared I might leave and join you in Denver. He only wanted what was best for me."

Hmm. Just as Eli had suspected.

"But what about what you wanted?" he asked with a brief glance in her direction. In this weather, he was unwilling to take his eyes off the road for long.

She took a deep inhale and let it go. "I guess we'll never know now."

True. It was water under the bridge. But Lizzie's voice sounded embarrassed, as if she hated confessing her father's duplicity. Because of the situation, Eli couldn't bring himself to be angry over Jeremiah's misdeed. Not when he had so many faults of his own to repent from.

"It's all right," he said. "I probably would have done the same thing if you had been my *dochder*. I can't blame Jeremiah for wanting what he believes is best for you."

She looked at him. "*Danke*. I appreciate your understanding."

"When I didn't hear from you, I figured you didn't love me anymore," he said. "I felt terrible about that, but then I realized I had to move on with my life. I… I met an *Englisch* girl and…and I asked her to marry me."

The words slipped out before he could stop them. Lizzie jerked around, her eyes round with shock. He wondered if he'd made a huge mistake by telling her, but also felt relieved to finally tell someone about Shannon. Because he feared their censure, he hadn't even told his parents about her.

"You…you were engaged to be married? To an *Englisch* woman?" she asked, her voice sounding small and deflated.

He nodded and suddenly the story poured out of him. He told Lizzie everything. How he'd given up on ever hearing from her again. How he'd met Shannon when she was working at the hospital as a pediatric volunteer. How gentle, kind and reserved she was and how they'd dated some time before becoming engaged. And then about the drunk driving accident after which she'd died in his arms.

He stared straight ahead and gripped the lead lines tighter as he spoke in a low, hoarse voice. "She was driving the car that night when a drunk driver hit us head-on. She survived the initial impact and I thought she'd be all right, but I… I couldn't save her, Lizzie. She was bleeding internally and I couldn't stop it. I prayed so hard, but *Gott* didn't answer me. He let Shannon die."

Lizzie must have heard the anguish in his voice, because she pressed her gloved fingers against her lips. He was surprised to see tears shimmering in her eyes.

"*Ach*, Eli. I'm so sorry for your loss, but I have no doubt the Lord was with you that night. We don't always understand His ways, but He has our best interests in mind. There was nothing else you could have done. It wasn't your fault. You know that, don't you?" Her voice was filled with sincerity, her eyes crinkled with compassion.

No, he didn't know that. He kept replaying everything in his mind, as if in slow motion. Trying to think of what steps he might have taken to help Shannon survive.

They were quiet for several moments, listening to the gusts of wind as white swirled around them. The falling snow was getting worse. Ginger lowered her head and trudged onward, her horseshoes biting into the slick sheet of ice covering the road. Without the protection of doors and windows, they would all be truly miserable right now.

"You must have loved Shannon very much," Lizzie said.

He nodded. "I did, just as I loved you."

She stiffened beside him and he feared she might be angry. But when he glanced over, he saw nothing but sympathy in her eyes.

"It wasn't your fault, Eli. Accidents happen and you can't save everyone. We have to trust in *Gott*. He knows what is best for each of us. You must believe that."

Somehow the conviction in her voice made him feel better. Yet, knowing how he'd broken her heart, he was surprised she was offering him comfort. If anything, he deserved her anger. But that wasn't her way.

"When you left, I was hurt to think that you could forget me so easily," she continued. "But now, I understand what happened. You wanted to know more about the world, to learn and grow. It was your choice to go and I mustn't judge you for that. It wasn't your fault that *Daed* hid your letters from me. And I can't hold a grudge against Shannon and the love you shared with her either."

"I… I tried so hard to save her," he said, trying not to let his emotions show in his wobbly voice. But he couldn't seem to help it. He had to quickly wipe his eyes.

"Of course you did." She rested a gloved hand on his arm, her touch consoling. "I know you did everything you could. But now, you should hand your pain over to the Lord. Give your grief to Him and be at peace."

She withdrew her hand and became very still, her brow furrowed in a troubled frown. She seemed so understanding. So supportive. It reminded him of when they were teenagers and she'd always put everyone else first. Her generous spirit had been one of the things he'd loved the most about her.

A particularly hard gust rocked the buggy and drew his attention back to the road ahead. He had to reach outside and clear the caking snow off the window. The wind buffeted them. For just a moment, he missed the comfort of an automobile's heater and defroster, not to mention the solid security of the larger, heavier vehicles. But a car wouldn't include Lizzie. Dear, faithful Lizzie.

He felt strangely calm sitting next to her. As he drew his arm back inside, he caught her worried look.

"I'll sure be glad when we're home," she said. "I thought we could beat the storm. I have to admit I'm glad you're driving instead of me."

In spite of her smile, her body seemed stiff and her demeanor reserved. Perhaps he was reading something in her manner that wasn't really there. As she shivered and pulled a blanket over her legs, he figured she was just worried about the weather. Yes, that must be it.

"You're *willkomm*," he replied, feeling better, yet feeling worse at the same time. Oh, he was so confused. He didn't know himself anymore. Didn't know where he belonged or what he wanted.

Fearing a truck might come barreling down the road and not see them in the storm, he pulled the horse as far over onto the shoulder as he dared. Through the white swirling around them, he could just make out the jutting edges of an irrigation ditch running parallel to the road. He eyed the reflective snowplow poles and mileage markers, using them as a guide to stay out of the ditch. As he concentrated on his driving, they didn't speak for several minutes. A comfortable silence settled over them, something he hadn't realized how much he'd missed... until now. But he had little time to consider the reason why as they came upon a car that had slid off the road.

Chapter Nine

Two thin lines on the icy road showed where the tires of the black car had skidded off the road. The vehicle's hazard lights blinked red. Through the flurries of wind gusting against the falling snow, Lizzie could make out the front fender hanging just above the irrigation ditch. Another inch and the vehicle would drop two feet and require a tow truck to drag it out.

Lizzie clutched the side of the buggy, a feeling of trepidation filling her heart. The last time she'd been involved in a car accident had not been pleasant. Even as she wished they didn't have to stop, she knew they must. They couldn't pass by someone in need.

Eli pulled Ginger to a halt just behind the floundered car. "Wait here inside the buggy. I'll see if we can help."

Pulling his black felt hat lower over his forehead, Eli opened the door and stepped out into the lashing wind and snow. Chilling air whooshed inside the buggy. As she looked out at several tall elm trees edging the road, their barren limbs covered in white, she thought the winter scene would be beautiful...if she were watching it from the safety of her kitchen window. But sitting inside a horse-drawn buggy, she couldn't help wishing they were anywhere but here.

Hunching his wide shoulders, Eli hurried toward the car. Lizzie's gaze followed him. For some odd reason, she felt desperate to keep her eyes on him. As if she'd lose him again if she couldn't see him anymore.

At the car, Eli leaned forward and someone inside the vehicle rolled down a window to speak with him. Although Lizzie couldn't hear their conversation, she saw Eli gesture toward the horse and nod several times.

"What's going on?" Awakened by the stop, Annie rubbed her eyes and sat up.

Marty leaned forward, her eyes wide with fear. "We didn't wreck again, did we?"

Lizzie swiveled in her seat and smiled. *"Ne, bensel,"* she reassured them. "There's just a car off the road and Eli is seeing if they need our help."

A strong surge of wind rocked the buggy. Staring out the thin windows, Annie shivered and her eyes welled with tears. "But I wanna go home. I don't wanna be out here anymore."

"Me either. Let's go home now," Marty cried.

Lizzie reached back and consoled both girls, pulling them close for a quick kiss on their cheeks. *"Ne,* my *liebchen*, we must help these people if we can. But don't worry. *Gott* will take care of us. And Eli won't let any harm befall us."

As she cuddled her sisters, she froze at what she'd said. Did she really trust Eli so much? Since he'd arrived home, he'd shown sound judgment, but she still doubted him. He'd told her about his *Englisch* girlfriend and her heart ached for all that he'd lost. But it hurt Lizzie deeply to know he'd loved someone else so much. That he'd made a life without her. Now he was back. But did she trust him to stay? She wasn't sure.

When he jerked open the door and leaned inside, she whirled around. His hat, shoulders and arms were covered with snow. Icy drops of water covered his face. He wiped them away with a brush of his hand, his breath puffing on the frigid air. Lizzie hated that he had to be out in this rotten weather.

"I'm going to see if Ginger can pull the car back onto the road. I want all of you to stay inside, out of the wet and cold," he said.

Lizzie nodded, grateful for his consideration. But something in her expression must have betrayed her thoughts.

"Don't worry. It's going to be all right. We're just making memories to laugh about later." He flashed her a confident smile, then shut the door.

Annie shivered at the blast of frigid air. "Brr! I'm glad Eli is taking care of this. I'd hate to be outside right now."

"Me too," Marty said.

Me three! Lizzie thought. Her respect for Eli grew when she saw that he didn't complain or shirk his responsibilities. He was a man who didn't flinch at what had to be done.

They watched as he unhitched Ginger from the buggy. An *Englisch* man in a pair of blue jeans and a light jacket got out of the car to help. Without a hat or gloves to protect him from the elements, the *Englischer* hunched his shoulders and mostly just shielded his face from the snow while Eli did the work. Lizzie figured he had no idea how to harness a horse let alone tie the lines to the car. In contrast, Eli moved with speed and confidence. She wondered how he could see what he was doing in the lashing storm. But soon, he had the horse hooked up and she couldn't help thinking that he'd become an amazing man.

He spoke to the *Englischer*, seeming completely comfortable around the stranger. While Lizzie preferred not to mingle with the *Englisch*, she supposed Eli was used to them and their strange ways. A part of her disapproved of his life among them, but right now, she appreciated his goodness and generosity.

Within moments, the *Englischer* climbed back into his vehicle and put it in Reverse. Through the rear window, Lizzie saw two young children peering out, their faces pale, their eyes round. A woman's face was visible, looking back from the front seat, and Lizzie realized an entire *Englisch familye* was inside the car.

With Eli directing the horse, Ginger leaned forward, her hooves digging into the snow as she pulled on the line. The animal's back was blanketed with white, but she seemed not to notice.

The vehicle's tires made a whizzing sound as they spun around. Finally, they caught traction and the car moved back a space. Eli led Ginger out of the way as the car came to a rest on the icy pavement.

"You see?" Marty nudged Annie. "Eli isn't worried one bit, so we shouldn't be either."

Annie nodded, huddling closer to her sister. "*Ja*, the *gut* Lord would want us to stop and help our neighbors, even if they are *Englisch* and we're afraid."

Tears filled Lizzie's eyes and she quickly wiped them away so the girls wouldn't see. Her siblings sounded so confident and grown-up that it touched her heart. She could learn from their generous and trusting example. Their words inspired her to have courage and believe in Eli too. After all, he'd stopped to help in spite of the hardship and discomfort to himself. He'd already done so much for her *familye* and many other people in their *Gmay* too. From all appearances, Eli was a good, devout Amish man. He'd suffered a lot recently. When he'd told her about losing his fiancée, he'd seemed so lost and hurt. Lizzie didn't have the heart to be angry with him anymore. She had to accept that he didn't love her. That he'd moved on and found another life that didn't include her. She should move on too. But would he stay? Or would he recover from his loss and decide the Amish life wasn't for him after all? Already, Lizzie cared too much about him. She told herself it was normal to care for everyone in the *Gmay*. But if Lizzie wasn't careful, she could get her heart broken again.

Eli climbed back into the buggy and breathed a sigh of relief. Conscious of Lizzie watching him, he blew onto his gloved hands, trying to warm them. Without being asked, Lizzie handed him a blanket. He wiped his damp face.

"Wrap it over your body. It'll warm you up quicker," she said.

"Danke," he murmured, startled to hear a croak in his voice. He coughed, hoping he didn't get hypothermia for his good deeds.

When he had the blanket packed tight around his upper torso and thighs, he felt better and shivered less. He cleared his voice and took hold of the lead lines. "Mark Walden and his *familye* are in the car. Mrs. Walden is five months pregnant and they're very grateful that we stopped."

Lizzie nodded. *"Ja,* it was the right thing to do."

He swallowed, grateful to be out of the wet and cold. "The Waldens are going to accompany us to the farm, just to ensure we arrive safely. Would you rather ride in their warm car while I drive the buggy?"

Lizzie shook her head. "That's very kind of them, but I'd rather stay with you." She glanced back at the girls, still huddled together beneath a heavy quilt. "I believe we are warm enough."

Eli wasn't surprised by her decision. He'd been living among the *Englisch* and was comfortable around them. But Lizzie wasn't.

"All right. They'll drive ahead of us, so that their lights can show the way."

He wasn't sure, but he thought he saw a flicker of relief fill her eyes before she looked away. Releasing the brake, he called loudly to Ginger, fearing the horse couldn't hear him above the storm. Either she caught his command or the animal felt the leads against her back, because she leaned into the harness, dug in her hooves and pulled forward. Eli felt the grating of the buggy wheels, frozen in ice. They gave way and were soon moving at a smooth pace. The black car drove in front of them, going slow. The bright taillights of the vehicle helped Eli see the way in the falling snow.

"I'll be glad when we're home," Marty sniffled.

"Me too. I don't want to do any more good deeds today," Annie said, her voice trembling.

"*Ja*, do you think we'll make it okay?" Lizzie asked.

Focusing on the road, Eli didn't look at any of them, but he felt the girls crouched forward between him and Lizzie. A little hand rested on his shoulder and he thought it must be Annie's. He imagined each child's eyes were wide with fear and a protective feeling filled his chest with warmth and compassion. He'd do almost anything to keep these three girls safe and wanted to reassure them all.

"Of course we'll make it," he said. "We're going very slow. Don't worry. With the Waldens' car to light the way, we'll be there soon enough." But a little doubt nibbled at his mind. Even at this snail's pace, he could see the Waldens' vehicle skidding on the icy road. Now and then, he could feel the buggy doing the same and he didn't want any mishaps to make matters worse. At this pace, the worst that could happen was they'd end up on the side of the road…unless a truck or car came up too fast behind them. That could end in catastrophe and he wondered if he should have insisted the girls ride in the safety of the car.

Everyone in the buggy was incredibly quiet. They each seemed to know that he needed to concentrate on his driving. In his heart, Eli whispered a prayer for their safety.

As they rode in silence, his thoughts began to wander. He wished he had the courage to confide another serious issue to Lizzie.

The day before, he'd received another letter from Tom Caldwell, his former employer in Denver. Tom had sent a new job offer for Eli to become an EMT supervisor. Before he lost Shannon, Eli would have loved to make such a career move. When he'd first read the letter, his heart had leaped at the proposal. It would be a wonderful way to use his skills to serve others. But then, he remembered the commitment he'd made to *Gott* and his *familye*. He planned to be baptized soon. He loved the Lord and wanted to stay in Riverton. Didn't he?

If only there was a way for him to work as a para-

medic and remain here among his people. But he didn't
see how. To be a paramedic, he'd need to keep his certifications current, which meant taking yearly classes and
using modern technology. Surely the elders of his church
would never approve of that, especially Jeremiah, who
was the minister of their congregation. Eli didn't even
dare ask. Not when he'd been home such a short time.
They might think he wasn't serious about staying. And
he was. Yet, he felt torn.

By the time they pulled into the yard of the Beilers'
farm, it was early evening and the snow had stopped.
They'd passed two big plows up on the county road and
knew the pavement would be cleared by morning.

Eli released a giant whoosh, his breath looking like
a puff of smoke on the air. He hadn't realized he'd been
holding his breath. They were safe. He'd kept his promise to Lizzie and the girls.

"We're home!" Marty crowed with delight.

"*Ja*, we're safe," Lizzie said, her voice a soft whisper.

Mark Walden waved as he slowly turned his car
around and headed back toward the county road so he
could take his *familye* home.

"But what if they go off the road again?" Annie asked,
watching their red taillights fade into the darkness.

"They won't. *Gott* is with all of us tonight and they're
driving nice and slow. They also have a cell phone to
call for help. They'll arrive just fine," Eli said, hoping
his words were true.

"*Ja*, we must trust in *Gott* to keep us safe, even when
we don't have a cell phone," Lizzie said.

Eli wasn't certain, but he thought he saw her lips
curve into a little smile. Her sense of humor made him
chuckle.

He pulled up in front of the dark house. "You take the *maed* inside and I'll take Ginger to the barn. I want to feed and dry her off *gut*. Then I'll head on home."

Lizzie's mouth dropped open. "But it's not safe for you to travel tonight. You should stay here until morning."

"It wouldn't be appropriate. I'll be fine. The snow has stopped. Once I get up to the county road, the plows will have cleared the asphalt all the way to my *eldres'* farm. And it would be unseemly for me to stay here tonight when you and the *maed* are alone."

She looked away, her gaze suddenly shy. "*Ach*, I hadn't thought about that. But you are right."

Eli nodded, wishing he dared take just a moment to seek her advice. Her compassion over Shannon's death had touched him deeply. Lizzie had always been so empathetic and kind. So obedient and wise. But he had no illusions. Lizzie would never approve of him asking their leaders to sanction his work as a paramedic. Especially if she knew he was considering accepting another job offer in Denver. Leaving Riverton meant abandoning his faith and *familye* again, something he hated to do. Because the next time he left, he knew he would never be coming back.

Chapter Ten

A freezing rain the next day, followed by another day of warm sunshine, cleared the snow and ice off the roads. A blanket of white still covered the valley and mountains surrounding them and another storm was on its way. Since they needed the water so badly for their summer irrigation, Lizzie wouldn't complain. Especially since they had good weather right now, when she needed it most. Standing in her father's hospital room in town, she glanced out the window and noticed the morning sky was still clear. They had just enough time to get him home. The chill air made her pull her heavy cape tighter around her.

"I don't know why you let Eli drive you into town. Couldn't you have come to get me on your own?" Jeremiah grumbled. He sat on the edge of the bed, fully dressed, his casted leg extended in front of him.

"*Ne, Daedi*. The weather has been too bad and I'm not sure I can lift you alone." She'd already told him about getting caught in a blizzard the night they'd helped pull the *familye*'s car back onto the road.

"What about Martin Hostetler? Couldn't he drive you into town instead of Eli?"

Lizzie clenched her eyes shut at the thought. Tall and slender, with bright red hair and a smattering of freckles, Martin was a nice enough man, but a bit too zealous for her. His outgoing nature and forward manner always unnerved Lizzie. He was too overt and outspoken for her likes. After Eli had left, it had taken a year to convince Martin that she wasn't interested in courting with him. The last thing she wanted to do was encourage him by asking if he would drive her into town to pick up her father.

"Bishop Yoder specifically charged Eli with looking after the farm and our *familye*. I'm afraid we have no choice but to accept his help," she said.

There. That was good. Surely her father wouldn't argue with the bishop.

"Has Eli...has he been spending quite a bit of time with you while I've been in the hospital?" Jeremiah asked.

"*Ne*, he mostly works outside or in the barn."

Not to mention her numerous efforts to avoid him.

After the doctor had instructed them on some exercises Jeremiah could do at home to help quicken his rehabilitation, she'd packed her father's few belongings into a bag. Eli had taken it outside as he went to fetch the horse and buggy. Her two sisters had tagged along with Eli, holding his hands and smiling. Now, Lizzie and her father were just waiting for an orderly to bring a wheelchair so they could wheel her father outside.

"So, he hasn't spoken to you about going back to the *Englisch* world with him?" Jeremiah peered at her with a look that said he didn't want to intrude, but he couldn't help asking anyway.

She snorted. "Don't worry, *Vadder*. Eli and I have no interest in each other anymore. He's been a tremendous help and looked after the farm, but he's been nothing but completely appropriate the entire time."

She didn't dare tell him about Shannon, Eli's fiancée—the proof that he'd fully moved past his old feelings for her. Though Eli hadn't asked her to keep the information private, she got the impression he had confided in her and she didn't want to betray that trust.

"*Ach*, what's taking so long?" Jeremiah looked at the door, a surly frown on his face.

Since her father was normally a gentle, patient man, Lizzie surmised that his weariness with the hospital was the reason for his impatience.

"They'll be here soon," she soothed.

Her own composure surprised her. But something had changed inside of her since Eli had told her about Shannon. When she'd reassured him that his fiancée's death wasn't his fault, a startling realization had struck her. She must exercise what she preached and hand her own grief and anger over to the Lord. It was what *Gott* expected from her. Eli had suffered enough without her condemnation too. But her heart still ached with the knowledge that he'd gotten over his love for her, and had been ready to build a life with Shannon. And that hurt most of all.

Thankfully, a young man wearing a blue smock wheeled a chair into the room at that moment.

"All ready to go?" the orderly asked in a pleasant voice. Lizzie could see from his curious gaze that he found their Amish clothing interesting, but he didn't say anything.

"We've been ready for half an hour," Jeremiah grumbled.

The orderly stepped forward, seeming unruffled by Jeremiah's bad humor. "Then let's get you on your way home. Remember not to put any weight on your casted leg."

Jeremiah nodded, reaching out as the orderly wrapped his arms around him to take the brunt of his weight before hefting him into the seat. An extender bar was lifted into place and Jeremiah's casted leg rested outstretched on the support.

"All ready?" The orderly smiled at Lizzie.

She nodded and he pushed the chair out of the room and down the long hall. Tugging her black bonnet lower over her forehead, Lizzie followed behind. As they passed Timmy's room, she glanced inside, finding the bed vacant. Jeremiah had told her the boy had gone home just before she'd arrived. Knowing the child was healthy enough to return to his *familye* brought a buoyant feeling to Lizzie's chest.

Outside, the frigid air caught her breath and she took a quick inhale. The horse and buggy were waiting at the bottom of the steps. The orderly wheeled Jeremiah down a side ramp sprinkled with ice melt. Eli hopped out of the buggy and came to assist.

"This young man can get me in just fine." Jeremiah gave Eli the cold shoulder by turning toward the orderly.

"Of course," Eli said, gracious as always but looking a bit snubbed by the rebuttal.

While Eli stood on the sidewalk, Lizzie stared at her father in amazement. She knew her father was suspicious of the other man, but what cause did he have to be so rude to Eli? It wasn't like her father. No, not at all. She sensed that something was bothering him and she had no idea what it was.

The orderly lifted Jeremiah into the buggy, then gripped the handles on the wheelchair and nodded farewell.

"Drive safely," he called.

Eli waved before reaching to help Lizzie into the back of the buggy with her two sisters. She looked inside and found that little Annie had twined her hand around her father's arm and beamed with pleasure to know he was finally going home.

As always, Eli took hold of Lizzie's arm so she wouldn't stumble on the wet footrest. Normally, she looked away and tried to ignore how his touch made her stomach quiver. But this time, their gazes met. In his eyes, she saw a flash of uncertainty, then it was gone and she thought she must have imagined it. After all, Eli was the strongest, most confident man she knew. Surely her father's temper hadn't rattled him.

Once Eli was inside, he took up the lead lines and slapped them against Billie's back. The buggy jerked forward as the horse took off at a slow trot out of the parking lot. While the little girls jabbered about their activities to their father, the adults were quiet. From the stiff shoulders of the two men sitting in front, Lizzie could feel the tension in the air like a thick fog. She understood *Daed*'s motives for keeping Eli's letters from her, but she didn't understand why he was offish toward Eli now. Unless *Daed* was like Marva Geingerich and feared Eli might leave again…and try to take Lizzie with him. He'd already asked Lizzie about it, so that must be the problem. But it wasn't becoming of *Daed* to be so judgmental.

The ride home seemed to take much longer than usual. By the time they arrived, all the adults seemed to be in a sour mood. The children, picking up on the tension but not understanding it, seemed anxious and confused, bewildered as to why the happy occasion of their father coming home wasn't being treated with more joy.

Without a word, Lizzie hurried up the front steps to hold the house's door open for Eli. Since she wasn't strong enough, *Daed* had no option but to let the other man help him inside. The night before, Eli had been kind enough to move *Daed*'s bed downstairs to the living room. Lizzie figured her father wouldn't be able to negotiate the stairs. Having him close at hand would make it easier to see to his needs too.

"I can remove your shoe so you can lie down," Annie offered as Eli deposited her father on the narrow bed.

Jeremiah sat straight as a board. "I don't want my shoe removed. I should be outside working."

Showing her sternest frown, Lizzie placed her hands on her hips and shook her head. "There will be no working or putting weight on your injured leg for several more weeks. The doctor said if you don't want to walk with a limp, you'll let the bones heal."

"*Ja*, and I'll take care of the farm work," Eli said.

Jeremiah glanced at the younger man. "What work have you already done?"

Eli stood in front of Jeremiah, holding his hat in his hands. While Lizzie helped her sisters doff their coats and gloves, Eli recounted a few of the things he'd done, including mending the fence, shoeing the horses and a myriad of other chores.

"And don't forget baling and putting away the hay," Lizzie said as she hung their coats in the closet. She headed toward the kitchen, wanting to be alone for some reason. With her sisters here to mind their father, she decided to start lunch.

"Humph," came her father's surly reply. "I'm glad you've been of use then. I guess you didn't forget how to bale a field during all that time you were living among the *Englisch*."

Again, Lizzie was surprised by the extent of her father's poor manners.

"*Ne*, sir. I remember very well how to plow and bale and I'm glad I could help you out," Eli replied.

Lizzie caught the teasing quality in Eli's voice. She'd never seen a man work as hard as he had worked for them. No doubt he was feeling amused by Jeremiah's skepticism. And that made her want to defend him to her father and she didn't understand why. Yes, she was grateful to Eli. His presence on the farm had brought her a lot of comfort. Because of him, her burdens had been eased but... Oh, she didn't know what to think anymore. Eli didn't love her anymore and all her crazy feelings would lead to nothing.

Whew! After getting the third degree from Jeremiah, Eli was glad to escape the house. Lizzie would call him for the noon meal soon, but he thought going hungry might be better than facing her father again. The man obviously didn't like him and Eli understood why. As teenagers, he and Lizzie had been inseparable. Everyone expected them to marry. But then, he'd left and Jeremiah had hidden his letters from Lizzie. No doubt the man feared, then and now, that Eli might contaminate her with his *Englisch* ideas.

Opening the barn door, Eli stepped inside, relieved to be alone. He wanted to feel angry at Jeremiah, but he couldn't. Losing Shannon had taught him a patience he didn't quite understand. He only knew that everyone was a child of *Gott*. Everyone made mistakes. But he deeply believed in the power of the Atonement and forgiveness.

Otherwise, he wouldn't have come home. And frankly, he was tired of being angry.

"Eli?"

He whirled around and found Lizzie standing just inside the doorway. Sunlight glimmered behind her, highlighting several strands of golden hair that had escaped her prayer bonnet. Her forehead was furrowed with concern. Wearing her winter cape, her porcelain cheeks had a rosy hue, as if they'd been kissed by the cold air. And for just a moment, he thought about taking her into his arms and kissing her. And that thought confused him. He still loved Shannon, didn't he? How could he be thinking about Lizzie when his fiancée had so recently died?

"I brought you something to eat," she said.

For the first time, he noticed that she held a tray covered by a white dish towel.

She came forward and set the tray on a wooden bench. Stepping back, she smoothed her cape, looking suddenly shy.

"I figured you wouldn't want to eat in the house today. My *vadder* isn't in a very *gut* mood," she said.

How insightful of her, but he didn't say so. *"Danke."*

Now! Now he should tell her about the job offer in Denver. He'd been pondering the letter he'd received from Tom Caldwell for days now, but still had found no answers. He was alone with Lizzie and it was a perfect moment to seek her advice.

"Are you all right?" she asked, her expression earnest.

"Sure. I'm fine." He smiled, hoping to alleviate her fears. It occurred to him that he hadn't seen her smile all day. She must have a lot on her mind too and he wished he could do even more to alleviate her load. He remembered how close they'd been as teenagers and a part of him wished they could share that closeness again.

She poked a clump of hay with the tip of her shoe. "I... I'm sure *Daed* will feel better tomorrow."

He lifted his head. "He's upset because I'm here. I've been living among the *Englisch* and he thinks I might corrupt you."

Her mouth dropped open. "He doesn't think that at all."

"Doesn't he?" he challenged.

She ducked her head, a mingling of acceptance and dismay in her eyes. "*Ach*, maybe a little bit. I'll speak to him."

"*Ne*, let it go. I knew when I returned that I'd have to prove myself again."

She met his eyes. "Can you blame him for not trusting you? You ran away. You've been gone a long time."

"*Ja*, you're right. I can't blame anyone for being upset with me. In fact, you might be even more disappointed when you hear that I've received a job offer in Denver."

There. He'd finally told her. He reached inside his hat and pulled out Tom Caldwell's letter. Handing it to her, he waited patiently while she read it through. Twice. Then, she folded the pages, put them inside the envelope and handed it back to him. The only betrayal of her apparent calm was that her hand visibly trembled.

"So you're definitely going to leave again," she said. It was a statement, not a question.

"I haven't decided yet."

She folded her arms, as if she were cold. Since she was wearing her cape and the barn was quite warm, he doubted that.

"But you must be seriously considering accepting the offer or you wouldn't have shown me the letter," she said.

She was upset. He knew it instinctively. He could tell by the way her spine stiffened and she lifted her chin slightly higher in the air. Given the circumstances, he couldn't blame her.

"*Ja*, my logic tells me the work in Denver would give me more opportunities than staying here. But I love my life here too. I love the farm work, I love my *familye* and I love…"

He shook his head, wondering what he was about to say. He wasn't sure. A muddle of thoughts filled his mind. He was still missing Shannon more than he could say, but she was gone. Now, he was here with Lizzie.

"What about your faith?" she asked.

He nodded and placed a hand over his chest. "*Ja*, I still have it here in my heart."

She quirked one eyebrow at him. "Do you? When you go back to Denver, how can you live your faith when you are apart from your *familye* and never join us at church? Just like a bright coal that is pulled away from the flames of a fire, you would eventually lose the warmth of your faith."

He caught a tone of reservation in her voice. But deep inside, he believed in *Gott*. His faith was all that had carried him through after Shannon had passed away. Before he could say so, Lizzie quoted an old Amish saying.

"If you must doubt, then doubt your doubts, not your beliefs," she said.

He heard the conviction in her voice, but no judgment. Her face looked passive, her voice so composed…just another one of her good qualities. Except when they had played volleyball or baseball, he couldn't remember hear-

ing her raise her voice. And he wasn't sure why he'd told
her about the offer or what else he expected her to say.
Of course she wouldn't want him to leave. Her faith was
strong and she believed families should stay together.

"You always were so straightforward and sensible,"
he said.

"Is that wrong? What else do you want me to say?"
she asked.

He hung his head. "I don't know. On the one hand, I
wish you'd tell me it's okay to live among the *Englisch*.
That I'm still a *gut* man and acceptable to the Lord if I
return to Denver. But a part of me also wishes you'd yell
and scream at me and tell me that you want me to stay
here with my *familye* and…"

You.

Now where had that thought come from? He wasn't
sure.

"*Ach*, of course I want you to stay here. We are your
people. You belong here. There, I've said it. But it didn't
make you feel any better, did it?"

No, it didn't. And he realized the problem wasn't
with his faith, his *familye*, or his work as a paramedic.
The problem was with him. He loved both worlds, but
hadn't accepted himself so that he could decide where
he wanted to be. Where he truly felt he belonged and
where the Lord wanted him to live.

"You…you won't mention this to my *mudder* or *vadder* or anyone else, will you? It would only upset them,"
he said.

A deep, wrenching sadness filled her eyes and he
thought for a moment that she was going to cry. "*Ne*, I
won't tell a soul. But, Eli, keeping it a secret will only

delay the inevitable. What do you want? Where do you want to be? Unfortunately, you can't choose both lives."

He couldn't answer. He honestly didn't know.

"I wish you felt a firm conviction of who you are and where you ought to be. Because once you know that deep inside, there will be no turning back and you will feel a deep, abiding joy and confidence in your life. I'll pray that you find that peace very soon."

She turned and left as quietly as she had come. He stared after her for a very long time, pondering her words. Wishing he could know for a certainty where he belonged. But no answers came.

Chapter Eleven

"I don't want to do it. I tell you, I don't need to exercise."

Eli heard the irritable words as he entered the back door to the kitchen and set a pail of milk on the table. Morning sunbeams glinted off the snow-covered fields and sprayed a ray of light through the window over the stainless steel sink. The little girls' happy voices carried from upstairs. Apparently they didn't have school today so the teacher could attend some meetings.

Across the countertops and table, a variety of large and small plastic bowls, brown bottles, powders, spatulas and long wooden molds covered with freezer paper had been set out in an orderly fashion. Eli recognized the molds as the same type his mother used to make soap and he figured that was Lizzie's planned work for the day. But she wasn't in here now.

"Leave me alone, I say." Jeremiah's unmistakable curt voice came from the living area.

"But, *Daed*, the doctor said you must do these exercises twice each day so you can regain your strength." Lizzie's pleading explanation was filled with frustration.

Knowing that Jeremiah didn't want him around, Eli turned toward the door. Like a coward, he planned to flee to the barn.

"And I'm not buying dumbbells either. I've lived my whole life without lifting weights. It's a bunch of foolishness, if you ask me."

"But, *Daed*, you've been in bed for weeks already. You need to move your muscles."

Eli paused at the back door, his hand on the knob. No, he was not going to interfere. This wasn't his business. He should leave them alone and return to his chores.

"*Daed*…please."

That did it. Turning, Eli walked into the living room. He had taken a couple of classes on physical therapy and understood the process. He could help, if Jeremiah and Lizzie would let him. If there was any way he could help ease Lizzie's frustration, he had to try.

Jeremiah was sitting upright on the bed, his legs extended on top of the covers with his casted leg cradled by two pillows. Except for his missing hat and bare feet, the man was fully dressed for the day. A breakfast tray, basin of water, toothbrush and shaving implements rested on the coffee table nearby, along with a towel and comb. Eli couldn't help thinking Lizzie was taking good care of her father.

Clearing his voice, he stepped near. "Can I help?"

Lizzie whirled around and the papers she was holding fluttered to the wood floor. Eli saw that they were covered with pictures, showing how to correctly perform a number of simple exercises.

"Eli! *Guder mariye*," she said as she quickly gathered up the pages.

He nodded respectfully, noticing her ruffled expression. *"Guder mariye."*

"What do you want?" Jeremiah looked away, as if dismissing him.

Since Eli had dealt with obstinate patients before, he didn't feel intimidated one bit. And knowing how hard Lizzie was trying to help her father, Eli decided to be blunt.

"I want to offer my services."

Jeremiah glared. "What are you talking about? You're already running my farm."

Resigning himself to being patient, Eli smiled tolerantly. "That's not what I mean. I'm trained and have worked with physical therapy patients before."

"You…you have?" Lizzie said, her eyes filled with startled wonder.

He nodded. *"Ja*, when I was trying to decide what field I wanted to go into, I took some extra classes. I thought perhaps I could help your *vadder* with his exercises."

"I don't need to exercise, nor do I need your help," Jeremiah replied, his tone a low rumble.

Hmm. Maybe Eli should try a different approach.

"Of course you need to exercise. As Lizzie pointed out, it'll strengthen your body. Without it, your muscles will atrophy from lack of use. Once you're able to get up and walk again, you won't be able to do the work. You'll be weak and winded. And then I'll have to stay here on your farm even longer."

Ah! That did the trick. Jeremiah's eyes widened and he stared at Eli with open shock.

Eli hated to use such tactics, but knew it was the only way to get through to Jeremiah. It couldn't be easy for a hardworking man like Jeremiah to sit around idle all day, dependent on the help of a man he didn't even like to keep the farm running. Up until the accident, he had led a vital, busy, self-sufficient life. No wonder he was so irritable.

Releasing a cantankerous sigh, Jeremiah pursed his lips together. "*Ach*, all right. Let's get on with it then."

Lizzie smiled and threw an expression of gratitude in Eli's direction. In her eyes, he could see that she understood what he'd just done. Reverse psychology, of sorts. But if it got Jeremiah to cooperate, then it was worth the effort.

"Do you have some unopened soup cans that weigh about one pound each?" Eli asked Lizzie.

"*Ja*, in the cupboard." Without asking what they were for, she hurried into the kitchen and soon returned with two cans of soup. She handed them to Eli, then stepped back.

Jeremiah eyed the cans with a belligerent scowl. "What are you gonna do with those?"

"Since you don't have any one-or two-pound dumbbells, you can lift cans of soup to exercise your arms. It's cheaper and just as effective…unless you're already too weak to lift them," Eli added, trying to needle Jeremiah into doing the exercises.

"Humph! Of course I can do it," Jeremiah said.

Eli thought he heard a muffled laugh coming from Lizzie, but didn't look her way. Jeremiah murmured something about looking silly lifting soup cans that Eli chose to ignore.

"Can you do this?" Eli proceeded to clasp a can in each hand and do several biceps curls. Then he handed the cans over to Jeremiah.

Conscious of Lizzie watching with interest, Eli waited as Jeremiah did the curls.

"That is *gut*, but what about doing it this way?" Taking the cans, Eli showed Jeremiah a variation of curls that would exercise different muscles in his neck, shoulders, arms and back.

"*Ja*, I can do all of them." Jeremiah took the cans and mimicked Eli in perfect fashion.

"That is very *gut*. But slow down just a bit and concentrate on working your muscles. Feel your movements and make them worth the effort," Eli encouraged.

Jeremiah did as asked and Eli counted out two sets of eight repetitions before they switched to a different exercise.

"I heard your doctor tell Lizzie that he wants you to aim for full weight bearing on your leg within three weeks. In order to do that, you should exercise your good leg too," Eli said.

He didn't want to confess that, while Lizzie was helping Jeremiah pack for his trip home, Eli had spoken with Dr. McGann out in the reception room at the hospital. Eli hadn't expected to help Jeremiah with his exercises, but he was naturally curious and so he'd educated himself on what the man needed to do.

When he glanced Lizzie's way, Eli discovered that she had vacated the room. The subtle sounds of tap water running in the kitchen and dishes clanking told him she was doing her morning chores. He continued to work with Jeremiah, coaxing the older man to lay flat so he could lift, push and stretch his healthy leg. Soon, they'd completed the variety of tasks the doctor had recommended.

"There, you're all done for the morning. But you need to do the same exercises this afternoon. It wasn't so hard, was it?" Eli asked.

"*Ne*, it wasn't hard," Jeremiah responded.

But Eli knew the man was covering the exhaustion he

felt. Jeremiah's breathing sounded heavy and his arms trembled as he tried to do extra repetitions of the exercises. Even just a few weeks of inactivity had left his body weaker, but Eli doubted the man would ever confess that out loud. At least, not to him.

"Tomorrow, try to do an extra set of each exercise. You'll soon find that the work gets easier and you'll be able to do more each day." Ignoring Jeremiah's cloudy frown, Eli spoke in a cheery, optimistic tone.

"*Ja*, I will do as you say," Jeremiah said.

Pleased by this admission, Eli turned toward the kitchen. "And now, I had better get on with my work. Send one of the *maed* for me if you need anything at all."

"I won't need anything from you," Jeremiah said.

Pretending not to notice the man's deep scowl, Eli hid a smile as he walked out of the room. As he entered the kitchen and saw Lizzie standing in front of the counter, he felt suddenly light of heart. The ties of her *kapp* hung loose against her shoulders and he was tempted to tug playfully on them. No, he better not. She was still on edge around him. But he had to admit it felt great to be needed.

Wearing goggles and a face mask, Lizzie set the heavy plastic bowl on the battery-operated scale and measured out the distilled water. When she finished, she reached for the jar of sodium hydroxide, or lye as it was commonly called.

As he spoke to her father, the sound of Eli's deep voice reached her from the living room. She paused a moment, trying to hear his words.

Glancing at the new recipe Abby had given her, she read through the list of ingredients again. Now where was she?

Eli's laughter caused her to glance toward the door. With a sigh, she picked up the recipe one more time. Glancing at the bowl of water, she shook her head in disgust. She'd barely started and had already made a huge mistake. She wanted to double this batch of soap, which meant she needed more distilled water. Why couldn't she seem to concentrate today?

Setting aside the lye, she picked up the water jug and added the proper amount to the bowl. She was too distracted by her father and Eli. Determined to focus on her work, she again reached for the lye. Removing the lid, she shook the container to get the white chips to fall out into the bowl.

"Lizzie?"

She jerked, splashing lye chips into the water. The caustic liquid spattered her hands and arms and she dropped the container of chips. Of all the foolish things to do…she'd forgotten to put on her rubber gloves.

Thankfully, the lye container thudded onto the counter top rather than spilling across the floor. The last thing she wanted was to clean up a big lye spill. But she flinched in pain as the corrosive alkaline solution burned her bare flesh.

"Ouch!" she cried.

Before she knew what was happening, she found herself leaning over the sink. A gush of fresh water rushed over her hands from the tap.

She stared at the stream for several moments, shocked by what had happened. Then, she looked up at Eli. He stood close, his face only a breath away. He held her hands, his touch gentle but firm.

"Is that better?" he asked.

"Um, *ja*, it is…"

She couldn't finish, barely able to gather her thoughts. Their gazes met and she couldn't have moved away to save her life. She felt locked there, held prisoner by her own suppressed longings. As if time stood still and he had never left Riverton and nothing bad had ever happened between them.

"Does it still hurt?" he asked, his voice slightly husky.

"What…?"

He repeated the question.

She blinked, trying to remember where she was. Trying to think. "*Ne*, I think it's fine now."

"Do you have some vinegar?" he asked.

"*Ja*." But she didn't move.

"Where is it? It'll help neutralize the lye and stop the burning."

"*Ach*, of course."

With water dripping down her arms, she reached into a cupboard and took out a bottle. Before she could act, he removed it from her hand and unscrewed the lid. He reached for a hand towel and tipped the bottle so that it saturated the fabric. Then he pressed it against the myriad of small splotches on her skin where the lye had burned her. Her nose twitched at the pungent scent of vinegar, but she felt instant relief.

Looking up, she found his lips were but a space away from hers. She felt his warm breath tickle her cheek. Felt the warmth of his fingers against her skin. It happened again. That magnetic attraction she'd thought was long dead.

"Lizzie-bee," he whispered, drawing nearer.

He kissed her. A soft, gentle caress that filled her with a yearning she had forgotten years ago. She closed her eyes and let herself go…

"Lizzie, *Daed* needs another pillow."

They jerked apart as Marty bounced into the kitchen.

Lizzie flinched and turned aside, clasping the dish towel with her hands. As Eli turned off the water faucet, she snuck a worried glance over at Marty, relieved to note that the girl didn't seem to notice anything wrong. But Lizzie still felt the strong emotions buzzing between her and Eli. Had the moment affected him as much as it had her?

"Of course. I'll get one right now," she said, swiveling toward the door.

This was a good excuse to get out of here right now. She stole a glance at Eli, trying to see his face and assess his mood. He ducked his head as he dried his own hands on the discarded towel, seeming completely composed. And it was just as well. After all, he was considering another job in Denver. He was planning to leave again. He had loved Shannon and didn't want her. Deep in her heart, Lizzie had always known he wouldn't stay. That the call of the *Englisch* world was too strong for him to resist. But she'd hoped and prayed he might find life in Riverton too compelling to leave.

Her decision not to let herself fall in love with him again had been wise. And yet, moments like this reminded her of how much they'd once cared for one another. It would be so easy to let down her guard and...

No! She mustn't think that way. Eli was leaving and that was that.

As she walked out of the kitchen, she didn't look back to see if Eli was watching her. But she didn't have to. She could feel his eyes on her just as surely as she lived.

Chapter Twelve

Eli lifted the full bucket of milk and moved it carefully out from beneath the Holstein. The cow stamped a foot and gave a low *moo*. A little of the frothy milk sloshed over the brim and Eli steadied his hold on the handle. He shouldn't have filled the bucket so full, but he'd been thinking about what had happened yesterday with Lizzie. He never should have kissed her. Never should have gotten so close to her. Not only was he still heartsick over losing Shannon, but he was seriously considering leaving soon. So, what had he been thinking?

Bending over one of the tall canisters, he poured the milk inside. At a sound in the doorway, he looked up, surprised to see Lizzie standing there. After what had happened between them, he would have thought she would avoid him like the plague. He blinked, thinking she was his imagination playing tricks on his mind. But no. She stood in front of the open doorway, her slender body silhouetted by morning sunlight.

"Lizzie-bee," he whispered her name, or at least he thought he did. He wasn't sure.

She wore a light blue dress, her black apron and white

kapp both crisp and perfectly starched. He caught a brief whiff of her scent, a subtle mixture of cinnamon and vanilla. He wasn't surprised. She was always baking something delicious to eat.

"Eli," she said.

"Lizzie," he spoke at the same time.

They both laughed with embarrassment.

After setting the bucket on the ground, he stood up straight. "Sorry. You go first."

She waved a hand in the air. "*Ne*, tell me what you wanted to say. My issue will probably take longer to discuss."

Folding her hands together in front of her, she waited with a firm, but serene expression. He never should have kissed her. Now, he felt like a heel. He'd simply forgotten himself in the moment. But he didn't want Lizzie to think he was using her. She already thought he was too worldly, too filled with pride. He'd be mortified if she thought he was taking advantage of her. But how could he explain what he'd done when he didn't understand it himself?

"I… I'm sorry for what happened yesterday. So very sorry. I've regretted it ever since and wanted you to know how bad I feel…"

She stiffened, then shook her head emphatically. "I'm sorry you regret it, but you're right. It was an accident. It never should have happened."

She turned away and he hurried to clasp her arm. He didn't want to drive her away. Trying to be gentle, he pulled her back around.

"*Ne*, Lizzie. I… I didn't mean it like that. I don't really regret our kiss. *Ach*, I do, but I don't. It's just that…"

"There's no need for you to explain. We won't discuss it ever again. Please just let it drop now."

He opened his mouth to say something more. Something that didn't sound so ridiculous. But she didn't give him the chance.

"I have a small request, if you wouldn't mind." She took a step back, her hands fluttering nervously for a moment.

He stared at her in confusion. That was it? They weren't going to discuss the kiss? She'd barely let him apologize. There was more he wanted to say. To clarify and try to help her understand. After all, she deserved an explanation. But since he didn't know what to say, maybe dropping the subject was for the best.

"What is it? Anything you need. Just name it," he said.

Okay, maybe he was overcompensating now. But he realized that he'd do almost anything for this woman. Anything at all. She'd earned his admiration and respect and he considered her to be one of the best people he'd ever been privileged to know.

"I would like to attend the quilting frolic over at Naomi's farm this morning. We will be working on some new baby quilts for Abby. The *maed* would like to go with me, to play with the other *kinder*." Her voice sounded hesitant, as if she feared he might think her desires were foolish or frivolous.

He nodded, delighted that she was telling him about a normal, mundane event. "*Ja*, you absolutely should go. It would be *gut* for you to get out of here for a while. The roads are clear and you should have no problems driving the buggy."

After all, tending to the demanding needs of a grumpy man like Jeremiah couldn't be easy all the time. It might do both Lizzie and the girls good to get out and have a little fun for once.

She frowned. "*Ach*, I have one problem, though."

His hearing perked up at that. Lizzie was actually confiding in him, seeking his advice. It was like they were real friends again. He hoped.

He stood close, looking down at her sweet face. "What is it?"

"While I'm gone, would you mind checking in on *Daed* now and then? I've prepared a lunch for both of you and put it in the cooler. When the time comes, if you wouldn't mind getting it out for him and, you know, seeing to his other needs, I'd greatly appreciate it." She shrugged, her cheeks flushing a pretty shade of pink.

Without asking for more details, he understood her meaning. "Of course. I'd be happy to look in on Jeremiah from time to time. I'm sure I can help him with anything he might need. And it might be fun to eat lunch with him today."

A doubtful frown pulled at her lips and he laughed. "Don't worry. We will both be just fine."

She showed a smile so bright that it made his throat ache.

"*Danke*, that would be great. But I should warn you. He's not happy about being alone for most of the day. He has *The Budget* newspaper and plenty of other reading material close at hand, but he may be a bit grouchy with you. I think he's got cabin fever something fierce. Are you sure you're up to spending time with him through-out the day?"

Her eyes were so wide and hopeful that he wouldn't have had the heart to deny her, even if he was so inclined. Which he wasn't.

"*Ja*, we'll be fine. You leave Jeremiah to me." He smiled, trying to convey a self-confidence he wasn't sure he really felt. He knew Jeremiah didn't like him anymore, but was determined to win him over. Maybe this was just what they needed.

"Will you be leaving soon?" he asked.

She nodded. "As soon as the *maed* are ready. They've just finished breakfast and are brushing their teeth now."

"*Gut.* I'll get the horse and buggy hitched up and bring them outside for you," he offered.

"*Danke.*"

She turned and walked away, a happy bounce in her stride. She didn't look back at him. He knew because he stared after her to see if she would. And though it made no sense to him, he couldn't help feeling a tad disappointed that she didn't.

An hour later, Eli reached a stopping point in his work and decided to check on Jeremiah. He fidgeted with his hat, feeling suddenly more wary than normal. In spite of speaking with Lizzie's father almost every day, Eli had yet to be alone with him. Since he'd returned from the hospital, there'd always been someone else in the room with them. Lizzie or one of her sisters. With someone else always around, there had been no opportunity for them to discuss that Jeremiah was the one who had returned Eli's letters.

Opening the back door to the kitchen, Eli stepped inside. He let the screen door clap closed behind him, purposefully alerting Jeremiah that he was here. Then he thought better of it. What if the man was napping?

"*Hallo,*" Eli called to the house.

He stepped into the living room, automatically glancing toward the bed. Jeremiah sat reclining against a pile of pillows, a newspaper resting beside him on the mattress. His left fingers still held the page. It looked as if he'd just lowered it there. He wore a pair of black reading glasses and peered at Eli from over the narrow frames.

"Did you need something?" Jeremiah asked, his voice still filled with a disapproving curtness.

"*Ne*, I just wanted to check on you, to see how you're doing." Eli forced himself to put a smile in his voice. After all, this man wasn't his enemy and he wished they'd never had any hostility between them.

"I'm doing fine." Jeremiah picked the newspaper up again, as if brushing Eli aside.

"Would you like your lunch now? It's about that time. Are you hungry yet?" Eli pressed.

Because he'd eaten so early that morning, Eli was famished and ready for the yummy meal Lizzie had prepared for them.

Jeremiah again lowered the paper to his lap and removed his glasses, setting them on top of a pile of magazines that rested beside him. He gazed at Eli for a few moments, his bushy eyebrows lifted in consideration.

"*Ja*, I could eat now. Why don't you go see what Lizzie prepared for us?"

Really? That wasn't so hard.

Turning, Eli returned to the kitchen. He went to the gas-powered refrigerator and opened the door, leaning down so he could peer inside. Sitting on the middle rack, he found two plates covered with plastic wrap. They each contained sandwiches made with thin slices of homemade bread and moist, thick cuts of meatloaf...probably leftover from last night's supper. A note lay atop a shoofly pie that said: *Enjoy*! As he got the plates out along with a pitcher of chilled milk, Eli's mouth watered in anticipation. He never doubted Lizzie's cooking skills. She would make some man an excellent wife.

He frowned. For some crazy reason, he didn't like the thought of her marrying someone else. And because of his relationship with Shannon, that didn't seem right.

He poured the milk and carried a tray of the food into the living room. As he set it beside Jeremiah, he didn't feel as nervous as before. That changed the moment he sat in a chair next to the elder man and took a bite of his sandwich.

"*Ach*, what are your plans for the future?" Jeremiah asked.

Eli coughed and took a quick swallow of milk to clear his throat.

"Um, I plan to live and work just as before," he said.

Jeremiah took a slow bite, chewed for a moment, then swallowed. During the entire time, his gaze never wavered from Eli. "Here in Riverton? Or will you return to Denver?"

Eli blinked, wondering if Lizzie had told her father about the job offer. He doubted it—she had said she would keep his secret. Until he was baptized into their faith, everyone in the *Gmay* was wondering if he would stay or go. For most everyone, Eli was able to brush aside their blunt questions. But something about Jeremiah's piercing gaze seemed to look deep inside of him for the truth. Because he'd always respected this man and because he was Lizzie's father, Eli couldn't lie to him. But how could he admit he didn't know for sure what he would do?

"I plan to stay."

Since he hadn't decided if he wanted to leave, he thought that was an honest enough response.

"*Gut.* I've seen the way you look at my *dochder*, and I'll admit I've been concerned."

What? The way he looked at Lizzie?

Eli tilted his head to the side. "I don't understand. I don't look any special way at her," Eli said, feeling totally confused.

Jeremiah snorted, then took another bite of food, chewed calmly and swallowed before responding. "I don't want you to hurt her again the way you did last time you left. Nor do I want her to run away with you. You sent her letters before. I imagine they asked for her to join you in Denver."

So. Here it was. The topic had turned around to the letters. Eli knew it would. Eventually. And he couldn't deny that he *had* asked Lizzie to come to him in those letters.

"I didn't run away. I just left," Eli said.

One of Jeremiah's bushy eyebrows shot up. "Is there a difference?"

"I think so. But are you referring to the letters I wrote to Lizzie, which you returned to me? Unopened? Without even telling her about them?"

Jeremiah met Eli's gaze without a single drop of shame in his eyes.

"*Ja*, those would be the ones. I don't want you to do that again. It would hurt Lizzie too much. She is a gut *maedel* and deserves better from her fiancé."

"We were only fourteen years old when I asked her to marry me."

"So? Why does it matter how old you were? Are you a man of your word or not?" Jeremiah paused, waiting for a response that didn't come.

Once again, Eli felt rotten inside. The foolishness of his youth seemed to keep haunting him.

"I regret hurting her more than I can say. When she didn't write back to me, I assumed she no longer wanted me and our engagement was broken," Eli said.

Jeremiah didn't respond to that. He simply looked at

Eli with that calm, unemotional expression of his. Finally, he picked up his fork and took a big bite of pie.

"I don't regret returning your letters and I'd do it again if the situation was the same," Jeremiah said.

Eli flinched at these words. He thought their conversation was over, but apparently not.

"I do regret that my *dochder* got hurt when you ran away to the *Englisch* world," Jeremiah continued. "I hope you've figured out who you are by now. Because no amount of education, no career or accolades of men, no wealth or worldly success can ever compensate for failure in your own home. Every man must live with the man he makes of himself. As you prepare for your future, I hope you'll never forget that. Especially where my *dochder* is concerned."

Every man must live with the man he makes of himself.

Eli hesitated, these words playing over and over in his mind. Since it was an old Amish saying, he'd heard it many times from his own father. But never before had it struck him with such powerful force. Such meaning.

He thought about the past, present and future, and wanted more than anything to be content with the man he became at the end of his life. To be able to meet the Lord without shame. To know he'd done his absolute best and kept trying even when he failed. To have as few regrets in his life as he could possibly make. But what did that have to do with Lizzie? They were no longer engaged and his future no longer included her.

Or did it?

Chapter Thirteen

Over the next few weeks, Lizzie and her *familye* settled into a routine. In the mornings and early afternoons, Jeremiah grudgingly accepted Eli's help with the simple exercises the doctor had recommended. When they drove into town to visit Dr. McGann, he was more than pleased by Jeremiah's progress.

Each evening, before he went home, Eli would come into the house to sit and talk with Jeremiah about his work for the following day. No longer did Lizzie's father speak to Eli with a gruff, disapproving voice, although he was still reserved around the younger man.

On this particular afternoon, the wind and a lashing rain buffeted the house, but Lizzie felt warm and cozy inside. Because of the stormy weather, she had dried the laundry on racks set up in the living room. As she folded each piece and laid it inside the wicker basket, she couldn't help eavesdropping on the men's low conversation. The little girls sat on the couch nearby, reading quietly to one another. Outside, dark clouds filled the sky. The rain had slowed to a smattering that hit the windowpanes. Lizzie glanced that way, grateful to be inside. As she lit a kerosene lamp and set it nearby on a table so the children could see more easily, she thought the moment seemed so tranquil. So relaxed and normal, but it wasn't. Not for Lizzie.

No matter how many days passed, she couldn't forget the kiss she'd shared with Eli. Every time she saw him, she became nervous and quivery inside. When she thought of how much he must still love Shannon, she felt completely confused. Why had he kissed her? Had he forgotten who she was? But more than that, why had she kissed him back?

"What about the disc plow? Have you sharpened the blades yet?" Jeremiah asked Eli.

The older man sat upright on his bed with several pillows to support his back. Eli sat nearby in a hard chair.

"*Ja*, I took care of that as soon as Lizzie and I finished baling and putting the hay away," came Eli's even reply.

"And the baler…does it need any maintenance?"

Eli shook his head. "*Ne*, but I cleaned it out *gut* and got it ready for next season. The harness required mending and I replaced several buckles. The *maed* helped me."

Jeremiah glanced at his younger daughters, approval shining in his eyes.

"The barn roof also needed a few repairs. I found your extra shingles and did the work before the storms hit," Eli said.

"*Gut, gut.* Tomorrow, I'd like you to check the fence again, if the weather isn't too bad. I don't want any of the livestock to get out."

"I will do so," Eli confirmed.

Hefting the laundry basket, Lizzie climbed the stairs. She felt a mixture of gratitude and uncertainty. Eli had become immersed in their lives, almost as if he was a part of their *familye*. And he wasn't.

He acted as if he wanted to stay in Riverton, but Lizzie knew he was still drawn to worldly pursuits. If only he could find his *Gelassenheit* and accept that he was born to be an Amish man. She wondered how his leaving might impact his parents and the rest of the *Gmay*.

And her.

Thinking about his eventual departure made her heart pound harder. She told herself it was because she feared for his salvation. Her faith would allow nothing less. She truly believed that, if he turned his back on their faith and left Riverton, his soul would be in jeopardy. And no matter how many times she told herself it was his choice, she still longed for a way to convince him to stay.

Inside the children's room, she placed their folded clothes tidily in their dressers. She crossed the hall to her room and looked up. A shoebox she did not recognize sat on top of her chest of drawers.

Wondering what it was, she set the laundry basket on the floor, then lifted the lid to the box. A gasp tore from her throat and she stepped back, covering her lips with the fingertips of one hand. Her thoughts scattered. Inside, tied together with a bit of string, was a hefty stack of sealed letters. Each one was addressed to her, the postmark from Denver several years earlier. Without asking, she knew these were Eli's letters. The ones her father had returned.

Reaching inside, she lifted out the stack, then closed the door to give herself more privacy. The bed bounced gently as she sat on one corner. Resting the pile of letters in her lap, she stared at them for at least five minutes. Her body trembled when she finally untied the string.

She withdrew the first letter, but her shaking hands immediately dropped it to the floor. Bending at the waist, she picked it up. What was the matter with her? After so many years, these letters should make no difference in her life. They shouldn't matter. But they did.

Obviously, Eli had put the letters here for her to find. Maybe she should return them to him, or burn them and forget they ever existed.

The envelopes had been arranged in chronological order. She told herself that, if she didn't read them, nothing in her life would change. She could go on the way she was, filled with heartbreak and doubt. And that's when she realized how comfortable she'd become with those two emotions as her constant companions.

She felt compelled to read. She had to know what Eli had said to her. The letters were a part of her somehow. A part of her life—and Eli's life—that she'd missed because her father had withheld them from her.

She slid her finger beneath the flap of the first envelope. As she pulled out the crisp pages and unfolded them, she took a deep breath, trying to settle her nerves. She immediately recognized Eli's scrawling handwriting. Her gaze scanned the words, a hard lump as big as a boulder lodging in her throat. Eli conveyed his regrets over leaving her without saying goodbye. He expressed his love for her and a wish that she would join him in Denver. He still wanted to marry her, if she wanted him. He would await her reply…a response that never came.

One by one, Lizzie read the pile of letters, dazed by Eli's explanations of his fierce desire for a college education and skeptical of his declarations of love for her. Toward the end, he conveyed the deep sense of loss he felt when she didn't write back, and returned his let-

ters unopened. In between, he discussed his schooling
and work as a waiter in a restaurant to make ends meet.
He looked mature for his age and had rented a studio
apartment that was small but clean and had room for
her. Every day, he walked to school, sitting in classes
that tantalized his intellect and convinced him more and
more of an eternal *Gott* who loved all his children un-
conditionally. Instead of weakening his faith, his education had strengthened his beliefs. Several times, he
asked why she wouldn't write to him. He begged her to
reconsider and join him in his *Englisch* life.

To marry him.

And then the final letter. Lizzie maintained her composure as she read Eli's deep sense of sorrow because
he realized he'd lost her for good. He said he understood
why she hadn't written him. That their breakup was his
fault and he couldn't blame her for not wanting a life
with him outside of the *Gmay*. She deserved a man of
faith who never questioned their leaders or *Gott*'s will
for them. It was time for them both to move on.

And that was the end.

Folding the last letter, Lizzie added it to the stack and
retied the string. She put the letters back in their box and
settled the lid over the top of them. Fearing her father or
sisters might find and read them, she slid them far beneath her bed where they wouldn't be discovered easily.

So, now she knew. She'd finally read Eli's letters. His
words were highly personal and gave her a new insight
into who he really was inside. And for the first time since
she'd known him, she finally understood his desire to
learn new things. And she was surprised to find that it
didn't make her angry anymore. Because she'd loved

him so much, she couldn't condemn him. She had to let him choose for himself, no matter how much it hurt her.

Taking a deep, settling breath, she smoothed her skirt and apron. A quick glance in the tiny mirror on her night-stand caused her to tidy her hair and adjust her *kapp*. Chores were waiting. She had to go on with her life. She couldn't while away the day by sulking here in her room. She had to go downstairs and tend to her father and sisters. She had to be strong and resolute. Firm in her faith and her place in the world.

She took a step toward the door. She clutched the knob, but couldn't make it turn so she could leave. She stared at the oak panel, her vision blurring. Something gave way inside of her and she burst into deep, trembling sobs.

It was time to go. The rain had finally stopped, the evening air filled with the crisp scent of damp sage. Eli had finished his work and harnessed his horse to the buggy, but couldn't seem to get inside and drive away. Instead, he stood at the barn doors, gazing out at the damp farmyard. It was already dark with not even the stars or moon to light his way home. Without being able to see them, he knew the sky was filled with heavy, black clouds.

For the sake of safety, he should get on the road now, before it got any later. *Mamm* and *Daed* were expecting him for supper. But he hesitated, wondering if Lizzie had read the letters he'd left in her room. Wondering if she might come out to speak with him about them. He'd watched her go upstairs and knew she must have found them.

As he surveyed the house, the lights in the kitchen

brightened and he knew she must be inside, preparing supper for her *familye*. Soon, Jeremiah would be up and walking again. His leg would continue to heal and he wouldn't need Eli's help on the farm anymore. Eli could leave, if he chose to do so. He could return to Denver and his old life there. No Shannon or Lizzie to welcome him. No love to share.

Completely alone.

Lizzie wasn't coming out to the barn. His stomach rumbled and he realized it was time to eat. His parents would be worried if he didn't arrive soon. Lizzie was occupied elsewhere. She probably didn't care about the letters now. He wasn't sure what he had expected. That she would read them and come running into his arms to declare that she still loved him? That she wanted to marry him and raise a *familye* with him here in Riverton? That wasn't what he wanted, was it? He was still in love with Shannon. Right?

He snorted and turned away, returning to his buggy. He'd always been so firm in what he wanted out of life. So convinced that the *Englisch* life was best for him. But now, he felt nothing but conflict. He was even starting to doubt his love for Shannon. Sometimes, he couldn't remember her face. All he could remember was Lizzie. And that wasn't right. No, it couldn't be.

Pulling on his warm gloves, he led the horse out into the yard and secured the barn doors. He climbed into his buggy seat and took hold of the lead lines.

"Schritt!" he called.

The horse stepped forward, pulling the buggy through puddles of water along the dirt road.

Eli figured his letters to Lizzie were too little, too late. In the time since he had written them, he'd fallen in love with someone else. It still hurt like a knife to his heart every time he thought about losing Shannon. But lately, he couldn't remember the shape of her eyes, or the contour of her chin. Whenever he thought about her, his thoughts turned to Lizzie. Which was foolish because she didn't care for him anymore. Not romantically, anyway. They'd both moved on with their lives. And yet, he couldn't help wishing…

He was being stupid! He had no idea why he'd kissed her. He'd been so embarrassed by what he'd done. So ashamed.

He turned the buggy onto the county road, pulling over to the shoulder. The horse trotted forward, eager to get home.

Every time Lizzie was in the room with him, Eli felt a deeper sense of guilt. Kissing her had been wrong on so many levels. His lapse in judgment hadn't been fair to either of them. It might lead her to believe there could be something between them again. That he still loved her the way he used to. And he didn't. Did he?

He remembered all the times when he'd thought Lizzie was rejecting his letters because she was disappointed in him. He thought she had returned them all to him. Because he'd turned his back on his faith and their love. And all that time, she hadn't even known that he had written to her. From her perspective, she must have thought he'd abandoned her completely, without any explanation. That he'd broken all his promises to her. That he'd chosen the world over her. And that wasn't true. He'd begged her to join him—had wanted to share the world with her. But that had been a foolish dream. Lizzie had never wanted a life anywhere other than here.

He shook his head. The letter from Tom Caldwell was

still folded inside his hat. He hadn't responded to the job offer yet. For the time being, Lizzie's *familye* still needed his help. But soon, Jeremiah would be back on his feet. So, what was holding Eli back? He wasn't sure, but knew he'd have to make a decision soon. And he'd need to speak to Lizzie as well. To tell her he was deeply, genuinely sorry for how things had not worked out between them. She deserved that apology and so much more. He only hoped she could find it in her heart to forgive him.

Chapter Fourteen

The day of Church Sunday was a pleasant surprise. The Sangre de Cristo Mountains were coated with snow, but down in the valley everything had melted off the roads and fields. The sun gleamed bright and surprisingly warm in the morning sky. Not bad, considering they were only a week away from Thanksgiving. As Lizzie hurried to gather the eggs, she thought it most fitting for the *Gmay*'s semiannual Communion meeting. It should be a day of enlightenment and confidence in the Lord. But for herself, she still felt overshadowed by qualms.

"Lizzie?"

She turned. Eli stood just beyond the open doorway, his dark hair shining against his sun-bronzed face. Wearing his best clothes, he held his hat in his hands. Seeing him brought a quick leap of excitement to her chest, but she tried to squelch it. She'd avoided him for a long time now. Perhaps today of all days, it was time to speak with him and let go of her harsh feelings. Instead of nursing her own broken heart, she should think about other people for a change…starting with Eli.

Carrying the wire basket filled with eggs, she stepped

outside and latched the door of the chicken coop. Then, she looked up into his eyes.

"*Guder mariye*, Eli. *Wie bischt du heit*?"

"I am *gut*, but I am worried about you," he said.

She took a deep inhale of the crisp air and let it go, reminding herself to remain calm. To trust in the Lord. And to forgive.

"Why would you be worried about me?" she asked, thinking she knew the answer, but not quite sure.

He looked at the ground, his chiseled profile so handsome that she almost reached out to touch his cheek. Almost.

"I… I owe you an apology," he said.

Yes, he did, but she didn't say that.

"For what?" she said instead.

His gaze met hers and in his eyes, she saw deep remorse there. "For so many things. For kissing you. For leaving all those years ago without saying goodbye in person. For not coming to see you when you didn't respond to my letters. For breaking off our engagement. For being a stupid, foolish kid. I was young and *dumm* and wanted a *rumspringa*."

She showed a sad little smile. "*Ach*, then you got what you wanted."

"*Ja*, but I regret putting myself first and not thinking about how my leaving might affect you and my *eldre*. I'm sorry for the pain I caused. I can't look back and regret my life, but I do deeply regret hurting you, both now and in the past."

Oh, did he have to say that?

"*Es tut mir leid*. Can you please forgive me for what I did?" he continued.

Here it was. The moment she'd been dreading. Forgiveness was a requirement of her faith. If she truly believed in Christ and the Atonement, then she must pardon Eli for any wrongs he'd done to her. Repentance wasn't just for her. It was for others as well. But still she hesitated, her pulse quickening as she pondered what to say. And yet, there was really only one response she could give.

"Of course I forgive you, Eli."

As she said the words, her heart seemed to open up and a breath of fresh air cleansed her pain-filled heart.

A wide smile spread across his face. A gorgeous smile that stole her breath away and turned her mind to mush.

Placing his hat on his head, he took her hand in his. "That's the best thing I've heard since…since I don't know when. *Danke*, Lizzie-bee. You've made me very happy."

He paused for a moment, his long fingers wrapped around hers. She showed a lame smile, trying hard to be positive and friendly. She withdrew her hand, still feeling the warmth of his skin zinging up her arm.

"Will you be ready for me to drive you and your *familye* to church soon?" he asked, still smiling brightly.

"*Ja*, but I'm afraid *Daed* still needs our help to get from the house to the buggy."

"I figured as much. I'll get the horse ready and come by to help you in about ten minutes. Is that enough time?"

She nodded, her mouth too dry to speak. Instead, she whirled around and headed toward the house. Hopefully her sisters were ready and *Daed* had finished the breakfast tray she'd left for him before coming outside.

As she crossed the yard, she looked up and saw her father peering at her from the window beside his bed. His forehead was crinkled in a troubled frown.

A flush of heat scorched Lizzie's cheeks. Surely he couldn't have overheard her conversation with Eli, but he must have seen him holding her hand. *Daed* might misunderstand and think the gesture was romantic. And it wasn't. No, not at all. But the last thing she wanted was to explain to her father that Eli had merely apologized to her. No declarations of love. No new proposals of marriage. No promises for the future. It was just a simple apology so Eli could clear his conscience before he left and returned to Denver. And that was all.

"Hallo," Eli called as he entered the front door to the Beilers' house. He glanced at Jeremiah's bed, but found it vacant, the covers pulled up over the pillow in tidy order.

The house smelled of cinnamon and he wondered if Lizzie had baked something special for lunch. But where was Jeremiah?

"Eli!" Marty came running from the kitchen, her warm winter coat tucked beneath her arm.

Annie pounded down the stairs, the ties on her *kapp* whipping at her shoulders. Both girls launched themselves at him in a tight three-way hug.

"Oof!" he grunted and staggered back with their impact, then laughed. "You're not happy to see me, are you?"

"Of course we are," Marty said with a grin.

"Look! I lost another tooth last night." Annie smiled wide, showing a gaping hole in the front.

Eli leaned over to look closely, realizing how much he loved these two little girls. It would be so difficult to leave and never see them again. And what would they think of him when they found out he was gone? He hated the thought that they might be disappointed in him.

"Wow! You've lost a lot of teeth lately. How many does that make now?" he asked.

"Two in the last month. Lizzie says I'm getting my permanent teeth in because I'm growing up so fast."

"*Ach*, I suppose that's true. You're almost as tall as Marty." He glanced between the two girls, comparing their height.

Standing straighter, Marty frowned at that. "*Ne*, she's not. I'm still the tallest. That's 'cause I'm the oldest."

Annie giggled, her sweet voice filling the room. "But not for long. Lizzie says if I eat all my vegetables, I'll grow up to be tall and strong. I might pass you up one day."

"You will not," Marty said.

"I might," Annie insisted.

The two girls engaged in a harmless pushing match and Eli reached out to separate them. "*Ach*, that's no way to treat one another. When you're older, you'll be the best of friends. I promise you that. Until then, be kind and take care of one another."

As the elder, Marty nodded, looking rather serious. The thought of leaving and never seeing them grow up to be lovely young women brought a pang of hurt to Eli's chest. How he would miss them.

"I'm sorry," Annie said, hugging her sister.

A movement caught Eli's eye and he looked up, seeing Lizzie standing in the threshold to the kitchen. Dressed in her winter coat and black traveling bonnet, she held a large basket hanging from one arm.

"Annie, it's time to leave. Go get your coat," she said.

The girl did as asked, hurrying to the closet.

Eli stood straight, contemplating Lizzie. Her cheeks were flushed, possibly from baking early that morning.

Her pale lavender skirts swished against her legs as she reached for a pair of gloves on the table.

"Where is Jeremiah?" he asked.

She jutted her chin toward the bathroom. "He insisted on bathing himself this morning. I couldn't stop him."

Eli widened his eyes. "He's not walking on his broken leg, is he?"

"*Ne, ne.* He's walking on crutches. He promised not to put any weight at all on his bad leg. He knows how important it is to let it heal." The concern in her voice belied her words.

Eli's gaze followed her as she walked down the short hall to the bathroom and tapped lightly on the closed door.

"*Daedi*, are you all right? Do you need any help?" she asked, leaning her cheek against the hard panel.

"*Ne!* I'm fine," came Jeremiah's muffled response.

A loud clatter and splash accompanied his words, lending doubt to his statement.

"Eli is here to take us to church," she said.

"I'll be right out."

Lizzie returned to the living room, tugging on her gloves. She helped Annie with her coat and tidied a short wisp of hair. Watching Lizzie lovingly caress each child's cheek, Eli thought she would make an amazing mother one day. And suddenly, he saw her with new eyes. No longer was she the young teenaged girl he'd loved and left. Now, she was a fully matured woman who understood her place in the world and was confident in her choices.

The bathroom door rattled and jerked open, releasing a blast of steam. Jeremiah stood there on crutches, holding his injured leg up so it didn't touch the floor. He was fully dressed in his black frock coat, his combed hair and beard slightly damp.

Lizzie set her basket aside and both she and Eli hurried to help the man as he hobbled forward.

"Danke," he said.

Eli flinched, surprised to hear such a gracious word directed at him. Not since he'd been home had he heard anything approaching gratitude from Jeremiah. After working for the man for almost two months now, maybe Eli was growing on him. Maybe Jeremiah didn't think he was such a bad influence on Lizzie after all. Of course, that would end if Eli returned to Denver. And though he knew Jeremiah didn't approve of him, Eli hated the thought of losing the man's respect. He hated to let him and elders of their church down. He knew what people in the *Gmay* would say about him. He could just imagine Marva Geingerich's response at church.

You see? I told you he wouldn't stay with us, she would tell everyone who would listen.

He could also imagine his mother's tears. His leaving would break her heart. And though his father would never show his emotions, Eli knew it would break his heart too. But he mustn't let that be his reason for staying. Whether he stayed or left must be purely between him and *Gott*. He would have to live with his decision for the rest of his life and he must make the choice that was right for him.

Jeremiah fell back into a chair, breathing hard while Lizzie reached for his winter coat. One of his crutches dropped to the floor with a clatter while the other leaned against the side of the chair. Eli picked them up, holding both crutches at the ready.

"Vie gehts?" Eli asked the older man.

"I'm just fine," Jeremiah said as Lizzie held up his coat and he thrust each of his arms into the sleeves.

"Does your leg cause you any pain?" Eli asked.

"*Ne*, it feels *gut*. But I hate this weakness. I can't hardly move without being out of breath. You were right. My muscles aren't as strong anymore." The man wiped his forehead, seeming a bit out of sorts.

"Don't worry. The weakness will fade," Eli assured him.

Jeremiah looked up, his eyes filled with hope. "You really think so?"

"*Ja*, I know so."

"I must do more exercises, now that I'm able to get up and walk on crutches. I need to get stronger."

"That is a *gut* idea, but don't overdo. Give your body time to mend."

Jeremiah blessed Eli with a coveted smile. And that alone made him feel incredibly happy inside. But it soon faded when he thought of the stern frown that would cover the elder man's face once he learned that Eli had returned to Denver.

"Are you ready to go?" Lizzie asked her father.

He nodded, reaching for his crutches. Eli helped him as he stood.

"Marty, get the door," Lizzie called.

Both little girls hurried to open the way so that Jeremiah could pass through to the front porch. Outside, Eli lifted Jeremiah down the stairs. He had spread ice melt so the path to the buggy wasn't slick. They all moved at a slower pace, but once Lizzie had retrieved her basket and they were loaded inside, Eli breathed a silent sigh of relief.

Taking the lead lines into his hands, he released the break and called to Billie. *"Schritt!"*

The horse stepped forward in a jaunty trot, as if understanding the happy mood inside the buggy. Eli held the lead lines in his hands and thought about how much he would miss working with horses and the other livestock once he was back in Denver. Already he was yearning for the feel of a plow as it dug into the rich, fertile soil. The excitement of the harvest. The pleasure of eating one of Lizzie's home-baked pies. But if he stayed, he would long for the work he was missing in Denver. The joy of helping someone survive a heart attack, or saving their life after a bad accident. He'd put years into his schooling and couldn't let it go.

Returning to the present, he mentally calculated how long it would take to drive to Bishop Yoder's farm. Once they arrived, there would be many strong men to lift Jeremiah out of the buggy. They'd be happy to help, always working together for the good of them all. He realized how much he would miss each member of the *Gmay*.

As he listened to the girls' happy chatter in the back seat, he was surprised that Jeremiah chimed in now and then. Yes, the man was definitely feeling better. And though he was still weak, he was growing stronger every day. Soon, he wouldn't need Eli to work his farm. Soon, Eli could leave Lizzie and her sweet *familye* behind and return to his *Englisch* life. Lizzie had helped him see that Shannon's death hadn't been his fault and while he still grieved for her loss, he was grateful he'd been privileged to know his fiancée, for however short a time. But he wouldn't let guilt hold him back from the direction his life needed to take. Being a paramedic was what he'd worked so hard for. It was what he wanted to do with his life. He had to go back to Denver. He just had to. Lizzie would understand even if his parents and the rest of the *Gmay* wouldn't.

There. He'd finally made the decision of what he should do. He would return to Denver right after Thanksgiving. It was the right thing to do. He knew it deep within his heart. So, why did he feel so gloomy inside?

Chapter Fifteen

Sitting in the back seat of the buggy with her sisters, Lizzy enjoyed this trip to church more than any other she could remember. Snuggled in her warm cape and mittens, she listened to her sisters' happy prattle and watched the beautiful scenery pass by the window. Tall mountains and wide-open fields covered with snow met her view.

Once they arrived at Bishop Yoder's farm, Eli hopped out to help her father. Without being summoned, numerous men and boys appeared, eager to assist. They lifted Jeremiah easily and carried him inside the spacious barn. Lizzie followed with her father's crutches, placing them nearby.

"Eli!"

Little Timmy Hostetler ran into the barn and made a beeline straight for Eli. The man turned, saw the boy and scooped him up and spun him around before pausing for a tight hug.

"There's my Timmy. How are you doing this fine day?" Eli asked.

Still in the man's arms, the boy drew back and placed

his hands trustingly on Eli's shoulders. "I'm great. Even *Mamm* wonders at my recovery."

David stood nearby, a satisfied smile on his lips. "That's right. Linda thought he was too wild before he got sick. Now, she can't believe how active he is."

The other men laughed, patting Eli on the back.

Nearby, Linda Hostetler nudged old Marva Geingerich. "What do you think, Marva? Look at all the *gut* things Eli has done. Isn't it *wundervoll*? Do you still think he's going to leave again?"

"Humph!" was all Marva said.

Lizzie would have laughed it if hadn't been so sad to her. Watching Eli mingle with members of their *Gmay*, she felt a burst of joy. They were a tight community, sharing one another's burdens and joys. It was so good that they had avoided several catastrophes and they were happy to have all their members here today. But more than that, she gazed at Eli, and a sudden, wrenching sadness filled her heart with pain. Because she knew he would be leaving soon.

Marva Geingerich had been right all along.

Turning away, Lizzie headed into the house where she assisted the other women with the food. Abby and Fannie welcomed her and she pasted a smile on her face, pretending all was well.

When they were called in to church, Lizzie stepped outside and walked to the barn. Taking her place opposite the men, she sang when appropriate and listened intently as the bishop explained the true meaning of *Gelassenheit*, the joy in submission to *Gott*. She'd fought her fears for so many years now, but longed for a calm heart. She'd forgiven Eli, but still felt like she needed to let go of her fears. And that's when she realized the difficulty was no longer with Eli, but rather with herself. Withholding her forgiveness had made her the sinner, but pardoning Eli had taken a giant leap of faith. In spite of her father's disapproval and knowing Eli would soon be leaving, her heart was softened and she finally let go of her anger and doubts.

Glancing over at Eli, she watched his expressions as he listened intently to the bishop's sermon. A mixture of yearning and torment filled his eyes.

Lizzie's heart reached out to him. He didn't have an easy task ahead of him. It would take a lot for him to turn his back on his parents and church and walk away again. To return to his *Englisch* life alone, without Shannon or anyone else to love and care for. Lizzie knew she could never have that kind of strength, but neither could she be angry with him for his choices. Because now, she had another huge problem to deal with.

In spite of her father's disapproval, in spite of her best efforts not to, she still loved Eli more than ever before.

So much for her vow never to let him break her heart again.

The morning before Thanksgiving Day, Lizzie walked out to the barn under cover of darkness. Planning to get an early start to her day, she would feed the chickens first. She needed the extra eggs for her pies, breads and cream fillings.

Crossing the yard, she snuggled her knitted scarf tighter around her throat. As she exhaled, she saw her breath on the air like the blast from a steam engine. The sun wasn't even up yet, but she couldn't sleep. Too many things waged a battle inside her mind. Preparation of her *familye*'s feast, finding extra time when her sisters weren't around so she could sew a new dress for each of them before Christmas and Eli's inevitable departure.

Inside the barn, she looked up, surprised to discover that Eli's horse and buggy were already here. Two tall canisters of fresh milk sat beside the door. Since he was nowhere to be seen, she figured he must have finished the milking and gone out in the field with the cows. But why was he here so early? Maybe he couldn't sleep either.

Going about her business, she removed her gloves and picked up a silver scoop. First, she dug it into the grain, then into the cracked corn before dumping it all into her bucket and mixing it together. The extra protein helped the hens keep laying eggs even with the colder, shorter days of winter.

Looking up, she saw Eli's jacket had fallen off the peg by the door. She stepped over and lifted the coat to hang it up and blinked when some papers fell open on the ground. She picked them up, surprised to discover another letter from Eli's old boss in Denver. The man named Tom Caldwell.

Glancing at the doorway, she hunched her shoulders, feeling guilty for reading Eli's personal correspondence. She should return the letter to his coat and forget she'd ever seen it.

Folding the pages, her eyes caught the words *job* and *excited for your return*. Unable to resist, she quickly scanned the contents, discovering that Tom Caldwell needed Eli's acceptance of the supervisory job with a start date of December 1.

"Lizzie?"

She whirled around and faced Eli, flustered to be caught in the act of reading his mail. "I…um, your coat was on the ground and when I picked it up, this letter fell out."

She quickly handed the pages to him. Never had she been more conscious of her lack of worldliness. Compared to the classes he'd taken at the university and the life he'd lived among the *Englisch*, she must seem so simple and unsophisticated.

He gazed at the papers in his hand, overly quiet and seemingly uncertain. "Did you…did you read it?"

She nodded, unwilling to lie. "I'm sorry. I didn't mean to pry. It was just lying there open and I…"

Succumbed.

"*Ne*, it's me who is sorry, Lizzie. I should have taken better care. I didn't want you to see this." He peered at her, his eyes filled with misgivings. "Are you angry at me?"

She hesitated, her heart filled with anguish. How she hated to lose him a second time. How she hated that he couldn't seem to find contentment here in Riverton. But she couldn't be angry with him anymore. What good would it do? She loved him and truly wanted him to be happy, even if it meant losing him.

"*Ne*, I'm not angry. In fact, I understand." Reaching out, she squeezed his hand and met his gaze with conviction.

"You do?" he asked.

She nodded, but didn't speak. Her throat felt like it was stuffed with sandpaper.

"You see why I want to go, don't you? It's a great opening for me, Lizzie. It's what I've always wanted and I'll never get this chance again. All of my schooling has been for this opportunity. I can't pass it up. You know that, don't you?" He sounded almost desperate to convince her. And for a moment, she thought he was really trying to convince himself.

She showed a sad little smile and nodded. "*Ja*, I know it's what you've always wanted the most. I wish you would stay here in Riverton, but I know you have a gift for helping others. I can't hold you back from reaching your potential, nor will I judge you or try to stop you from following your heart. You have to decide for yourself. And I promise to support you in whatever life you choose, even though my place is here in Riverton, with our people. I care so very deeply for you and I just want you to be happy. Even if that means we'll never see each other again."

Before he could respond, she leaned upward on her tippy-toes and kissed his cheek farewell, then whirled around and raced back to the house. She didn't stop until she was safely inside her room where she closed the door and lay upon her bed to have a good, muffled cry. She would send the girls out to feed the chickens and gather the eggs later on. But even if the house was burning down around her, she didn't think she could face Eli again. She meant everything she had said to him. And right now, his happiness meant more to her than anything else, even if it meant she had to let him go.

Eli stood where Lizzie had left him. He stared at the open doorway, transfixed by the sight of her slender back as she walked away from him. Knowing he would never see her again. He couldn't move. Couldn't breathe. An overwhelming feeling of deep, abiding loss and grief pulsed over him again and again, like the crashing of tidal waves buffeting the shore. Lizzie was gone. All he had to do was finish his chores and go home. And the day after Thanksgiving, he could catch a bus back to Denver. It was what he wanted.

Or was it?

Lizzie wouldn't be there. He'd never see her again. Never hear her laugh or see her smile. Never be able to seek out her advice or hear his name breathed from her lips in a sigh of happiness ever again. And it was his own fault. He'd made this happen. With his thoughtless, selfish desires to chase the world.

But maybe, just maybe, it didn't have to be like this. He had one chance to make this right. To change the outcome. And suddenly, his life came into focus. It was as if a panoramic view opened up to him with his past, present and future life right before his eyes. Finally, he could see it all and understood what he wanted most above all other things.

His heart was filled with absolute confidence in what he must do. But he must do it now.

Turning, he reached for his coat. His course was set. He'd made up his mind and knew just what he wanted out of life. But he better not blow it this time. Because his eternal happiness was depending on what he did within the next ten minutes.

Chapter Sixteen

Over an hour later, Lizzie waited until she heard her sisters rustling around in their bedroom before she went downstairs and started breakfast. Finally the sun was up and she could stop staring at the ceiling in her room. She couldn't lay on her bed feeling sorry for herself all day long. She wiped her eyes and blew her nose and took hold of her composure. Within a week, Eli would be gone back to Denver and she'd never see him again. She had to accept that and move on.

"Why are your eyes all red and puffy?" little Annie asked when she came into the kitchen.

The girl's *kapp* and apron were askew. Lizzie adjusted her sister's clothing before turning toward the stove. "I think I might be catching a cold."

Which was partly true. She'd been sniffling even before her talk out in the barn with Eli that morning.

"*Guder mariye,*" Jeremiah called as he hobbled into the room on his crutches.

He smiled as he kissed Lizzie on the forehead, then scooted back a chair and sat down.

"*Guder mariye, Daedi,*" Lizzie said.

She watched him briefly, wondering if it was too soon for him to be getting around on his own. But since he never put any weight on his injured leg, she figured it was all right.

When Marty joined them seconds later, Lizzie set a meal of scrapple, bacon and thick-sliced bread on the table, then took her seat and bowed her head for prayer. As they ate, she responded automatically to questions and nodded to the conversations around her, but didn't really listen. Later, as she went about her day, she felt like she was moving in a fog. Her bones were achy, her chest filled with a painful emptiness. Maybe she had caught a cold after all. Surely it had nothing to do with losing the love of her life. Again.

"Do you want me to see if we have more eggs?" Marty asked later that afternoon.

Lizzie felt a tad guilty for sending the girl on another errand, but she had been avoiding the barn at all costs. She couldn't see Eli again. She just couldn't.

"I'm afraid I do need two more eggs," she said.

Nodding obediently, Marty did as asked. She returned minutes later with three fresh eggs.

"That's all there is. I hope that's enough to make your pies," Marty said as she set the eggs carefully on the counter.

Lizzie didn't look up from the batter she was whipping with a whisk. "*Danke, boppli.* I think this will be enough."

"*Gut!*" The girl reeled around and headed back to the living room. Lizzie knew she had a new book she wanted to read and decided to let her go. After all, it was Thanksgiving tomorrow. Except for the mandatory work of milking and feeding the livestock, they all planned to take a break from their other chores.

Once her pies sat cooling on the counter, Lizzie decided she needed some fresh air. Wrapping her cape around her, she stepped out on the front porch where she wouldn't be seen from the barn by Eli. Sitting in an Adirondack chair, she took several deep breaths, letting the frosty air cool her heated cheeks. It had gotten hot in the kitchen and she was grateful for this short break.

When she finally turned to go back inside, she glanced at the mailbox sitting at the edge of the lawn. The red flag was up, signaling to the postman that he should collect a letter to mail. That wasn't right. She had placed no letters there.

Planning to lower the flag, she stepped down off the porch and hurried over to the box. Inside, she found a sealed envelope from Eli to Tom Caldwell in Denver.

Her heart sank. No doubt the letter was Eli's acceptance of the job offer. Out of a selfish desire to keep him there in Riverton, Lizzie thought about taking the letter and destroying it. But that wouldn't be honest. Her personal integrity wouldn't allow her to do such a thing. Besides, destroying the letter wouldn't change Eli's decision. Instead, she left the letter right where it was and closed the door to the box. The red flag was up and she didn't lower it. The postman would pick it up within the next few minutes. But now, her heart felt even heavier than before. She'd seen the proof with her own eyes. Eli was leaving. She would never see him again.

Turning, she returned to the kitchen where she forced herself to focus on cleaning the turkey for their big feast tomorrow afternoon. In spite of it being Thanksgiving, she was having serious difficulty counting all her many blessings.

She tried to think of all the things she was grateful for. Her *familye* and their good health. The *Gmay* and all her many friends who genuinely cared about her. Good, nutritious food and the plentiful moisture they'd had to nourish their crops for a bountiful harvest next fall. It was all so wonderful. So grand and glorious. Other than a husband and *familye* of her own, she had everything an Amish woman could want. Perhaps she would one day meet another good man she could love and respect. Someone who would love her in return. But right now, she just couldn't feel any joy. Maybe in the near future. But not today. Not when she knew she would never see Eli again.

The following morning, Lizzie didn't feel much better. In spite of her sisters' happy banter, she carried a heavy heart as she prepared a Thanksgiving feast for her *familye*. In fact, she didn't feel like celebrating. She felt like crying. But the Lord wanted her to have joy, so she pasted a smile on her lips and forced herself to be in a good mood. But deep inside, she felt empty.

While her sisters set the table, Lizzie mixed the stuffing. It was filled with celery, sage and onion, and her nose twitched with the wonderful aromas. When it was time, her father helped her stuff the turkey. Once it was in the oven, she set the timer and glanced over at the counter. Hmm. Where had Marty gone off to? She was supposed to be peeling the potatoes. In fact, where was Annie? She had been given the task of cleaning the broccoli. Her vacant step stool stood in front of the kitchen sink, but no girls were anywhere in sight.

"Marty! Annie! *Kumme helfe*," she called, turning toward the door.

Jeremiah stood there on his crutches, his casted leg

held up from touching the floor. She had to admit, she was delighted that he was getting around so well. Because of Eli, the exercises had really helped and she must thank him for...

She paused, her brain spinning. Eli was leaving. She couldn't thank him. He wouldn't be at church next Sunday, nor would he be back at the farm to help her father with his chores.

"Where are those *maed*?" she asked, her voice rather brusque as she dried her damp hands on a clean dish towel. She stepped toward the living room, trying to see past her father's shoulder. He just stood there in the way, not bothering to move at all. Of course, he wasn't very light on his feet these days, but the least he could do was step to one side and let her pass.

"Lizzie," he said.

"Ja?" She glanced at his face, trying to skirt around him.

He lifted a hand and she drew up beside him. Caught between the fingers of his right hand was an envelope.

"What is this?" she asked, peering at him.

She didn't have time for nonsense. Not if he wanted his Thanksgiving dinner to be served on time.

He rotated the envelope so she could see her name on it, perfectly written in Eli's angled scrawl. She didn't take the letter. No, she couldn't.

"This is for you," Jeremiah said. "It's from Eli."

"Ja, I can see that." She backed away, turning toward the sink. Trying to ignore the heavy beating in her chest and the sound of her own pulse pounding in her ears.

"He wanted you to have it. Because I hid his other letters from you, I promised him that I'd deliver this one to you personally." Jeremiah's lips twitched with laughter, but she didn't find anything humorous about it.

"I don't want it. Take it away." She made a pretense of cutting more celery for the cranberry salad she was making. Why would Eli write another letter to her? It was bad enough that he was leaving right after Thanksgiving. After all, they both knew he must report to his new job by December 1. There was no explanation required this time, so there was no need for him to say goodbye in a letter too.

Jeremiah hobbled over to her, standing beside her. "Lizzie, I want to make amends for hiding your other letters from you. Please, take this letter and read it right now."

The command in her father's voice caused her to pause. She stared at the envelope, knowing it was a farewell letter. She didn't want it, but realized her father was going to hound her until she took it. Whisking it from his hand, she tucked it inside the waist of her apron and returned to her celery. Tears filled her eyes as she cut a stalk into cubes with a knife. When a new Amish bride was planning to marry, she often grew extra celery for all the many foods she would prepare for her wedding feast. But there would be no such banquet for her.

"I'll read it later," she mumbled.

"Lizzie. Read it now." Jeremiah gripped one of her hands, holding her movements still.

She flinched when she saw Bishop Yoder standing beside the refrigerator. When had he entered the room? And what was he doing here? Why had he come here on Thanksgiving Day? It must be serious.

"Bishop Yoder?" she croaked out his name.

"Read the letter, Lizzie," he said.

Confusion fogged her brain. Something was very, very wrong for both men to be here, pushing her to read Eli's letter. Perhaps Eli had already left Riverton and the bishop wanted her to help convince him to return. But she knew that would be futile. Eli had made his choice. She would not beg him to come home. It would be too humiliating. Too pathetic for her to do such a thing. But her father and Bishop Yoder were still standing there waiting for her.

Dropping the knife and celery stalk into the sink, she again dried her hands, then reached for the envelope and slid her finger beneath the flap to break the seal. She hesitantly pulled out the single page and spread out the creased folds. As her gaze scanned the words, her heart did a myriad of flip-flops. She gasped, unable to believe what she was reading. Without a word, she brushed past the two men and hurried into the living room, then out onto the porch.

Eli! Was he here? Or had he already left the farm? She glanced around, looking for any sign of him. Hoping. Carrying a prayer inside her heart.

"Who are you looking for?"

She spun around. Eli! He was here. He'd been sitting on an Adirondack chair, but came to his feet as he spoke to her. He whisked off his hat, holding it in his hands. In his eyes, she saw a mixture of uncertainty and hope.

She stared at him, her throat too clogged to speak. Confusion filled her mind and she didn't know what to say.

"Who are you looking for?" he asked again.

"You," she croaked.

"Did you read my letter?" he asked, stepping closer.

She nodded, a raft of tears clogging her throat.

"Then you know. I'm not going back to Denver," he said.

She swallowed hard, still gripping his letter in her hand. "You're…you're not?"

"*Ne*. In fact, I mailed my rejection letter to Tom Caldwell just yesterday. I'm not going to accept his job offer after all."

"You're…you're not?" she said again, thinking she must sound irrational and foolish.

"*Ne*, I'm not. That's why I invited Bishop Yoder to accompany me here today. You see, yesterday, when you turned and hurried away from me, something cold gripped my heart."

She blinked, trying to clear the tears from her eyes. "And what is that?"

"For a third time in my life, I was about to lose the woman I loved. And I couldn't allow that to happen again. I was devastated when Shannon died. And watching you walk away was like that all over again. I couldn't lose you too. Not again. I know on my deathbed I won't be thinking about my education or my career. I'll be thinking about you. And what good would my life be if you're not a major part of it?"

She shook her head, not understanding. Not daring to hope she was hearing him correctly. "What are you saying, Eli?"

"Just that I love you, Lizzie. I love you so very much."

The letter she still clutched in her hand said the same things and so much more. She hadn't heard him say those words in many long years. But now, he said he wanted to stay in Riverton. That he wanted to marry her. She licked her lips, not daring to believe his words.

"I… I don't understand."

"I know. I didn't understand myself, until yesterday. You see, over the past couple of months, I've experienced your strength and abiding faith, and I now feel a deep sense of peace in my heart. I could return to my *Englisch* life in

Denver and forever lose you and the other things that matter most to me. Or I can remain here and always wonder if I made the right choice. In all honesty, I had planned to leave. But then, I started thinking about all the things I would miss. And most of all, I would miss you more than I could stand. Without you, nothing else matters to me."

He paused, taking a deep breath. She forced herself to breathe too. To remain quiet and let him finish what he was saying.

"I don't want to live without you, Lizzie."

"You don't?"

"*Ne*, I don't. I realize that each of us has been given a *wundervoll* gift. The right to choose who and what we want to be. We both have the option of staying or going. I've finally made peace with *Gott* and I want to stay. Because I love you and my faith more than anything else in the world. This is where I belong. I know that now."

A surge of joy almost overwhelmed her. She could hardly believe she'd heard him right. "Oh, Eli. Do you know how long I've waited to hear you say these things? I've never stopped loving you. I tried to pretend that I didn't, but it was no use. I'm sure that's why my heart has been in so much pain. Becoming your wife and raising a *familye* with you here in Riverton has always been my fondest dream. But…but what about your career as a paramedic?"

He showed a thoughtful frown and looked down at his feet. That alone told her he still felt misgivings about quitting his profession. Yes, he could still help others in the *Gmay* now and then with their medical ailments, but it wouldn't be the same. If he stayed in Riverton, he wouldn't be a paramedic anymore and they both knew it.

"You've worked so hard and you love your work," she

said. "I can't ask you to give that up. You say you love me now, but what about five, ten or fifteen years from now? If you must abandon your career in order to be here with me, I fear you might come to resent me for it. I don't want you to settle for something you may regret later down the road. And I don't want you to have to choose between me and your career. I want you to be happy. To feel confident that you have the best life right here with me."

He didn't speak for several moments, his eyebrows drawn together as he considered her words. A heavy sense of loss settled in her chest. Yes, she believed he truly loved her. Maybe he had never stopped. But loving one another didn't mean he would stay. Not if he couldn't have all that his heart desired.

"You and the Lord are all I need to be happy," Eli insisted. "When you turned and walked away from me yesterday, I knew that more than anything. I won't lose you, Lizzie. Not again. I have made my choice. My work as a humble farmer, future husband and father are every bit as important as being a paramedic in Denver. I will remain here with you. I know deep in my heart that it's the decision the Lord would want me to make. It's what I want too."

"Ahum!"

They both turned and found Jeremiah and Bishop Yoder standing behind them on the porch. Lizzie hadn't even heard them come outside. Through the living room window, she could see her two sisters peering out at them. Could she have no privacy at all?

Annie pressed her nose against the glass pane, looking as if she might cry. Jeremiah leaned against the outer wall, his crutches beneath his arms as he held his injured leg up off the wooden floor. Both men wore serious expressions, their foreheads creased with concern.

"I'm sorry to interrupt, but I think I might be able to clear up a few fears you both might have," the bishop said.

Lizzie's ears perked up at that. Eli faced the two men, but she could see the doubt in his eyes.

Bishop Yoder lifted a hand and rested it on Eli's shoulder. "When you came to see me yesterday and told me you wanted to stay, I was worried that you might change your mind yet again. I wanted to know what was truly in your heart. Since you returned home, Deacon Albrecht, Jeremiah and I have been watching you closely. Of course, Jeremiah has had his concerns. He has feared you might hurt Lizzie again, or draw her off with you into an *Englisch* life. But it has been our fondest hope that the two of you might discover you are still in love, and then choose to marry and start a *familye* here in Riverton. Now that we know what you really want, I have a proposal for the two of you."

Lizzie blinked in confusion. What Eli really wanted was to be a paramedic. What could the bishop have to say that would impact that?

"The church elders and I have discussed your paramedic training at length," the bishop continued. "You have done so much *gut* work for our people with your healing skills. Since our farms are scattered far outside of town, we would like you to maintain your certifications and continue to assist our people as a paramedic."

Lizzie gasped. Had she heard right?

"I have taken the liberty of speaking with the hospital administrators in town. Dr. McGann and Dr. Graham have both voiced their support and I have confirmed that they will work with you. They are pleased with the impact you have had in getting the Amish to receive necessary medical care. The hospital will even pay you a fair salary to serve as a paramedic. I know for a fact that Lancaster County and Pennsylvania have Amish paramedics and firefighters who serve their people. Our need here in Colorado is just as great. *Ach*, so you see? When we exercise faith and bow to *Gott*'s will, He blesses us with more joy than we can ever hope for."

A halting laugh burst from Eli's throat. "*Ja*, Bishop Yoder. You are right. I never expected to feel so much joy. I... I can't believe this is truly happening. I can remain here and work the career I have chosen, but..."

Eli spun toward Lizzie. His eyes were filled with happiness and eager anticipation. Reaching into his hat, he pulled out the job offer from Tom Caldwell and ripped the letter in two before placing it in her hands. Lizzie gazed at him with stunned amazement. She barely noticed as her father and Bishop Yoder turned and quietly went back inside the house and closed the door. Out of her peripheral vision, she saw the men pulling the little girls away from the window. Finally, she and Eli had a moment alone together.

"Lizzie, you hold my heart in your hands," Eli said. He squeezed her fingers, his gaze searching hers. "I'm not going anywhere. I belong right here in Riverton, with you. Say you'll be mine. Make me the happiest man in the world. I want us to be married just as soon as I'm baptized. Please say yes."

A movement from the window caught Lizzie's eye. She glanced over and saw her father nodding his approval from inside the house. She almost laughed. So much for privacy. But it wasn't as if she needed his prompting to find her answer. If her father approved of this man, then so must she. Especially when marrying Eli was what she'd always wanted.

With tears of happiness dripping from her eyes, she enfolded Eli in a tight hug. "*Ja*, I will, Eli. *Ach*, I will!"

A shout of delight came from the living room. Her *familye* and Bishop Yoder were inside, celebrating this thrilling news. And what more could Lizzie want? This Thanksgiving, she had found so much to be grateful for. So much to praise the Lord for.

"I love you, Lizzie-bee." Eli pressed a gentle kiss to her lips. His eyes were filled with wonder and love.

"And I love you, Eli. So very much."

She heard the front door open and the squeak of the screen door as her sisters rushed outside to congratulate her. With Eli's arm securely wrapped around her shoulders, she faced her father and the bishop. Both men smiled wide with pleasure. With Eli by her side and her *familye* surrounding her, Lizzie felt such deep contentment that she was overwhelmed with joy. Truly *Gott*'s redeeming love had mended their broken hearts. He had made them whole again. And Lizzie could ask for nothing more.

* * * * *

WE HOPE YOU ENJOYED THIS BOOK!

Love Inspired®

New beginnings. Happy endings. Discover uplifting inspirational romance.

Look for six new Love Inspired books available every month, wherever books are sold!

Save $1.00

on the purchase of ANY
Love Inspired® or
Love Inspired® Suspense book.

Available wherever books are sold,
including most bookstores, supermarkets,
drugstores and discount stores.

Save $1.00

on the purchase of ANY Love Inspired® or Love Inspired® Suspense book.

Coupon valid until December 31, 2019.
Redeemable at participating retail outlets in the U.S. and Canada only.
Limit one coupon per customer.

52616482

Canadian Retailers: Harlequin Enterprises Limited will pay the face value of this coupon plus 10.25¢ if submitted by customer for this product only. Any other use constitutes fraud. Coupon is nonassignable. Void if taxed, prohibited or restricted by law. Consumer must pay any government taxes. Void if copied. Inmar Promotional Services ("IPS") customers submit coupons and proof of sales to Harlequin Enterprises Limited, P.O. Box 31000, Scarborough, ON M1R 0E7, Canada. Non-IPS retailer—for reimbursement submit coupons and proof of sales directly to Harlequin Enterprises Limited, Retail Marketing Department, 22 Adelaide St. West, 40th Floor, Toronto, Ontario M5H 4E3, Canada.

5 65373 00076 2   (8100)0 12431

U.S. Retailers: Harlequin Enterprises Limited will pay the face value of this coupon plus 8¢ if submitted by customer for this product only. Any other use constitutes fraud. Coupon is nonassignable. Void if taxed, prohibited or restricted by law. Consumer must pay any government taxes. Void if copied. For reimbursement submit coupons and proof of sales directly to Harlequin Enterprises, Ltd 482, NCH Marketing Services, P.O. Box 880001, El Paso, TX 88588-0001, U.S.A. Cash value 1/100 cents.

LICOUP47014

*On her way home, pregnant and alone,
an Amish woman finds herself stranded
with the last person she wanted to see.*

Read on for a sneak preview of
Shelter from the Storm *by Patricia Davids,
available September 2019 from Love Inspired.*

"There won't be another bus going that way until the day after tomorrow."

"Are you sure?" Gemma Lapp stared at the agent behind the counter in stunned disbelief.

"Of course I'm sure. I work for the bus company."

She clasped her hands together tightly, praying the tears that pricked the backs of her eyes wouldn't start flowing. She couldn't afford a motel room for two nights.

She wheeled her suitcase over to the bench. Sitting down with a sigh, she moved her suitcase in front of her so she could prop up her swollen feet. After two solid days on a bus she was ready to lie down. Anywhere.

She bit her lower lip to stop it from quivering. She could place a call to the phone shack her parents shared with their Amish neighbors to let them know she was returning and ask her father to send a car for her, but she would have to leave a message.

Any message she left would be overheard. If she gave the real reason, even Jesse Crump would know before she reached home. She couldn't bear that, although she didn't understand why his opinion mattered so much. His stoic face wouldn't reveal his thoughts, but he was sure to gloat when he learned he'd been right about her reckless ways. He had said she was looking for trouble and that she would find it sooner or later. Well, she had found it all right.

No, she wouldn't call. What she had to say was better said face-to-face. She was cowardly enough to delay as long as possible.

She didn't know how she was going to find the courage to tell her mother and father that she was six months pregnant, and Robert Troyer, the man who'd promised to marry her, was long gone.

Don't miss
Shelter from the Storm *by* USA TODAY
bestselling author Patricia Davids,
available September 2019 wherever
Love Inspired® books and ebooks are sold.

www.LoveInspired.com

Looking for inspiration in tales
of hope, faith and heartfelt romance?

Check out **Love Inspired**® and
Love Inspired® **Suspense** books!

New books available every month!

CONNECT WITH US AT:

Facebook.com/groups/HarlequinConnection

 Facebook.com/HarlequinBooks

Twitter.com/HarlequinBooks

Instagram.com/HarlequinBooks

 Pinterest.com/HarlequinBooks

ReaderService.com

Love Inspired.

Love Inspired®

Discover wholesome and uplifting stories of faith, forgiveness and hope.

Join our social communities to connect with other readers who share your love!

Sign up for the Love Inspired newsletter at **LoveInspired.com** to be the first to find out about upcoming titles, special promotions and exclusive content.

CONNECT WITH US AT:

Facebook.com/groups/HarlequinConnection

 Facebook.com/LoveInspiredBooks

Twitter.com/LoveInspiredBks

LISOCIAL2019